THE DISAPPEARANCE

ALSO BY J. F. FREEDMAN

House of Smoke

The Obstacle Course

Against the Wind

Key Witness

J. F. FREEDMAN

THE DISAPPEARANCE

A DUTTON BOOK

DUTTON
Published by the Penguin Group
Penguin Putnam Inc., 375 Hudson Street, New York, New York 10014, U.S.A.
Penguin Books Ltd, 27 Wrights Lane, London W8 5TZ, England
Penguin Books Australia Ltd, Ringwood, Victoria, Australia
Penguin Books Canada Ltd, 10 Alcorn Avenue, Toronto, Ontario, Canada M4V 3B2
Penguin Books (N.Z.) Ltd, 182–190 Wairau Road, Auckland 10, New Zealand

Penguin Books Ltd, Registered Offices: Harmondsworth, Middlesex, England

First published by Dutton, an imprint of Dutton NAL, a member of Penguin Putnam Inc.

First Printing, October, 1998
10 9 8 7 6 5 4 3 2 1

Freedman, J.F.
The disappearance / J.F. Freedman.
p. cm.
ISBN 0-525-94425-7 (acid-free paper)
I. Title.
PS3556.R3833D57 1998
813'.54—dc21 98-26999
CIP

Printed in the United States of America
Set in Plantin

PUBLISHER'S NOTE
This is a work of fiction. Names, characters, places, and incidents either are the products of the author's imagination or are used fictitiously, and any resemblance to actual persons, living or dead, events, or locales is entirely coincidental.

This book is printed on acid-free paper. ∞

for Al Silverman

The weather had been raw and miserable virtually every day for two months; this was the worst winter in a couple of decades, way worse than those of '95 or '82, a continuous, relentless, El Niño–driven hard-falling rain from right after Christmas all through January and February, torrential sheets of cold piercing needles crashing down days at a time without cessation, soaking the ground past saturation, waterlogging everyone and everything. Wet-dog smell stunk up houses, cats sprayed and crapped behind couches because they wouldn't go outside, everywhere indoors reeked of mildew, a decaying-newspaper rot. There was widespread flooding of basements and low-lying dwellings—people in those houses and apartments who hadn't sandbagged properly, mostly lower-incomers who could least afford any loss, saw some of their most precious possessions—family photographs and records and heirlooms—ruined by mud and water, or washed right out of their dwellings. Turbid runoff flowed through the creeks and streams, joining contaminated effluent from broken sewage lines and cracked septic tanks, the force of the water a full-on raging swollen urban river, cascading down the streets and roads, at times climbing to a level of four or five feet in the streets that didn't have good gutters and storm drains. Those foolhardy enough to be driving down these overwhelmed streets in the middle of one of the heavy downpours would see the water rushing past their car windows. Several cars were floated clear off the road, crashing into parked cars or washing up on the sidewalk, where they had to be abandoned.

Uprooted oaks and eucalyptus, big ones, old ones, their root systems rotted out, fell in the middle of main thoroughfares. Massive palm fronds littered the streets, literally closing off some roads. Power outages were common—a wide swath of the busiest commercial area downtown lost power at 9:30 on New Year's Eve. Most of the restaurants had to close down early; people fought their way home and watched the mess (those who hadn't lost power themselves) on the local television news.

There were fewer drunken accidents. That was one of the only consolations.

Finally, the rains stopped. Everyone immediately began spending as much time outside as possible.

The ground was still soaked. It would take another month to dry out, but the worst was over.

ONE

DAY ONE

The moon, two days past full, hangs low and forbiddingly cold, diamond hard in the late winter dead-of-night sky. A thirty-knot wind swooping out of the northeast earlier in the evening, blowing as hard as the summer Santa Anas, has brought the temperature down almost to freezing, which rarely happens this late, mid-March, people aren't prepared for it, even though they should be, given the terrible winter this new year has brought forth.

It's late now, well past midnight. Nothing is moving on the streets. All the lights are out in all the houses.

The girl sleeping on the futon hears a noise, a dull thump, like a body bumping into something. The sound is just loud enough to bring her to the edge of consciousness, somnolently turning her head to look up from where it's buried in a pillow.

There are three fourteen-year-old girls sleeping in the bedroom, eighth-graders having their little slumber party. They have been together most of the day, from mid-afternoon. Emma's mom dropped them off downtown a couple hours before dark.

They cruised the Paseo Nuevo mall, bought some tops and shorts at Nordstrom and The Gap, followed that with dinner at California Pizza Kitchen, and finished off downtown by going to a movie at the Metro 4 down the street (an R-rated movie with Johnny Depp, they brazened their way in with attitude, the movie people let the ID deal slide as long as you don't look like a sixth-grader). Emma bought the tickets. She's fourteen, going on twenty in her head, mature-looking for her age, with an innocent sensuality that oozes from her.

Their parents have just started letting them out at night on their own, as long as they're in by a reasonable hour. They are growing up fast.

Between the time they had dinner and the time they went to the movie they flirted with some older boys who were at their school before moving on to high school—Bolt or Thatcher or the public high school—but then they danced away, giggling and whispering. They liked the attention, but they aren't dating yet. Except for Emma, and her dates are secrets only her very closest friends share.

Their parents have given them plenty of money on top of their allowances (these mothers and fathers who comprise various combinations of married, separated, and divorced adults have their own weekend agendas which don't include their children, they are all, in their own self-wrapped-up ways, happy the girls can take care of themselves for an entire evening), so they cabbed home and watched *Mad TV* followed by *Night Stand*, a stupid-humor takeoff on a talk show. The guy who hosts the show lives in Montecito, the same as them. The girls have seen him in Starbucks, hunched over the *News-Press*, nursing a latte. Probably checking out his reviews. He's a minor celebrity, nobody to get excited about, not when there are real celebrities all over the place, John Cleese walking on the beach, Michael Douglas having lunch at Pane e Vino, Jodie Foster buying wine and brie at Von's.

They've stayed up way late, past midnight. After they were done watching TV, they went outside and smoked. Emma's house has a huge yard, more than two acres of manicured lawn and beautifully trimmed trees and voluptuous flowerbeds you can get lost in it easy, especially at night. Smoking is new to them—they know kids who have been doing it from when they were ten or eleven or even younger, but these are mostly Chicano public-school kids. At fourteen, though, eighth or ninth grade, lots of kids smoke, it isn't that big a deal.

Big deal or not, they don't want their parents to find out. They don't want the hassle of dealing with their parents about shit like that.

Glenna, Emma's mom, knows that Emma smokes. She hasn't

actually caught her daughter with the burning evidence in her mouth, but she sees the signs. She doesn't like it, but she doesn't hassle Emma too much about it, like other mothers would, so most of the time the girls hang out at Emma's house. Glenna looks the other way about lots of things regular mothers wouldn't—having boys in the house when there aren't any adults around, watching any videos or TV shows they want no matter how R-rated-raunchy they are. Glenna is a woman of the '90s, she wants her daughter to be one, too. So she cuts Emma a lot of slack.

The house—it could truly be called a mansion, Montecito is full of houses like this—is one-story, the bedrooms located in two separate wings from the rest of the house. Emma's bedroom has French doors that open onto a flagstone patio, from which a path leads down the full acre of rolling lawn to the swimming pool and bathhouse. When the girls came back to Emma's room they took off their shoes and left them outside.

One of the French doors is open. The moon, just past full, bathes the doorway and part of the bedroom in pale yellow shadowy light.

Is something moving in the room? A person?

Whatever it is, it is out the door, pulling the door closed behind it, crossing the patio.

The girl feels she must be dreaming, a dream within a dream, the kind of dream that feels incredibly real, the kind of dream that if retained at all is always a nightmare in the remembering.

She isn't used to smoking and staying up so late, the way Emma and Hillary, the third girl in the slumber party, are. They're faster than her—she was tremendously flattered and surprised when Emma inexplicably decided, at the beginning of the school year, to admit her into her circle of friends.

Still, she's the third of the threesome. Which is why she is sleeping on the futon on the floor while the other two are in the twin beds. Not that she cares. Being in this company is enough, it doesn't matter where you sleep. Futons are fun, like camping out.

In her dream the French doors are now closed, the room is tranquil, empty. The moon shines on the carpet, a small shimmering pool. The figure is gone.

Then nothingness. The girl rolls over in her sleep and her unconscious mind goes blank.

Hillary and Lisa don't wake up until after ten—normal teenage weekend behavior. Emma isn't there; her unmade bed is rumpled. They figure she's gotten up earlier and gone out.

They lounge around in the room for a while, not sure what to do—go out into the house and look for Emma, or wait for her to come back. They watch some television, get dressed, wait.

Finally, hungry and bored, they wander through the house to the kitchen. Glenna—Mrs. Lancaster to the girls—is sitting on a stool at the island, drinking black coffee and reading the *New York Sunday Times* magazine. Her angular, striking face is devoid of makeup, and her straight black hair is pulled back in a ponytail; her long, slender feet are bare. A tall, athletic woman, she was awake early and played tennis for two hours on her private court with her coach and a friend.

"Emma still sleeping?" she asks casually, her eyes going back to her article. "How late were you guys up, anyway?"

The girls look at each other. "She's already got up, Mrs. Lancaster," Hillary says. "We thought she was in here."

Glenna shakes her head. "I haven't seen her all morning." She glances at the clock on the wall. It's almost 10:30. "She must be in the shower." She turns a page. There's some great clothing coming out this spring. She needs a trip to New York in the near future.

"We used her bathroom, Mrs. Lancaster," Lisa pipes up. "She wasn't in it."

Glenna cocks her head for a moment, thinking. "Well, she's around somewhere." She lays her magazine aside and favors them with a smile. "She isn't much of a hostess, leaving the two of you to fend for yourselves. Do you want any breakfast?" She gets up from her perch, crosses to the refrigerator. "There's fresh orange juice, bagels, croissants. Do your parents let you drink coffee?" Without waiting for a reply she pours two small glasses of juice. "There's cereal, if you want it. In that cupboard," she points across the room.

Lisa hesitates before she speaks. "I had this really weird dream last night. More like a nightmare."

Glenna smiles. "That's what happens when you stay up too late. You're disturbing your biorhythms."

Lisa nods, uncertain. "It was like I woke up in Emma's bedroom, just the way it was when we went to sleep? And the door to the outside was open, and somebody was in there?"

Glenna looks at her more seriously. "Are you sure this was a dream?"

"I thought it was."

"Tell me what you thought you dreamed. Or saw," she says, becoming agitated. "What time did you think this was? In your dream."

"I don't know. It was really late. Like maybe morning, almost."

Glenna crosses to her. "Did you see something, Lisa?" Her eyes locked onto the girl's. "Look at me, Lisa. What did you see?"

It's early in the afternoon. Glenna and the girls had combed the property looking for Emma. When they didn't find her, Glenna called the police who referred her call to the county sheriff's department. She'd been reluctant to do so, but nothing felt right, and she figured it was better to err on the side of caution.

"What exactly did you see, Lisa?"

They are in the study of Emma's parents' house: Lisa, Hillary, Emma's mother, and the police detective. The detective from the sheriff's department, a big man with a hairbrush mustache, has asked the question. He's asking all the questions. Ninety-nine times out of a hundred, the missing kid blithely breezes in and wonders what all the commotion's about, but you still have to go through the drill.

Lisa is scrunched up on a couch, pushing hard against it. If she could force herself into it, through it, she would.

She's scared. She feels they're all angry at her. Like it's her fault Emma isn't here.

Glenna Lancaster crosses over and sits next to Lisa, taking the girl's fluttering hand. "It's okay, Lisa," she says soothingly, reassuringly. "What can you remember?" she asks the shaking girl.

Lisa shrugs, more of a wriggle. "I . . . it was really dark. Something was moving, I thought. I mean I thought I saw something. But it was pretty dark," she ends lamely.

* * *

An hour later Doug Lancaster arrives at his home like a whirlwind, the tire-squeal of his turbo Bentley on the circular Italian-tile driveway announcing his arrival. Hair askew, still in his golf clothes, he charges into the house.

"What?" he asks Glenna, who has jumped up and runs towards the door, intercepting him in the front hallway. The entryway to their house is eighteen feet high; the massive front door was custom-built of imported Hawiian koa wood, with floor-to-ceiling beveled windows on either side of the doorway refracting muted rainbow-colored light upon the marble floor.

The Lancasters had built the house a decade ago. They'd been painstaking in making sure everything was exactly as they desired. One example—Glenna and her designer had gone to Italy twice before they found a quarry that had the right marble for the entryway floor. She had supervised every detail of the construction, relentlessly pushing the architect and myriad contractors every day for a year and a half, seven days a week, driving everyone crazy. She went through the three best contractors in the country before she was done; but she got the house the way she wanted it, which is the only way she knows to do things.

"She's missing," she tells her husband. "Emma—"

"You already told me that on the phone," he interrupts her impatiently. "What's the deal? I mean how do you know—I mean what's—" His tongue can't keep up with the pace of his anxiety.

"Calm down," she says forcefully. "Come in and talk."

She steers him into the study, where the police detective, a man named Reuben Garcia, has been waiting for more than two hours. Contacting Doug in Santa Monica was no small feat—he hadn't been in his hotel room and it took forever to get through to him on the back nine at Bel Air Country Club, where he was playing golf with some of the heavies from NBC.

Hillary is gone now. Her parents came and hustled her away. Lisa, the cause for this alarm, is still there: Garcia wouldn't let her leave until Doug Lancaster could get home and hear her story, fragmentary as it is, firsthand. Garcia doesn't want any problems later on down the line, such as an irate father with a ton of clout becoming upset because he didn't hear the story himself from the mouth of this small, increasingly terrified fourteen-year-old girl.

Susan Jaffe, Lisa's mother, is with her daughter. Lisa is her only child. They live alone in a small house in the affordable area of the lower Riviera, in Santa Barbara proper. Susan and Lisa's father have been divorced for a long time. Susan's raised her daughter on her own, and done it while going to Santa Barbara College of Law at night. She's worked for the county for six years now; her salary is decent, enough that she can afford to send her daughter to Elgin, the best private middle school in the area, which is where Lisa met Emma.

Still, Susan makes less in a year than Doug Lancaster draws in salary per month. His salary is for show: he owns four television stations, including the local NBC affiliate, his flagship station. He has a lot of power and he isn't shy about using it, generally for good reasons—he isn't a bully. But the power is there, and everyone who knows what's going on in this town knows it, including Susan Jaffe, a county employee, and Reuben Garcia, a local deputy.

"This is my husband, Doug Lancaster," Glenna says to Susan and Garcia. "Susan is Lisa's mother. You've met her, haven't you?" she asks her husband, whose pulse rate is coming down slightly, now that he's finished his frenzied drive up the coast and is in his own house.

"I don't think so. Hello," he says, offering his hand.

"We met at Elgin School," Susan Jaffe corrects him. "Last parents' night. Your daughter and mine were in the play together."

"Of course," he responds quickly, diplomatically. "You'll have to forgive me. I'm kind of discombobulated right now, since I don't know what's going on." He doesn't remember the woman at all; she's nice enough looking in a generic way. Much like her daughter, cowering next to her on the couch. "Your daughter was very good in the play, as I recall."

"She had a small part, but she was good, I agree."

"So what's the deal?" Doug says now, having dealt with as much of the amenities as he's going to. "Are we sure Emma couldn't have gone out earlier, with a friend or something? You're positive she hasn't called, and in the rush no one picked up the phone?"

Glenna, biting her lip, shakes her head impatiently. "There were no calls. I'm sure."

Garcia answers the other question. "We've had calls out to everyone we can think of who knows your daughter, Mr. Lancaster. We're concerned."

Doug rocks back on his heels. "What do you mean?" he asks slowly, sounding dumb to himself as the words come out of his mouth.

Garcia extends his hand towards the mother and daughter sitting on the sofa. "Lisa here might have seen something."

Doug looks at Lisa. "Seen something?"

"Sit down," Glenna tells him. She steers him to an armchair across from the sofa where the girl sits.

He folds himself into the chair, his eyes fixed on the small girl eight feet across from him, who is shrinking into herself as he stares at her.

"Tell Mr. Lancaster what you saw," Garcia instructs Lisa. "What you think you might have seen," he corrects himself. He isn't committing to anything, not yet.

The sound of the bump brought Lisa out of a deep sleep, the deepest part of sleep that comes about two hours after you first lose consciousness, where whatever primitive sensors are working make you feel like you're a hundred feet under the ocean, all murky and indefinable.

It took her a few seconds to realize where she was. Then she knew. She was in Emma Lancaster's bedroom, sleeping on a futon.

She was groggy. Her mouth was dry. She wished she'd brought a glass of water to bed with her, but this was only her second sleep-over and she wouldn't know how to get to the kitchen from here in the dark, she'd probably trip an alarm and freak everyone out.

She could make her way to Emma's bathroom. She could drink out of the faucet. She rolled over on her side, started to push her quilt down off her body.

Someone was in the room.

The door leading to the outside patio was open. Someone was standing in the room, at the foot of the twin beds. Light was coming in the door from outside, moonlight. Like a dull spotlight shining into the room.

Whoever was standing in the middle of the floor had a bundle in his arms. A large bundle, like a person wrapped up in a blanket.

The person was tall. He seemed tall, anyway, from her position on the floor, looking up. She couldn't tell what he was wearing, but maybe a windbreaker, a dark thigh-length jacket.

She lay as still as she could.

The man carrying the bundle moved towards the open door. As he reached it he turned for a moment and looked back at the room, not a full turn, not enough for her to see a face. She could only see a fragment of an outline.

The figure turned away and walked out the door. He closed the door behind him and was gone.

She was suddenly exhausted. Her limbs felt like they were bound in cement, and she was scared, too, scared of the unknown, whatever it was. She was too tired to move, and even though her mouth was hot and dry she didn't get up, not even after there was no one standing in the room anymore.

She rolled over again and fell back asleep, almost instantly.

When she woke up hours later she vaguely remembered it, but she thought it had been a dream.

Garcia prompts her. "What did the intruder look like?" He has already heard it, all she knows or can remember, but he wants Doug Lancaster to hear it himself, from the witness directly. He wants to protect his ass from whatever might come down later.

"Tall."

"Right. Tall. What else?"

"He was—"

"It was a man? You're sure of that?" Doug Lancaster interrupts her. He's sitting on the edge of his chair, fidgeting, his knee involuntarily dancing.

"I . . . I'm pretty sure. I'd say almost sure." She's scared of Emma's father. He is staring at her like he could look right through her.

"Let her finish," Glenna admonishes her husband, putting a restraining hand on his shoulder. "This has been terrible for Lisa. And terrifying."

He nods, taking a deep breath to calm himself. "I'm sorry, Lisa. Go ahead, please."

"Was there anything else he was wearing you can remember?" Garcia prompts the girl again.

"A baseball kind of hat," she says.

"Could you see his face at all?" the detective asks, getting excited.

"Not really. I could see some of his hair sticking out the back."

His enthusiasm drops. "Dark hair or light?"

She squirms in her place. Her mother has a protective arm around her shoulder. "I couldn't tell. It was dark."

"Someone, probably tall, probably carrying a bundle that might have been someone wrapped up in a blanket. Hair long enough to be sticking out the back of his hat. Anything else?" Garcia continues his probing. "Could you tell how old this intruder might be? A teenager? Or someone older, like my age, or Mr. Lancaster's?"

She looks from one man to the other. "It didn't look to me like a teenager."

"Can you be any more specific? Twenties, thirties, forties, whatever?"

She shakes her head, eyes averted to the floor. "I hardly saw him. His back was to me. It was dark, and I was asleep, and I was really groggy, you know?" The words are coming out in a scared, scrambled rush. "I don't . . . I wish I . . ." She stumbles to a halt.

"And whoever it was that was wrapped up in this blanket, if it was a person," Garcia goes on. "Was it struggling? Did it look like it was moving or fighting?"

Lisa shakes her head. "It was still. It wasn't fighting. She," she adds, then catches herself. "I mean . . ."

Doug Lancaster stands up. "I think that's enough for now," he says, coming over and putting a hand on Lisa's shoulder. "There's nothing more you can remember, is there?" he says soothingly, a father who has a daughter this girl's age.

"I just have one other question," Garcia says, almost apologetically, now that Doug Lancaster has flexed a little muscle on this girl's behalf. Which is a hell of a nice gesture, considering the man's daughter is missing and may have been kidnapped.

Lisa turns to him, her face a scared-to-death open book.

"What he had in his arms. That looked like it was in a blanket." He doesn't want to ask this question, but he has to. "You think it might have been Emma?"

"It might have been," she answers. "I wasn't thinking anything like that. Not till later," she adds, glancing over at Mr. and Mrs. Lancaster, who look like they've been whacked really hard on their heads with a baseball bat. "But it looked pretty big, the way he had it kind of over his shoulder. So it could have been." She turns her look away, half to her mother, half to the floor. "It was big enough to be a girl."

The clothes Emma wore last night are scattered teen-fashion on the floor. Emma's purse is on top of her bureau.

"Is there anything missing of your daughter's that's obvious?" Detective Garcia asks.

"Her keys," Glenna answers. "She always kept them in her purse. They aren't there."

"You checked?" he asks.

She nods. "I thought maybe it was a robbery," she says. "But her wallet's still there. There's money in it. The only thing I can see missing is her keys." Her eyes mist. "Her key ring was a miniature Maltese cross. We bought it in Greece last year, when we were there on vacation."

It's late in the afternoon. Darkness is approaching, the sun dropping fast in the sky. The Lancaster house, high in the hills off Santa Ynez Road, has views to the city and ocean below, a sweeping vista extending from Port Hueneme, fifty miles to the southeast, to beyond the Goleta wharf thirty miles up the coast.

Half a dozen sheriff's deputies, specialists in this type of work, have converged on the property. Bob Williams, the sheriff, arrived an hour ago, when Detective Garcia made the determination there was a strong probability that Emma Lancaster had been taken forcibly from her home by a person unknown.

Williams will oversee this investigation personally. Montecito has no police force of its own; investigations such as this one fall under the jurisdiction of the county sheriff. Williams will coordinate with other local law enforcement agencies, but it's his show to run. He's an acquaintance of the Lancasters—not socially, of course, but professionally. It's a small county, so everyone who's important knows everyone else who's important. And Doug Lancaster isn't merely another wealthy, important person, he's the leading media heavyweight in the area. Every politician in the state, from the governor on down to the local level, wants to be—*has* to be—on his good side. The alternative could be a quick return to the private sector.

If this turns out to be a real kidnapping, as opposed to something else, some rebellious juvenile action, for example, it will be a high-profile one: the daughter of a wealthy family that has high public recognition.

The sheriff's deputies, some uniformed, some in plainclothes, are clustered in small groups in the backyard. There is a gazebo anchoring one corner of the property, with a duck pond at the other end. The pool and poolhouse complex, which has a sauna, jacuzzi, weight room, and party area, are tucked away against the eastern property line. Although it hasn't rained in a week now, the grounds are still oversaturated from all the water they had to absorb. Because of the dampness, there are muddy footprints crisscrossing the back patios, including the one outside Emma's bedroom, the various flagstone walkways around the trees under which Smith & Hawken Adirondack-style wooden benches are tastefully deployed.

A team of forensic experts have been studying these various sets of footprints since they arrived. Almost all of the prints will be accounted for, they know from past experience; they've worked countless locations like this one. Some of the prints are from steel-toed work boots, others are from rubber-galosh types, and there are some running-shoe prints. All are the trackings of gardeners, pool men, other physical laborers. None of these shoe prints have unique enough markings to be able to single out the one that would have been worn by the abductor who entered Emma Lancaster's bedroom in the darkest hour of the night. If, that is, she was abducted.

"Here's some fresher sets." One of the forensic cops is pointing out to another detective, his partner, footprints that lead onto Emma's bedroom patio from the lawn. The shoes the girls wore when they went out are strewn near the doorway.

"Three sets," the other cop observes quickly.

"Three girls, three pairs of shoes, three sets of prints," the lead cop agrees. "Stands to reason."

They follow the prints across the expanse of lawn, where they wind up at the stairs of the gazebo, the farthest point from the house. "Still just three girls," the senior cop observes quickly. He's a good tracker, he's part of the county search-and-rescue team. He's tracked and found lost children and hikers all over the Los Padres National Forest to the north. Compared to that kind of tracking, this is child's play.

"Let's see what they were up to," he says. Presciently, he adds, "Whatever they were doing, they didn't want mommy or daddy to know about it." He heads up the stairs, his partner following.

The scuffed wooden floor of the gazebo is littered with cigarette butts. A stack of Coke, Pepsi, Dr Pepper, and Snapple bottles and cans have been haphazardly pushed into a corner. There are a few beer bottles and cans scattered among them as well.

"My college dorm room wasn't this grungy," the lead cop observes.

The other picks up one of the empty beer bottles. "Sierra Nevada. These kids have taste. Money, too."

"It's what their parents drink," his partner says. He stands at the gazebo railing, looking at the back of the sprawling house, the clusters of detectives combing it for clues. "A place this size has three or four big refrigerators. You could take a truckload of beer out and no one would ever miss it."

His partner spies something in a crack in the floor. "What have we here?" he asks aloud, bending down to pry the object from between two floorboards with the point of a key. "Check this out." He holds the roach up to the other cop's face.

The lead man squints at the found object. "Big fucking deal."

"It isn't licorice."

"Go by Santa Barbara Junior High any day during lunch break," the forensic officer says. "This is the least of what they're indulging in. Anyway, who says it's one of the girls—or any of this shit, for that matter? It could be some of the servants, a gardener. Places like this have a gazillion people working at them."

The other man drops the roach into a plastic bag. "Worth checking out."

"Oh, yeah. We've got to."

While this is going on outside, Sheriff Williams is inside the house interviewing Doug and Glenna in a private study away from the working cops.

"When was the last time either of you saw your daughter?" he starts out.

"When she came home last night," Glenna says straight away.

"What time was that?"

She thinks for a moment. "About a little before eleven, I guess. I wasn't looking at the clock. I had people over. Her curfew's eleven, she's good about making it."

"Do you know how she got home? Did a friend bring her, one of the mothers of the other girls?"

Glenna shakes her head. "She took a cab. They did. The girls."

"You know that for a fact? Maybe she told you that because they were with a boy? Or some boys? That you wouldn't be happy about them being with? Or even if you didn't mind who the boys were, but they wouldn't want their mothers to know about it?"

"Emma's only in the eighth grade. She doesn't date." She takes a sip of wine. It's her second glass. She needs it to keep her nerves under control, so she doesn't all of a sudden start screaming. "Besides, she hit me up for the cab fare. Twenty-two dollars."

Williams makes a note. "Do you remember what cab company?"

"No. I didn't go out to pay them. She did."

"Does your daughter take cabs fairly often?"

"No." Glenna glances at Doug. "Normally one of the people who work here picks her up—if we can't," she adds hastily, not wanting to come off as a rich, uncaring parent.

"But not last night?"

"They were busy with other things," she says, feeling apologetic and not liking it.

"How large a staff do you have?" the sheriff asks. "That live here?"

"We have four people who live with us, and staff is too formal a word. There are two that drive her. I gave both of them the evening off. Emma knew to catch a cab ride home if she couldn't get a lift from one of her friends."

"That doesn't count the gardeners," Doug Lancaster interjects.

"The gardeners don't live here," his wife answers. She feels defensive about all the people who work for them, although she knows she shouldn't; she pays them well, people love working for her. Everyone gets a bonus at Christmas, even if the revenue from the stations is down.

"How many gardeners are there on a steady basis?"

"Two," Glenna answers.

"How many times a week do they come?"

"Every day during the week," she says, beginning to feel annoyed. "They don't work weekends unless it's a special occasion, a party for charity, things like that."

Another note. "I'll get their names later. Could you tell me what you yourself were doing?" he asks her.

"I was hosting my monthly women's consciousness group," she informs him.

Williams waits for her to go on.

"A dozen or so women. We pick a different topic each month and we talk about our experiences on that topic. Personal stuff—feelings, emotions, things that matter to us. It's normally Tuesday nights, but this month worked out better for Saturday."

"The other women in the group were here when the girls got back from downtown?"

"Yes, they were here."

The women's group broke up around twelve-thirty. Glenna called good-night to Emma and her friends, volubly chattering away in Emma's room behind the closed door. Glenna doesn't intrude on her daughter's space. It's important to Glenna that Emma have her own space and her mother's confidence in her, with no prying or spying.

Glenna did her bedtime preparations and was asleep by one.

"And you didn't hear anything later on?" Williams asks. "No out-of-the-ordinary sounds?"

"No. I slept straight through until seven-thirty. I'm usually a light sleeper. If there had been anything loud, I'm sure I would've heard it. The master bedroom is on the opposite side of the house from the other bedrooms."

Williams starts to say something, then decides not to. "If you could give me the names of those women," he asks her. "It might be helpful."

Glenna nods. "I'll make a list for you before you leave."

"Appreciate that." He turns to Doug, who's sitting immobile, cracking his knuckles, looking impatient. That's okay, Williams thinks, let him stew a bit. "And you, Mr. Lancaster?"

"The last time I saw Emma?" Doug isn't drinking. He feels like one, a stiff one, but he doesn't want to drink with the police here.

"Yes."

Doug thinks for a minute. "Yesterday morning? Did I see her then? You know, I don't remember now. I think so, but maybe I didn't."

"When was the last time you could definitely say you saw her?"

"Friday night," Glenna answers for him. "Two nights ago. We all had dinner together, the three of us."

"That sounds right," Doug agrees.

Williams scribbles in his notebook again. Looking up, he asks, "And you were where last night, Mr. Lancaster?"

"L.A. Beverly Hills, to be specific, until pretty late, then I was in my hotel in Santa Monica."

"L.A.?"

"I had a business meeting," Doug explains. "Some of my affiliate associates from the network were out for the weekend from New York and Atlanta. We worked Saturday, had dinner Saturday night, then some of us played golf this morning." He paused. "That's where my wife finally tracked me down, on the golf course."

"Right," Williams responds, his face betraying no interest. "You'll give us the names?"

"I don't carry a cell phone on the course," Doug adds apologetically. Then he rattles off the names of the men and women he had dinner with last night, the name of the hotel he stayed at, the names of the others in his golf foursome.

Williams writes it down. "That's all we need for now. We'll be looking around for a while. If we find anything, we'll come and tell you."

As the sheriff is leaving the room, Doug stands in the doorway, blocking his exit. "That was some pretty inquisitive questioning just now," Doug says, not bothering to conceal his displeasure. "I almost felt we were under suspicion of something, the way you were probing." The intensity of his voice forces Williams to look at him. "I understand you have to find out what's going on, but what was that? Or am I misreading you?"

The sheriff responds directly. "You weren't misreading me."

Glenna's intake of breath is sharply audible. Her husband puts a supportive arm around her shoulders.

"We have to do this," Williams explains. "Anytime a family member is missing, particularly a child, the other family members are the first ones to be"—he fumbles for the right word—"suspects," he finishes. "Like the Ramsey family, back there in Colorado. I hope you understand."

"Maybe I do," Doug answers slowly, tightening his grip on his wife's shoulders as he feels her tense up. "But I sure as hell don't like it."

"Yes, I can understand that," Williams says. "But we have to do it," he repeats himself, uncomfortably holding his ground. "This is the way it works with every police department in the country."

"If you say so." Doug isn't conceding anything.

"It's for your benefit—sir."

"Our benefit? How in the hell is that?" Doug's angry. His daughter's missing and the cops are screwing him and Glenna around. Don't they have better things to do, like figuring out who did this? If, in fact, she really was abducted, which by now he has to believe. There aren't any other plausible options.

Williams keeps his cool. Doug's is a normal reaction. "In a kidnapping without any witnesses, family members are the first suspects," he explains patiently. "*Especially* in a situation without any witnesses."

"There was a witness," Glenna protests. "Lisa saw it. Detective Garcia took her testimony. You know that."

"She didn't see anything," Williams says dismissively. "A tall white man. No face, no nothing. It could be her father," he goes on, looking at Doug.

"Hey!"

"I'm not saying it's you, Mr. Lancaster," the sheriff comes back, "but we have to look at that. It's how we're trained, and with good reason. Or it could be one of your staff, or someone else who's worked around here and knows the lay of the land."

"It wasn't anyone who works for us," Glenna says adamantly. "I'm sure of that."

"Don't be sure of anything," Williams cautions her. "For your own good. You're a high-profile family, you're in the media, there are people out there you might have—excuse my French—pissed off."

Doug starts to answer in the negative, but stops himself. "You're right about that," he concedes. "Anyone who has control over a piece of the media is going to make enemies," he says, as much for his wife's benefit as the police's. "I'm sure I have." He pauses. "I know I have."

Williams puts a consoling hand on Glenna's forearm. The woman's skin is cold to his touch. She could be going into preliminary shock. He'd better have a doctor check her out.

"We're inoculating you, okay?" he says to them. "If your daughter really has been abducted, there's going to be a lot of heat coming down. We want you to have a clean bill of health so you aren't hassled later, in case things turn out . . ."

"To be ugly." Doug Lancaster finishes his sentence for him.

Williams nods. "This is for *your* good—believe me when I tell you that."

Glenna too nods slowly. Her breath is coming hard. "I hear you."

"Good." He's going to call a doctor, right now. He'll get the name of the family physician from her husband, out of her hearing. "I know you didn't have anything to do with whatever happened," he assures them (and himself). "This way we're all protected, you and us."

"I understand."

As he's about to leave, Williams catches himself. "There was one thing I meant to ask you and it slipped my mind."

"What's that?" Doug asks.

"You have an alarm system here, don't you?"

"Of course we do."

"If an outside door to your daughter's room was open, wouldn't that have tripped the alarm?"

Doug nods, comprehending. He turns to his wife. "Was the alarm set? Do you remember setting it?"

She thinks, her fingertips pressed against her forehead. "I thought I did. After Audrey left—she was the last one to leave." She thinks some more. "I'm sure I did. I always do."

"You couldn't have forgotten this time?" Williams probes.

"I suppose I could have, but I'm usually diligent about that."

"Who was the first person up this morning, Mrs. Lancaster? Who would've gone outside."

"I . . . I suppose I was. Although one of my people could have, earlier. I did go out for the papers myself."

"Was the alarm set when you went out?"

"I . . ." She shakes her head. "I honestly don't remember. I do it by rote. I just . . . don't remember," she says, feeling feeble and stupid and guilty.

"It's not a big deal." Williams, sensitive to her feelings, stops the questioning. He hands Doug his card. "My home phone's on here," he points out. "If you can think of anything, if anything comes up, call me. Anytime. I mean that." He pauses. Here comes the hardest part. "Particularly if anyone contacts you."

Both parents visibly flinch.

"Oh, God!" Glenna buries her head in her hands.

"Is that . . . what you expect?" Doug asks. He forces the words out. "What we should expect?"

The sheriff doesn't mince words. There's no point. "If it's a kidnapping for ransom, yes."

"When would . . ." Doug begins. He stops, unable to continue.

Williams shakes his head in resignation. "There's no way of telling. It could be later tonight, tomorrow morning, a few days from now. Or . . ." He stops.

Doug says the unspoken: "Or never."

"That almost never happens."

Glenna breaks down crying, loud mournful sobs. Her husband puts his arm tight around her. "It's okay, honey," he whispers as soothingly as he can. "It's going to be okay. We don't know for sure yet what's going on." The sheriff's card is burning a hole in his palm. He pockets it. "Thanks in advance for what you're doing," he tells Williams hollowly. "I realize we're not handling this as well as we should be."

"You don't have to thank me for anything, Doug," Williams says, calling the man by his given name for the first time since he's been here: an attempt at making a consoling gesture. "And please, no apologies. Nobody should have to apologize for anything they say or do under circumstances like these. I'd be acting the same way if it were my daughter."

On the books it isn't an official kidnapping yet. Emma's only been missing about nine hours (fourteen or fifteen if you believe Lisa's story about the intruder). More important, there's no ransom demand, and no evidence of foul play. But the police are busting their asses anyway; they don't want to get behind in the count, to have this blow up in their faces if it turns out, as they're increasingly fearful it might, to be the real thing.

Williams stands in a semicircle with his detectives. "Anything special?"

The men who tracked the girls' footprints to the gazebo fill him in on what they found—the beer cans, the cigarette butts. Every item up there will be gathered and gone over with a fine-tooth comb.

"They were having a party. We'll dust the cans. Hopefully they'll have prints on some of them—besides the girls' and people who have a reason to be there."

The other one shows the roach in the Baggie.

Williams is dismissive, as the man's partner was. "That doesn't mean anything. Even if they were smoking that stuff, so what? It doesn't have anything to do with this." His arm sweeps the area. "And how are you going to get prints off a girl who isn't here? She's too young to have a driver's license, she's probably never been fingerprinted in her life."

* * *

He's getting antsy. This isn't progressing the way he wants it to. Not that he expected it would, but he wants something, something he can take to this family, to the entire community, when they find out.

"Over here."

Williams turns towards the voice. A woman detective named Jeri Bryan is standing about fifteen feet off the patio that's outside the presumed kidnap victim's room.

"We almost overlooked this," Jeri says. "Be careful," she warns, "there's only one that I've found—so far. Don't step on it," she cautions.

Carefully, almost daintily, the sheriff walks over to her.

"Here." She squats down, points to the edge of a gravel walkway that starts where the patio ends and leads around the house to a gate in the fence that surrounds the property. Sheriff Williams hunches down next to her. She shines her flashlight on the ground.

One footprint. A partial of the left foot. A man's shoe, pretty large. Someone who was walking on the gravel, where he wouldn't leave a track. But he misstepped slightly, this one time.

"See this?" She points to a mark in the tread pattern, in the middle of the print.

Williams gets down on his hands and knees in the damp grass, bending over so that his face is inches from the impression. Jeri points to the mark with the tip of her pencil. There's a sharp, deep half-inch gouge that cuts across the connecting treads, all the way through to the foundation sole of the shoe.

"Probably caused by stepping on some sharp object," she hazards. "Like a knife, the edge of a rake, or it could've come from digging with a shovel that penetrated the tread." She looks up, catches the eye of the forensic detective who followed the girls' footprints to their gazebo hideaway. "Take a look at this, Frank."

The expert squats next to her and the sheriff. He stares at the footprint, then stands up. "This is good. It's pretty fresh."

Williams stands beside him. "Let's cast it, yes?"

"Definitely."

"Good work, Jeri," Williams compliments Detective Bryan.

"Someone would've found it, sooner or later," she says modestly.

"If one of us hadn't stepped on it first and obliterated it." He turns to his troops. "We may have caught a break here, people. Let's capitalize on it."

The detectives intensify their search, looking for similar prints. Within minutes, now that they know what they're looking for, two more are found—one near the gazebo, almost hidden in some tall grass, and another closer to the gate.

While they're carefully making impressions of the shoe prints, like paleontologists sifting for dinosaur bones, another detective comes out of the house and says something low into the sheriff's ear. Williams looks up. Then he follows the detective back into the house, into Emma's bedroom.

Doug and Glenna Lancaster are in the room. They both look stricken. "I think we figured out what happened to the alarm," Doug says, his voice forlorn. "Follow me."

He leads them out of the room into the hallway. On the wall, right outside the door, is an alarm panel.

"This panel is for this wing of the house," Doug explains. He points to the lights that are flashing green. "The alarm's been turned off."

Williams looks at the panel soberly. The girl did it herself. She turned off her alarm when she and her friends went outside for their little fun and games. Then she forgot to turn it on when she came back in. What teenager who'd been smoking grass and cigarettes and drinking beer would remember?

"Maybe the abductor turned it off," Glenna mumbles, hating that word: "abductor."

"That's possible," Williams concedes. "But if he did, he'd have to know about it, and the code. Which brings us back to this being an inside job, if in fact she was kidnapped, which we shouldn't jump to, not yet."

He'll tell them about the partial footprint and the girls' tracks leading to the gazebo later, after his people have left. Right now they need a breather.

Doug Lancaster, standing behind his wife, starts shaking his head.

"Yes, sir?" Williams asks.

"No one turned this off," Doug says. "No one except Emma." He looks at Williams. "She was outside, wasn't she? She and her friends—after she said good-night to her mother. They went outside, didn't they?"

Williams looks at the man. There's no point in being indirect now.

"Yes, Mr. Lancaster," he answers. "We believe they did."

The police photographer takes infrared pictures of the floor of Emma's room to see if the unique footprint they found outside might have left a mark in the carpeting that would be invisible to the eye but discernible to high-tech photography. Outside, the casts of the potentially case-breaking shoe prints are bagged. Then the deputies load everything into their cars and vans, and leave.

The sheriff puts a tap on the telephone, with a direct connection to FBI regional headquarters in Los Angeles. If anyone calls regarding Emma's disappearance—a kidnapper with a ransom demand, an anonymous tipster, or anything else—they'll be ready to jump into action. Doug and Glenna are instructed how to handle this—keep the caller on the line as long as possible, and don't do anything that will spook a prospect into hanging up prematurely or, even worse, running away from the situation altogether. If a ransom demand is forthcoming, the sheriff's people, with FBI and state police assistance, will come back and set up a command post in the house. For now, though, that isn't necessary or advisable. If (again *if*) it is a kidnapping, whoever did this might be watching the house, or having it watched. The police don't want to spook him.

The abduction (*potential* abduction, everyone hopes) is under wraps for now, but that will change, maybe as early as tomorrow morning. A reporter from the *Santa Barbara News-Press*, the local daily, picked up the incident from the open police lines and was outside the mansion earlier in the evening, hoping to find out if there was a story. Doug refused the reporter's request to come out and give him anything, and the sheriff was similarly mum. "No comment" was his only comment as he got into his car and drove away.

Sitting in his oppressively quiet house, Doug Lancaster thinks about how to handle this. He has to do something—this is news, it can't be stonewalled, he won't be able to keep the lid on for more than a day. If anything, that it's happening to his family makes it all the more newsworthy. He's going to have to deal with it, even though that's the last thing he wants to do.

He telephone-conferences with Jane Bluestine, his station manager, Wes Cobb, the head producer of his news team, and his top anchorman, Joe Allison. They decide to put out a short, innocuous announcement on tonight's eleven o'clock news: there was an incident at the home of a prominent Montecito resident, involving a possible missing juvenile. That's all. Overnight they'll polish the story, hope for more details—a phone call or other communication from the kidnapper, some kind of breakthrough on the evidence (flimsy as it is) that was discovered at the site, a possible profile by the police psychologist who's been called in to go over the known facts and come up with the kind of person who might have done this. Already the police are all over their computers, checking for known sex offenders who might be in the region, anyone recently released from a prison in any of the western states, anyone missing from parole, anyone who could plausibly be the abductor. Maybe by six o'clock tomorrow morning, when the early local news hits the air, they'll have something, more than they have now.

Regardless of what they have, they're going to have to go with it. And then, Doug Lancaster knows, he and his family will be living in a glass house.

Glenna and Doug are bunkered in the smaller of their two studies. Doug has his drink now, a healthy shot of Laphroig. Glenna's on her fourth glass of chardonnay. They stare at each other, at the phone, but they don't talk.

Doug makes one call, to Fred Hampshire, his lawyer. Hampshire is shocked at the news. He offers to cut out of the dinner party he's hosting and come over immediately, but Doug demurs. There's nothing Fred can do. There's nothing anyone can do right now, except hope and pray. They'll get together tomorrow, after the police have sifted through the evidence they've collected and come up with a plan of action.

Occasionally the telephone rings, in a normal fashion. None of these calls are about Emma; no one outside of the immediate parties knows what's happened. The police discussed the situation with Lisa and her mother, and Hillary and her parents. This is a very delicate matter; if word were to get out prematurely, or the wrong way, it could have disastrous consequences.

Among the few people who have heard about Emma's disappearance are their household employees. Shortly after the police arrived in force, Doug called Maria Gonzalez, their house manager, at her home, and asked her to return immediately. When she did, he told her what had maybe happened.

She immediately started rounding everyone up. They're all here now, whether or not they have the weekend off. They move about the house unobtrusively, quiet as phantoms. They have talked about this with each other, professing to each other that it's a mystery to them. Emma is precocious and headstrong, they all know that, but she's never been in any real trouble—no brushes with the law, even for ticky-tack stuff, never been known to take drugs. The word that there was marijuana found in the gazebo is a mild hiccup, nothing more, and finding it there doesn't mean Emma or her friends were indulging.

If anyone was out there smoking, the majority of the staff think, it would have been Glenna. They know she indulges with her artistic acquaintances from the growing film and television colony that's migrated up here in the last decade.

Maria raps lightly on the door to the study, pokes her head in. "Would you like something to eat?" she asks solicitously. She's been with them for more than ten years; they're almost as important in her life as her own family, Emma as much a daughter to her as her own children.

Glenna, rooted to her spot on the sofa, shakes her head. Doug gets up and walks to the door. "We're not hungry, but thanks, Maria." He pauses. "Make sure no one uses the first two phone lines, okay?" he reminds her for the umpteenth time.

He doesn't have to say why. They all know to stay off the phones.

"Of course, Mr. Lancaster. Let us know if you need anything." She closes the door behind her.

He comes back and sits next to his wife. "This could be completely different from what we think." The bullshit sticks in his throat, even as he speaks it.

Her eyes are bloodshot as she stares at him. "How?" she asks hoarsely. "She's never done anything remotely like this." She swigs the last of the wine in her glass. "Lisa saw it, for Christsakes!" she rants. "Has everyone forgotten that? She saw Emma being carried out of the room!"

Doug nods. That's irrefutable, however the police want to spin it. The girl was only half awake and she didn't actually see Emma in the blanket, that's the only straw they can grasp at for now.

If there was someone in there—and all the evidence is pointing to that and only that: a missing girl, an awakening but still lucid witness, the disturbing footprint on the pathway that leads to one of the outside gates—what else could this be?

Nothing else. Emma's gone. Someone took her.

DAY TWO

Neither of them sleeps all night. Until about eleven, the telephone rings intermittently, normal social calls from friends. Not the call they're awaiting, hoping for, dreading. Doug fields these calls; Glenna's in no shape to talk to anyone. He gives the same rote answer to each caller: "Glenna's asleep, and I'm expecting an important long-distance business call, so I have to keep the lines open."

Finally, at four o'clock, Doug makes Glenna take a sleeping pill and puts her to bed. She's out before he pulls the covers over her. Then he shaves, showers, puts on a good suit, white shirt, and tie (he often goes to work in khakis and golf shirt, he's a notably laid-back boss), and drives the deserted streets to his television station.

He takes Cabrillo Boulevard, the road that runs along the beach. It's still dark out, but there's enough moonlight to see the palm trees lining the road, swaying sentries against the nighttime sky. The beach stretches a hundred yards from the bike path that parallels the road and the ocean. The water is flat, baby waves lapping up onto the sand. Beyond that, looming in the gloom, are the Channel Islands, twenty miles offshore.

He leaves the beach and drives up into the hills where his station is located. KNSB, Channel 8 on the television dial from Thousand Oaks to Monterey, is one of the most profitable regional television stations in the country. It and the other stations Doug owns have made him a multimillionaire. As "media moguls" (a term Doug despises), he is rich beyond any possible human need, want, or desire—which is a plausible and compelling reason why their daughter, their only child, is missing. They have a lot of money to buy her back, if that's what this is about.

Doug has never gone in for superelaborate security: the ever lurking bodyguards just out of one's vision, the security firms patrolling one's home twenty-four hours a day, the major video setups and other kinds of surveillance that some of his wealthy acquaintances swear by. That stuff happens to other people, he's always thought, people with high profiles like politicians, film stars, ball players.

Now he's about to become one of those people—he and Glenna and (pray God) Emma. From now on, regardless of the outcome of this affair, their lives won't be as unconsciously free and mobile as they always have been. They're going to be, if not celebrities, notorious. Their pictures smeared across the pages of the *National Enquirer*, that kind of shit.

It's starting to hit home how heavy this might get.

Normally at this time of the morning the station runs a skeleton crew, the minimum needed to get out the prenetwork news and feature program. The day really kicks in around 8:00 and goes until 11:30 P.M., when the nightly news is done.

Today, however, his top people—Jane, Wes, Joe—are already there when he arrives. As soon as he walks in the door, Doug feels the tension. He's aware that everyone at the studio—cameramen, floor managers, whoever's there—is uneasily checking him out. That's normal; he's the owner. But this is different.

It takes on a life of its own, he thinks. It's like an invisible gas. You think you can contain it, but it finds all the nooks and cracks and oozes out, escaping into the world.

He's used to *broadcasting* the news, not *being* it. He'd better get used to it, he realizes with a pang. Glenna is going to have a hard time with this: reporters coming around, hovering at the edges of the house, waiting for her to come out so they can take pictures, ask questions. Television cameras in their faces—some of them their own.

He and his keys meet in the conference room. It's half an hour to airtime for the six o'clock news show. Everyone offers condolences.

Jane Bluestine hugs him. To his surprise, he hugs her back harder than he'd have thought he would. They're all solicitous, but careful—they're walking on eggs here.

Wes Cobb hands Doug the morning *News-Press*. "The local section," he says tersely.

Doug turns to the second section of the paper. The story is on the top page, in the lower right-hand corner. He skims it quickly. The phrases "missing girl" and "possible kidnapping" leap out at him. His heart takes a hard thud in his chest.

The reporter got someone to talk. Doug feels a surge of anger coupled with a blast of impotence at not having been able to snuff it; he should've been more aggressive with the guy, except that would have been counterproductive.

But that's Doug the father who's upset, not Doug the newsman. The man reported a story—that's his job.

At least there are no pictures, and his family's name isn't specifically mentioned, although the catchphrase "the daughter of a prominent Montecito family in the communications industry" narrows the players. Fortunately, because it's Santa Barbara, most readers will assume it's a show-business family.

No one knows what to say initially, so Doug takes charge. "This is a story, it's out there, we have to cover it," he starts out. "The question is, how do we handle it?"

"Where are you, Doug?" Jane asks. "I mean with the police, not personally."

"They don't know anything yet, but they're pretty certain"—God, it's hard to say the words—"that it's a kidnapping." He pauses. "I am too, I'm afraid."

He fills them in on what Lisa Jaffe saw, and the gathering of material that might be evidence but may well come up dry.

Wes, the producer, a hardheaded pragmatist, speaks out. "Until events tell us otherwise, we have to treat this for what it's worth. We can't give it any more or less importance because it happened to you, Doug."

Doug nods. "I agree."

Wes has the morning story lineup in his hand. He looks it over. "There was a gang-related murder on the west side last night," he says, reading the items sequentially. "There's seismic retrofitting on Highway 154 on the Paradise Road bridge, starting at seven this morning, that's going to have traffic from the valley backed up to Santa Ynez. That's a biggie—people are going to want to know how long the delay's going to take, if they should divert all the way over to 101. We have Tina with a remote out there, we'll go to her live."

"We should lead with that," Doug offers, "and then come back to it at least once more the first half hour, then twice between six-thirty and seven. I think," he adds diplomatically. He doesn't run the news operation. He's free with his opinions, but that's why he hires pros.

Wes and Jane agree. They don't need to let the boss know that his suggestion is unnecessary, especially not today.

"Lead with the murder."

Joe Allison has been standing off to one side listening. He's the top anchorperson for the station, a rising star. Two years ago he was doing the local news in Cheyenne, Wyoming; two years from now, or less, he will be anchoring the 6:00 news in L.A. or New York or Chicago, or even working nationally, pinch-hitting for Tom Brokaw, sitting in on the *Today* show, doing the weekend news. Barely thirty, he's photogenic, authoritative, aggressive, and smart. He came out of Northwestern's journalism school M.A. program as a print reporter; he's a good writer, and he knows how to tell a story the right way.

"Then your story, then Highway 154," he says to Doug.

They all readily agree. It didn't take a rocket scientist to figure that out, but someone had to make the call. Joe did.

"Would you like me to do the piece?" Joe asks. "I'm here, I might as well do something."

The regular morning anchor is Wendy Gross, a competent if inexperienced young woman. She does a good, crisp job, but she isn't part of the core group and doesn't need to know the particulars of this. They'll clue her in regarding Joe's uncustomary involvement at the last minute.

"Sixty seconds?" Wes asks, regarding length.

"Or longer, if needed," Jane says. She hesitates. "Do we go with footage?"

The station had a team at Doug's house last night. Tina Jones, who's going to be at the Highway 154 scene this morning, did a brief standup, but they didn't use it on the eleven o'clock news. The footage is innocuous, Jane tells Doug—a dark house with some sheriff's department cars parked in front. Even people who know Doug's house might not recognize it.

Everyone looks at him.

"I guess so," he says grudgingly, feeling trapped. He has to—this is public news, particularly since the *News-Press* has put out a story. "But no footage of me or my wife, and no pictures of my daughter. Or her name," he adds emphatically.

"Are you sure?" Wes asks. *Meaning, are you sure we shouldn't be more specific?*

Doug takes a deep breath. "Fuck it. Name us. Just don't belabor it." They have to be professional, even if they're the victims. He has a sudden insight into how people must feel who have had this public scrutiny happen to them. No wonder people hate the media, the way they lay open wounds.

"You can proof the copy for me," Joe offers. "If something's offensive, we'll excise it."

"Write it like it was anyone," Doug tells him. "We can't bend this to suit our needs." He forces a smile. "Okay, people. Let's go to work."

Upstairs in his office, he shuffles through some papers, trying for a few moments to take his mind off what's happening to him. The office is a small space for a man of his stature. The only vanity touches are a few pictures on the walls of him with various notables—Governor Wilson, Senator Feinstein, Vice President Gore. The nicest feature of this office is the view, which looks down to the city, the harbor, the ocean. On a clear day he can see to the horizon. It's still too dark now to see much of anything.

He can't focus. He's too antsy. Jesus, he thinks. This is really happening. His child is gone, taken away. Every parent's worst nightmare.

* * *

Doug calls Sheriff Williams.

"I saw the *News-Press* story," Williams says. "They sure didn't waste any time," he says bitingly.

Doug tells him about the story the local station is doing this morning.

"I hope we have something by tonight."

That's all Williams can say? Doug is pissed, angry. "No one's called the house." There's an extension of his home telephone here at his office, as there's one of his office at his house—his public and private lives can't be divided.

"I'll let you know immediately if anything turns up on this end," Williams says. "I'm going to put a car in front of your house, to keep the lookie-loos and kooks away."

"Thanks. I appreciate that."

He touches base with Hampshire, his lawyer, then calls his house and speaks to Maria. Glenna's sleeping; she'll be out for hours with the pill he gave her. She needs to sleep; there's no point in stressing her out any more than she is. She'll find out about what's happened overnight soon enough. "Call me when she wakes up. And don't let anyone talk to her before I do," he emphasizes.

The story goes on the air. It runs two minutes. As soon as it wraps, Doug goes onto the floor and thanks the crew. He and Joe Allison talk briefly. For what it was, it went well. No histrionics, no doomsday predictions. A missing girl whose parents are grieving and worried about her, and hope that whoever carried her away from them will bring her home unharmed.

Emma Lancaster's disappearance is the first story after the first commercial break on the *Nightly News* on NBC, Doug's home network. It's seven at night in New York, four in the afternoon in Santa Barbara. Joe Allison does the standup in front of the Lancasters' house. Sheriff Williams is interviewed briefly: there are, as of now, no clues, and no one has been in touch with the family.

Doug and Glenna watch the live feed via satellite from inside their house. Glenna is a wreck. She slept until one in the afternoon, by which time Doug had done whatever he could do at the station and had come home to be with her. She was going to need his physical presence as much as possible, that he knew.

Fred Hampshire watches with them. He and Doug have to talk about this, formulate a strategy. Doug can't sit by passively and wait for events to unfold, they both agree on that. He's going to have to take some action, force the issue.

There have been requests for interviews from the other networks, CNN, Turner Broadcasting, Fox, the *New York Times*, *Los Angeles Times*, *Washington Post*, as well as the supermarket muckrakers. Hampshire issues a blanket statement to one and all: "No interviews, no intrusions on the family." Earlier in the day he hired a security agency to keep everyone at bay.

It's getting dark. Husband, wife, and lawyer sit in the study. "What do you want to do?" Hampshire asks.

"What *can* we do until someone calls and tells us what they want?" Glenna laments.

Hampshire steeples his fingers. "What if whoever did it doesn't call?"

"Why wouldn't they call?" she says, wild-eyed. "Isn't that the point? To get money from us?"

"The kidnapper might not want money," Hampshire says somberly.

The ramifications of that fall on her like a slab of concrete from twenty floors. "Oh, no!" she wails. "That can't be!"

"You have to face the possibility that whoever did this didn't do it for money, Glenna," he says. "There are a lot of fucked-up, crazy people out there. He might just have wandered in, seen her, and taken her."

She starts crying uncontrollably. Doug pulls her to him, squeezing her in a fierce embrace. "That's theoretical, honey," he says, trying to soothe her while shooting a murderous glance at Hampshire, "but it isn't what happened. Somebody wants money. He knew who we were, and that we can pay whatever it takes."

"How do you know that?" she rasps hoarsely. "We don't know who did this, so how do you know what he wants, whoever he is!"

He holds on to his composure—he has to, he can't handle his daughter being abducted and an out-of-control wife too, if he isn't in control himself. "It's a feeling, honey," he says as gently as he can. "I have to go with my instincts, there's nothing else I can do right now. Or you."

"Well, my instincts tell me something horrible has happened to her," she cries. "That she's somewhere out there in pain, waiting for us to come and rescue her. *And we aren't doing a goddamn thing about it!*"

DAY THREE

"Good evening. My name is Doug Lancaster. I'm the owner of KNSB."

Doug is seated at the anchor desk staring into the camera, the TelePrompTer on top scrolling down. He's in a dark business suit and has had makeup applied, something he's never done before, even on the rare occasions when he has addressed a television audience, but another sleepless night, mostly spent holding his hysterical wife in his arms, has created monster raccoon rings under his eyes and given him an unhealthy pallor. For this presentation he wants to look healthy and in control, so he went with the pancake.

"I am speaking to you tonight for a very personal reason."

It took an entire day to write this speech. Joe Allison and Jane Bluestine helped him, and Fred Hampshire vetted it to make sure Doug didn't say anything of a legal nature that could come back to haunt him later. He practiced reading the speech off the TelePrompTer several times, to make sure it would go smoothly.

Off to the side he can see himself in the monitor. Forcing himself not to look, so he won't be more self-conscious than he already is, he draws a calming breath and launches into it.

"Two nights ago my daughter, Emma Lancaster, was taken from her bedroom in our home. By now, many of you have heard about that, on this station and others, as well as in the newspapers. Several of you have called in to the station with condolences, sent letters and faxes, and e-mailed us. My wife and I are extremely grateful for that support.

"To this moment, however, we have had no communication whatsoever with the person or persons who took her. While the police, sheriff's department, state police, and FBI have all been working around the clock to try to find her, they have not come up with any clues."

He straightens himself in his chair—here comes the punch line.

"Tonight, here and now, I am taking the special step of using this public forum to offer a reward of two hundred fifty thousand dollars for Emma's safe return. I will pay that reward to anyone who can give us evidence that will enable us to find her alive and unharmed. If anyone out there watching knows anything about Emma, and you don't want to reveal who you are, we can arrange a way to get you the money without anyone knowing about it. I have discussed this with the police, and they have assured me that they will not interfere with this in any way."

A photo of Emma, taken at their resort home at Telluride over the Christmas holidays, comes up on the monitor. Doug glances at it out of the corner of his eye before proceeding. "This is what Emma looks like. She is fourteen years old, five feet four, weighs one hundred and ten pounds, and has light brown shoulder-length hair and hazel eyes."

Seeing her picture up there causes the words scrolling down the TelePrompTer to begin looking fuzzy to him. He forces himself to concentrate, to get through this without losing it.

"Most importantly," he says, fixing the lens with the firmest look he can muster, "if you are the person who took my daughter, I am asking that you return her safely. That's all. I give you my word that I won't try to pursue you in any way. I will do whatever you want me to do. I will pay you any way you want. I can even transfer money into an untraceable foreign bank account if that would make you feel more secure."

He's losing it—he needs to get this over before he breaks down.

"Please," he says, hearing the begging in his voice and not caring, "if you know anything about my daughter Emma's whereabouts, call us at this toll-free number." He glances at the monitor again as the 800 number comes up on the screen, and he reads it aloud. "If you are the man that took her and are afraid of how to get yourself out of this, call us. We are not monitoring this line. I repeat, the police are not monitoring this line. Your call will not be traced. Just call us, please. We'll do anything you want. Anything."

He comes to the end of his speech. He feels his voice beginning to crack, but that's all right. He can't hold his emotions in check any longer.

"Emma," he says. "If you're watching this, sweetheart, don't give up. Your mom and I and everyone we know are doing everything we can to find you." His eyes begin to tear. He has to get off.

"And we will."

DAY FOUR

A massive manhunt is set in motion, all up and down the Pacific Coast. Dozens of suspects are brought in for interrogation, not only from California, but from all over the West—Oregon, Washington, Arizona, Nevada. Every man with a history of sexual deviance, assault, or abduction is rounded up and questioned fiercely. Boys from all the local high schools she might have known, men who in any way had an association with her, even the choirmaster at St. Martin's Episcopal Church where she sang in the Sunday choir, are talked to.

Tens of thousands of flyers are distributed. People from the community, all kinds of people, people the Lancasters have never met in their lives, volunteer their time to hunt for Emma. In Goleta alone, at least a hundred people show up at the search command headquarters at the sheriff's substation to team up and go out looking. People search the hills, the beaches, every crack in every sidewalk from Los Angeles to Monterey.

While this is going on, the police lab finishes analyzing all the stuff they took from the gazebo, the footprint that was found outside Emma's room, the pictures taken of her room and the immediate surroundings.

"We didn't get any prints we can't account for," the sheriff tells Doug the day after the televised appeal. He has come to the house to present the bad news. "If this was a premeditated snatch, he was probably wearing gloves."

"If this was premeditated," Doug retorts, "why haven't we been contacted?"

"To mess with your head," the sheriff answers succinctly. "So that when he finally does get in touch, you won't be thinking of any retaliation."

"Well, it's working. My wife is on tranquilizers around the clock, and I'm wiped out."

"Hang in there, Mr. Lancaster. You've got to keep yourself together."

"Why? Why do I have to keep myself together? Why should I have to?" Fuck this presenting-a-calm-face-to-the-world shit. This is his child they're talking about.

"Because he might be watching you. Or having you watched."

Whoa! That's heavy. He never thought about that at all.

"If someone took your daughter because of some slight in the past, whether it's real or not, they could be playing all kinds of games with you."

Doug buries his head in his hands. "That's insane! What kind of bastard would do something like that? I can't think that way. It'll drive me crazy trying to figure out who would do something like that."

"Don't let it," the sheriff admonishes him. "And *do* start thinking that way. Because right now, we don't have a thing. Not one clue. Believe me, this is driving all of us up the wall."

Doug forces himself to calm down. "All right," he agrees. "I'll start putting together an enemies list."

There is a noteworthy detail that has come out of the evidence analysis. "There were condoms in that debris we found in the gazebo," Williams tells Doug. "Somebody was using the place as a love pad."

Doug is incredulous. "Are you serious?"

Williams nods. "All the same brand. The lab's going to do an analysis of the semen. I'll give odds they're all from the same person." He gives Doug an inquiring look. "Any guesses on who it might be?"

"No, but I'm damned pissed off about it. If there was one rubber, I guess it could've been from someone who was here for a party or something and snuck off, but several means someone who's here on a steady basis." He thinks for a moment. "Should we get semen samples from all my male employees?"

"That might be helpful," Williams says, "but not legal. Anyway, what connection would that have with Emma's disappearance? We have to keep our focus."

Doug shakes his head in frustration. "Where does this all lead us?"

"Hoping for a break" is the only answer the sheriff has to give him.

DAYS FIVE AND SIX

Another day goes by. Still no word.

The story is covered by every media outlet in the country. Doug patiently sits and gives interviews—he abhors the notoriety, but he'll do anything that might help. Maybe someone has seen Emma but wasn't watching television or reading the papers the first couple of days, or has seen her but, for whatever reason, is reluctant to come forward. More pressure from the media might do the trick.

There is some solace in going to work. It keeps him from sinking into self-pity. There is a world out there and he is a part of it, regardless of anything. And by getting out of his house he sees how much sympathy for him and his family this has engendered. Sometimes, coming home at night when it's dark, he will see groups of people standing near his house holding candles, conducting a silent vigil. He doesn't know these people, has never met them. Yet here they stand, mute support for his family and his daughter's safe return from whatever hell she's living in.

And there are ribbons. Yellow ribbons, thousands of them. Tied to trees all over the city. Every palm tree along Cabrillo Boulevard, the street that parallels the beach, has a yellow ribbon tied to it. He feels incredibly grateful and thankful to all the people who have done this work. And who are out there every day in search parties, looking for Emma.

DAY EIGHT

Eight days after Emma Lancaster's abduction from her Montecito bedroom in the dead of night, two UCSB college students, one male, one female, intrepid hikers, are making their way up the trailhead of Hot Springs Canyon. It's a tough climb; the trail is still muddy from the winter's rains and hasn't been cut back by the Forest Service since the fall. But they've wanted to get out for over a month, and they're experienced, so they plunge along, breaking trail if they have to. Moose, their black Lab, races ahead of them, then behind them, then ahead of them again.

They keep to one side of the stream. It's running full, and has been since before Christmas—too full and fast to cross. The rocks you'd normally use as stepping stones are either submerged or too slippery to step on. A fall and you'd be wet, cold, and likely injured.

The trail switches back, and they climb up single file, the actual width no more than two feet, barely wide enough to traverse. The dog, running ahead, is barking loudly, racing up and down in a small circle near where a piece of the trail has recently collapsed under the pressure of the water. Old tree roots protrude under the caved-in ground, and water from the stream has diverted to cut a new stream running parallel with the main one.

"How are we going to get around this?" the girl asks. She's a healthy outdoors lady, freckle-faced even in winter.

"Ford it, I guess," the guy says. "It doesn't look too deep." He looks down. "Go ahead, lead the way. It's only knee high."

"*You* lead the way. I don't want to get soaked if it's too deep." She peers into the dark, muddy water. "It looks deeper than that to me. Up to my thigh, anyway." She sticks one leg in. Immediately her leg is wet all the way to the bottom of her shorts. "Too high," she declares.

"Damn. I wanted to get to the top," he says, disappointed.

"Can't today," she consoles him. "We'll come back next week."

She turns to head back down the trail, shifting to one side to avoid their dog, who is running in a tight circle, barking at something off to the side, slightly up the hill. "Moose," she calls to him, "leave the rabbits alone. Or whatever it is. If it's a skunk, boy, you're riding home in the trunk. Come on, now, move your ass."

The dog keeps barking, going out of his doggie mind.

"What?" she exclaims with some annoyance. She wanted to go to the top too. Now they have to walk back, and they've got a stupid barking dog who doesn't want to come with them.

"Come on, dammit," she says, reaching for Moose's collar to pull him, and as she reaches out, she slips on the soft mud that's collapsing under her feet. Instinctively she puts her hand out to break her fall.

Her hand hits something hard, like a tree root or a rock. Except it has soft covering on top of it, like moss. But it isn't moss. She knows the feeling of moss.

She gropes into the underbrush. It's long, whatever she's put her hand on, and . . .

She screams.

Sheriff's vehicles, the coroner's wagon, paramedic trucks, all converge on the scene as soon as word goes out over the police scanner that a girl's body has been found. The police set up a cordon around the scene, keeping everyone out, including the press.

Sheriff Williams doesn't have to look at the body. He knows.

Emma has been dead for days. The coroner ascertains that immediately. Probably within twenty-four hours of when she was abducted.

The body is already in an advanced state of decomposition due to the weather.

The crime scene has been polluted due to all the people that have converged on it. Even so, there are footprints, not fresh ones, that scream out as soon as they're discovered by one of Williams's men.

The left shoe print with the gouge in the treads. The same shoe print that had been found outside Emma Lancaster's bedroom.

Whoever had left that print at the Lancaster house had left it here, as well. Which means that whoever had been there had almost certainly brought the body of Emma Lancaster here.

Her abductor. Her killer.

Williams drives to the Lancasters' home to tell Doug and Glenna, dreading what's coming. He isn't going to tell them this over the telephone. He's barely out of his car before they rush outside to meet him.

"Is she—?" Glenna starts to ask, then she sees the expression of grief on the lawman's face.

"Emma's body has been found," Williams tells them immediately, before they can have any hope. Better not to arouse hope, even if only for a microsecond, he knows from past, distressing experience.

"Aaaaahhhh!" Glenna starts keening, a low animal moan, eyes rolling back into her head, her body swaying, then collapsing in sections, a slow free-fall. Doug lunges, grabbing her and preventing her from hitting the ground. He lifts her in his arms. Her body is shaking uncontrollably now.

He carries her into the house and lays her on a couch in the dark living room. (The house has gotten progressively darker every day, as Glenna has been closing curtains against the life outside.) He spreads an afghan over her supine form. She'll sleep for a while, he thinks, a defense against a reality that is too much for her to handle.

DAY NINE

News of the discovery of Emma's body spreads like wildfire. Within an hour the house is surrounded by television crews and teams of reporters. Doug has called the station and told them. Now he stands in front of his house facing a barrage of reporters. He looks into the bright lights of the television cameras, a platoon of microphones held out towards him to catch his words.

"I have a brief statement to make, but I won't answer any questions." He straightens his shoulders against the onslaught of emotion. "As you know by now, our daughter Emma—our only child—has been found dead. The police assume she was murdered. There will be an autopsy done to determine the cause of death."

He pauses to collect himself. "My wife and I are in shock. I cannot begin to describe how deeply hurt and wounded we feel. As painful as our lives have been since the night Emma was abducted from our home, it is nothing compared to how we feel now, because until now we could hold on to some hope that she was still alive and would be returned to us. Now that hope has been shattered."

He stops again, to pull himself together, as much as he can.

"I have only a few things to say. The police have assured me that the hunt for Emma's killer will not diminish. Instead, they will intensify their efforts to find out who did this, and bring him to justice. In that regard, I am doubling the reward I offered last week. I am now offering half a million dollars for information that will lead to the arrest and conviction of the inhuman bastard who stole my daughter's life—from her and from us."

A *woosh* rises from the assembled reporters and their entourages—talk about a story! This is going to flush out every weirdo and freak who envisions getting rich off a family's grief. And it may even help in finding the kidnapper—half a million dollars will loosen a lot of lips that know secrets meant to be buried. Most people would turn in their mothers for a sum like that.

"The other thing I want to say is, now that this ordeal is over, my wife and I want to be left alone. I know that we are semipublic figures, and that we ourselves are members of the media, and that we are, and unfortunately will continue to be, news. But, please, folks—this is a horrible time for us. We ask that you act decently, and give us some space to try and put our lives back together."

A few reporters, not heeding his entreaties, begin to shout questions at him. But he turns his back on them and goes into his house.

The television reporters, including one from his station, do their standups with the house in the background. Then they all pack up and leave, and the house stands alone in darkness.

The postmortem comes back two days later.

Glenna and Doug are in their house. Williams stands in front of them, feeling incredibly ill at ease. When he saw the coroner's report an hour ago he couldn't believe it, but Dr. Limones, the county coroner, assured him that there could be no doubt the findings were accurate.

Williams has the document with him. He reads from it. "Cause of death was from an object striking the head."

"Was she sexually assaulted?" Glenna asks hoarsely.

She's been up and around since yesterday, after she woke up, first from the sleep-shock of hearing the news, then from the sedative their doctor had given her, she decided she couldn't keep doing this—denying what had happened and opting out from living. Now she sits on a couch with Doug, steeling herself to hear the worst. Emma's dead, so whatever happened, it's in the past.

"She had . . ." Williams pauses. "There is evidence of sexual activity."

Glenna moans.

Williams looks pained. "But not necessarily forced entry," he says quickly.

She looks up sharply. "What do you mean?"

"There had been penetration," he stammers. He dreads what he has to say next. "The coroner's conclusion is that the sexual activity . . . may have been consensual."

Glenna goes ballistic. "Are you insane?" she cries. "She was fourteen years old! She was kidnapped from her bedroom! She's only been having her period a year, for Christsakes! Let me see that." She tries to grab the autopsy report from his hand.

Doug restrains her. "Glenna, don't." He looks at Williams. "Is this true?" he asks incredulously.

"I'm afraid it is."

"Oh, man!" Doug pushes the heels of his hands up against the tops of his eye sockets. "This is going to turn the search for her killer in a whole other direction, isn't it?"

"I don't know," Williams answers truthfully.

"Doesn't this indicate that whoever took her might have known her?"

"It might. It's certainly a possibility we have to consider."

"Oh, man, this is . . ." Doug doesn't know what to say to this excruciating piece of information.

"She was sexually active." Glenna's dull voice pulls him around. "Those rubbers up in the gazebo. Someone was using them on her. With her," she amends.

"For what it's worth, I don't think her having been active has anything to do with the other," Williams says.

"You just said . . ." Doug says.

"That it might influence the investigation? That whoever took her might have known her? It's theoretically possible, but my cop's gut instinct tells me it isn't. I think this was either an act done by a sexual deviate, or a kidnapping for money that went wrong."

Doug has been pacing the floor. "Who's going to know about this?"

"That's up to the district attorney. He can seal the report and keep it confidential. If he thinks that's in the public interest," he adds pointedly.

Ray Logan is the D.A. Doug knows him well—the station endorsed Ray in the special election that was called after the popular incumbent, Luke Garrison, abruptly announced he was resigning, walked out of his office, and disappeared off the face of the earth. Ray owes Doug.

"Anything else?" he asks Williams. "What about leaks from the coroner's office? Or yours."

"I'm the only one in my department who's seen this," Williams says stiffly. "And the coroner's office is pretty good about keeping their mouths shut."

"Good," Doug says. "Because sullying her memory won't serve any useful purpose. Someone out there kidnapped her and killed her. That's what this is all about, isn't it?"

"Yes, Mr. Lancaster. That's what this is all about."

Doug and Ray Logan talk on the phone. Logan extends his heartfelt condolences. He hopes to God the police catch the sonofabitch who did this.

The autopsy report regarding the death of Emma Lancaster is sealed, in the public interest.

After the first few weeks, when no suspect in what is now a kidnapping and murder is found, the media frenzy subsides. Doug goes back to work, Glenna starts going out into the world again, they try to patch together the pieces of their splintered lives.

A few months go by. Despite the allure of Doug's reward offer, there are still no legitimate leads.

The ongoing strain is taking its toll on their marriage. The knowledge that Emma had been sexually active haunts Glenna. She can't stop talking to Doug about it. She tells him that not knowing about such an important part of her daughter's life, when she had thought they were so close, so mother-daughter bonded, tears at her insides.

And she can't stop talking about her persistent conviction that Emma's being sexually active was in some way tied to her abduction. In her wild fantasies, she tells Doug, she imagines Emma being a willing partner in her disappearance, imagines that the whole thing wasn't a kidnapping at all.

Doug doesn't want to hear that. He's in denial about it. You don't sneak out to have sex while two of your friends are sleeping in your room, then wind up being found murdered five miles away, hastily buried off a virtually inaccessible trail. This was a kidnapping, pure and simple.

More and more they find themselves going in different directions.

Sheriff Williams comes to the house on a Saturday afternoon after lunch. It's a few days before the beginning of summer. Their gardens, tended to perfection, are in full color—the only brightness in their lives anymore.

The three sit by the pool. "So far we haven't been able to develop any leads, nothing useful at all," Williams tells them somberly.

Their faces register dismay and despair. "So her killer's never going to be found," Glenna says dully. She's lost fifteen pounds since this ordeal began. Her face, although still striking to look at, is all bones and angles.

"Never say never," Williams says. "Sometimes things come up. Later."

"By accident. Chance."

He nods slowly. "We can't manufacture something that doesn't exist."

Doug sees him out. "Thanks for all your help," Doug says.

"I'm sorry we haven't done better," the sheriff apologizes. "Truly sorry."

"You've done your best. And like you said, something could still turn up. My reward still stands. Make sure people don't forget that."

The two men shake hands. "Good luck, Mr. Lancaster," Williams says.

Luck will have nothing to do with this, Doug thinks. He keeps the thought to himself.

★ ★ ★

Glenna files for divorce the week after Labor Day and moves to a condominium on Butterfly Beach, near the Biltmore Hotel. They put the house up for sale. Doug stays in the house until it's sold. The sale is finalized the week before Christmas.

Emma Lancaster's kidnapping spawned a multiple tragedy: one life gone, two others ruined.

A year goes by. Whoever abducted and murdered Emma is still at large. No leads have ever panned out, no perpetrator has ever been arrested.

A YEAR LATER

Joe Allison, cruising down Coast Village Road after midnight in his Porsche turbo, is styling. Earlier in the evening he had dinner with Nicole Rogers, his girlfriend, a stunning woman befitting a star newscaster, who is finishing the last semester towards her law degree at Pepperdine, commuting down the coast to Malibu. Now, a Cohiba double corona in hand, the balls-to-the-walls twelve-speaker stereo blasting UB40, he's feeling awesome.

The dinner was a celebratory event. A month ago, his agent negotiated a contract for Joe to be the 5 P.M. anchor at KNBC, the network's station in Los Angeles. This evening's six o'clock newscast was his valedictory performance at KNSB.

Doug Lancaster joined Joe and Nicole for dinner. He was sorry to see his star anchorman leave, but Joe's ascension had been inevitable from the day he started work at the station. Joe was going places, and Doug was happy to have been a part of it.

Joe's yearly fee is going to start in the medium six figures, with a $125,000 signing bonus. And they promised him a good crack, down the line a year or so, at some of the network's most prestigious showcases—the *Weekend News*, subbing on the *Today Show*, doing live remotes on the *Evening News*. Tom Brokaw called Joe personally during the negotiations to congratulate him on this upward career move, even joshing that he'd better start looking over his shoulder.

Joe and Nicole aren't spending the night together, as they usually do. That's the only downside to his new job—she isn't coming with him. She has a life here, and she isn't ready to give it up. And he isn't ready for that kind of commitment either. The career's got to come first; the personal life will go on hold.

He doesn't know how long the revolving red lights have been flashing in his rearview mirror. He hasn't had that much to drink, but he isn't confident he can go under .08 percent on a blood-alcohol test. You don't need much booze in your system to test positive—he's done many a news story on this issue.

"I'll need to see your driver's license and registration, sir," the cop tells him, shining his flashlight into the window. The cop takes a closer look. "You're Joe Allison, right? From Channel 8."

Joe smiles at the officer. This might be a small pond, but he's a big fish in it. "That's me," he says brightly. Tone it down, man, he thinks to himself, you're giving it away. "I wasn't speeding, was I?" he asks as conversationally as he can. "I'm usually good at staying at the limit." Pulling his wallet from his hip pocket and handing over the driver's license, he fumbles around in his crowded glove compartment for the registration. The light isn't very good. "How fast was I going?" he asks again.

"You weren't speeding, but you were weaving over the double yellow line. I'm going to ask you to step out of your car onto the sidewalk, sir, so I can Field test you for sobriety. After you find the registration." A beat. "This is your car, isn't it?"

"Yes, it's mine." He digs more frantically in the dark compartment. This is pathetic; he needs to throw three-quarters of this shit out. His head buried halfway under the console now, he continues his line of patter, speaking slowly, carefully enunciating each word. "I'll tell you right now, officer, I have had a few drinks." Cop to the small indiscretion now and avoid the larger consequence, that's the smart strategy. His name in the paper or on a police report is what he wants to avoid. Not the best way to impress your new bosses down in Los Angeles.

"After the test, sir." The officer's right hand is resting lightly on his hip, above the gun. He's beginning to get impatient. "Do you need some help?" He starts to shine his flashlight into the car.

"Got it." Damn! He was panicked for a minute there. Bad enough he wasn't driving a straight line. Not producing his paperwork would do him in for sure. Although in truth he feels his driving was fine, but maybe he swerved—once. He wasn't paying attention.

He hands the slip to the cop, who looks it over.

"Okay. Now step out, Mr. Allison."

Slowly, carefully, Joe gets out of the car. As he opens the door, the cop's flashlight catches a reflection off something lying on the floor behind the seat.

"Excuse me, sir," the officer says tersely. "What's this?"

"What's what?" Allison turns to look behind him.

There's a bottle of Maker's Mark bourbon on the floor. It's half empty. "Turn around, sir," the cop says harshly. "Come up here onto the sidewalk, and place both hands behind your head." Keeping his eyes on Joe, he bends down and picks up the bottle. "Having an opened bottle of spirits in a vehicle is illegal, Mr. Allison."

Joe's startled. "Hey, I don't know how this got here," he protests. "I don't even drink bourbon."

"Do as I say."

Joe backs off. How did that get there? "The parking lot attendant must've left it there, because it isn't mine, I swear to God."

The officer pats him down. "Please sit down on the ground, sir, with your hands behind your head." He opens the passenger door, shining the flashlight on the floorboards and under the seats.

"That isn't mine," Joe protests again.

The cop ignores him. He starts rummaging around in the still-open glove compartment, taking items out and laying them on the seat.

"There's nothing in there." The sidewalk is damp; his ass is getting wet through his trousers, and he's sweating like a bandit under the arms.

The officer has almost finished searching through the pile of bills, old registrations, used food wrappers, and assorted other junk. All the way in the back, almost buried in a crease in the lining, he feels something like a key. He shines his light into the recess, pushing some of the junk aside so he can pull it out and see what it is.

A couple of house keys on a short key ring attached to a funny-looking cross. Expensive, the cop thinks, tossing the keys in his palm. Why does this seem familiar?

Then he remembers.

Joe is brought to the police station. He doesn't have a lawyer in town; he's never needed one. He tries to call his agent in L.A., but Scott's on the red-eye to New York.

At least they've got him in a single cell, not sharing with anyone else.

The key ring belonged to Emma Lancaster. Her mother had bought it for her in Greece, when they were on vacation the summer before last. The summer before she died.

It's after one in the morning. Bert Sterling and Terry Jackson, who had been the lead detectives on the kidnapping case, are called at home. They dress hurriedly and come down to the station. Sheriff Williams is also summoned and comes in.

Joe has already been Mirandized out in the field which he assumed had been on the DUI and open-bottle violation. The arresting officer wasn't specific. The officers talk about what they should do.

Williams is cautiously optimistic—what an incredible stroke of luck. "We've got to be really careful here. We don't want to blow this." He thinks about what to do. He calls the district attorney, Ray Logan.

Logan listens intently as Williams fills him in over the phone. There are good reasons to consider Joe Allison a prime suspect, both men agree. The key ring, of course, is a damning piece of evidence. Allison knew the Lancaster house and property well; he'd been there dozens of times. He may well have known the alarm-system codes. And as ugly as the prospect might be, he could be the guy who was fucking Emma—he's great-looking, charismatic, exactly the kind of man a young girl just learning how to fall in love would go for.

Logan gets to the jail in less than twenty minutes. "What do you think?" he asks the sheriff.

"I think it could be him," the sheriff says. "That key ring . . ."

"A big piece, anyway," Logan agrees. He ponders the options, then says to the sheriff, "Let's talk to the man." He thinks a moment longer. "And I want to send one of your men to his house. I'll call in the search warrant."

Williams turns to Sterling. "Go get 'em, slugger. You know what we're looking for."

A deputy unlocks the door to the holding cell where Joe's been stashed. Joe jerks awake from his light slumber. "What's going on?" he asks.

The deputy offers no explanation. "Follow me."

He leads Allison out of the cell block into the interview section and places him in a small, windowless room. In the middle of the room is a government-issue table with three beat-up metal chairs. There's also a video camera hidden in the corner of the ceiling that Joe doesn't know about.

"Have a seat. Someone'll be in shortly."

Joe looks around at the drab surroundings. What the hell's going on? he thinks.

Terry Jackson comes into the room, closing the door behind him. He's wearing sweatpants and a UCSB varsity basketball sweatshirt, the easiest things to throw on when he got the call. He's a lanky black man in his late thirties; he played small-college basketball upstate and is known for his booming laugh and needling humor.

"Mr. Allison. Terry Jackson. I'm a detective here in the department. I watch you on television."

Joe grimaces. "I feel like a jerk."

"Yeah, I can understand. You shouldn't have been drinking and driving, man."

"I didn't have that much to drink," Joe protests, but not too hard. These cops hear that a million times a day, he knows. Better to play it cool.

Jackson drops into a chair on the opposite side of the table from Joe, turning it around. He folds his arms on the scarred chairback, leans forward comfortably. "You shouldn't be in here," he says.

"Well, okay." That's good to hear, coming from a cop. "That's how I feel, too."

"So what I'd like to do is, I'd like to ask you a few questions and send you on your way, if that's okay with you."

Joe lets out an audible sigh of relief. "That's fine."

"Good." Jackson leans further forward. "The officer read you your rights, right?"

Joe stares at him quizzically. "What are you talking about?" he asks.

"Out there in the street, when you were stopped." Jackson's smile is open. "I can't talk to you at all if you haven't been told your rights," he explains. "It's the law."

"Well . . ." Joe's hesitant. This is the first time in his life that he's been in a jail cell. He isn't following this clearly—he's too nervous.

Jackson stands up, heads for the door. "Listen, if you've got any kind of problem with this, it's not a big deal."

"Wait a minute." Joe stops him. "Am I going to be released now anyway?"

Jackson stops a step from the door. "That I can't do," he says. "But it's no big thing, you'll be sprung sometime later this morning."

No way. He wants out now. There could be a reporter or someone who knows him around in the morning, and then he'd really be screwed.

"That's okay," he says before Jackson can leave. "He read me my rights."

Jackson turns back to him. "And you're all right with that?"

"Sure, I'm fine." He smiles. "I have nothing to hide."

Jackson sits back down again. "That's good, Mr. Allison. A little cooperation from you, a few pieces of information, and we can wrap this up." He takes the key ring, which is in a Ziploc bag, out of his pocket and places it on the table between them. "This belongs to you, that's correct?" he asks, taking the key ring out of the bag and passing it across the table.

Joe reaches out and picks the key ring up, looks at it. He hadn't seen the arresting officer take it out of his car. "No. This isn't mine."

Jackson seems surprised. "It isn't?"

"No. I don't recognize it."

Jackson sits back, his arms crossed in front of his chest. "That's weird."

"Why?"

"Because we found it in your car."

"Well, it isn't mine. Somebody must've left it in there." First the bottle, now this? What's this all about?

"Like who?" the detective asks.

"I don't know," Joe answers truthfully. "I have a million people riding in my car. Anyone could've tossed it in there."

In an adjoining room Logan and Williams are watching over the video feed.

"He's handling this well," Williams comments; he's nervous as hell about this. "If he's our man." Doubt is starting to creep in.

"He's a television personality," Logan reminds him. "He's trained to be cool under pressure." He pauses. "And to lie when it's convenient."

Inside the interrogation room, Jackson is pressing. "Man, you let anybody rides with you mess around in your glove compartment?" he asks with a disbelieving smile. "I don't let anyone in my box, not even my old lady. I got my car phone in there, gasoline credit cards, all kinds of personal stuff. Come on, man," he says jocularly, "a guy like you?" He winks at Joe. "You're not going to let anybody rummage around in your personal stuff, I know that for a fact."

Joe shrugs. "I don't keep my personal things in there. What is the point of all this?" he adds.

Jackson changes the subject. "Tonight was your swan song at the station, so I hear."

"Yes. I'm moving to Los Angeles."

"Ooooh," Jackson croons. "Tough city. Too big for this small-town boy. But if you want to get to the top, you got to make the move, right?"

"Yes."

"Guess your boss'll be sorry to see you go. Mr. Lancaster."

"He knows it's a good career move. That's the way it is in our business."

Jackson shakes his head in sadness. "What a terrible thing that family's gone through. And they never did find out who did it. We take that personally in this office," he adds, as if defending the entire department.

"You're right," Joe agrees. It was a terrible tragedy. He knows—he and Glenna have talked about it. Since her marriage broke up, she and Joe have spent time together. She needs someone to talk to, and he's a sympathetic listener.

"You were pretty close to them."

"I still am. I've talked to Mrs. Lancaster about it. Moving ninety miles south isn't going to diminish our friendship."

"That's good, that's good." The detective stares at Joe for a beat. "That young girl, their daughter. I heard she was a hell of a nice kid."

"She was a wonderful kid," Joe says forcefully.

"A little headstrong, though? We've heard stories she used to sneak out and meet up with boys, right under her parents' noses."

"I wouldn't know about that," Joe answers stiffly. He's uncomfortable talking about this kind of personal thing regarding the dead girl, especially with someone he's never met before.

"You never heard any of that?" the cop asks.

"No."

"But you were friends. Not only with the parents, but with the girl too."

"Well, sure," Joe admits readily, "Emma and I were friends, despite the difference in our ages. She was very mature for her age."

Jackson sits back. "I'm about done here," the cop says. "A couple more questions is all. Not about your deal," he adds, "that was an accident. We're not going to bust you on that. We don't want you going down to L.A. starting your new job with a cloud over your head."

Joe sags with relief. That's what he's been waiting and hoping to hear. "Thank you," he says to the cop. He's revised his attitude about the officer—he isn't a bad guy, he had a job to do.

"That kidnapping still bugs me." Jackson leans forward again. "I was one of the detectives working on it, and us not solving it, it just . . . it sticks right here," he says, pointing to his Adam's apple.

"I can understand that."

"You were around the house all the time, weren't you," Jackson says suddenly by way of left field.

"A fair amount."

"You were probably there the day she was snatched."

"Not that day, no. I hadn't been there for about a week, as I recall. All the rain, there wasn't much going on in the way of parties and whatever."

Jackson files that away in his mental computer. "Did we ever interview you?"

"Yes."

"Regarding your whereabouts and so forth."

"Yes." They hadn't pressed him—he obviously wasn't a suspect.

"Did the officer who questioned you ever ask your opinion of who might have done it?"

"Of course."

"What did you tell him?"

"That it had to have been some sick bastard."

"That was before or after her body was recovered?"

Joe thinks a moment. It's been over a year ago now, and everything then was crazy, no one was thinking straight; he certainly wasn't. "Before, I guess. Although it could've been after," he says with confusion.

"I could check that out," the cop says. "Not that I have any cause to," he adds quickly. "Now that it's over, and there's been a year to cogitate on it, who do you think did it? I don't mean a specific person," he clarifies, "there's no way you could know that. I mean what kind of person. Crazy or sane? A stranger . . . or someone she knew?" He's staring into Joe's eyes, pupil to pupil, as he's asking these questions.

"I don't know." Joe stifles a yawn. Jesus, he's exhausted. He doesn't have his watch, they took it off him along with the rest of his stuff, but he guesses it must be three or four in the morning. "Look. I've answered all your questions, like I said I would. Now I'd like you to let me go, like you said you would." He stands up. "A deal's a deal. I've kept up my end, I'd like you to keep up yours."

Williams and Logan, watching this over the closed-circuit, wince. "He's right," the D.A. says. "Legally, we can't hold him any longer."

"I'd better pull my boy at Allison's place," Williams concedes. "I don't want him there when he shows up." He picks up the telephone to dial Detective Sterling's pager number.

Before he finishes, Sterling comes flying through the door.

There's a knock on the door to the interrogation room. Jackson opens it. Sterling is on the other side. He says something into Jackson's ear.

Jackson exits the room without a word of explanation to Joe, firmly closing the door behind him. The lock clicks; it sounds like a gunshot to Allison's ears. He's starting to get freaked. What kind of number are these guys running on him? Why have they left him alone?

Jackson joins the others in the viewing room. He sees a paper bag on a table in the corner of the room. Sheriff Williams strides over to it and dumps out the contents: a pair of running shoes. He picks the left shoe up. "Check this out."

The shoe has a cut-mark in the bottom of the sole, as if sliced with a knife or the edge of a shovel: a solid match to the cut-mark on the shoe print left in the ground outside Emma's bedroom, and at the trail where her body was found.

Jackson high-fives Sterling. "Great work!"

They've also found some condoms, the same type as the ones discovered in the Lancaster gazebo the first night they searched the place. Williams, who knows something important that none of the others knows, treads lightly with them.

"This is a popular brand," he says cautiously. "In and of themselves they don't mean anything."

"Unless . . ." Sterling doesn't finish his sentence.

"Don't go barking up a tree you don't know where the branches are," Williams says sternly, cutting off any further discussion. "We have everything we need without any wild conjecturing."

He's going to call Doug Lancaster right away. And Glenna too. An end, finally, to this senseless, horrendous tragedy.

TWO

After you go a couple of hours north of San Francisco on Highway 101, past Ukiah twenty miles or so, you hang a left onto California 20, an old winding road that leads through dense woodland, most of it in Jackson State Forest. Ten miles before you get to Bartstown on the coast, you take a right, going north again now on County Road 97, a narrow two-lane lush with greenery on both sides, stands of pine and cedar and giant redwood, wildflowers and wild vines bursting into color at this time of year, early spring, after it has been raining all winter and the ground is bursting with life.

The road forks and you bear left onto Parris Road, which is almost never traveled unless you live on it, which hardly anyone does. It winds up and around the low green felt-covered mountains, moving into higher ground, switchbacking in ever narrowing circuitous loops and curves. The road is poorly maintained, potholed in many places; you have to be careful driving it or you could be plunging several hundred feet down a chasm. Even the few locals who regularly use this road drive it respectfully. Still, there are one or two fatalities on it every year, marijuana farmers hauling their product who fail to negotiate an unmarked curve on a moonless night.

After surviving this road you turn off, a hard right, onto an even thinner one which is little more than badly laid asphalt-gravel mix on hard-packed clay. In the winter it can be impassable for weeks at a time. You take this road three miles, to the ninth driveway off to the left.

"Ah!" the old man says to himself, "he really lives to hell and gone." If he'd known the drive up from Oakland, where he rented his Dodge Stratus, was going to be so treacherous, he never would have come. You'd think the man he was coming to see would have warned him, knowing his age. Picked him up in Ukiah. Some gesture of civility.

At the entrance to the driveway there is a thick rust-speckled chain that hooks into two iron poles set on either side of the narrow road, next to a weather-beaten tin sign on a wooden post on which is hand-painted in big block white paint letters the warning PRIVATE PROPERTY. KEEP OUT. THIS MEANS YOU—I SHIT YOU NOT. Under which, in a smaller, different hand, someone has spray-painted "He really means it!" The sign is riddled with bullet holes.

The chain is down now, lying slack across the entrance road.

The old man phoned two days before and informed the dweller of this hostile property that he was coming. Otherwise, he is sure, the chain would be firmly in place, barring access to any and all that might be tempted to violate its borders.

Judge Ferdinand De La Guerra, now retired, sits in his idling car for a few minutes, looking up the hard-packed dirt-gravel that leads to the house. Was this a smart idea? At the time he decided to come, it had seemed like a pretty good idea; of course, the fact that there were hardly any other options available, none that he could think of, anyway, rendered the decision moot, pretty much.

The judge emeritus is a sixth-generation Santa Barbaran, a direct descendant of one of the original land-grant families. There are buildings and streets all over the county named after the De La Guerras. Until a couple of decades ago, men like him ran the show. They decided how much new business would be allowed to come into town, who ran for mayor and city council, how the pie was going to be cut up. That isn't true anymore; democratization with its sloppy, anarchic style has taken over, which is okay, a democracy has to be democratic, he knows that and believes it, even if it means not as much gets done, and what is accomplished costs a lot more.

The problem is, getting democratic doesn't mean more people

share the control. It only means that different people have it now—the ones who are willing to put in the time, serve on the committees, hold the lesser offices, and so on. His people used to do that, too, but in their spare time; they had businesses to run. Now being a politician is a full-time occupation.

The other people who are in control now, besides the new breed of politicians, both on the right and on the left, are those with money, many of whom haven't lived in Santa Barbara for very long. Doug Lancaster is one of them. Not only is he rich as hell, he has the power of the media, because he owns a big piece of it. And he and his former wife certainly put in the time, there's no disputing that. The symphony, Music Academy, art museum, history museum, you name it, they get involved. Good people doing good things who wield considerable power. Which is the reason the old man has flown and then driven up here today.

He looks at his watch. Almost five-thirty. He drives up the narrow, rutted, winding road, profuse with wild plant life. Finally, after about five minutes, he comes to a clearing in which Luke's house sits amidst blankets of native grasses and wildflowers. Built of redwood, with a goodly amount of glass wrapping around, the house sits low to the ground, spreading and enveloping its piece of the property, rather than imposing a will. It reminds the old judge, in its own way, of the adobes of the Southwest that seem to grow up from the earth, rather than having been arbitrarily placed on it.

The dogs—of course there would be dogs, three of them—come running out at the sound of the approaching car. They don't look particularly fierce, but you never can tell. Around here, people establish elaborate lines of defense, dogs being some of the first soldiers you encounter. Then electric fences, elaborate camouflage, and finally guns.

Luke knows the old judge is coming. So these should not be attack dogs. Still, the old man sits in the car waiting for the owner of the dogs to show.

Instead of the man he has come all this way to see, a woman appears. Medium height, slender, nicely built. Striking features, long dark hair in a thick braid down her back. She's wearing loose-fitting

Levi's, a Bridges To Babylon 1997–98 tour T-shirt, and shower flops. She peers towards the car, waving a tentative welcoming hand.

"You have to be Judge De La Guerra." Her voice is low, rich, tinged with a trace of south of the border.

"Yes," he calls back in answer.

Two fingers to her mouth, she whistles loudly through her teeth, and the dogs sit down on their haunches, red tongues lolling out.

"They're harmless," she says. "Strictly for show."

The old man gets out of the car, stretches. His body doesn't like car trips like this one anymore; he stiffens up easily. He reaches his hand out as the woman approaches.

"Riva Montoya," she introduces herself.

"Ferdinand De La Guerra."

"What do they call you?"

He smiles: She's direct. He likes that. "Fred. Judge. The old coot."

"Welcome to our casa, Fred. Come on inside." She heads off towards the house. Hastily he grabs his overnight satchel and briefcase from the backseat and follows her. She's a lovely sight to follow, the judge thinks. The guy could always pick them. Especially Polly, until that went south.

"You want a beer, glass of wine, something stronger?" Riva asks.

"I'd better put some food in my stomach before I have anything like that to drink," he says. "I passed on lunch. I wanted to make sure I gave myself enough time to get here before dark, in case I got lost."

"Well, then, you've come to the right place," she says heartily, leading him into the kitchen through the back door. Different pots and pans are bubbling on the stove, and inside it as well—a collage of enticing aromas.

"I'll be right with you," Riva tells him. "Look around the house, make yourself at home. Luke had a crisis to tend to; he ought to be back any decade now."

The house is built in a modified hunting-lodge style: a long main room with the kitchen at one end, then dining area, living room, partially separated den at the far end. A hallway leads back off the living room section to the bedrooms.

The interior walls have been adobe-plastered. More than a dozen paintings, mostly California landscapes, hang on the walls, and there are bookshelves all over the place, books falling out of them onto the floor, bookmarked, old, dog-eared. Off to one side there's a huge stereo system; several speakers are set high on the walls around the cavernous room. A big-screen TV is visible in the study.

"We've got the mother of all satellite dishes," Riva calls out from the kitchen as he stands in the center of the living room taking it in, "so if you've got to satisfy your CNN or *World News Tonight* jones, you're covered."

"Thanks," he replies absentmindedly. What a place! The ultimate backwoods house.

Riva comes into the room carrying large wooden bowls filled with guacamole and salsa and a basket of chips that smell homemade. "Dig into this," she says graciously, "and let me know when you want something liquid. I make a killer margarita, if I do say so myself." She moves towards the front doorway, balancing the food on her arms and hands. "But you know what?" she says, leading him outside, "it tastes even better when you're sitting on our front porch."

She's right—the vista is absolutely breathtaking. From his aerie De La Guerra looks out over thousands of acres of virgin forest, mostly redwood and huge ponderosa pine, rolling down the sides of the low mountains until fifteen miles in the distance the village of Bartstown sits tucked up against the Pacific. The ocean, an almost infinite variety of greens and aquamarines and blues and whitecaps, extends 180 degrees south to north, stretching out to a hundred-mile-deep horizon. At this time of day the low light of the westering sun, some of it clear, some refracted through the cloud cover, is changing in color as it starts its final descent, transmuting from pale yellow to blood orange, casting shifting patterns of light and darkness on the water. Even from here he can see the high waves foaming up on the rocky beach.

Sitting in a battered Adirondack chair, De La Guerra scoops up a hearty dollop of Riva's guacamole on a chip, dips it into the salsa, and wolfs it down. Man, spicy! But delicious. "Whew!" His tongue starts dancing around in his mouth. He hadn't realized how hungry he was. Judicious with the salsa after that first fiery bite, he scarfs several more of the avocado-laden morsels, hunkering over the bowl so as not to drip any onto his trousers.

The edge off his hunger, the bowl of guacamole perched in his lap, the old man stretches out and contemplates the extraordinary scene. Why would anyone want to leave this? he thinks to himself. Not a comforting thought—he doesn't want to go home empty-handed.

"Why're you here?" she asks him suddenly.

"Yeah," comes a man's low drawl out of nowhere. "You planning on hanging with us for a couple weeks?"

Startled, De La Guerra almost drops the bowl. Luke Garrison has materialized on the porch, from where, the judge knows not. He squints as he looks up at the man beside him, the sun coming over his shoulder, backlighting him. "Don't you know better than to sneak up on an old man with a heart condition?"

"Come on, you'll outlive us all, Freddie," Luke drawls, looking down at his former mentor. "You look pretty damn good for an old fart. Downright healthy."

"I'm doing all right," the judge agrees, at ease now that his appetite's been appeased and his host has shown up.

Luke Garrison. He hasn't seen him for almost three years, since Luke left Santa Barbara. If he hadn't known who this man standing next to him was, he wouldn't have recognized him on the street. Always clean shaven, Luke sports a beard now, a bad-boy goatee. His hair, as straight and straggly as Neil Young's, is hanging loose considerably past his collar, and, the judge notes with shock, an honest-to-God ruby stud is prominent in his left ear. He's wearing an unraveling-at-the-cuffs black cotton sweater over a plain pocket T-shirt, greasy jeans, scuffed work boots. Even his voice is different—low, slow, guttural, like John Wayne with a hangover.

"Well," De La Guerra says, "are you sure you're Luke Garrison? You don't look like any Luke Garrison I know."

"You start a new life, you make changes. Inside as well as what you're seeing."

Riva comes onto the porch carrying a tray with a pitcher of margaritas and three salted glasses. "Is it cocktail hour yet?" she inquires rhetorically, setting the tray down on a side table next to De La Guerra's chair.

"Officially," Luke says, smiling at her. "And I for one can use this."

He pours three glasses full to the top and hands one to her, one to his guest. "To my number-one mentor, supporter, and ball-buster," he toasts, lifting his own glass in tribute. "It's good to see your old bones again. I think." He clinks glasses with the old man, knocks his drink half down in one long swallow.

His guest sips his drink. It's good: a De La Guerra from Santa Barbara knows how a margarita's supposed to taste, this one is the real thing. "It's good to see you too, even if you have reinvented yourself."

"Dinner's in half an hour," Riva informs them. "I trust you're not one of those squeamish wimps who won't eat my homemade rabbit stew."

"With relish." He smiles at her. Neat lady, this one. True to form for Luke Garrison, for whom looks were always only the surface of the package.

"Your timing is perfect, sweet thing," Luke says to Riva, apropos the imminent sunset. He eases his sinewy frame into a companion chair of his guest's.

"I try." Topping up her drink, she goes back into the house, leaving the two men alone on the porch.

De La Guerra contemplates this utterly relaxed person. He's never known Luke to be so cool. What, he wonders, besides appearance and a relaxed personality, makes him different from the man he knew three years ago, back home, when he was the golden boy who had the world by the balls.

Luke knows what the old judge is thinking. And it gets him thinking, too, back to the way it was at the beginning.

Growing up, he wanted to be a cop. A professional ballplayer too, of course, all boys dream about that. As he got into his teens and read adventure books, he envisioned being either an architect or an archeologist, where he could travel to exciting places and have wonderful experiences. But the cop thing, that hung in.

His neighborhood shaped his desires. East end of the San Fernando

Valley in L.A., Latino/blue-collar-anglo mix. Mother and two sisters, father longtime flown the coop, whereabouts forever unknown. A lot of kids he ran with got into trouble, but he stayed clean, because of sports, mostly; he was a good athlete as a young boy, he played the usual seasonal sports, football being his best. All over his neighborhood he'd see the drugs, the crime, he didn't want any part of that. He wanted to help stop it, if he could. Which is what cops did, so the idea of being one was natural. And he was smart, he worked hard at school—he wanted out.

His hard work got him a scholarship to UC Santa Barbara. Dean's List, All-American in water polo, big man on campus. He loved Santa Barbara, it was heaven on earth. Adios San Fernando Valley, forever.

With a college education, his aspirations were raised. The dream of police work was too limiting; you don't climb ladders this high so you can pound the streets for twenty years. He went to Stanford Law School, graduated in the top ten percent of his class, made Law Review. He still believed in order, and had come, as he made his way through the same law school that had produced so many great jurists, to love and revere the law.

He clerked for a federal judge in San Francisco for a year, a plum job. Then he moved back to his adopted home, Santa Barbara, and joined the county prosecutor's office.

He was an assistant D.A. for six years, rapidly working his way up to being the number-one trial lawyer. Along the way he was offered partnerships in several of the big law firms in town, all of which he turned down.

He liked his job. He liked being in the vortex. He especially liked putting bad people in prison. He wanted to make a difference. He felt he did.

The incumbent D.A. retired, Luke ran for the job, he won. It was a slam dunk—everyone in the community, left, right, and center, supported him. He was thirty-one years old.

Over the next decade, despite living in a county with a population of less than 320,000 (as opposed to L.A. County, for instance, population 9,000,000), he developed a statewide reputation. He was the prosecutor who almost always won the big cases: the murders, huge drug deals, headline-grabbing trials involving famous celebrities and their assorted perversions. He attracted great young lawyers—his staff of forty assistant prosecutors was one of the best in the state. Even some young people graduating at the top of their classes from quality law schools all over the West—Stanford,

USC, UCLA, Whittier—would forgo offers at major private firms to come to the central California coast and work in the Santa Barbara D.A.'s office.

By the time Luke was forty he was a local legend, and his name recognition in the state was shooting up the charts. The powers that be were talking of him as a possible attorney general, congressman, even governor someday. Earl Warren had gone that route, why not Luke Garrison? He was the complete package—good-looking, charismatic, smart, and tops at his job.

And he was married to a terrific woman whom he'd known since their undergraduate days at UCSB. Polly McBride was beautiful, charming, very smart. A pediatrician at one of the large clinics (she'd gone to Stanford Medical School so they could be together), she had her own career independent of his. They were a smashing couple. Everyone assumed they were devoted to each other.

They didn't have kids. They were planning on it, though not yet—right now there wasn't room for kids in their busy careers. But they were going to, that was a given.

Like many couples where both parties have successful careers, they didn't actually spend much private, intimate time together. Luke was a demanding boss; he asked a lot of his staff, and gave back more. Seventy-hour workweeks were the norm in his office. Entire weeks would go by when the only time he and Polly would see each other was over a hurried cup of coffee in the morning, or in bed at night, falling asleep exhausted, together physically but not emotionally, in their souls.

She turned forty three months after he did. The ticking sound of her biological clock was becoming deafening in her ears. It was now or never for getting pregnant. But Luke wasn't ready, which meant it would be too late for her, she'd be shut out.

Luke went up to Sacramento for a week-long conference. When he came home, she had moved out and filed for divorce. She had been seeing another man for a year. Someone who had time for her.

He was blindsided.

Right behind that crushing blow, there was more to come. A man who was awaiting trial on a gang-related murder charge confessed to another murder that had happened a dozen years before.

Luke knew the old murder case well. Several years earlier, when he had been the chief litigator in the office, he had convicted another man, Ralph

Tucker for that murder. It was a vicious crime, with aggravated circumstances, which meant it was a capital offense.

The case had been open-and-shut as far as Luke was concerned. It didn't matter to him that the defendant steadfastly maintained his innocence—they all do. The case went through all the appeals, up to the Supreme Court. After almost a decade of sitting on death row in San Quentin, Tucker was executed, one of only four in California since the death penalty had been reinstated.

At first Luke was sure the confession was phony. It had to be. The confessor, with nothing to lose, since he had a rap sheet several pages long and was going away forever anyway, was looking for a kind of perverse notoriety. Luke would blow a hole in his story you could drive an eighteen-wheeler through.

Except it turned out this confession was genuine. Luke had convicted and executed an innocent man. No one blamed him but himself, the guilt and remorse kept him up, night after night.

Santa Barbara's a small city. You can't escape your past. His wife was gone, his reputation was blistered. He felt trapped. He had to get out, find a new life.

He quit his job in the middle of the term. Everyone tried to talk him out of it, but he didn't pay attention to them. He sold his beautiful Craftsman house near the Mission and moved to northern California, where he promptly dropped out. As far as he was concerned, his lawyering days were over.

But that didn't last, because he couldn't make a living doing anything else. He tried farming a piece of land he bought, but it didn't work out. Though he liked working the land, he wasn't a good enough farmer to pay the bills, especially in an area where the major and only viable cash crop is marijuana.

Reluctantly he started practicing law again, but far differently from what he'd done in Santa Barbara. A one-man practice, he doesn't need help and he doesn't want it. He attracts clients straight-arrow lawyers don't care for, because they're hard to defend—obvious criminals with no redeeming features, drug dealers, outlaw bikers, perverts of various stripes. Mostly he works on contract for the county, taking public defender overflow or helping out in cases where the expertise of a top legal mind is needed. He makes enough money doing this work to survive okay. Money and status aren't important to him anymore.

His former friends in the legal profession who have kept up with what he's doing can't figure him out. Not only did he throw away an incredible career, but he's on the wrong side now. Of course every accused deserves a good defense—the system would break down otherwise. But Luke had been a hell-bent-for-leather prosecutor, super-gung-ho in pursuit of protecting society from the scumbags. Now he's fighting to keep the worst of those people out of jail.

Dinner is fabulous. Along with the rabbit stew there are homemade biscuits and a salad from the garden. Luke opens a bottle of a reserve Napa cabernet from the wine cellar. "Nice vino, eh?" he asks the judge.

"It's wonderful. I didn't know you were a connoisseur."

"I like the good stuff, but I didn't buy it. It came with the property," Luke says enigmatically.

They finish the meal off with fresh strawberry pie. "This was wonderful," the old man compliments Riva. "Thank you very much."

"Luke appreciates a good meal. I like to keep him happy."

"Which you do," Luke tells her. He begins to clear the table.

"I'm going over to Mabel's," Riva says. She knows the men need to talk privately. "I'll be back in a couple hours. Have a pleasant evening," she says to De La Guerra. "I've made up the guest room."

"Thank you. Again."

"Mañana." She pecks Luke on the cheek and is out the door. A moment later they hear the low rumble of a truck with glasspacks start up and drive away.

"Very nice woman," De La Guerra comments as he follows Luke into the long living room. There's a fire going in the massive stone fireplace, even though it isn't that cold out. "How did you find her?"

"I defended her significant other on a murder charge."

The judge cocks an inquisitive eyebrow.

"A dope dealer's dustoff. One scumbag offing another. Territorial. I got it knocked down to second-degree." He hands the older man a glass of port, sits in a leather easy chair with one of his own. "He pulled eight to twelve over in Soledad. With his record it should've been life without parole, so he was grateful."

He sweeps the large room with his arm. "He was a real cutie. Before he was nailed, he signed everything over to her, so the ATF and IRS assholes couldn't grab it, and it would be here for him when he got out. It was hers in spirit anyway, she'd done all the work putting it together, all the paintings and books, the good-taste stuff. She's kind of a backwoods intellectual, you might say." He sips from the '85 Taylor's port he's poured for them. "She'd known he wasn't one hundred percent legitimate, but not dirty to the extent he really was—he told her he was in the jewelry import–export business, she wanted to believe him, life was nice, so she bought into it. I'm not saying she's an angel or anything, but she wasn't part of his deal. I know that for a fact," he says, a trifle defensively.

He continues. "They'd been drifting apart for a while, before he offed the other guy. She and I had made a connection during the trial, I'm not going to kid you about that, we were hot for each other, but nothing came of it, you don't mess with the old lady of someone in the joint. It's also unethical, he was my client. But I'd see her, we'd have coffee, I'd commiserate with her."

"So how . . . ?" The judge indicates his surroundings.

"Like I said, he was a cutie, pushed the envelope hard. He'd screwed over various other bad people in his day, it's an occupational hazard. One of them took advantage of my guy's vulnerable position and put out a jail contract on him. Razorblade to the jugular, clean as a kosher butcher. No one knows who did it, sad to say. I don't know how hard they actually investigated the killing. Prisoner bites it, saves the state money."

He stretches out in his soft leather chair. "So now Riva's a grass widow, in a manner of speaking, and this is legally hers, and then comes the inevitable—we got together. Not the cleanest love affair in the world, but I didn't do anything I'm ashamed of. If he was still alive I'd be living down in the flatlands and we'd have had our dinner at Taco Bell. Anyway, that's the story of my being here."

He knocks back some port, leans back, contemplates De La Guerra over the rim of his glass.

"You've changed, Luke," his guest says gravely.

"Yeah, Fred. I have." He sips his port, rolling the sensuous liquid around in his mouth. "So now let's hear your spiel. You haven't come all the way up here to eat rabbit stew and drink wine with me."

"I need to buy a lawyer."

Luke stares at him, then laughs, a good belly guffaw. "You know a thousand lawyers. You had to haul ass five hundred miles to say this to me?"

De La Guerra leans forward in his chair. "You're aware of this kidnapping and murder case back home last year?"

"We're talking about the Lancaster girl?" He gets a nod from the judge. "I know a bit about it. I didn't follow the case all that much. I don't watch too much TV and I don't read the papers. I live a different life up here than I did back home." He sips his port. "They caught the guy who did it on a fluke, right?" he says to De La Guerra. "Some close friend of the family?"

"Yes. His name is Joe Allison. They have an open-and-shut case."

Luke's laugh is mirthless. "We've both heard that one before, Freddie. Why do you think I'm hanging my hat up here?" He pauses. "Besides Polly."

Hearing Luke name his former wife, the old man feels acutely uncomfortable. "I know, Luke." Now it's he who pauses—a long, uncomfortable silence.

Luke pours himself another drink. "So what do you want from me, anyway?"

De La Guerra sinks into the deep leather. "I came up here to ask you to take Joe Allison on as a client."

Luke puts his glass aside, comes over to his mentor, puts a hand on his shoulder. "You know I'd never go back, especially for a pathetic case like this one. C'mon, Freddie, you know that's a no-win situation."

"That's how everyone feels. But I had to come up here and ask you."

Luke stares at the old judge. "I must be getting dense in my incipient middle age. Why are you coming to me? There are good criminal defense lawyers in Santa Barbara. I'm out of that loop," he reminds him.

"None of the good ones want the case."

Luke nods sagely. "Because it's a stone-cold loser and not one lawyer worth a damn in Santa Barbara will take it. No one wants to have his name associated with a case that smells as bad as this one sounds like it does."

De La Guerra shakes his head. "That's not why. Doug Lancaster has asked every lawyer in the region not to take Allison as a client."

"That's a father at work," Luke says. "A father with a lot of clout."

"Yes."

"So why pick on me?" Luke says again. He feels a chill coming upon him. This is terrible, the last thing in the world he would have wanted to hear. He crosses the room and throws open the French doors that open out onto the porch. It's dark now. Far below he can see the lights of the small town of Bartstown, above his head at least a thousand stars. "Because I'm not in the loop anymore," he says. "I don't count. Therefore I can be bought. Is that what you mean here, Fred?"

De La Guerra comes out onto the porch and stands alongside the younger man, bracing against the wood railing with his arthritic hip. He couldn't live up here—the air is too cold, too wet. He'd freeze up like an engine that had run out of oil. "You've got it wrong. Nobody thinks Allison is innocent. But *he* says he is, he's adamant about it."

"So what?" He's getting mad now; they want to haul him back into the tar pit, suck him in. It's been three years, and he's still recovering. "They're all innocent," he says contemptuously. He may be on the other side now, but that doesn't make criminals any less guilty, certainly not the ones he's been defending.

"If Joe Allison goes to trial with a run-of-the-mill lawyer, and gets convicted, there will always be a doubt," De La Guerra explains. "The appeals process will drag on interminably. If he's convicted—"

"You mean '*when*'?"

"—it might be overturned on a technicality. And there will be those who will say he was railroaded." He puts a hand on Luke's forearm, as a father would a son. "We can't have that. It could be Ralph Tucker all over again."

Ferdinand De La Guerra was the judge in that case. He, too, was scarred.

Luke jerks his arm away. "We? The great omnipotent 'we'?"

De La Guerra knows Luke has to vent; he keeps his silence.

"And why should I do this?" *Jesus Christ, you old bastard, how dare you do this to me?* "Whoever takes this case is going to be vilified."

"Because you're the only lawyer I know who doesn't care about his standing in the community. And because you know what can happen. And because you're as good as they come. Are those good enough reasons?"

Luke doesn't answer.

"There's money," De La Guerra offers. "You can use money, can't you?"

"Don't I look like I'm doing okay?" Luke asks in anger.

The old judge knows he's angered Luke, but he has to speak his mind. "Luke Garrison living with the girlfriend of a drug dealer who's in prison for murder? That isn't you. You may have gone native, Luke, but that isn't you."

"It is now."

"No. I don't think so. I think this is a facade, this Luke Garrison. The real Luke Garrison loves justice. Finessing a murder charge for a drug dealer . . ." He lets the rest go unsaid.

Luke leans against the railing, staring up at the stars. He loves the way you can see so many stars up here. Some nights he mans his telescope for hours, getting lost in these stars. "Just out of idle curiosity," he asks. "Not that I want to get involved in this crap." He turns to De La Guerra. "Who's going to be prosecuting this?"

"Ray Logan. Personally."

Luke grimaces. "His ticket to ride."

De La Guerra nods.

"But of course." He bites at a piece of cuticle on his thumb. "Who's going to pay for this defense? Capital murder case, that's big money."

"Allison has a hundred and twenty-five thousand dollars of his own, and he'll find more if he has to. He doesn't qualify for a public defender, and he wouldn't take one anyway. He wants a quality litigator who knows his way around a courtroom."

Luke wraps a comforting arm around his mentor's shoulders.

"It's great having you up here, Freddie," he says warmly. "I've missed you." He leads the older man back into the house. "But not enough to fall on my sword in front of Ray Logan and the rest of the world."

Lying in bed awake, staring at the ceiling upon which the moon, shining through the high uncurtained window, makes rivers of light that lap rhythmically from corner to corner, Luke is aware of Riva, also awake, naked like he is, her back to him. She isn't confident enough in their relationship to feel comfortable intruding on whatever's going on inside his head. They have been living together for months, but they're not partners like that.

"You're awake too."

"Yes," she says, grateful that he is letting her in.

"Do you know why the old man came up here?"

"He wants you to go back to Santa Barbara for some purpose, I assume."

"He wants me to take on a case."

That's enough of an excuse to roll over and face him. "What would be the point of that?" She looks at his profile, trying to figure out what's going on. She wants to get inside him. He has not yet let her; they're good as far as they go, but they don't go as far as she would like.

She's in love with Luke, and doesn't want to lose him.

"There's good money in it."

"That's the reason? Are you boning me?" She's a plain talker; in her world you don't put doilies under your teacup.

Now he turns so they're looking at each other. "The reason would be ego," he admits. "So I could kick some hometown ass." He looks away again. "To show the bastards they didn't run me out of town," he confesses to the wave pattern on the ceiling. "I left of my own accord, and now I'm coming back the same way."

"That sounds good, Luke. It's also a lie."

He's still having a conversation with the ceiling. "Yeah, but if I say it enough, maybe I'll start believing it myself. Which I need to do," he adds, "at some point in this lifetime."

"Why do you want to hurt yourself when you don't have to?" she asks. Then she says, "Aren't you happy here? Reasonably happy?" She doesn't want to say that—it's pushing him into a corner—but she can't help herself.

He turns back to her. "Yes, I am."

"But a man's gotta do what a man's gotta do."

"I can't live off you indefinitely, Riva. I've always felt guilty about that."

"You live with me in a house I'm lucky enough to own which the feds would've confiscated if you hadn't pulled off the defense you did," she tells him in exasperation—how many times have they had this stupid conversation? She sits up. Her breasts are small, lovely in shape; the nipples, long and slender like her fingers and toes, stiffen from the sudden contact with the mild chill in the air. "Stop beating yourself up about that, okay? And me. And stop using it as an excuse to feel sorry for yourself. You don't have anything to feel sorry for, Luke. Your wife left you. It's not the end of the world." She touches his temple with the tips of her fingers. "Look to your future, Luke, there's plenty there. The stuff back in Santa Barbara's over. That's why they call it the past."

He sighs. "I'm hung up on self-image, I guess. I left with my tail between my legs."

"There's other ways to resolve that, and you know it."

"Oh, yes, I know it. I don't know that I'm going to go back and do this. It sounds like a stone-cold loser to me, and when I go back—make that *if*—I want to make sure I'm covered in glory. An up-front done deal."

"Then you'd better not go back yet," she says sagely. "And that's me talking without even knowing what your old friend's hocking you about."

Enough with the talking. This conversation isn't doing anything for either of them except making their heads hurt and driving a wedge into something that isn't that strong to begin with.

She rolls onto him, rubbing her chest against his, kissing him on the mouth. Down lower she feels him becoming aroused—almost, she thinks, despite himself.

She does the work. He doesn't fight it, that's the best he can do with all these conflicts fighting for space in his head. In his heart, too.

* * *

Breakfast is light—coffee, muffins, fruit—and early. Riva sets the ingredients on the kitchen table. She's dressed in a tailored skirt, high-necked silk blouse, pantyhose, low heels. With her lipstick and makeup in place she's striking enough to be a model in *Vogue*. "I've got a five o'clock class, so I won't be done until seven."

"Maybe I'll come in and we'll have dinner down there."

"Let me know." She shakes De La Guerra's hand. "It was nice meeting you. I hope you're not trying to talk him into something he'll regret." There is no smile in the voice as she says this.

"So do I," the old man answers truthfully. He hadn't known Luke was with a woman. A good woman. He might not have come, had he known.

The glasspack mufflers trumpet Riva's departure. Luke pours coffee for De La Guerra. "She's a bail bondsman in town," he explains. "She used to be a paralegal, but the murder thing screwed that up. She's a survivor, is what she is."

"I like her, Luke."

"She likes you, too, but she isn't happy you came up here. Not with that crappy offer you made me."

"I gathered that. I'm not sure I am, either, now that I've seen what you have here."

Luke spears a piece of melon. "I don't know what I have here, Freddie," he says. "Whatever it is, it isn't the whole picture," he adds candidly. "I'm smart enough about myself to know that." He takes a bite off the end of his fork. "And if what's here's the right thing, it'll still be here whether or not I go down to S.B."

The old man takes a thick sheaf of papers from his briefcase and lays them on the table. "This is the indictment and all the corollary material," he says. "In case you want to look it over."

"I'll think about it, Freddie. No promises."

De La Guerra starts the engine on his rental car. Luke grips the old man's shoulder through the open window. "Don't be a stranger, now that you know the way."

"You too." He feels tears welling in the corners of his eyes. As he gets older it seems they come more easily—an intimation of mortality, he's sure. Then he says what he's wanted to say since he saw Luke last night, and saw what a changed man he's become. "You can't live in your pain forever, Luke. Sooner or later you have to face your demons and conquer them."

First her last night, Luke thinks, now him. Opposite sides of the same coin. "Why do I have to?"

Because of who you are, the old man thinks. But he doesn't say that. "See you again, I hope," is all he says.

"See you."

The old man takes off down the long driveway. In the rearview mirror he sees Luke watching him. He turns his attention ahead for a moment, to make sure he doesn't run off into the ditch.

When he looks in the mirror again, Luke is gone.

Riva's crying; she can't help it. "You're an asshole."

He knows he is. "I'm merely going to go down and take a look around," he says, disgusted with his own evasion even as he hears it coming out of his mouth. "I haven't been back in a long time. I want to see my old friends."

"Yeah, right. Like you've been dying to go back and see all your old friends. What were their names again? I don't recall hearing about one of them."

Since De La Guerra left, Luke has spent the day reading the material, his interest slowly but surely captured. Like the old firehorse whose ears prick up when he hears the alarm go off, the combative juices have started percolating.

It's a great case for the prosecution—he would hit this one out of the ballpark with one hand tied behind his back. The key chain and running shoes are damning pieces of evidence, overwhelming. And Allison knew the girl, knew his way around her house. What more could a prosecutor want?

Granted, there are a few holes in it. There are holes in every case. These are technical holes, nothing substantive at the core, barely enough for a crafty defense lawyer to start to build a defense around.

Make that the shell of a defense; there would have to be more than technical holes to mount an honest-to-God defense.

But then he has to step back and look at reality. *Who are you kidding?* he says to himself. The only way the prosecution's case could be any better would be if Allison had actually been caught in the act of killing her.

Luke lays the material aside. He's deceiving himself if he thinks this has any kind of a chance. The guy is guilty.

Get real with yourself: this case isn't what's pulling you in. It's the past that's talking to you, dude, whispering in your ear. The voice from the grave of Ralph Tucker, the guilty man you prosecuted and sent to his death, who was innocent after all.

He can't imagine he ever will get over that. His old mentor, Judge De La Guerra, can't either, which is why he came. And why Luke will drive down there and talk to Joe Allison, the hapless defendant.

It can hurt Riva, a woman who loves him who has taken a big risk in doing that. The problem is, he doesn't love her, not enough. Not the way she loves him, not with the depth. He is still, after three long years, too unresolved about Polly to love another woman that way.

Face up to your demons, the old man had admonished him. That's what he wants to do.

Riva isn't buying that excuse, not for one second. "You want out," she said when he'd told her his plans. "You didn't even know it until that old man came up and gave you an excuse, but you do."

He doesn't know if that's true or not, but there is something tearing at him and he has to go and check it out. "I'll be back in a week."

"That's why you're packing for a year."

"In case I have to stay longer than a week." Hearing these phony words come out of his mouth, he feels ashamed. At least don't lie to her. She deserves more than that. "I'll call you tonight."

"Don't hold your breath waiting for me to answer the phone."

Luke motors into Santa Barbara in the glasspack-muffler pickup truck, a 1965 Dodge with a ridiculously huge V-8 that gets six miles to the gallon. The truck is pulling a U-Haul rental cube in which are an old Triumph Bonneville motorcycle, bought when he moved up north and changed his life, and a surfboard. If nothing else comes out of this, at least he'll get in some righteous surfing.

De La Guerra has booked a suite for him at the Biltmore—Joe Allison is footing the bill, why not go first class? Allison also wrote out a check for five thousand dollars, which will cover Luke's other short-term expenses and buy a few hours of his time. In the unlikely event Luke stays with this, his fee will be three hundred dollars an hour, plus living expenses and other necessities, such as a private investigator. Three hundred an hour is top money for Santa Barbara. Luke warned De La Guerra that if he was coming back, he was coming back in style, first class. Allison, through De La Guerra, was happy to pay the freight.

"He has no choice," De La Guerra candidly admitted when Luke phoned and said he'd come down for a look-see: no promises, no commitment, just a meet-and-greet. "I'm glad you're coming, Luke, and if you decide it's hopeless, or not for you, I'll understand."

Luke decides to pass on the Biltmore. For now, he wants to maintain a low profile. His presence in town will be known soon enough, but as much as he can, he wants to stay out of the limelight.

He takes a room at one of the nondescript motels on Upper State Street and checks in with De La Guerra. They'll get together in an hour, then tomorrow morning he'll drive over to the jail to see Allison. He helps himself to a vodka from the minibar, sits on the edge of the bed, and dials long distance.

The answering machine picks up. Riva's voice, cool and efficient. "At the tone leave your name, phone number, the time of your call, and we'll return it as soon as we can." Plus a new line, just added on. "If this is you, Luke, go fuck yourself."

He decides not to leave a message.

Luke sits across the table in an interview room in the county jail from the accused. Allison is wearing puke-green prison sweats and carpet slippers. His hair, which used to be immaculately blow-dried, is unwashed and matted, and his complexion is gray, like moldy bread. No one would mistake this specimen for a star newscaster, Luke thinks as he eyeballs Allison critically.

Allison is also sizing Luke up. This man used to be the district attorney? He looks like the white inmates here in the jail—the bad-asses. "I've heard a lot about you," Allison says. His voice is shaking. "Thanks for taking my case."

This poor bastard isn't going to handle prison well, Luke thinks. Not at all. "I don't know if I'm taking your case, Mr. Allison," he says. "I have to know more than I know now before I decide."

The prisoner's face collapses. "But Judge De La Guerra told me—"

"I don't know what Freddie told you," Luke interrupts, "but he doesn't speak for me. I told him I'd review the material and meet with you and think about it. That's all. I thought that was made clear to you."

Allison nods slowly. "Yes, it was. But I thought—"

"You're hoping, is what. Right?"

Another slow nod. "I guess so."

"Let me say a couple things. One, don't get your hopes up. About my involvement in this or not, about what the outcome is going to be regardless of whether I take it or not, about what I can do for you, or any lawyer can do for you. Two, don't ever lie to me. I'm going to be asking you a bunch of questions today and over the next few days. Tell me the truth, even if it's brutal and you think it could hurt your chances. Anything you tell me is confidential and can not be used against you, ever. That's whether or not I stay on this as your lawyer. Okay?"

Allison looks like he's about to start hyperventilating. "Yes."

"You don't look good," Luke says. "Were you on any medication on the outside?"

"No."

Having opened that door, Luke momentarily goes off on an important tangent. "Do you do any drugs, other than prescription? Recreationally?"

Allison starts to say no, catches himself. "I smoke a little pot." He looks around involuntarily.

"We're not bugged," Luke assures him. "What else?"

Allison hesitates. "If there's some coke at a party, I might do a line. I don't buy it. That's rare," he adds hastily.

"Do people in the community know you do drugs?"

"Excuse me," Allison answers, "I don't 'do' drugs. I just told you that. Once in a while, that's all. I'm not a user, okay?" he adds testily.

Luke disregards the man's annoyance, real or feigned. "Anyone who might come forward and testify against you in that regard?"

Allison takes a deep breath, nods. "Glenna Lancaster knows. We've been around drugs together, at parties."

"At their house?"

"A few times. A few of us would sneak off, out in the far end of the yard. Doug didn't know about any of that," he adds piously.

"Glenna Lancaster," Luke muses. "I doubt she wishes you well."

"The Lancasters want to see me dead," Allison says flatly.

"Why shouldn't they? Their daughter's been murdered and you're accused of doing it. I'd feel the same way if I were them, and so would you."

Defiantly: "Except I didn't do it."

"Hold that thought." Luke admires how the guy isn't backing down—but it's early in the game, and he doesn't have an alternative. "That's another thing, very important: don't volunteer anything unless you're asked. Especially not to anyone except me, or whoever your lawyer turns out to be."

Another tortured nod. Allison's head feels as heavy as a bowling ball, and this gonzo-looking lawyer isn't helping his disposition. And the questioning about the drugs—what was that all about?

The prisoner paranoia kicks in hard. Luke Garrison used to be the district attorney for the county. An ass-kicking prosecutor, from what he's heard. Maybe he's a plant, sent in here to try and snake a confession under the guise of being a defense lawyer.

They wouldn't have the balls to do that. And Judge De La Guerra has vouched for him. That's good enough. It has to be.

Luke opens a folder in which he's jotted some notes. "Let's get some basic information. Where were you the night Emma was kidnapped? Do you remember?"

"Have you read the statement I gave the police?" Allison asks. "I told them the same thing a year ago that I told them a few weeks ago."

"Yes, I read it, and that doesn't matter now, because what you tell the police and what you tell your lawyer might be two different things. So, do you remember?" he repeats. He doesn't bother to mask his irritation.

Almost as if reading off cue cards, Allison recites, "I was out to dinner with some friends. We were together until after eleven. I dropped my girlfriend off at her place and went home and went to bed."

"You didn't stay with your girlfriend?" Luke asks, almost prompting Allison to say yes. If they had been together all night, this case would have a very different complexion.

"We spend some nights together, but not all. That night, we didn't."

"How many nights a week were you spending together then?" Luke asks. "You and . . ." He leafs through some notes.

"Nicole Rogers." Allison saves him the searching. "Four or five."

"So this was only one of a couple nights in the week you didn't spend the night together?"

"Yes."

"Any reason you didn't spend that particular night together?"

Allison shrugs. "There probably was. There were times when we wanted some space, other times when one of us had something to do later."

That's a losing remark—any prosecutor would tear that one in half. Especially since they spent most nights together. A believable inference would be that he had plans for later that night, and had to be alone. Plans that included Emma Lancaster.

Allison breaks into his thought process. "Now that I recall," he suddenly remembers, "Nicole had a study group going with other students in her class at law school. Either she was going to get up early, or she needed time that night to prepare. One or the other. Maybe she would remember."

Luke makes the note. That could help—at least give Allison a decent reason for not being with his woman on that night, when his normal pattern was the opposite.

He lays the folder aside. Fuck the details, he needs to get to what this case is about. "There are three pieces of damning evidence against you. The shoes, the condoms, and the key ring."

A Sisyphean nod. "I know."

"How are we going to account for those? Those are three smoking guns, Joe. Usually one is enough, and they have three."

Allison bows his head, running his fingers through his greasy hair. "I don't know."

Luke looks at him sharply. "Are the shoes yours?"

"I don't know. I had a pair of New Balance once, but they disappeared before the kidnapping."

This is a disaster. "Disappeared? Jesus, man, can't you do better than that?"

"No." Allison's tired, baffled. His head drops against his chest, his neck moving like it's lost its muscularity. This is a man who has suffered a catastrophe of monumental proportions and doesn't know why. Jail time has taken a tremendous toll on him. Luke has seen and heard other men like Joe Allison in this situation. They're so unprepared for something like this, they almost shrivel up and die right before your eyes.

He hopes Allison can hang on to his defiance. Especially if he, Luke, decides *not* to take this case. "The shoes were found in your closet."

Allison nods.

"So what you're saying is, someone snuck your lost shoes into your closet and planted them?"

Another nod. "What else could it be?"

That you did it, asswipe. A pair of shoes linked to the abduction, were just found in Allison's closet, but a year ago had *disappeared* before the kidnapping? What am I doing here? he thinks. "How many people have keys to your guest house?"

"I don't know. Half a dozen I gave keys to, like Nicole and my cleaning lady. And whoever had it before me. I didn't change the locks." He looks at Luke, smiling ruefully. "I don't always lock it anyway. It's back behind the house I rent from. They have good security."

"Not good enough," Luke notes, "to stop whoever went in there and planted them and left without being spotted."

Allison looks up sharply.

"That skepticism you heard from me is what any reasonable man or woman would think," Luke says. "Such as the kind you're going to have on your jury." He goes on. "What about the key ring in your glove compartment? That was a plant, too?"

"Any parking attendant could get in there," Allison points out. "Hotel, bar, restaurant. Plus I park it at the station, people are coming and going all the time. Not a big deal to reach in."

"You're a trusting soul."

"Not anymore," Allison replies darkly. "You don't believe what I'm saying about somebody planting all this on me, do you?"

Luke leans back, considering his answer. "It's pretty far-fetched, okay? If you didn't kill her, then you're right, somebody could have planted that stuff on you, to frame you. It's going to be hard to convince a jury of that, I have to be honest with you."

Allison nods in understanding, but then says, "If I had done it, why would I have kept the shoes and the key ring? Why would I have held on to the only evidence that could connect me with the murders? It doesn't make sense."

It doesn't make *logical* sense, that's true, Luke thinks. But the abductor wouldn't know the shoes were evidence. That information was never made public. As for the key ring, there are plenty of reasons a guilty man might keep it as a remembrance of a past relationship, or an arrogant nose-thumbing at the authorities: You're never going to catch me.

He doesn't say what he's been thinking. He says, "There are always reasons. It could be nothing more than carelessness."

"Or it could be a plant," Allison retorts stubbornly.

"Yes. If you're innocent, it likely was."

"What about the bottle of bourbon the cop that stopped me found on the floor behind the seat of my car?" Allison asks, pressing his thought process.

"What about it?"

That opened bottle was the reason for the search in the first place. If it hadn't been in Allison's car, they wouldn't be sitting here in this funky jail, one having traveled hundreds of miles against his better judgment, the other about to go to trial for his life with odds hovering between slim and none.

"I don't drink bourbon. I haven't drunk bourbon since college.

Anybody who knows me knows that. So it couldn't be mine. And if that wasn't mine, what about the other stuff?"

Good question. "That may have been left there by someone else," Luke concedes. "But it's a big stretch from a bottle on the floor to a key ring hidden in the back of a glove compartment and a pair of shoes stuck way back in your closet."

He stands up. "That's enough for today, Joe. Unless you have anything else to tell me . . . that you haven't yet told me, or anyone else."

"Like what?"

"Like have you been completely straight with me?" Before Allison can form an answer he offers his hand. "I'll try and drop by tomorrow. If you can remember who had keys to your pad, that'll be helpful."

Allison also rises. "So you're taking my case?" he asks too eagerly.

"Slow down, Joe. I told you I wanted to check things out, meet with you. I still have work to do on my end before I can decide. This was one step, but there are others."

Allison slumps. "When are you going to decide? I have a right to know that."

"Yes, you do." He thinks about the question. "Today's Tuesday. By the end of the day Friday. One way or the other."

He checks in with De La Guerra by phone, informs the old man of his misgivings, says he'll discuss this further after he's gone through the police reports again.

"It doesn't look promising," he warns the judge. "He has no alibi for the hours when the girl was snatched, and this whole attitude of his that everything was planted, it sounds like a stretch to me, Freddie. The shoes particularly. It would take some real adroit planning to get those shoes in his closet after having made sure there was a print left both at the kidnap scene and where the body was found. And for them to have been discovered a year later? Off a fluke arrest? What're the odds on all that coming together? By denying ownership so lamely, he's painting himself into a corner I don't think I could get him out of. No lawyer could." He pauses. "I'll hand it to him, though—he's got guts, the way he's maintaining his stand on the shoes."

De La Guerra, on the other end of the line, grunts noncommittally. He will not be an active participant in this; his tie is emotional. If Luke will do it, his job is finished. If not, he hits the road again, a prospect he isn't looking forward to. "It's been known to happen," he says in gentle persuasion. "For all we know, the police had the shoes already, they had the key chain in his car, they decided to help things along a bit."

"No," Luke protests strongly. "I was in the power seat a long time here," he reminds De La Guerra. "I never saw that kind of corruption, and neither did you. The cops here will push the envelope, all cops do, but breaking the law that way, I'd have to have definitive proof before I'd entertain that."

"I'm sure you're right," De La Guerra agrees.

They talk a bit more, how Luke is doing back in Santa Barbara after his self-imposed exile, other things. Luke will do some homework tomorrow and keep De La Guerra abreast of his findings and where he thinks he's heading.

Luke shaves, showers, lays out a clean change of clothes. He puts on a white soft-cotton collarless shirt, cord trousers, a tan linen sports coat.

He takes a taxi to Meritage, a restaurant whose owners he used to know. He can sit alone at the small counter in the back room, eat his solitary meal, have a couple of glasses of good wine. He won't be disturbed: not many people know he's in town, and a casual look wouldn't reveal his identity. He's a changed man, and not only in his visage. Buffing his snakeskin cowboy boots and pulling his hair back into a neat ponytail, he sets forth into the night.

A Ketel One on the rocks, a light meal—small Caesar salad, shrimp risotto, a glass of Foxen pinot noir. Tomorrow, for the third or fourth time, he'll dig into the evidence against Allison—the police reports, how the evidence was handled, anything else that's there. Maybe there's something he's missed. He has to give this an honest shot—he can't help it, it won't work for him to do it any other way.

The restaurant is three-quarters full. Couples and foursomes sit at tables covered with Irish linen tablecloths; a single pink rose adorned with baby's breath in a slender cut-glass vase graces each table, alongside a candle in a brass ship's candlestick. A fire's going in the fireplace in the main room, the light low and soothing. He sits with his decaf cappuccino and a glass of port, feeling the alcohol spreading comfort and warmth in his body. He's tired—he'll sleep well tonight.

On the other side of the room, a party of eight are finishing their meal—six men and a couple of women, from their attire professionals who came here directly from the office. They have been loud and boisterous in a good-natured way, trading insults and raucous opinions. Luke, his back to them, hasn't been paying them attention.

They debate their bill briefly, a couple of credit cards are thrown down. Then a voice cuts through: a voice too familiar for Luke not to notice.

You can run, but you can't hide. Luke knocks back the last swallow of port, pushes up from his bar stool, and crosses the room to the dinner party.

It's been three years. Ray Logan has put on a good twenty pounds, making his Newt Gingrich-like doughboy face even rounder. Balding, pink to the point of translucence around the ears, Ray looks the stereotype of the well-fed barrister.

"Hey, Ray. How're you doing?"

The assemblage turns to look at him, at first without recognition—who the hell is this?—then with slack-jawed disbelief.

"Luke?" This is Ray Logan finding his voice.

"Hello, Ray."

They're all staring at him like he's a brother from another planet. They're all senior deputy D.A.'s, almost all of whom were recruited by him, and worked for him, and took their marching orders from him blindly and with fierce commitment.

A few of them mutter "hello" and "Luke." Then Logan's loud voice supersedes: "Jesus Christ!"

Luke smiles. "Something the matter?"

"You look like . . ."

"What?" He's grinning fiercely.

"A biker."

"A biker? I do own a motorcycle. So does Jay Leno. What's that mean?"

"It means you look like a bad actor. Certainly not a professional lawyer."

The grin dies. Luke stares at Ray, then at the others. He knows them all except one woman and one man, the youngest in the group. Hired since he left. But they'd know who he is; oh, yes.

"How are you all doing?" he asks, his eyes sweeping the group.

They stare back at him. A mixture of respect, fear, anxiety.

Logan is composed. "I heard you were back in town," he says. "That you're thinking about hiring on as Joe Allison's lawyer."

"You heard it on the grapevine?" Luke asks coolly. "Well, obviously I am back in town," he continues, "and I'm full of life."

"If you're thinking of taking Joe Allison as a client, you're full of something and it isn't life," Ray Logan says to him.

"I thought the trial hadn't happened yet," Luke says evenly.

Logan shakes his head in dismissal. "Only technically." He looks Luke over again. "What're you doing here? How did you get into this?"

"Judge De La Guerra asked me to come down and peruse the situation," Luke drawls. His voice and everything else about him are getting under Logan's fair skin, which gives him pleasure.

"He should know better than to stick his nose into this."

"My impression was that he was an emissary for the establishment. People like you, Ray."

"You're laboring under a false impression, Luke."

Luke looks the group over again. They used to be as loyal to him as Hannibal's troops. Now they're looking at him like he's the enemy.

He's the enemy now.

Ray Logan reaches out and puts a soft, plump hand on Luke's shoulder. It's almost a gesture of affection. "You don't want to get involved in this, Luke. It's an absolute loser. This is as strong a case as I've ever been around." He searches for Luke's eyes with his own. "Look at the evidence I have. You'll see it. You know what to look for, better than any of us."

Luke smiles. "Thanks for the vote of confidence, pal. If I take this case," Luke replies, holding Logan's stare, "I'll remember you helped persuade me."

Logan stiffens. "I heard you changed, Luke. We all did. But we didn't think you'd gone off the deep end." He pauses. "Run across Polly since you've been back in town?"

The question takes Luke by surprise. The expression on his face reveals everything Logan wanted it to.

Luke's former assistant lets fly his harpoon. "When Polly sees you, she'll know she made the right decision."

He sweeps out of the restaurant with his entourage flowing behind him, leaving Luke nailed to the floor, shaking in rage and pain.

Before dawn he arises from a restless sleep. The freshly pressed pants and newly laundered shirt are carelessly flung over the burnt orange Naugahyde chair that is jammed into the near corner of the small motel room. Underwear and socks lie balled up in another corner, hastily pulled off and flung away.

Crusty with sweat, his armpits stink—he hadn't opened the window or turned on the phlegmy air conditioner, so the air overnight has turned warm and stale, like pond water becoming stagnant. He had tumbled into sleep on top of the covers, naked, teeth unbrushed.

After leaving the restaurant the night before, too keyed up with exposed nervous emotion to go back and work, he walked into the center of town and wandered through the Paseo Nuevo mall, mingling with the sparse midweek nighttime crowd. He ambled through both large chain bookstores, Borders and Barnes & Noble, catty-corner across State Street from each other, leafing through magazines and paperbacks but not buying anything, then walked a block over to Anacapa and down to the Paradise.

He sat at the bar of the Paradise from ten until closing, midnight. The television was tuned to ESPN, featuring wrapups of the day's sports and a recap of the weekend's PGA tournament. Sitting at the bar, watching the tube, he drank five margaritas.

He was high, but not close to drunk. He never gets drunk, he knows his limit. During the cab ride back to the motel he has the driver detour to the Albertson's on upper State, where he bought a pint of Fundador Spanish brandy and a large box of Famous Amos chocolate chip cookies.

Back at the motel he watched the tail end of Leno and part of Conan O'Brien and ate cookies and drank brandy. When he got undressed and went to bed, he doesn't remember exactly. Time wasn't particularly important.

Now he drinks half a large bottle of Mountain Spring water without pausing, pisses at length, brushes his teeth, flossing last night's grunge out. He needs water from the source, the sting of the spray on his face.

Standing on the beach at Rincon Point, fifteen miles south of town in Carpinteria, he sees the sun starting to rise to the east, already a strong, soft, rosy explosion. Red sky at morning doesn't apply here: storms rarely hit this part of the Pacific, and when they do, they're tropical tails from the south or Hawaii.

Today's waves are small ones, not the ones that have made this beach a famous surf spot, but good enough to get wet over. Wearing his ancient wetsuit, he paddles out on his board past the shore break and sets up at the edge of where the outer waves are forming.

He rides for a couple of hours, nothing higher than three-footers. There are few other surfers out here. The mild surf report has kept most of the regulars in bed.

He didn't come expecting big waves, or needing them. He came because he needed to feel the water of the ocean on him. Up north he does this a couple of times a week. The waves are big there, sometimes fifteen or twenty feet. Those he handles gingerly, usually passing them by. He's your basic okay surfer, not a lifer by any means. But he loves it, the communion with this watery vastness. Even when he'd become the D.A. and was the epitome of workaholism, he would come out early in the morning, weekends mostly, and paddle out into the water and catch some waves.

As he's throwing the board into the shell of the pickup truck and is peeling off his wetsuit, a splinter of sunlight momentarily blinds him. Looking to the cliffs above, he sees a shadow moving out of his line of sight. The figure has a pair of binoculars around its neck.

Someone's watching him. He doesn't know why he thinks that,

since there are other hardy souls out here, but he knows it to be true. He's being spied upon.

Someone from Ray Logan's office? No. That would be overkill. They know he's in town, what would they be watching him for? He isn't dangerous. As far as he knows, no one is aware that he's in town except Logan and the others he encountered last night, Joe Allison, and Ferdinand De La Guerra. By midmorning, of course, Logan will have spread the word about his return home; he will speak of Luke in a jokey, dismissive manner, like the toadstool that he is, forget that he's an important elected official now; to Luke, who was his boss, he's still and forevermore shall be a nerd, a dweeb.

He wonders if Ray Logan has called the Lancasters. If Doug Lancaster has been scaring prospective lawyers off, as the judge said, he certainly wouldn't want Luke, a former local icon, getting involved.

As soon as he thinks that, he dismisses it. Doug Lancaster wouldn't stoop to spying on him. The man has too much class.

But someone was there, watching him. He's certain of that. Not a comforting thought. Because he might be defending a man accused of a crime? A terrible crime, to be sure, but are the passions against Joe Allison so high that his lawyer will also be a pariah and a target?

Jesus, he just got back to town. All this is happening awfully fast.

He didn't ask for this job. He sure as hell isn't going to put himself in harm's way for it.

Late morning in the jail, after having come back from surfing, showered, breakfasted at the Carrow's across the street. His meeting with Joe Allison is a desultory affair. "How well did you know Emma Lancaster?" he asks.

"How well?" The prisoner shrugs. "Pretty well. Like I said, she was mature for her age. You could talk to her like an adult."

"When would you talk to her?"

Another shrug. "At the house, mostly. Sometimes she'd tag along to the station with her dad. She was interested in broadcasting. I think Doug was fantasizing about her coming into the business someday."

"There were always other people around? When you and she were together?"

Allison frowns. "Is somebody saying there was a relationship of some kind between me and Emma?"

"Not that I've heard," Luke tells him. "But if there was, I've got to know it. I don't want to wind up getting blindsided."

Allison can't mask his hopefulness. "So you are going to get involved?"

"I said, don't get your hopes up. I still don't know. I don't know how to defend you yet, and if I can't figure that out, I can't take your case."

Allison laughs nervously. "I'm being set up. Isn't that obvious?"

"Maybe to you," Luke responds, "but not to the rest of the world."

"What about you?" Allison challenges him for an answer.

Luke doesn't avert his eyes from Allison's stare. "I don't know. I don't know you well enough yet to know. But what I do know is that this setup business is a crummy defense. It reeks of desperation. I'd feel uncomfortable if that's all I went into a courtroom with." He gets up. "I need to study on this more. I'll give you an answer day after tomorrow, okay?"

"Do I have a choice?"

"No."

Back at the motel, early afternoon. Going over the material again.

The shoes and the key ring. How do you finesse those? Maybe one, but not both. If, as Allison claims, they were both a plant, whoever did it would have to have intimate access to Allison's personal life, and also would have to be both incredibly clever and extraordinarily lucky. The evidence sits unknown for a year, then is recovered on a fluke? In another week Allison would no longer have been living in Santa Barbara. Even if the stuff had been found, it would have happened in another jurisdiction whose authorities wouldn't have known what they meant.

Sitting in the room's one decent chair, the front door left open to let in fresh air and lift his spirits, he studies some recent photos of Emma Lancaster. If he'd encountered her and was told she was seventeen, he would have believed it.

He asks himself a basic question as he studies the material. What does Joe Allison have in his favor? What could a reasonable defense be built upon? Not a *plausible* defense, necessarily, something clear and logical; plenty of the best defenses have come from left field, built on any manner of preposterous premises. But reasonable in the sense that you can get a jury to believe it, or at least believe that it's possible, and thus cast reasonable doubt.

Start with the key ring in the glove box. It's Emma Lancaster's, of that there's no doubt. It is, without question, the single most important piece of evidence in the case, because it concretely links Emma with Joe Allison. Unless, as Allison is asserting, it was a plant—which no jury in the world is going to buy, not as a stand-alone entity. Either he or the deceased put it in there. And if there is a connection between them, beyond that of the boss's daughter and an employee, it's a connection that has only negative implications. What would a fourteen-year-old girl be doing in the company of a thirty-year-old man? Maybe he gave her a lift somewhere, she accidentally dropped the key ring in the car, he threw it in the glove compartment and then forgot about it?

Selling that would be a bitch, but there might be room to maneuver around it. Allison had been Mirandized, but not as a suspect in the kidnapping/murder. There's a big difference between a drunk driving charge and premeditated murder. They should have been clear with him about that. That would be an argument that might have merit.

And the shoes. Again, Allison seems to have crawled out on a limb and then sawed it off behind himself. By denying any possibility that he could have left the shoe print in a reasonable and believable situation, he has screwed himself.

If he decides to take this case (still highly unlikely), there are other avenues he must explore, starting with the sealed autopsy report. *Why was it sealed? Was there something in it that reflected badly on the victim?* More specific information about how she was killed. A blow to the temple with a sharp object, that's what was officially declared. The sealed report would have more informed speculation. Was the killer right- or left-handed? Dozens of specifics that could help point the finger away from Joe Allison. Or towards him; Luke doesn't figure

Ray Logan is going to try this case without having as much of that shit buttoned down as he possibly can.

He looks up from his reading. It's late in the day, almost eight. He's weary from fighting the material. There are no positives in it. Some of the negatives are less bleak than others, that's about it.

He's hungry. Dinner at the beach would be nice. He'll make sure there's no one in the restaurant he knows—he doesn't need any more stress. And then straight back to the room, watch some TV, go to bed. Sober.

He knows the back of her head better than the back of his own hand. He's looked at it a lot more. They're strolling ahead of him along Cabrillo Boulevard near Los Baños swimming pool, a man and a woman and a small child in a stroller. He's parked his motorcycle on the beach side of the street, is waiting for a break in the traffic to cross over to Emilio's, where he's going to have his solitary dinner.

He freezes. Don't turn around, he prays. Keep walking, away from me.

The woman, full of intuition, feels his vibe like a shock wave. She turns and looks back over her shoulder, her body pivoting to profile.

She's pregnant. Her stomach is stretched out like it's packed with a medium-sized watermelon.

Their eyes meet at thirty yards. Despite the changes in how he looks, there is no moment of nonrecognition—Polly knows him instantly. Her hand goes to her mouth.

He can't move, can't speak. He sees her hand come down, her mouth moving: "Luke." But whether she actually says it aloud and the wind carries it away so he doesn't hear, or she silently mouths it, he doesn't know, it doesn't matter. For he finds his legs, unsteady as a sailor's on dry land, and has turned from her and is walking away, down the sidewalk in the opposite direction, as quickly as he can.

Fifty interminable yards and he finds the will to stop, turn around and look. She and the man, her new husband, are walking away from him, their heads close together, talking quietly. The man glances over his shoulder and Luke looks out to the ocean, studying the sand and the tepid incoming tide.

His throat is a bilious vessel. He chokes the puke down.

When he's finally able to turn and look again they're no longer in sight. He stands there for several more minutes, locked in place, waiting for his heart rate to come down. Then he walks back, fires up the old motorcycle, and rides straightaway to the motel. Whatever appetite he had is gone.

This won't work. He was stupid for even coming down here and checking it out. His old mentor baited him, and he rose to it like a starving trout. Bad enough that the case against his client-to-be (in his dreams) is an absolute loser—Clarence Darrow and Johnnie Cochran and Gerry Spence all rolled into one couldn't salvage Joe Allison's hide. But seeing Polly, that was the kicker. He'd thought, after three years, he could handle that.

Well, he can't. If someone fired a 12-gauge round into his gut, it couldn't hurt any more than the pain he felt last night, seeing her with her new husband, her baby, and another one on the way.

When he left Santa Barbara, it was for good reason. It's time to leave again.

He's having breakfast with De La Guerra. Over eggs, home fries, and coffee, he details for the older man why he can't take Joe Allison on as a client.

"He says he isn't guilty. Fine." He slathers strawberry jelly on his sourdough toast. "Unfortunately, all the evidence says otherwise. This is an absolute loser, Freddie. A hog-slaughtering. If I'm standing next to him, there'll be blood all over me." He mixes egg yolk with potato and sausage, forks the mixture in his mouth.

"You saw Polly yesterday." The former judge is eating light, a fruit bowl and dry toast.

Another forkful of food stops in suspension halfway to Luke's mouth. "How do you know that?" he asks slowly. Jesus, this city is infinitesimal!

"She called me last night."

"She called you?"

"She assumed, correctly, that if you were here and in touch with anyone, it might be me." He pauses, sips from his coffee. "I didn't tell her the reason you were here."

"Good." No, awful. He's losing his appetite again.

"If running across your former wife sets you off like that," De La Guerra goes on, "you'll never be able to come back here again."

"That's . . ." He hesitates, but has to admit it—it's the truth. "I was hurt, okay? These things take time."

"Three years should be enough time."

"It was an accident, the way I ran across her." He's rationalizing like a tap dancer skittering across the stage. "I wasn't expecting it, I wasn't prepared. I can handle seeing her, I just need some preparation," he adds lamely.

"Now that you have, the next time should be easier," De La Guerra says blandly. But his eyes, intense over his coffee cup, give him away.

You're setting me up, you bastard, Luke thinks. As if I don't have enough problems with that loser client you tried to book for me.

He did what Freddie asked him to do, and wanted him to do: saw Joe Allison, and saw Polly. He can leave Santa Barbara with a clear conscience.

"Could be," he answers. "But since I'm not taking the case, it isn't going to matter." He sits back in the booth, munching on a piece of toast and sipping coffee.

"Is it the case?" De La Guerra asks, not willing to give up yet. "Or is it Polly?"

"Both," Luke answers truthfully. "And neither, not stand-alone." He holds his coffee cup up as the waitress passes bearing a hot pot; she freshens it for him. He adds some half-and-half, another spoonful of sugar. "If I thought I had any chance with Allison, I'd hang around. I'd love to lock horns with Ray Logan. I intimidate the shit out of that little twerp, I could see it in his eyes when we met, even after three years. If this case had any chance, I could push him so that he'd blow it. I know that. On the other hand, if I was cool with Polly and me, I might stay anyway; as you said, the money's good and I'm not expected to win."

He slides back against the corner of the booth—now that he's made his decision, he feels better. He hadn't realized how much pressure he'd been putting on himself, from the moment he'd driven into town. It's as if a steel band that was tightened against his head has suddenly been cut loose.

"I've got a life, and it's getting better. You saw it." He leans forward. "I'm trying to achieve peace. What's wrong with that?"

The old judge carefully arranges his cutlery by the side of his plate. "Nothing." He hesitates. "What if there was more money? Another hundred thou, let's say."

Luke laughs. "Money can't buy me love. Or make this loser into a winner."

"That's it, then."

"Yes, Freddie. That's it."

The old man signals for the check. "You have to do what's right for you."

"Thank you for finally seeing that."

Fumbling in his wallet for some bills, De La Guerra looks over at Luke again. "I think you could do a good job defending Joe Allison. Better than anyone he's ultimately going to get. But that's your choice, and I respect it," he says sincerely. "You did what I asked you to do; I can't ask more."

Luke is touched by the humility in the remarks. "I'm sorry, Freddie. But it doesn't work."

"That's all right. Like I said, you tried. The others I asked . . ." He looks at Luke. "You had to know I asked other lawyers about this."

"I figured you had." So he wasn't at the top of the list. At least he was on the list. Given his history over the last three years, that isn't bad. Still, he feels a sting.

The waitress hands De La Guerra the check. He gives her a twenty. "Keep the change." He looks at Luke. "Are you going to tell him, or do you want me to?"

"I'll do it. He paid me, I should tell him."

"You still have some class," De La Guerra says dryly.

"Not much. But I try." He smiles.

De La Guerra starts to get up from the booth, then changes his mind. "That's not what bothers me," he says. "Taking this case, or not taking it." His eyes, rheumy with age, focus on the younger man's face—a face that's undergone some strong changes, and not only cosmetically. "It's your fear of Polly, of seeing her." He leans forward on his elbows. "You have to deal with that, Luke," he says softly. "You have to confront it."

Luke goes rigid, leaning away from De La Guerra. "Why, Freddie?" he asks harshly.

"Because you won't be free until you do."

"That's bullshit!" Luke explodes; but not loudly. He doesn't want a scene in here. He came to this town in anonymity; that's blown now, but he can leave with some privacy. "I don't have to. Okay? I don't have to confront it. I can avoid it—her. Like I've been doing successfully for the last three years."

He stands up. Looking down at the old judge, he says, "I'm doing the best I can. It isn't perfect, but it's good enough for me. I've accepted that imperfection in me, all right? And if I can live with it, it's going to have to be good enough for you, and her, and everyone else in this town."

"It's me. Don't hang up. Please."

He sits on the edge of the bed in his motel room. It's the third time he's called Riva. The first two times he got the answering machine; he didn't leave a message because he knew she wouldn't listen to it.

"I'm coming home."

There's silence from her end. Finally: "When?"

"Tomorrow." He would have left today, but he hasn't gotten over to the jail to see Allison and give him the bad news. A small procrastination, but who's perfect? He'll pack up tonight, give Allison the bad news first thing in the morning, and hit the road.

"What happened?" He can hear the caution in her voice, the protectiveness.

"It didn't work out." He takes a breath. "And I miss you."

That's a lie. He missed her, but not enough to bring him back if the case had more of a chance or he hadn't choked on seeing his ex-wife.

But it's an okay lie, a good lie. Because it makes her feel better.

He can feel the softening over five hundred miles of telephone line. "I've missed you too."

"I'll see you tomorrow."

"I'll be here."

He's going to have a stellar dinner tonight on Joe Allison's money with no recriminations before, during, or after. He calls over to Citronelle and books a table by the window, overlooking the ocean and the harbor. He feels good; a calmness suffuses him. He's made the right decision.

The dinner proceeds leisurely. The food is wonderful, the service unobtrusively exquisite. Lovely wines by the glass complement each course. The view is great, it's a clear night, he can see, out the windows of the third-floor dining room, all the way to Santa Cruz in the Channel Islands twenty miles away. Even the lights from the offshore oil rigs, pollutants for three decades, twinkle like bright Christmas tree ornaments, offering a benign, serene delectation.

Luke's comfortable eating alone. When he entered, he cased the place thoroughly to make sure there wasn't anyone present that he knew. He wants a quiet, peaceful meal to end his brief sojourn here; he's had enough stress in these few days.

No such luck. The way things have gone, he should have known. But at least he got all the way through the meal before his serenity was broken.

"I've been wanting to talk to you."

Luke looks up from signing the credit card receipt. Doug Lancaster, his posture almost that of a supplicant, is standing beside his table.

Why isn't he surprised? Everything that's happened to him since he got here has had an inevitability to it; why should this final night be any different? Because he wanted it to be?

"Hello, Doug," he says.

"Hello, Luke. Long time no see."

Luke starts to say, "It could've been longer as far as I'm concerned." But this man is different, he remembers. "I never got to tell you how sorry I was about what happened," he says. The guy lost his only child, for Godsakes. And once upon a time he was your friend.

"Thank you."

"I didn't notice you in here or I would've come over and said hello," Luke lies as he stands up.

"I didn't eat here," Doug tells him. "I came over to see you." He pauses. "I wanted to wait for you to finish your dinner," he says, letting Luke know he is being gracious.

"I appreciate that," Luke says. You could've waited another day, he thinks; then you wouldn't have seen me at all.

"I understand you're taking on Joe Allison's defense."

Luke stares at him. "This is an improper discussion, which I'm sure you know," he says evenly.

"I do know that. But I'd like to speak to you about it anyway."

"No."

Doug carries on. "You and I used to be friends, and now my daughter is dead and my marriage is over. Please let me talk to you for a minute—as two old friends. Off the record."

They have drinks in a small private bar off the dining room that is empty except for them. "I'll be straight and to the point," Doug says. "I don't want you taking this case."

"I'm not the first lawyer you've said this to, am I?" Luke says, knowing the answer but wanting to hear how Lancaster handles it.

"As a matter of fact, you are." Doug smiles tightly. "The others—there were three of them before you—I contacted through emissaries. But I felt I should speak to you directly."

"I suppose I should be flattered, but I'm not." This is bad, so bald-faced. The guy has big *cojones*, give him that. "Since we're off the record, I should warn you that this is an obstruction of justice. You'd better watch your ass."

"But since this conversation is off the record, it isn't happening, is it?" Doug replies.

"It's good seeing you again, Doug. I wish we could've met under better circumstances. But I have to be going." He starts for the door.

Lancaster stops him. "What's Allison paying you?"

He doesn't know, Luke realizes. He doesn't know I'm not taking the case.

"I heard between a hundred and two hundred thousand," Doug says.

"That's none of your business, and you know it."

"Making sure my daughter's killer is brought to justice is my business, Luke." He's a man who's used to having his way. "Please don't tell me otherwise."

"We're finished here, Doug."

Lancaster stares at him. "Think about it, Luke. We're friends. Joe Allison murdered my daughter, far beyond any doubt. Please don't take this case."

Luke doesn't reply. He takes the elevator downstairs to the lobby.

"Excuse me. Are you Mr. Garrison?"

He turns. A young woman, obviously a hotel employee, comes to him from behind the check-in counter.

"Yes," he answers.

"A gentleman asked me to give this to you," she says with a practiced, sterile smile. And with that, she presses a legal-size envelope in his hand.

"What did he look like?" he starts to ask, but she's already marching back to her workstation.

He hefts the envelope in his hand. It's light. Crossing the room to a quiet corner, he sits down in a wicker chair and rips the envelope open.

The cashier's check, signed by an officer of the issuing bank, is made out to Luke Garrison for $200,000. There's no direct link from the check to Doug Lancaster.

Shoes in hand, he walks along East Beach at the water's edge, feeling the cold, wet sand on his feet. The check is in his hip pocket. His first impulse was to rip it up and throw it away, but then he calmed down.

Two hundred K. A small fortune, although Doug Lancaster can easily afford it—he offered a larger amount as reward for finding his daughter, when there was still hope that she was alive. I could retire on that, given my present lifestyle, Luke daydreams. Stick the money in an offshore bank account, don't even pay taxes. Live up north with Riva, do some light lawyering on the side, indulge myself in new and exciting hobbies while collecting dividend checks from the investments of the clandestine money.

He mulls over his options.

He can take the money and run. He was going to leave anyway; why not leave with two hundred thousand untraceable dollars in his pocket? That would be the most cynical choice, but so what? The law is a shitty business much of the time. Might as well make some money at it.

He can give the money back, and leave as planned. That would be the honorable thing to do. He's been paid for his brief sojourn down here; he's no better or worse off than he was a week ago.

The problem with that is, it isn't true. He *is* worse off than before he came down, much worse. Regardless of whether he keeps Lancaster's blood money or gives it back, he's fucked here. They're going to be laughing at him behind his back. The old king of the hill, now deposed, who's afraid of taking on a tough case, a case he's not assured of winning. That would be Ray Logan's aria, and he'd sing it to the multitudes.

Doug Lancaster's reaction figures to be more complex. If he keeps the money, he'll be a serf, someone a rich man can buy off. Worse than that, he'll be an outcast in his profession, a lawyer who would abandon a client for money.

If, on the other hand, he doesn't take the money but simply leaves town, he'll be just another putz who doesn't have the smarts to come in out of the rain.

And then there's Polly. They loved each other for a long time; part of him still loves her. Will he forever be incapable of being anywhere near where she is?

An hour ago it was all so clear.

He walks as far as Stearn's Wharf. The wooden slats, wet from nighttime fog, feel slimy-slippery under his bare feet. He puts his shoes and socks back on, continues walking until he's at the end of the pier, where he sits on a cold wooden bench and watches some Chicano kids fishing for perch.

The more he thinks about what Doug Lancaster did just now, the more enraged he feels. How dare that bastard try to buy him off? How dare he think he can? He was going to leave, yes, but not for money. Now it's a cloud over his head, and it will not go away.

Before tonight he had options. Now, thanks to Doug Lancaster's unyielding need to obliterate his daughter's killer, he doesn't. And no one except him will know why.

"I can't come home tomorrow after all."

A long silence on the other end of the line. Then: "Why?" She's groggy from being woken up, he hears the fog in her voice.

"I've gotten boxed in here, Riva. I can't leave now, not yet. It's impossible to explain."

"Give me an estimate."

"I can't."

"So you're staying. You're taking that stupid loser case."

"I have to."

She starts to say "fuck you" and slam down the phone once and for all, but she doesn't. "We'll talk about this tomorrow," she says instead.

This is a good woman. Better than he deserves. "I'll call you." He wonders how much blood she drew, biting her tongue.

The knocking at the door is soft at first, then louder. He sits up in bed, looking at his watch on the nightstand. A quarter to six. Who could this be? he wonders.

"Just a moment," he calls out. Slipping into a pair of Levi's, he stumbles to the door and opens it.

Riva's standing there. He gapes at her.

"Aren't you going to invite me in?" she asks. "Or do you have company?"

"Oh. Yeah, of course." He moves aside so she can enter.

She stands in the middle of the small room, giving it the once-over. "Just like home," she says wryly.

"Not hardly. What are you doing here?" Jesus, does she look

good. It's a long haul, she must have flown straight here as soon as she hung up.

She stares at him. "If you can't beat 'em, join 'em. If that's all right with you."

He doesn't deserve an act this kind, he thinks. But he'll take it.

They undress, him the jeans, her everything she has on. Then they're in bed, all over each other, and it isn't the sex that matters, it's the lovemaking.

Hours later. He goes out to Starbucks for coffee and scones. They sit up in bed, naked, drinking their lattes. He explains about what happened to change his mind, telling her everything, including the fiascos with Logan and Polly. She listens intently, quietly.

"You need help," she informs him after he finishes his entire recitation.

"I know. There's going to be a ton of investigative work, research—"

She shakes her head. "Up here." She taps him on the temple.

"Yeah." He leans over and kisses the nape of her neck. She scrunches her shoulders—she's sensitive there. "I do," he says.

She's here for the duration. "Hershel'll baby-sit the place till we get back. He's done it before. The animals love him." Hershel is one of their neighbors, an older man who's grown dope going on thirty years now but is serious about taking care of business.

She'll put her bail-bond business on hiatus, handle what she can by fax, long distance, and occasional trips back there. With her background, she can do basic investigative work for him. If she stumbles onto a piece of sleuthing that becomes too complex, involving special technology and so forth, they'll hire out.

He doesn't have a clue as to how he's going to defend Allison, because (a) so far he hasn't figured out a workable defense, and (b) he hasn't tried to, because he wasn't taking the case.

"You'll figure something out," she says.

"I'd better."

"It's your job," she reassures him. "Dealing with all the backstabbers in this town, plus your own demons, that's going to be your real work. Work those things out, and Allison's defense will take care of itself."

He isn't sure that he can handle either. But at least he isn't alone now.

It feels good, her being here. Much better than he would have thought.

The meeting with Allison is almost anticlimactic—for Luke, if not for Allison, whose gratitude is almost embarrassing. "I can't tell you how appreciative I am," he gushes.

"We'll see how you're feeling about me in six months," Luke says brusquely, jerking the prisoner back to earth. "Let's start with the basics. How much money do you have?" He has a contract for Allison to sign. They're in a lawyer-interview room. He shoves the contract across the table.

Allison, although taken aback by the aggressive questioning, answers gamely. "A little less than a hundred twenty-five grand, my bonus from NBC. They wanted it back, but I'd already cashed the check. I gave you five thousand as an advance, and I spent a few bucks before I was arrested."

"No property, stocks, other investments?"

"About fifteen thousand in the market."

"Cash it out. What about your car? What's that worth?"

Allison gulps. "About forty thousand, although I owe twenty-five."

"Sign it over to me. I'll sell it. Whatever's left goes in the kitty."

Allison blanches. "I'm not going to have anything left," he whines.

Luke rests his elbows on the table. "If you're convicted, which is the odds-on choice right now, that isn't going to matter, is it? Getting the best defense I can give you is going to cost money, more money than you have. So whatever you have, it's mine now. To spend on your behalf."

"What if there's some left over afterwards?" Allison asks naively.

Luke roars, a real belly laugh. "There won't be, don't worry."

He doesn't mention the two hundred thousand Doug Lancaster gave him. He's still trying to figure out what to do about that. He wants to keep it—serve the bastard right. Riva isn't sure. She isn't averse to handling shady money, she lived with a drug dealer. But Luke isn't that kind of man, and she doesn't want him tarnished.

He laughed, talking to her about it. "From fearless prosecutor to small-time drug lawyer to a scofflaw pocketing a cool quarter-mil, almost. What could be more the American dream than that?"

"That isn't you," she said. "Not yet. Hopefully, never. I didn't exchange one scumbag for another, Luke. Don't you know that?"

Still, two hundred thousand undeclared and untraceable dollars is not small potatoes. She knows how to launder money, if that's what they ultimately decide.

That's for later. "I'm going to spend a few days going over the transcripts of your police interview," Luke tells Allison. "Next week you'll be formally arraigned—they've been waiting for you to get a lawyer. Then it begins." He stands up, offers his hand. "Don't ever lie to me," he informs his fresh client again. "Do exactly what I tell you, always. And no matter what, never doubt me."

Allison shakes Luke's hand. Taking the proffered ballpoint, he signs the contract without reading it. "Whatever you say. My life's in your hands."

The last thing Luke wants to hear.

THREE

How do you plead?"

"Not guilty, Your Honor."

As Luke assumed, the courtroom is filled to capacity. There's a large media contingent, with stringers and reporters from the national newspapers and television networks, whose trucks are parked outside on Anacapa Street, where the broadcast reporters will have the photogenic courthouse as a backdrop when they do their standups. Doug and Glenna Lancaster are there, of course, Doug sitting in the first spectator row behind the prosecution table, the ex-wife farther back. They are there as two separate entities with one common purpose, rather than as a team.

Doug Lancaster stares at Luke with unvarnished venom. Luke can't blame him—he's defending the man accused of kidnapping and murdering the Lancasters' only child, and he's sitting on two hundred thousand dollars of Doug's money, money he was supposed to have left town with.

Too bad. He's here to do a job.

Glenna Lancaster, dressed all in black, no makeup, is also looking at him, but with more of a wary, suspicious gaze than one of hatred or anger. She shifts her focus to Joe Allison, a foot to Luke's left at the defense table. She's wearing her hair shorter than she used to, Luke notices. He's also reminded of how attractive she is, and how tall—

he's over six feet, and she's almost his height. From the pictures he's seen of Emma, she looked a lot like her mother.

The rest of the audience are people who are interested in this case for what are, essentially, voyeuristic reasons. Many are lawyers Luke used to know, some of the best lawyers in town. They're curious about his self-imposed exile, and whether he has anything left after his fall from grace. The fraternity of criminal-defense lawyers is a tight one, but none of these men and women are on Luke's side. Even with the long hair and beard (he removed the earring), in this city Luke Garrison will always be the prosecutor.

Riva sits in the rear of the room scoping things out. She's wearing a calf-length charcoal gray skirt slit to reveal most of her long, attractive thigh as she sits with one leg crossed over the other.

Luke's only other ally, Judge De La Guerra, isn't in attendance. He doesn't want the situation to get any more inflamed than it already is, and he knows that if he came, it would be. Ray Logan and Doug Lancaster, among others, are royally pissed at him for having recruited Luke.

Nicole Rogers is not in the room. Luke finds that intriguing, even though he hasn't met her yet.

Joe is seated, having made his plea. The accused is wearing a good suit. He's had a haircut and looks much as he did when he was the Channel 8 news anchor: a decent, intelligent man, not a kidnapper/murderer. But Luke knows that won't matter. In the hearts and minds of everyone in this room except him and Riva and maybe a few die-hard contrarians, Allison has been tried, convicted, and sentenced to everlasting hell.

The case is being heard by Judge Prescott Ewing, the senior judge on the superior court bench. Like everyone else, he is mystified to see the county's former star prosecutor—a man whose office tried scores of cases in his courtroom—standing before him at the table on the other side of the aisle.

When Luke came in yesterday to Ewing's chambers for the prearraignment meeting along with Ray Logan, Ewing hadn't been able to conceal his curiosity and dismay. "This has an otherworldly quality," he remarked to Luke. He couldn't help but ask, "Are you sure you want to do this?"

"I'm sure," Luke had answered.

Ewing stares at the indictment in front of him. "How long will it take you to prepare your defense?" he asks Luke.

Without hesitation Luke answers, "Six months, Your Honor."

Ray Logan, seated at the prosecution table, rises swiftly from his chair. "Six months?" He glares at Luke. "That's ridiculous, Your Honor. The People are prepared to go to trial right now!"

Ewing turns to Luke. "Do you need that much time?" he asks skeptically.

"I just came into this, Your Honor," Luke replies. "I don't know yet. This is a capital case with the death penalty as an option," he says forcefully. Putting a hand on his client's shoulder, he stares at the judge. "A case of this importance should not be rushed to trial."

The conviction and sentencing of the man wrongly sent to the gas chamber is still remembered, especially in the legal community. But that was when Luke was standing up for the People.

Things are different now. With scarcely a moment's hesitation, the judge swings his gavel. "Four months," he says abruptly. Looking to his clerk: "Schedule case number B-1694, *People versus Joseph B. Allison*."

Outside the courtroom, in the Mexican-tiled hallways and the exterior garden courtyard, rumor and innuendo and gossip run rampant. Most of the people here have not seen Luke Garrison in three years, and his radical change, both in appearance and attitude, is disconcerting. A few of those emerging from the courtroom sidle near him as he stands outside the main courthouse door, exchange strained greetings as they pass.

"How are you?" he says to one and all, shifting his weight from one foot to the other. "Good to see you." Rote salutations, recited mechanically. He doesn't make real eye contact with anyone; there's no one he wants to get close to. He's already rebuffed the various reporters—he'll hold a small press conference shortly, he tells them. Until then, no comment on anything.

Riva, having detoured to the ladies' room, comes trotting down the steps. "Ready?" she asks.

He nods. "Let's go." Out of the courtroom, a familiar safe haven, he's antsy, anxious to get out of here: he's acutely aware of being the curious and critical object of a hundred pair of eyes. And not only him, but also this unknown, rather exotic-looking woman with him: Lover? Cocounsel? Associate?

Let 'em guess. Whoever needs to know will figure it out. Taking Riva's arm, he begins to lead her away through the throng. Then a low concentrated murmur causes him to turn and look back at the large entrance door.

Doug Lancaster has emerged from the courthouse. He's flanked by a group of his friends and supporters, including Fred Hampshire, his lawyer. They're immediately swarmed on by the reporter-horde. Questions fly at Doug, cameras and microphones are thrust in his face.

Hampshire holds up a hand for order. "No questions for Mr. Lancaster now," he says crisply. "He'll talk to you later."

Looking towards the street, Doug spies Luke and Riva watching him. For a brief moment his face tenses, then he regains his equilibrium.

"Are you happy that the case is finally getting under way?" This from one of his own field reporters, a young, generically attractive woman.

The smile comes on. A serious smile, the face he presents to the world in this matter. "Yes, Doris, I am. We all are. It's time to bring justice and closure to this painful event."

Behind him Glenna Lancaster, with her own small entourage, has emerged from inside and is moving away. As some of the reporters head towards her, two large men sporting close-cropped hair and designer sunglasses, off-duty cops hired as bodyguards for the occasion, block access to her. She sweeps past Luke and Riva. Without a backwards look she gets into the backseat of a Lincoln Town Car with heavily tinted side windows.

"Interesting-looking woman," Riva comments as she watches Glenna's car meld into the traffic heading down Anacapa.

"Yeah," Luke answers distractedly. He's focused on Doug, still holding court on the steps.

"We need to talk."

Luke turns. Fred Hampshire has snuck up behind him. His voice is stealthy, edgy; even Riva, standing alongside Luke, can barely hear him.

"What about?" Luke says, turning away, his eyes again fixed on Doug Lancaster.

"Money."

"What about it?"

Riva has moved away a discreet distance. She doesn't want any part of this.

"We want it back."

A minuscule smile creases Luke's mouth. Still not looking at Hampshire, he says, "I don't know what you're talking about."

"You're not seriously thinking of keeping it." The lawyer's voice is lower, with a lot of threat in it.

"Like I said, Fred, I don't know what in hell you're talking about."

Fred Hampshire's face goes crimson. "Listen, you wise sonof—"

"*You* listen," Luke says, cutting him off. Keeping his voice low, calm, he says, "My heart goes out to Doug and Glenna. Losing your child, especially under these circumstances, has to be the most horrible thing that could ever happen to someone. And I understand that they want her killer to be brought to justice—which is why we're going to trial. You're a lawyer. You know that. And you also know the system has to be allowed to work legitimately, without perversion or coercion."

He's getting heated up: mostly show, to tweak the family lawyer. "If, for instance, your client tried to buy a lawyer off from defending someone—we're talking hypothetically here, in case you're wired, which would be illegal but not uncommon—he would be committing a major felony that would get him sent to jail for a long time. A good lawyer such as yourself would advise said client never to try something as stupid as that. Beyond that, as I said, I don't know what you're talking about. And if I hear another word from anyone about this hypothetical bullshit, I'll file a complaint that will embarrass the hell out of you people, which won't help anyone."

Leaving Hampshire fuming on the sidewalk, he takes Riva's arm and walks her away. A few television reporters, pole mikes and remote cameras thrust forward, try to get a last-minute quote as he and

Riva climb into the old truck, but he fends them off with a polite but firm "no comment."

They sign a month-to-month lease on a small house on Mountain Drive high above the city, furnishings to be provided by Bekins on a monthly rental. The telephone company puts in two lines, and they're set. It's a little box, but the views are great—the entire city, harbor, Channel Islands, the ocean stretching to the horizon. It's similar in feel to their house up north, a soothing womb to come home to at the end of a trying day, of which there will be many.

Finding suitable office space takes more time. Most of the private lawyers in town, those who practice criminal work, either don't like him or are scared of him or both. He was their enemy, their nemesis, the man who kicked their asses and took their names. It's only three feet to cross the aisle in the courtroom from the prosecution table to the defense side, but the psychological distance is vast, almost immeasurable.

And there's the Doug Lancaster intimidation factor. Doug has already talked, conned, wheedled, and intimidated the good lawyers out of getting involved. Not that any of them needed much persuading—the overwhelming feeling is that this is going to be the Branch Davidian of trials. No lawyer in the area who's got anything at all going wants an association with this, even as innocuously and indirectly as renting out some offices. Doug Lancaster is an eight-hundred-pound gorilla. Why piss him off when he's only trying to do the right thing for his daughter's memory and the community's redemption?

The old judge comes through. The Anacapa School of Law is a night and weekend law school for people getting their degrees in their spare time. They expanded recently, and have a vacant suite. There's an adequate law library, computer hookups, students eager to pitch in for stuff like research if the need arises. The ex-judge is on their board of directors, so getting the space is a done deal.

Four days after Luke stands up in court for the first time with his client Joe Allison, he's ready to go to work.

* * *

Both he and Riva are up with the sun. It's hard to sleep well the first few nights in a new place, and their bedroom faces southeast, so the new-day sun, arising over the south-facing coast like a fresh egg yolk, shines full into the windows. They could close the wide paint-peeling wood shutters, but they both like the feeling of open space.

They separate; they won't see each other until the day's end, when they'll meet up someplace for a drink, checking with each other on their cell phones, to recap the day's events, then maybe dinner out, or pick something up and bring it back here or, for him, to his office.

He heads to town, parks at his new office, and strolls three blocks over to the courthouse, where he files a discovery motion to obtain Emma Lancaster's autopsy report. The method of killing, as he understands it, is cut-and-dried, but maybe there's some off-center wrinkle that might point him in a helpful direction.

The clerk behind the counter instructs him to check back towards the end of the day, or maybe tomorrow. Sealed files, whether autopsy reports or others of a criminal nature, aren't in the computer.

"For protection against unauthorized access," she explains.

"That's a good idea," he says dryly. He knows about that policy. He instituted it, when he was running the show.

He walks down to Figueroa Street and into police headquarters. They lead him through the maze and sit him down in a small holding room, where he waits to interview the officer who arrested Joe Allison on the DUI charge. Passing through the entrance, signing in with the officer of the day, and following his escort through the hallways, he sees familiar faces. He nods to them, they nod and grunt in return. None of them do anything to make him feel welcome. He used to be their poster boy, their hero—they'd bust the bad guys, he'd put them away. Now, like most everyone else in town, they wish he'd never come back.

Elton Caramba, the cop who stopped Joe Allison and put all this in motion, sits across the small wooden desk from Luke. He just came off his shift, but he's alert, buttoned-down, his uniform still crisp after eight hours riding around in a patrol car.

Luke originally asked Caramba, a short, contentious ex-Marine with a discernible chip on his shoulder, to meet him at his office at the law school, but the cop preferred his own territory. Luke acquiesced:

interviewing the other side's witnesses is always a touchy situation. Arguing over where an interview will take place isn't worthwhile.

"Good morning, Officer Caramba. Thanks for taking time to talk to me."

Caramba shrugs. He's got his story straight. He's been over it enough times.

Luke knows the cop hates his guts. The law says you don't have to be interviewed in a criminal case, but police department regs say otherwise. The position is that the police work for everyone, prosecution and defense. So you cooperate. But that doesn't mean you have to bend over and open wide.

Normally, an assistant D.A. would be sitting in; advising Caramba. It's SOP whenever a police officer is questioned by a defense lawyer. But because of Luke's former position, Logan had decided, after some deliberation, not to have one of his people present. Most of the current assistants worked under Luke, and there might be some embarrassment. Deeper than that is Logan's desire to let Luke know that they have nothing to fear from him, nothing to hide. Their cops don't need that kind of protection. All they have to do is tell the truth. And they will.

Luke opens the folder with the cop's information. Looking up, he asks, "Where were you when you saw my client's car on the night you arrested him?"

"When I first spotted him?"

Luke nods. "Yes."

"I was in my patrol car on Coast Village Road."

"Driving or parked?"

"I was driving."

"Towards him, or in the same direction?"

"In the same direction."

"So you came up behind him." Another glance at his notes. His notes, like all lawyers', are work-product, protected by confidentiality—he never has to show them to anyone. But he doesn't like to take copious notes while he's interviewing; it breaks the flow, and tends to make the interviewee uptight, knowing that every word he (or she) is saying is being recorded for posterity, usually to be used, in the case of hostile witnesses such as this one, against him.

Later, right after the interview, he'll flesh them out.

"Yes." The cop answers.

"And you followed him for a while."

"A short time."

"How long is a short time, Officer?"

"Ten, fifteen seconds."

Luke frowns. "That isn't much time."

"It was enough for me," Caramba says without any hesitation.

"Was he speeding?" He already knows the answer—he wants to find out, as soon as possible, if this particular officer shades things, either out of reflex, nervousness, or plain attitude. He won't press whatever he learns now—the information will go into the mental file, to be used later when needed.

Caramba starts to say something, changes his mind, says, "No."

"Then why did you stop him?"

"He was weaving."

"Could you describe 'weaving' for me? How you personally define it, out in the field?"

"Not driving a straight line. Crossing the double yellow line. You use your common sense. And your experience."

"Right. So Mr. Allison was weaving back and forth across the double yellow line? That was the main reason you thought he might have been impaired?"

Another short hesitation. "Yes."

Luke waits a moment before asking his next question. "If you only followed him for ten or fifteen seconds," he says, "how many times could you have seen him weaving back and forth across the double yellow?"

The cop squares himself in his chair. "A couple."

"A couple?" Luke says dubiously. "In ten or fifteen seconds?"

"Once would've been enough. I do this for a living—*sir.* I'm trained to spot this sort of thing. Better too early a stop for a DUI than too late. If I'm wrong, I apologize and I'm on my way. Most drivers appreciate that attitude, even if they are over the limit."

Luke changes the subject. He's going to have this cop on the stand, he knows that already, and he has enough information on this part of the story for now. "You pulled him over . . ."

Without further prompting, Caramba gives a dry, by-the-numbers description of what went down: He pulled the car over, the driver seemed flushed, impaired, he was talking loud, the usual symptoms. Then he (Caramba) spotted the opened whiskey bottle on the floor of the car, which prompted him to search (legally) for other possible violations.

Luke listens with half an ear—he knows what the guy's going to say, almost word for word, before he says it. A parrot on a perch.

"And that's when I found the key ring in the back of the glove compartment," the cop says, finishing that part of his recitation. "I remembered it because it had been described to us when we were out searching for her. Since the keys were one of the few personal items missing then," he adds, wishing he hadn't; he wants to give the facts and that's all, no editorializing or embellishing.

"Uh-huh. When did you read Mr. Allison his Miranda rights?" Luke asks casually, changing directions. "Before or after you found the key ring that turned out to belong to Emma Lancaster?"

The cop blinks. "After," he says.

"And was that before or after you field-tested him for sobriety?"

Another blinking, several fast ones, as if the blinking brings up the correct answer. "Before. I mean . . ." He realizes he's been caught. He stops talking.

"Hmm." Luke rises, stretches.

The cop stares at him impassively.

When Luke sits down again, he says, "Don't you normally wait until *after* you've found out if they're over the limit or not before you read them their rights? If they're not over the limit you're not going to bust them, so you don't have to read them their rights, right?"

For the first time in the session the cop squirms in his chair, just a small movement, but enough for Luke to know that the guy is feeling uncomfortable. "Yeah, normally that's how you'd do it."

"So reading him his rights was about finding the key ring, rather than any DUI thing."

Reluctantly, the cop answers. "Yes."

"Because you recognized the seriousness of it. The potential seriousness of it."

Again, reluctantly, "Yeah."

Luke casually leafs through the file. "I think that's all I need, Officer," he says. He stands and offers the man his hand. The policeman, rising on his own feet, takes it with dubious hesitation.

"Oh, one last thing," Luke remembers. "When *did* you test Mr. Allison for whether or not he was over the limit? Did you field-test him out there on the street, or did you wait until you got back to the station?"

"I didn't test him in the field," the arresting officer, a career foot-soldier who will never rise higher than his present station, says as flatly as he can. But presented with the opportunity to boast a little, he can't help but add, "At that point I had bigger problems to deal with."

Okay, so the cop was lying. That it was a lie of omission rather than commission makes it less of a lie, but in the black-and-white-morality sense it's still a lie, because it isn't the full truth. The cop didn't inform Allison, when he read him his Miranda rights, that he was a possible suspect in an unsolved murder.

The first chink in the armor. Only a technicality, one that no judge, certainly no judge sitting on the bench in this county, will listen to. But it's a beginning, a possible handhold.

The sheriff's office is reluctant to hand over the videotape of Allison's interrogation. But they have to, so he gets his hands on it and watches it at home with Riva.

It's nighttime. They're sprawled on the floor of their sparsely furnished living room in the rental house, watching the tape on the VCR and eating take-out Chinese.

"They were playing fast and loose with the rules, Riva. They didn't tell him he was under suspicion for Emma Lancaster's murder. He thought all he was sweating was a DUI, which is only a misdemeanor. They don't normally book someone on that, unless he's falling-down drunk, which Allison clearly wasn't."

"Can you use that?" she asks.

"Probably not, although I'll raise it." He remotes the tape off. "It's too nebulous, and they did read him his rights. It's SOP cop stuff. I could only use it if there was other malfeasance on top of it, and I doubt there was."

She maneuvers some noodles with her chopsticks. "You used to do that stuff, didn't you? When you were running the show."

He nods. "Like I said, it's SOP. You have to get the confession, you don't want to scare the pigeon off. It's easier now than it used to be. The courts've given the prosecution much more leeway in interpreting that stuff."

"So how does it feel?" She pours him more chardonnay. She's wearing shorts and one of his T-shirts. Looking up at her long legs from his supine position on the floor, he feels a growing horniness.

"Being on the other side?" He quaffs some wine. "Mildly weird, but it's not that important. Sooner or later you have to get down to guilt or innocence, and all the 'side' stuff gets sifted out. All this jury swaying and jury nullification stuff you read about, it rarely happens. It won't in this case," he predicts, "because there aren't any unique circumstances. No racial issues, no money issues."

"But it's so inflammatory. All this stuff feeds the fire, doesn't it?" she asks.

"Of course. Goes with the territory."

He follows her into the kitchen. She rinses their plates in the sink. Handing him a towel for drying, she looks at him closely. "Luke—do you think he's guilty?"

"The evidence points to it."

"But what do you think?" she persists.

He puts the dried plates in the cabinet. "He's my client. The least I can do for him at this point is be open-minded."

"It sounds to me like you do," she counters, trying to get him to commit. "Think he's guilty."

They go out onto the porch with their glasses of wine. It's a balmy night, they're comfortable sitting outside. In the low distance the lights of the city and the harbor sparkle and flicker.

"From up here it feels like we're home," she says. "Especially when it's dark out."

"This is my home," he reminds her.

"Used to be," she reminds him.

"Used to be," he agrees. Reverting to the other train of thought she raised, he says, "If it was a kidnapping, why wasn't there a struggle? I keep coming back to that."

"Maybe she was still asleep."

"Yeah. It's logical, but it doesn't feel right. I've got to pin that down more."

Riva says what she's thinking, what he's been thinking. "Or she knew him."

"That feels more right."

"She knew Joe Allison, didn't she?"

"Oh, yeah." That is what's most upsetting to him. "But if it was him, what in the world would that say about them? What kind of relationship does that say they had?" He runs a finger around the rim of his wine glass. "God forbid, if there was something going on between them, was it even a kidnapping at all?" Continuing that train of thought, he adds, "But if there was something going on between them, why would he kill her?"

Lisa Jaffe, dressed in the outfit she wore to school—holed-at-the-knees baggy overalls over a Wet Seal T-shirt and sockless black Converse All-Stars—sits cheek by jowl with Susan, her mother, on the canvas-slipcovered couch in their small living room, tightly gripping her mother's hand for support. Luke and Riva sit across from them, a small Mexican-tiled coffee table from Pier One separating the two groups. Luke can sense her nervousness. He knows she's been seeing a psychologist since the murder, but wonders if it's done much good.

The house is not impressive, nor is the street on which they live. A small clapboard house in need of paint in a neighborhood of like houses. The people in this neighborhood are working-class, a lot different from the rich folks in Montecito like the Lancasters.

Luke has brought Riva with him to soften the impact. Observing the witness's mother sitting next to her anxious daughter, the woman's mouth set in a tight line, he knows that having her accompany him was a smart move.

He takes the file containing Lisa's statement from his briefcase and opens it, laying it on the coffee table in front of him. "This won't take long," he assures mother and daughter. "We appreciate your seeing us."

Susan gives him a tight nod. Lisa stares down at the open file as if the flat papers inside it might come alive and attack her.

"We have a few details to clarify," Riva says by way of opening the questioning. Luke has introduced her as his "colleague," leaving any specific designation deliberately vague. He's already prepped her on what he is hoping to find out. Her asking the questions will make it easier for Lisa to speak freely.

"Lisa has to leave for ballet rehearsal in half an hour," Susan says. Meaning: don't drag this out.

"That's fine," Riva says in a soft, calming voice. She picks up Lisa's statement. "Initially you weren't sure if this had happened or if you were dreaming it? Is that correct?"

Lisa looks at her mother, who nods. "Yes," the petite girl says in a small voice. "But it wasn't. I said that because I had been very tired. We'd been up late and I got woke up, so for a minute I didn't realize where I was, since I wasn't in my own house," she goes on, rambling from nervousness.

She looks closer to twelve or thirteen than fifteen, Luke thinks, observing her. He wonders if she's even started menstruating yet. Certainly anything having to do with sex would be foreign and scary to her, even more so a year ago.

"You're positive, then, that what you saw was real, and not a dream," Riva says.

"Yes. It was real."

"The man—it was a man?"

"Yes, I believe so."

"Had her in his arms."

"Yes."

"Actually, what you told the police was, someone who must have been a man had something in his arms that must have been Emma, is that right?"

The girl, twitching like a nervous rabbit, glances at her mother.

"Go ahead," Susan Jaffe tells her daughter, her irritation at this uninvited intrusion into their lives clear and unambiguous. Luke, watching the interaction, knows she won't consent to having her daughter interviewed again; they won't have another chance to question her until she's actually on the stand at the trial.

He's okay with that. There's only one important detail he wants to nail down.

"Yes," Lisa says timorously, answering Riva's question about what she had told the police.

"But at the time you actually witnessed this—at about three or four o'clock in the morning, after having been abruptly awakened from a deep sleep—you didn't know it was Emma wrapped up in that blanket, is that right?" Riva asks, keeping her voice low and soothing.

"Yes," the girl admits.

"You never actually saw Emma's face?"

"No."

"Or the man who took her."

Lisa draws breath. "No," she admits. "I didn't see him."

"He had a hat on that covered most of his face," Riva reads from the file. "Do you remember telling the police that, Lisa?"

"Yes," the girl answers quietly.

"Let me see if there's anything else," Riva says, looking to Luke for prompting. He makes a twisting motion with his hand. "Oh, yes," Riva says. "You went to Emma's house from downtown in a taxicab, right?"

"Uh-huh."

"Who let you into the house?" Riva asks. "Was it Mrs. Lancaster, or was it someone else? Or was the door unlocked?"

The girl blinks. Thinking about that, she scrunches her eyebrows in a frown, then says slowly, "I don't . . . Emma unlocked the door, I think. Nobody let us in," she says with more certainty.

"So either the door was unlocked, or she used her house key," Riva continues the thought.

"I guess."

Riva glances at Luke. He nods. "I think that's all we need for now," she says, closing the folder and handing it to Luke. Bending closer to Lisa, she says, "That wasn't too bad, I hope."

"No, it wasn't too bad," Lisa admits. She's relaxing her vigilance, now that the questioning's over.

"May I ask one question?" Luke says. He's on his feet, stuffing the file into his thickly filled briefcase.

"What?" the girl says, freezing up immediately.

"This man who was carrying this figure in the blanket. Did he have anything else in his hands, like some clothes, shoes, a purse. Anything like that?"

Lisa thinks for a moment, closing her eyes and scrunching up her forehead again. "No," she says, opening her eyes and looking at him. "I don't remember anything like that."

Sitting outside the Jaffe house in the old truck, Luke ponders what Lisa Jaffe has just told him. "If Emma Lancaster unlocked the door that night, that means she had her keys with her. And then she's carried away. So how does the key ring get out of the house and into Joe Allison's car a year later?"

"Unless the door was unlocked and she didn't use her keys," Riva responds.

"Okay, that's one possibility, although in her statement to the cops, Glenna Lancaster went to pains to talk about how they were security-conscious." Thinking, he goes on, "Or another possibility, Emma had a duplicate set of keys. Not far-fetched. And she did know Allison, so she could have lost her keys in his car some earlier time, told her mother she lost them and didn't remember where, and got a new set."

"Except her mother made a big point of telling the police that *those* keys were missing," Riva reminds him. "Specifically. They were the only items she could definitely remember as missing, because of the sentimental value."

"So unless Emma was asleep when her abductor snatched her, she went without a struggle," he recaps. "And her missing keys might not have been missing when they were supposed to be missing."

"Which takes us back to her knowing who did it," Riva reiterates. "And going with him willingly."

"Man, I hope to God there's no evidence that points to Joe Allison having some kind of secret relationship with that girl," Luke says apprehensively. His finely tuned lawyer's antennae are quivering, feeling something percolating out in the corner of the ether where justice is sometimes served, sometimes subverted, but always jacked around. *Why the fuck did you take this dumb case? You come back for a sure thing, not a thousand-to-one shot.* "Because that would be the coffin nail from hell."

Riva turns to him. "You're the pro at this, not me. But if I were you, and that was bothering me half as much as it's bothering you, I'd ask him."

It's a sealed envelope, with a warning on the cover: *The opening, reading, examination, or any other use of this document by unauthorized persons will result in criminal penalties.*

He's authorized, Riva isn't, he'll share it with her anyway, and with anyone else he needs to share it with, if there's information in it that has a bearing on his case. Sitting at his desk, he slashes the envelope open. By the time he's finished reading the first paragraph, he's starting to shake.

Riva notices. "What's the matter?"

"Emma Lancaster was pregnant."

"Oh, no!" She's as shocked by this information as he is.

This is incredible, he thinks, reading the report. This revelation is going to throw his investigations and his entire defense posture—not that he has one yet—into chaos. A fourteen-year-old girl is carried away willingly (in his mind, he's almost positive of that now) from her bedroom. It almost certainly had to be by the man she's been having sex with, who got her pregnant.

This case is going to take a broader path now. He's going to have to explore Emma Lancaster's life in much greater depth and detail than he'd planned. Who she was seeing, where she was seeing them, who could have known she was pregnant—did her parents know, for instance? Did her abductor know she was pregnant? Was he the father of her unborn child, who upon hearing of this disaster panicked and killed her?

Fundamentally, this case is no longer merely about defending Joe Allison; its now about Emma Lancaster's short life, how she lived, and why she died.

So here's another problem for you, Luke my boy, he thinks to himself. If Joe Allison, your client, was fucking Emma Lancaster, a fourteen-year-old girl, then very likely he's the one who killed her. What does that mean to you, defending a man who was screwing a girl that young? Where is your moral compass? Do you even have one? And if you do, and he is, what can you do about it, since you're now his lawyer, until death or the end of this trial do you part?

It's a warm night, with a southwestern offshore flow bringing unusually high humidity. Riva, cooking the first dinner in their new digs, has thrown all the windows open, and the high, wispy breeze filters through the small house, keeping it cool and comfortable.

Judge De La Guerra has been invited to be the guest of honor. A widower who eats most of his meals at Birnam Wood, his golf club, the judge was happy to accept. He sits in the lone good rental chair and sips one of Riva's killer margaritas.

Luke, sprawled on the couch, his own large tequila libation in hand, drops the latest bombshell in his mentor's lap. "Do you think Ray Logan is stupid enough to think this autopsy report would be kept sealed permanently?" he asks.

Without hesitation: "No. Of course not."

"Then he has to figure Allison's who knocked her up," Luke thinks out loud. "Logan could've handed the goddamn file over, or at least alerted me to its contents. There is such a thing as professional courtesy." He thinks further. "We're going to have to find out if the lab did any DNA testing on her, and if they did, are they going to request that the court have Allison tested. Hair, skin, particles, anything."

"That would simplify things," De La Guerra observes.

"There's no way in hell I'm going to let him get tested," Luke says. "I'd fight that all the way to the Supreme Court." Thinking through that, he goes on, "Actually, if they were going to, they would've done it by now, I suspect, or at least raised the issue. If whoever screwed her that last day used a rubber, like what they found up there in the gazebo, there wouldn't be any sperm to provide DNA proof."

Riva brings dishes of food into the small dining room, which is tucked into a bay window. Outside, the city and ocean glow with the lights of the stars and the moon and a thousand houses. They dig in, piling their plates high with rellenos, rice, beans, tortillas, salad.

The judge beams at Riva. "This is delicious," he tells her.

"Thank you, kind sir." A wide smile lights up her face.

"So now my defense strategy is about looking for who shtupped Emma Lancaster," Luke says, not joining in their bantering. "Assuming it wasn't Allison."

"You have to clear up that assumption with your client," Riva chimes in. "And that it was only one man."

"That's true," Luke says. "Christ, if it were to turn out she was a round-heeled little tramp, that would be brutal." He pauses. "But good for us," he has to admit.

"Yes, it would certainly help your defense," De La Guerra agrees. "An eighth-grade girl from a good family with that kind of background? Damn good cause to raise reasonable doubt."

"Yep, it would help," Luke agrees, "and you know what? I would hate to get an acquittal with that kind of defense."

"Your job is to get your client off, not to judge him or the methods that might be used," De La Guerra counters.

Luke shakes his head. "No." He puts his napkin down; he doesn't want to eat any more now, his stomach can't handle the conversation. "That's how the establishment works, how they teach you in law school. But I didn't come back here after all this time and expose myself to ridicule and snide charges of obliquity to win a case at any cost." He drinks some of the zinfandel he's poured with dinner. "I came back here to do the right thing, or nothing at all."

De La Guerra raises his wine glass in toast. "Hear, hear."

"Are you mocking me?" He turns and looks at Riva, who's smothering a smile with the back of her hand. "You too? Are you both mocking me?"

"We love you, Luke. Even when you are chasing crazy dreams."

"So now I'm Don Quixote? Jousting at windmills?"

"No," De La Guerra says. "Just a man who's got religion and doesn't know how to act on it. But you're doing a good job of learning," he adds. He reaches over for the wine bottle. "May I?" he asks Luke.

"Of course."

He pours a few ounces. Swilling the dark liquid, looking at it up against the overhead ceiling light, he says, "I think you should act on Riva's suggestion. Confront Allison directly. Ask him if he and Emma were having sex."

Luke nods. "I can put the question to him, but I know he'll flat-out deny it, whether it's the truth or not. He'd be crazy to admit to that."

"At first glance, maybe, but not necessarily. If he really was her lover, why kill her?"

"Because she found out she was with child and she was going to turn him in as the father," Luke answers. "Bye-bye career, hello the rest of your life in Soledad."

"Yes," De La Guerra responds. "That's a good, plausible reason. But if he says he wasn't, if he swears it, wouldn't you give him the benefit of the doubt, unless you found out otherwise? Everyone else in this county has already tried and convicted Joe Allison of murder," he reminds Luke. "The least you can do is *not* convict him of something he hasn't been accused of."

Joe Allison, three days unshaven, wearing his prison sweats while sitting in the attorney-client holding room, looks at his lawyer like he's insane. "Sleeping with a fourteen-year-old girl?" he asks incredulously. "Do you really think I'm that sick?"

"It happens thousands of times every day," Luke says calmly. He's sitting back, trying to ascertain the truthfulness of Allison's reaction as it plays out before him. "You hear it all the time. Teachers with students, fathers with daughters. Young girls these days're much more sexually sophisticated than they've ever been."

He expected his client to deny it, but is there a twinge of guilt there, a millisecond of caught-off-guard-ness before Allison can recover and pull the shade of deceit down over the truth?

He doesn't think so. This reaction seems genuine and spontaneous.

"I wasn't sleeping with Emma," Allison says straight. Then the ramifications of the question sink in. "Are you telling me someone was? Emma had a sex life?"

"Not only did she have a sex life, she was three months pregnant," Luke says.

Allison rocks back on the molded plastic chair. "That's . . . unbelievable!"

"Yep," Luke agrees.

"So I guess that means you're going to try and find out who was sleeping with her."

"Yes."

"That could be who killed her, right?"

"It's a strong possibility. The only one I can think of."

Allison rocks in his chair. "I'll level with you. She came on to me. Hard. Christ Almighty, she looked like she was sixteen, and acted older."

"So what exactly *did* you do with her, Joe?"

"I . . ." Allison is squirming in his seat. "I gave her a few kisses and hugs. You know, like an uncle would."

Luke shakes his head. "Like an uncle? C'mon, man, what did I warn you? About telling me the truth?"

Allison looks away. "Okay. We made out a couple of times." Forcefully, he adds, "But that's all. I did not sleep with her. I did not get her pregnant. And I wasn't anywhere near her house that night." He whines: "She initiated it."

"And you just couldn't resist. Sounds like she was a seasoned seductress," Luke says sarcastically.

Allison shakes his head. "She was full of teenage juice, but underneath it all she was an innocent kid, despite everything," he says sadly. "She was only in the eighth grade." He calculates in his head. "If she was pregnant, that means she was getting it on even earlier, like thirteen."

Luke nods. "But not with you," he challenges Allison, one more time. "Even though the rubbers they found in your place match the ones they found up in the Lancaster's gazebo."

"That was a plant," Allison says. "That's so obvious it's pathetic. Ask my girlfriend, Nicole. She'll tell you I've never used that kind."

Luke gets up. He's heard enough on this subject from Joe Allison. "I'm planning to."

Doug Lancaster's lover, Helena Buchinsky, is the wife of the head of Mason/Dixon Productions, one of the major independent film and television companies in the country. Dark, Rubenesquely voluptuous—she has Armenian, Turkish, Greek, some Czech or Polish in her ancestry—she lies on the deck of her Trancas beach house wearing nothing but a pair of men's boxer shorts, her body wet with her own perspiration, suntan oil, Doug's sweat. You can smell the reek of sexuality coming from her, not a body smell, a life force.

They made love as soon as Doug drove his Jaguar convertible down the coast highway from Santa Barbara, in the guest bedroom, where they always have sex when they're at this house, their preferred place of assignation, since the Buchinskys don't have full-time live-in help here. She won't make love with him in the bed she shares with her husband (the same rule applies to her primary house in Brentwood, where she and Doug meet rarely, it's too dangerous), not for moral reasons or to spare her husband some small indignity, however unknown to him, but because she doesn't want to take the chance of something foreign being left behind that could be found and used against her. Her prenuptial agreement with Ted, her husband of nine years, specifies only a few reasons he can cut her out of her community property and support, should they divorce. Extramarital sex is the main one, and while she and Doug have been lovers for many years, since long before he and Glenna split, she is ever vigilant. She assumes Ted has her watched from time to time; he may even have pictures of her naked with Doug. But the actual act of sexual congress, she makes sure that's hidden from the world.

Helena knows Doug is worried and preoccupied with the arrest of the man who killed his daughter, and the trial that's on the distant horizon. She knows everything Doug knows: he confides in her more than he ever confided in Glenna. *You can always talk to the lover better than the mate, she thinks. It's the same with her and Teddy, they don't talk about squat.* She knows about the botched bribe. She knows his daughter Emma wasn't a virgin, that her killer might have been her lover. She knows of Doug's anger and concern over it, both that it happened and, even worse, now that she's dead, that the knowledge will become public. And she knows that her lover fears Luke Garrison as an opponent, a man with nothing to lose who for the last three years has lived a life straight out of the '60s: turn on, tune in, drop out.

"How're you doing?" she asks. She speaks in a thick New York accent, as street-sounding as Cathy Moriarty, the actress who played Jake LaMotta's wife in *Raging Bull* and, more recently, Harvey Keitel's in *Cop Land*. She loves those movies—it's her old neighborhoods. Cathy's a friend from way back.

"Good, now," he says, running the fingers of one hand along the inside of her thigh closest to him.

"That's good," she responds, sliding her hand down her leg to cover his, stop its stimulating journey. They've had their fuck for the day, it was fine, she doesn't want to get turned on again. And even though her stretch of beach is private and inaccessible, the deck sheltered with darkly tinted glass walls that you can see out of but not in through, and the house itself tucked into a secluded alcove and elevated from the beach, she's still careful when they're outside.

"I mean in general," she says, "not the last half hour." She scratches her behind where the sweat's making it itch. "Get me a Coke, will you?" She points vaguely towards the inside, separated from the deck by open French doors.

Doug, wearing a bathing suit, gets up and pads into the house, reemerging a moment later with a liter of cold Coca-Cola from the refrigerator, an open bottle of Absolut, and a couple of glasses filled with ice. He knows the layout of this house well, he's been coming here for a long time now. Dropping down next to her, he hands her the Coke and a glass, pours a couple of fingers of vodka into each glass, drinks from his.

"In general . . ." he says.

"You think he's gonna investigate."

He stares at her. She's in her soothsayer mode, which is usually right on the money.

"You," she says to him. "This lawyer. He's gonna try to find out what everybody was doing that night, anybody that could've had

access to your property. That's how he's gonna work it for his client, right? See if somebody else could've killed Emma. If their time can't be accounted for," she adds, staring at him.

Nothing wrong with her brain, Doug thinks. It's one of her attractions, all the contradictions in her personality. Along with her blunt directness.

"Yes," he agrees, "that would be a strategy a good lawyer might take."

She drinks some Coke, crunching a piece of ice in her teeth. "It's hot today, isn't it?" She smiles at him. "Can you account for all your time that night?"

He stares at her. "Yes," he says slowly, "I can account for my time that night." He pauses. The unspoken hangs between them like a sea-soaked net, an onerous veil. "Yes, I can."

"Are you going to be okay with that? Keep it quiet?"

"I can account for my time," he repeats firmly.

"Then all you have to worry about is making sure Joe Allison gets convicted."

"That's not all I have to worry about, but that would solve most of my problems," he agrees. "And bring closure to Emma's memory," he says with genuine sadness.

She pulls him to her, his head jammed against her breasts, his mouth grazing the salty nipples, which brings an involuntary shudder from her. "That's gonna happen," she tells him with assurance in her heavy Bronx patois. "There will be closure for your daughter. For Emma."

Sitting in the living room, the windows thrown open to catch the end-of-the-day breeze, Luke and Riva watch the tape of Joe Allison's interrogation by Detective Terry Jackson of the Santa Barbara P.D. Luke takes notes, pausing the tape when he wants to write down a salient point.

"So he admits to a mutual attraction, but no sex," Riva says. Luke has filled her in on his session with Allison. "I hope he isn't sand-bagging you."

He turns to her. "So do I, sweetness. So do I."

"Well, it makes him a crummy person, but not a murderer."

Luke nods. "He isn't on trial for being a crummy person."

"But you wish he were squeaky-clean."

"Yeah. Defending men like him doesn't make me particularly happy. But someone has to."

After watching the tape twice, all the way through, Luke clicks the VCR off. "This is a pretty slippery interview," he remarks.

She looks to him for clarification.

"They never told him they suspected him of anything other than drunk driving," he explains. He has the transcript of the interview on his lap.

"But wasn't that the point of the questioning? That they thought he was involved in the kidnapping, because they found the key ring in his car?" she asks.

"Exactly." He thinks for a moment. "I need to find out if the cop out in the field explained that to him, when he gave him the Miranda warning. I'll bet the farm he didn't."

"What does that mean?"

"They misled him. They lied to him, actually. As soon as you suspect someone of a crime, you have to warn them of that. From what I'm seeing"—he holds up the transcript and points to the blank television screen—"they didn't. They violated his rights in a very fundamental way."

"Could they have told him before they brought him into that room for questioning?"

Luke shakes his head. "You saw the tape. Allison didn't have a clue." Brandishing the transcript, he adds, "He had no idea they were connecting him to Emma Lancaster's murder. None. They didn't even tell him it was her key ring."

He gets up and goes to the refrigerator for a beer. "Want one?"

She shakes her head.

He twists the cap off, licks the rim, starts pacing the room. "This is bullshit. Ray Logan was there. What the hell was he thinking?" Shaking his head, he says, "I know exactly what he was thinking. He wanted the goods on Allison and he didn't want to fuck things up with a warning. He was afraid Joe would clam up and they'd lose the moment."

"What are you going to do?"

"I have to go to the judge on this. I'm going to interview that cop, Jackson, and Sheriff Williams too, but there's no acceptable explanation for this. You have to inform a suspect of his rights, that's basic."

"If it turns out they violated his rights, what happens?" she asks. She can feel his agitation and excitement. It energizes her, seeing him in this mode, the professional on the job.

"I'm not sure," he says. He sits on the edge of the couch guzzling some beer. "Technically, their whole justification for arresting and charging him is tainted. They can't use any evidence they got from him."

Her eyes widen.

"It *should* be thrown out," he says vehemently. "But I can't see any local judge doing that, can you? Ewing'll look for any wiggle room he can find." He smiles sardonically. "Can you imagine the screaming that would rise if this were thrown out on a so-called technicality? There'd be a mushroom cloud ten times the size of Hiroshima."

"So what are you going to do?" she asks.

"Check it out. Put them on notice that I won't tolerate it. File a motion for dismissal at some point, if I have to." He gets up again, paces around the room—he thinks better on his feet. "I have to put them on notice that they can't do this." He pauses, taking another hit from his bottle of Sierra Nevada. "I don't want to get drawn into Allison's paranoia, but there's some fishy stuff going on here. You can make a case out of anything if you twist stuff around enough. I need to dig deeper into this, going back to why Allison was even stopped in the first place."

He finishes his beer, obliviously pokes his pinky into the bottle's neck. The bottle swings from the end of his hand like a swollen appendage. "You don't bring a charge like this by taking shortcuts. This thing ought to stand on its own merits, clean as a whistle. Otherwise, the whole structure crumbles." Realizing his finger's stuck in the bottle neck, he pops it out. "And I'm starting to get itchy to throw a stick of dynamite into the middle of their celebration."

★ ★ ★

Luke's meeting with Jackson is frustrating. It's obvious that the detective, under a veneer of civility (a thin veneer), loathes Luke, the turncoat prosecutor. It's not because Luke's now working the other side of the aisle; that's a common enough occurrence in both directions that it is no cause for latent animosity or disdain, although it is a rare thing for the head man to make that move. It's who, in the eyes of this policeman and of everyone else who knew him when he was Luke Garrison, county district attorney, he has become. It's the air of hostility that Luke emits unconsciously, the attitude, which to Jackson's antennae preceded Luke into the room, that all the people who used to make up his professional and, to a great extent, social world are out to screw people over, that's their secret agenda, and only he and a select few others, who know the real truth about how the law works and the innate corruptness and rottenness of the legal system, can expose it and make it right. And have the courage to do so.

Luke senses this feeling. He's encountered it before. It's ridiculously overblown and simplistic and he doesn't agree with it, not too much of it, but he acknowledges that it's part of his makeup now. It pisses him off to be stereotyped that way, but he knows it's useful. It puts people on the defensive, off balance. *This guy is crazy, you don't know what he's going to do.* Unpredictability can be a powerful weapon.

"Did you inform Mr. Allison of his rights?" Luke asks, jumping right in. "The right to remain silent, the right to have a lawyer, that anything he said could be used against him? Did you tell him those things?"

"He'd already been Mirandized," Jackson says smoothly. "The officer in the field did that. It's on record."

"I know. But did you tell him the reason you brought him in was because he was a suspect in an unsolved murder? He thought he was in here under a DUI."

The cop shrugs. "I'm not a mind reader, sir. I don't know what he thought."

"Fine. But you thought he might be connected to Emma Lancaster's kidnapping and murder."

The cop shakes his head. "Not initially."

Luke stares at him. Jesus, what chutzpah! "Your people found her key ring in his car, he was brought in here, you questioned him for over half an hour, but you didn't consider him a suspect? I find that hard to believe, Detective."

Another practiced shrug. "I said not initially."

"Then what did you think?"

"That he might have some information that could help us."

"What kind of information could that have been?"

"If someone had given him those keys, and he could remember who it was, that might have been the killer, or someone who knew the killer. That was my initial reaction."

Luke smothers his incredulity at the answer, and at the man's audacity in giving it. "Not that Joe Allison was involved, but that he might know someone who was involved," he repeats Jackson's assertion, wanting to make sure he's hearing this right.

"That's correct."

"Then why didn't you tell him that?"

"Tell him what?"

"That the keys belonged to Emma Lancaster," Luke patiently says, "and you were hoping he could remember how they got in his car so you could find out who killed her. Wouldn't that be the logical approach?"

He waits for a response, an involuntary reflex reaction. There is none.

"Unless he was a suspect in your mind, and you didn't want to give the game away," Luke continues.

"I question people my way," the detective answers. "You might prefer a different approach. That's how I work."

This is going nowhere, Luke sees that clearly. The man isn't about to budge off his story.

"When did Allison's status change from that of an innocent party who might know something that could help your investigation to that of the prime suspect in the investigation?" he asks.

"When we found additional evidence pointing at him."

"So then he became a suspect, and you told him he was a suspect, and informed him of his rights."

"Exactly," Jackson says. "As soon as he became a suspect, we told him, and informed him of his rights under the law."

Luke nods. "But if that's the case, explain something for me, Officer."

"Detective," Jackson corrects him.

"Sorry," Luke answers. "*Detective.* Explain to me—De*tec*tive—why the sheriff's office searched Mr. Allison's residence if he *wasn't* a suspect? How did you get a search warrant if he wasn't a suspect? What did you tell the judge who issued it—'we've got a guy in custody who isn't a suspect in a murder case, but we want to search his home anyway because he might be if we find some evidence to prove he is'? That's kind of ass-backwards, isn't it?"

He knows what the search warrant said—he's read it. It was a fine piece of obscurity and double talk—just enough factual information to allow a judge reason to issue it, but not enough to be successfully challenged at some later date, such as now. These guys are pros, Luke knows. They don't break the law, but they push it as far as is possible. Nowadays, you don't get convictions if you don't. At least that's their thinking—screw the civil libertarians, bad people need to be put away. A good cop figures out how.

The *shrug* again. He must practice that move in front of a mirror, Luke thinks. "It was a precaution," Jackson says. "To make sure. The judge agreed with us."

My ass. "You know what's interesting?" Luke says.

"What?"

"Caramba, the cop who arrested Allison, *did* think he was a suspect."

For the first time in their meeting Jackson reacts, shifting his weight in his chair. Subtle, but Luke notices it.

"Who says that?" the detective asks carefully.

"He did."

"He did?" Jackson seems genuinely surprised, taken aback. "When?"

"When I talked to him about it."

Jackson thinks about how to react. "I think you misunderstood him" is the answer he comes up with.

"No, I didn't."

"A cop in the field doesn't make those kinds of judgments."

"It's what he told me."

"He was mistaken," the detective says firmly.

"He was mistaken about his own judgment? How is that possible?" Luke asks.

"He was mistaken about—" Jackson stops. Any answer he gives will be the wrong one. The right answer is no answer. "Whatever Officer Caramba thought doesn't matter," he says, changing directions. "It's up to the detectives to make those decisions. And the brass." He leans forward, stares hard at Luke. "We did *not* think of Joe Allison as a suspect when we began talking to him. Period."

Luke leans back. This is as far as he goes today. "One more thing," he says as a preamble to departing. "What was the result of Mr. Allison's sobriety test? I haven't been able to find that."

Jackson blinks. "I'm not sure," he says cautiously.

"Didn't you tell me he was brought in here on a DUI?"

"Yes."

"Which means he was tested, right? And since you were holding him, he tested over point zero eight, correct?"

"I'm not sure," Jackson says again.

Luke furrows his brow. "Let me get this straight. You questioned a man about an unsolved murder that had this entire city up in arms last year and you don't know if he was drunk or sober?"

"I—"

"If he was sober," Luke continues, curtly interrupting him, "if he passed the test, you had no grounds to hold him, correct?"

Jackson doesn't answer.

"Legally, you had no grounds to detain Mr. Allison, is that right, Detective Jackson?" Luke asks again, this time with steam.

"Legally . . ." Again, a shrug.

"But since you were holding him, he had to be drunk, yes? You told him you couldn't release him until the morning, when he would go before a magistrate. That's on the tape of your interrogation, *Detec-tive.*" He draws the word out with scorn.

"So?" Jackson says defensively.

"So was he drunk or was he sober?"

Jackson keeps quiet.

"You don't know, do you?" Luke stands and gathers his papers into his briefcase. "Because you never tested him."

★ ★ ★

As the crow flies, the distance from the Lancasters' former house, where they lived when Emma was kidnapped, to Puerto Salle Street on the west side is less than five miles; the financial, social, and lifestyle differences are immeasurable and vast, almost two separate countries in the same city. Puerto Salle Street, where Maria Gonzalez, the Lancasters' former house manager, lives with her husband and four children, is one hundred percent Latino, the average family income is less than twenty-five thousand dollars a year, and some families are on AFDC and food stamps.

For the most part, the people who live on Puerto Salle Street have jobs and work hard at them. Their houses are modest wood-frame-and-stucco structures no more than forty feet apart, in some cases considerably less; if you want privacy you shut your windows and keep your voices low. In this neighborhood, where everyone knows everyone, that's uncommon. The houses are neat and trim, in good repair—no peeling paint coming off the exterior walls—the small patches of front yard are manicured, borders etched cleanly, walkways graveled, bricked, or paved. Most of the houses have flowers around the perimeters, with stone birdbaths and statuettes adorning the lawns. There are large cactus plants in abundance, flowering jacaranda, red and orange bougainvillea vines clinging to fences. It's a community of families; during the day when school's out there are always kids chasing each other across the street, riding bikes, skateboards, rollerblades, throwing balls and frisbees.

Luke and Riva pull up in front of Maria's house. When Luke phoned to set up this meeting and get directions, Maria's English seemed fine, not even much of an accent. But Riva's Spanish still might come in handy. Besides, he's always felt it's good policy to have a woman present when interviewing another woman. It makes for a more comfortable environment, and there's never a question later about harassment.

They sink into overstuffed armchairs in her small, cluttered living room. She offers them lemonade; they accept. Then she sits opposite them on the sofa, folds her hands in her lap, and waits.

"Thank you for taking the time to meet with us," Luke begins. "I know it must have been a difficult time for you. The events of last year." She's younger—to his eye in her early thirties—and prettier than he'd somehow expected. Her dress and accessories are fashionable, understated. She was the head housekeeper of a multi-million-dollar estate, he reminds himself. She learned from that.

"Very difficult." She nods in agreement. "I loved Emma like I love my own children."

"We understand," Riva says, joining the conversation. She won't speak Spanish to this woman, it would be patronizing. Also unnecessary. "How long did you work for the Lancasters?"

"Ten years."

"Since Emma was—four?"

Maria nods. "I raised her up from a small child," she says proudly.

"You aren't employed by either of the Lancasters now, are you?" Riva asks.

Maria shakes her head. "They're divorced now, and . . ." She hesitates.

"Yes?" Riva prompts.

"I decided not to," Maria continues. "Mrs. Lancaster asked me to come work for her in her new house, but I didn't want to."

"Because of Emma, and the circumstances?"

The woman takes some time before answering. "Things changed."

"Did you and Mrs. Lancaster not get along as well after what happened?" Luke asks, taking a flyer.

She nods. "Mrs. Lancaster changed after Emma died."

"That's understandable," he says. "She suffered a great tragedy."

"Yes." She pauses. "Mrs. Lancaster was very good to me. When I went to work for her, I was an illegal. Under the wire. She helped me bring my husband here, helped us get our green cards. I owe my life to Mrs. Lancaster."

That kind of loyalty can be blind, cause a shading of the truth. He'll have to watch for that with her. He takes from his briefcase a sheet of paper on which he's written some questions. "What was the situation like in the Lancaster household before Emma was kidnapped?" he asks. "Was it a happy situation? Did everyone pretty much get along with each other?"

"It was normal. For that kind of family," she adds.

"That kind of family?" He glances over at Riva, who's listening intently. "What does that mean?" He drinks some lemonade. It's good, made from real lemons, not a mix.

"Rich, involved in many things, always on the go. Emma spent more time with me than with either of her parents," she tells them.

Not uncommon, he thinks. "How many times a week did the family eat dinner together?" he asks.

"One or two. Emma usually had dinner with me, because her parents didn't get home early enough. They both had busy lives."

"You lived in, is that correct?" he asks. "You have your own family?"

She nods. "I have three children. That was another reason I didn't want to work for Mrs. Lancaster anymore. She wanted someone to live in, even though there were no children to take care of. I want to take care of my own children now." Answering the first part of his question, she says, "I came and went. Some nights I stayed all night, some nights I left after Mr. or Mrs. Lancaster was home, or sometimes I just left. There were plenty of others there to look after Emma. She was getting older, she didn't need someone to watch out for her as much anymore."

She did that night, he thinks. But knowing what he knows now, or thinks he knows, would it have mattered?

"When you said 'that kind of family,' " Riva kicks in, "did you mean anything else besides their busy schedules and their money?"

"I don't know what you mean," Maria says to her, a sudden evasion in her voice.

Riva struggles up from her chair and goes over and sits down next to Maria. "Was it a happy place? Did they get along well?" She pauses, looking directly at Maria. "Or did they fight?"

Maria takes a deep breath, sighs heavily. "There was . . . they didn't get along so well, not all the time."

"What did they fight over?" Riva asks, gently pushing the woman.

The woman squirms uneasily. "Different things."

Riva inches closer to Maria. Their knees are almost touching. "Did they fight about—how shall I put it—relationships either one had with someone else? Lovers?"

Maria nods. Riva glances at Luke, who's right with her. "Did they fight quietly, or yell at each other, or . . ."

"Mr. Lancaster did not yell."

Luke asks, "Were they ever physically violent with each other?"

"Sometimes she would hit him, or throw things," she says. "Only a couple of times." Looking across the room at him, she asks a question of her own. "What difference does that make? What does that have to do with Emma's killer, sitting there in jail?"

"*If* he's the killer," Luke corrects her. "He hasn't been convicted yet."

"The police say he did it," she says passionately. "They have the evidence."

He lets that pass. Emma Lancaster's death was as hard on her as it was on Emma's parents, this he knows.

"Did they fight about anything else?" he asks, pursuing the previous line of questioning.

The woman's brows knot up. "Sometimes Emma and her mama fought. All teenage girls fight with their mothers," she adds quickly, as if she's upset with herself for letting a bad genie out of a bottle.

Luke doesn't let her off the hook. "What did they fight about?"

Maria turns away from him.

"Did they fight about men?" he asks. "About men or boys she might be seeing, that her mother didn't approve of?"

Maria nods slowly. "Sometimes."

"Emma was seeing some boys her mother didn't approve of?" *Or men?*

"She thought Emma was too young to date."

"But Emma did. Behind her mother's back," he guesses out loud.

Another nod. "Yes."

"And when Mrs. Lancaster caught her, she yelled at her?"

"They yelled at each other," Maria says. "Emma was very headstrong. She did what she wanted. Her mother couldn't discipline her."

Glenna told the police, on the day Emma disappeared, that Emma didn't date at all. Now this woman, who knew Emma as well or better than her mother, is saying the opposite. And that Glenna knew about Emma's seeing boys (and men?) and fought with her daughter about it.

She isn't going to give him any more—she's already angry with herself for being this forthcoming on the subject.

"Were you at the house the entire night when Emma was kidnapped?" he asks, changing direction for safer territory.

Maria shakes her head. "No. I was there pretty late, because Mrs. Lancaster had her friends over, and Emma didn't come home until after eleven, but I did not stay all night."

So she wasn't on the premises when the abduction and murder actually took place. No, not the murder—that would have taken place somewhere else, off the muddy trail where Emma was found, or closer to it.

He's almost done, only a couple more questions. "Was Mr. Allison a frequent guest at the Lancaster house?"

"Yes." She nods. "He was there often."

"To see the Lancasters."

"Yes. He was friendly with both of them."

"What about Emma? Was he friendly with her?"

She moistens her lips. "I think . . . I think Emma had a crush on him."

"Did he ever . . . did you ever see him . . ."

"Did Joe Allison ever make a play for Emma?" Riva says, bailing him out. A woman asking a woman, easier.

Maria smiles, remembering. "They flirted with each other." The smile goes away. "She was fourteen years old. And he worked for her father." She pauses. "There were enough adult women interested in Mr. Allison that he didn't have to worry about a fourteen-year-old girl."

"Are you saying Allison was involved with women besides his girlfriend?" he asks. "Do you know that for a fact?"

"I don't know about that," Maria Gonzalez says stiffly. "Perhaps you should ask Mr. Allison."

Thanks, he thinks to himself, but I already did.

Nicole Rogers has a willowy figure and a heart-shaped, heartbreaking face. Her hair, blond with tinted highlights, falls softly over her shoulders. Allison was sleeping with her, Luke thinks. Some guys have all the luck.

But that's not true. Far from it. He's with a terrific woman himself, so there's no jealousy on that score, just the normal testosterone kick. And Joe Allison's in jail awaiting trial for murder.

No one has all the luck. Not all the good luck.

She's invited him to meet with her in her small office. She's an associate at Meyers and Harcourt, one of the largest law firms in town, a practice that's mostly corporate clients, including some of the oil conglomerates. She's been here six months, since she passed the bar.

She's dressed lady-lawyer style. A suit with a skirt, dark blue. An ivory blouse buttoned to her neck. Sensible heels, opaque hose. A woman who doesn't downplay her attractiveness but keeps it in check—at least at the office. She meets him in the reception area and walks him to her cubicle in the back, passing several large offices on the way. They sit facing each other across her desk.

"What kind of law are you practicing?" he asks conversationally.

"Whatever's needed," she answers. "Mostly I do research for the senior partners, to get a feel for everything we do. I want to move into environmental law eventually."

"Big field around here," he comments. "For or against?" He knows the firm's bias, but they work both sides of the issues.

"The big money's with the big companies," she says. "I'm not in it for the glory."

Practical. He isn't going to have to play games with her. "What can you tell me about Joe Allison?" he asks, beginning his formal questioning.

"Can you be more specific?"

"Sure. Let me start from the end and work back. Do you think he could have done this?"

"*Could* he have done it?" she says in a tone that indicates she's asked herself that question already. "I guess so—theoretically."

"You can't alibi him for that night." Allison's already told him she couldn't, but perhaps her take on it is different. He has to ask the question anyway, because if she's called to the stand, the opposition will.

She shakes her head. "We were together that evening, but we didn't spend the night together, so no, I couldn't."

"Do you think he did it?"

Another negative shake. "No."

"Why is that? You seem certain."

"Joe isn't violent. He never made a threatening gesture of any kind towards me, in the year and a half we were going together. Towards anyone. It's not in his nature." She ponders the rest of her answer for a moment. "I can't imagine Joe doing something like that."

"Killing someone?"

"Kidnapping her."

"What if he wasn't kidnapping her?"

She looks at him quizzically.

"What if it was consensual?"

"You mean . . . Emma going with him willingly?"

"Yes."

She sits up in her chair. "Why in the world would you think that?"

"Because it's possible, in fact likely, that Emma Lancaster knew whoever it was who took her out of her room that night."

Big exhale. "I didn't know that."

"It's becoming the most likely explanation. The young girl who saw it happen told the police Emma didn't struggle. She told me that, too. So you have to think of that possibility."

She thinks about it. "Would that be—" She stops herself, as if debating whether to pursue this line of thought, then continues. "Are you talking about sex? A sexual involvement?"

"It's possible."

She sits back. "I wondered about that. Not with Joe, I could never see that. But it's there, I guess. No one wants to think that or talk about it," she says, "but I have thought about it, and I'm sure other people did, too."

"Are you seeing Joe now?" he asks. "Have you been down to the jail?"

"No." She shakes her head. "I haven't been to see him."

"Are you going to?" Then: "Do you want to?"

"I'm not going to. And I do want to, but . . . I'm not going to."

"Is there a particular reason?"

"We'd stopped seeing each other. The night he was arrested was our swan song."

"What was the reason? Or reasons?"

She doesn't answer for a moment. "We were going in different directions," she says at length.

"Careerwise?"

She nods. "Yes."

"Are there others?"

She looks away.

It hits him—the simplest explanation is often the best. "Was Joe seeing someone else? Is that the reason you broke up with him?"

She turns back, her chest rising under her proper lawyerly blouse. "Yes."

"You know that for a fact."

A shake of the head. "I don't know it for a *fact*. I don't have physical proof. I never caught him with another woman." She gathers herself together. "But I know he was."

"For how long?"

"I don't know."

"For a while?"

"I think so. Yes."

"Do you think he was having an affair with one woman, or was he playing around?"

"I think one woman."

"But you never saw him with her. Whoever she is. Was."

She combs her hair with her fingers, a nervous gesture. "No."

"You weren't suspicious? Or jealous?" Jesus, you have a woman like this, why would you screw around? "You never followed him, tried to find out?"

"I didn't want to find out," she says flatly.

That's the most human explanation anyone can give. "I'm sorry. I don't know what else to say." Her little office has one small window which doesn't open; it's getting warm. Normally she would keep the door open, he thinks.

"Me too." She plays with a paper clip. "That's why I'm not going down to see him."

"Do you think he knows that you think this?"

She shrugs. "I don't know. Probably. Don't you generally feel guilty when you're fooling around? Afraid of being caught? We weren't married, but . . . I thought we were being faithful to each other."

He waits a bit before asking the next question. "Who do you think this other woman is? Do you have any suspicions?"

"No one I'm willing to name."

He'll get back to that later. There will be other interviews, and if he comes up with a name and says it to her, she'll be straight with him. She seems like a decent person. Still, they were lovers, so there's something there. There always is.

Something from one of his conversations with Allison jogs his memory. "You know what else I want to ask you? I just remembered this. You probably can't help me, but you know about the running shoes the police found in Joe's closet? The ones that matched the shoe print they found at the Lancaster house the day after Emma was kidnapped?"

"Yes?"

"Joe claims he misplaced them before that night. That he couldn't have been wearing them, because he didn't have them anymore. Did he ever say anything about that to you?"

"As a matter of fact, he did."

"He did?"

She nods. "We were out jogging, about a week before, and he had a new pair of running shoes on, and I asked him what was wrong with his old ones, because he liked them, they fit him well, and he told me he couldn't find them, that he must have left them at the gym or someplace." She thinks for a moment. "I thought he'd misplaced them and found them later."

"Maybe he didn't misplace them," he says. This is a break.

"Maybe he didn't," she says. From her tone he knows she doesn't think Joe lost those shoes at all. But at least it's on the record that he told someone else that he had, before the kidnapping.

He's just about run out of questions. "One more thing. This is a delicate question, but I have to ask it."

She smiles at him. She is very attractive, no getting around it. "You're supposed to be fearless," she says lightly.

"I wish." He stands. "The condoms that were found where Joe lived. Was that the brand you used?"

Her smile shuts off abruptly. "I used a diaphragm. We didn't use those things."

"But if you thought he was having an affair, weren't you worried about . . ."

"HIV? We stopped making love then. I lied to him that I'd developed an allergy to the diaphragm and couldn't. He bought that."

"So you stopped having sex before you split up?"

"It was only for the last month," she says. "When I finally faced up to my suspicions enough to act on them." She laughs involuntarily, a nervous, mirthless sound. "Pink rubbers? Where would they have come from, Mary Kay Cosmetics? If Joe had put on something that ridiculous, I would have been hysterical with laughter, and we never would have made love." She pulls herself together. "If they were his, he was using them with another woman."

"He claims they were planted there."

She stares at him. "What's the significance of a particular brand of contraceptives?" she asks.

This is going to come out anyway, so he might as well tell her. He'd like her to be an ally. He—his client—is going to need friends. "The same brand was found on the Lancaster estate. In the gazebo at the back end of the property." He braces himself. "Used ones. Someone had been using the gazebo for a"—he almost says "fuck"—"love pad."

She gasps. "Oh, that's bad."

"Yes, it is. That's why my question is important."

"I feel terrible for Joe," she says. She's fighting her emotions now, her voice beginning to break. "My life isn't part of his anymore. But the fact that a particular brand of condoms was found in his bedroom and the Lancaster property doesn't mean he killed anyone."

He's been riding his motorcycle around town. It's easier to find parking spaces than with his big truck, and he enjoys riding it. He had parked it in an alley a block from Nicole's office.

He stops in his tracks as he rounds the corner of the building. Then he sprints forward.

The classic Triumph is in ruins. Whoever trashed it did a thorough, brutal job. The tires have been slashed, the seat has been pulled off, the instrument panels have been broken, hundreds of glass shards litter the asphalt. Wires have been pulled out and cut, a spaghetti bowl of twisted plastic and copper. And something heavy, like a sledgehammer, has laid siege to the block, splitting the heads clear off, then smashing the pistons and cylinders into metal mush.

He slumps on his knees next to the wreckage. "You motherfucker!" he screams to the unknown executioner.

Then he sees the note. Big, crude block letters, written with a child's crayon on butcher paper: GET OUT OF TOWN WHILE U CAN! WE DON'T WANT ANY HIPPIE DOPE-SMOKING BABY-KILLER LAWYERS HERE! And a few other similarly sophisticated lines he doesn't bother reading.

The hero who did this noble deed left his note unsigned.

Enraged, he starts to crumple it up and throw it away, but the police will need to see it. He springs to his feet instead, looking from one end of the alley to the other.

Except for him and the remains of his machine, the alley is deserted.

"Did you file a police report?" Riva asks him.

"For what it's worth." He's still shaking inside, he's so angry. "They practically laughed in my face. I'm sure the note's already in the circular file."

"Who do you think did it?"

"Somebody who doesn't like me, I guess."

They're walking along the beach, Butterfly Beach near the Biltmore, watching the sun go down. The motorcycle, the hundreds of pieces of it, sits in a bin at Precision Motorcycle Works on Salsipuedes Street. The shop owner, Gentle Ben Loomis, a 350-pound former outlaw biker turned semilegitimate, didn't sound sanguine about the old Triumph's prospects for survival.

"This is a rebuild from the ground up, and the bitch is, they don't make parts for this model anymore. Triumphs are dinosaurs, bro. I'll check around the country on the handy-dandy Internet, see what parts are available, but I wouldn't be holding my breath." He'd looked at the box of parts tenderly. "I love these old bikes, man. Beautiful pieces of art. Sculpture they are, truly. Even if they ain't born in the U.S. of A." Preparing Luke for the worst, he'd said, "If I were you, ace, I'd be looking to buy me a Harley. Get you a Soft-Tail—smooth, smooth ride. Not like that old beast you were rasslin'."

They walk along the water's edge, getting their feet wet on the foam. "Have you thought some more that you shouldn't have taken this case?" she asks.

"Yes, I've thought about it," he admits.

"Are you worried?" She bends over to pick up a piece of beach glass, a bottom of an old bottle, milky blue like a cataract eye, the jagged edges smoothed off from the water's long caressing. She drops the glass into her pocket.

"Pissed is what I am. Cowardly goddamn act. Whoever did it hit me where it hurt, I won't deny that." He picks up a scallop shell and sidearms it at the water, where it skips three times before sinking.

"I'm worried," she tells him.

He stops and faces her. "About someone coming after me?"

"Yes."

He dismisses the thought with a wave of the hand. "Nobody's going to come after me, they're going to come after my shit. Fuck with my head. It's bullshit, baby shit."

"I hope you're right." She scratches at a sandflea bite on her calf. "Do you think Doug Lancaster could be involved?"

He stares at her in surprise. "Doug Lancaster? Don't you think a pissant act like this is beneath him?"

"You're defending the man he's convinced killed his daughter. He tried to buy you off, and you haven't returned his money."

"Nah." He dismisses that idea. "Doug Lancaster wouldn't pussyfoot around. He'd come at me straightaway. Which I'm assuming he will, sooner or later, but not like this. He's going to want me to know he's on my ass, he isn't going to be anonymous about it. This was the act of a coward." He takes her hand as they walk slowly towards the sunset. "Coming after me would hurt the case against Joe Allison, not help it. Even a pit bull like Ray Logan wouldn't stomach that."

They stop and watch the last mushroom-topped sliver of the sun dive into the ocean. "It's a beautiful world we live in, Riva."

She squeezes his hand. "I know. And I want to enjoy it with you. For a long time."

He squeezes her hand back. That's the best he can do.

She sleeps now and he, awake, sits on the porch with a cognac that he hasn't touched, the night winds flowing up off the ocean, ruffling the hair on his bare arms and legs. He thinks about his life and the moment of it that he's in and how he got to this place and what the point of it is. If there is one.

Some of the specifics he thinks about are his age, over forty; his marital status, divorced; how many children he has, none. He's going in the opposite direction—the fear is that it's the wrong direction. From solid, upwardly moving career to almost no career; from alleged storybook marriage to no marriage; from defending law and order to—what? Opposing it?

No, that's not it, he's not against law and order. He is against corruption, and he sees it everywhere, he's become obsessed with it. Obsessed, outraged, consumed. And that way lies madness, almost certainly. And paralysis.

There are different ways to fight and not give in, and there are different battles. This battle he's presently engaged in has heavy Don Quixote overtones. It's masochistic in some way, and he's afraid he's beginning to enjoy the pain and, furthermore, believe that he deserves it. That he's supposed to be doing a lifetime of penance because of an accidental mistake, a miscalculation—an honest mistake, one that anyone in the world would have made. Except "anyone" didn't make it, he did. And it came from his ego, his inability at that time to admit, or even know, that anyone else's ideas or opinions might have merit and value, and that he needed to look at his own more deeply.

But it was an accident. It wasn't as if he'd fabricated or suppressed evidence against Ralph Tucker. He did everything right, clear and above board.

In the end, it turned out wrong, all of it. That can happen with accidents. Especially when you're convinced, in your heart, that you know the immutable truth.

In the old days, his corps of detectives would have done much of the sleuthing: who was with whom, when and where. But since his entire case (unless something startling comes out of the woodwork) is going to be based on the theory of a frameup, he needs to talk to everyone who's involved. He wants to see the expressions on their faces when they answer tough and uncomfortable questions, so he can get a feel for the big picture.

He approaches Mr. and Mrs. Wilson, the owners of the property from whom Joe Allison rented his guest house. An elderly couple, longtime residents, they are activists on various environmental issues in the county—oil exploration, land development, urban encroachment.

He phoned ahead, they're expecting him. They come out to meet him as his car pulls into the driveway, a hearty couple, full of energy. The woman, who has steel gray hair cut short and looks vaguely Scandinavian in origin, is half a head taller than the man, who looks vaguely southern European and is bald.

"How is Joe?" Mrs. Wilson asks solicitously, right off the bat.

"This must be so hard on him," Mr. Wilson chimes in right behind her.

"Yes," Luke says noncommittally. These people seem to like Allison. That's good.

"We don't think Joe did this," Mrs. Wilson says with force. They're walking up the path to the house from the driveway. The path is lined with flowers in a lovely, cluttered, English-countryside, helter-skelter fashion. "Everyone else in town does," she says with aggressive cheerfulness, "they've already convicted him, but we know Joe. We know he couldn't have done what he's accused of."

"Why not?" Luke asks, intrigued. Could these people have an alibi for Allison that he isn't aware of?

"Because he isn't that kind of person," the husband answers, bringing him back to earth. "He isn't capable of violence."

Anybody's capable under the right circumstances, he's been around enough violence to know that. Still, it's good that Allison has some people on his side.

Their living room is furnished like a Hollywood idealization of a Swiss chalet. It's overdone for Luke's taste, but charming, like the Wilsons. "I only have a few questions, so this will be short," he says.

"First of all, I don't suppose you can account for Joe's whereabouts the night of Emma Lancaster's kidnapping," Luke says.

Both shake their heads in unison. After several decades of marriage, they move and think alike. "We go to bed early," Mrs. Wilson says. "We were usually asleep before Joe ever got home."

"Celebrity like him, he was out on the town nearly every night," Mr. Wilson adds.

"I didn't think so," Luke rejoins. "But I do have a question I hope you can help me with. You knew Nicole Rogers, didn't you? Joe's girlfriend?"

Mrs. Wilson beams. "Very well. She's a nice young woman. Always helpful in my garden."

"She was here a goodly amount of time?"

"Quite a bit, yes," the old lady answers. "We looked forward to her visits."

"And she spent some nights here. With Joe."

The Wilsons exchange a glance. "Yes," Mr. Wilson says. "Mind you, we don't pry into other people's lives, including our tenants. They're adults, they have a right to their own privacy."

"Sure." They misunderstood his intention. "She wasn't here that night, though, correct?"

"I don't think so," Mrs. Wilson says. "If she had been, Joe wouldn't be in jail, would he?" she asks.

"No," Luke admits ruefully. "He wouldn't."

"She was here so many nights," Mr. Wilson says. "To have missed that one night out of so many . . ."

"I know. It's too bad. But she wasn't," he goes on briskly, "so we have to defend him anther way. Let me ask you this: Did Joe bring other women here? On a regular basis?"

Mrs. Wilson nods. "Oh, yes." She looks over at her husband.

"He did?" He tries to keep his eagerness in check. "Do you know who any of them were?"

"There was only one woman," Mrs. Wilson says, "who was here on a regular basis." She emphasizes the word "woman."

"Would you happen to know who she was?"

Mr. Wilson answers. "His boss's wife, Mrs. Lancaster. She was here quite a bit, until Emma was kidnapped. After that we hardly saw her anymore." He hesitates. "She was the only other mature woman."

A major brain cramp seizes him. Was Joe Allison having an affair with Glenna Lancaster? Could that be possible? "Was she a guest of Joe's in the evening as well as during the day?" he asks timorously. Fleetingly, he thinks, "Why the phrase 'mature woman'?" A generational thing obviously.

"Occasionally," Mr. Wilson says. "Not that we pry into our tenants' affairs," he's quick to add.

"Was Mrs. Lancaster around when Nicole Rogers was here, too? The two women were here together?"

Mr. Wilson looks to Mrs. Wilson for guidance. "I'm often gone during the day, so I wouldn't know," he explains.

His wife shakes her strong-featured head. "I don't recall seeing the two women here at the same time," she says thoughtfully. "There were never two women here at the same time. That's odd, isn't it?" she poses to Luke.

"Coincidental, I'm sure."

Back in jail. Same lawyer-client room. Luke's beginning to hate this space, the dirty off-white walls, the scarred chairs and table, the overhead fluorescent light that makes everyone's face look green. The room is designed this way for a reason, to discourage intimacy and foster depression. He knows, because he was privy to the design when he was the *jefe*. It works, he's thinking, sitting in it opposite his client.

"So here's a question out of the blue," he says. He waits a minute to ask it, while Allison looks at him blankly. "Were you and Glenna Lancaster having an affair?"

Allison, startled, sits up. "What are you talking about?"

Luke points a don't-bullshit-me finger at the man. "Simple English, ace. Were you and the mother of the girl you're accused of kidnapping and murdering sleeping together?"

Allison hesitates before answering. He chooses his words judiciously. "I wouldn't call it an affair, but we did have sex together," he admits. "A few times," he adds.

Luke's enraged. "You were sleeping with Glenna Lancaster and you withheld that from me? How long did it go on?"

"A while. On and off. It was only a few times," he repeats.

"How soon after you went to work at the station?"

There's no movement for a moment. Then Allison answers, his voice low. "A couple months."

"A couple of months? You've been fucking her for, what—two years, man? That's not an affair, that's a relationship."

"It was neither," Allison retorts sharply. "We were friends, but it wasn't romantic. We played tennis together, we jogged together. Jock things, mostly. That was how we spent our time together, not fucking. Look," he continues, "Doug Lancaster was fucking around for years. She knew about it but she didn't want to know, you know what I mean? Great lifestyle, great marriage on paper, movers and shakers in the community, the whole nine yards. So she swallowed it. Even if it was a dead-end situation. Until I came along, and she had someone to confide in. That's what it really was. The sex was incidental."

Tell that to a jury, Luke thinks. "So instead of doing something about taking care of her marriage, she seduced you?"

Allison shrugs. "She's an attractive woman. And she was lonely. There's a limit to how much resistance you can put up."

"Obviously none, in your case. And you're a liar. You've been lying to me since the day I met you. Which was the one thing I warned you never to do." He pauses. "Did Glenna know? About you and Emma? Your make-out scene, as you call it? Or was there more? I don't know what to believe from you now."

"There was nothing more than I told you," Allison declares. "And no, Glenna didn't know about anything with me and Emma. I took great pains to make sure of that, as you can imagine." He goes on. "Actually, she had gotten to the point, right before Emma was killed, that she was about to pull the plug on the marriage, regardless of the consequences. We talked about it. She saw a lawyer about it." He leans forward. "I told her she ought to confront Doug and try to work it out."

"And tell him about you and her, too?" Luke scoffs. "Doug Lancaster not only would've fired you, he'd have blackballed you from the business. You'd be doing the weekend weather in Nome, Alaska, if you got lucky."

"I know," Allison admits.

"You're lying to me again. You didn't try to talk her into coming clean with her old man. You talked her *out* of it, didn't you?"

Allison's no-answer says everything Luke needs to know.

"Did Nicole know?" he asks.

Allison shakes his head. "She wasn't concerned that I might have slept with Glenna a few times. That wasn't the problem."

"She'd had enough to pull the plug once you decided to move south and give her the out, didn't she?"

An unhappy nod. "It was our close friendship she didn't like. Time taken away from her. And that's the truth."

Luke takes a deep slow-down breath. This is too surreal. "How did Glenna take your leaving town?" he asks. "Losing her favorite—it sounds like only—confidant?"

"She was upset."

"Upset? She wasn't angry? She didn't think you'd led her on? She wasn't harboring any romantic fantasies?"

Allison shakes his head emphatically. "We hadn't slept together for a long time—not since Emma's murder. Besides, she knew how careers like mine work."

"She may have known in her head, but that doesn't mean she took it okay, does it?"

Allison nods. "All right—she took it badly."

"Was she planning on coming down and seeing you once you were set up in L.A.?"

Allison shakes his head. "I told her we had to end it—our friendship. We both had to start anew."

"That's pretty callous. You're a prince, Joe."

"No," Allison says sharply. "My behavior with Glenna was anything but callous. She had no one to turn to. I was a lifesaver for her for a long time, believe me."

Luke gets up and paces around. "I don't know what to believe anymore. You've put us in a terrible position, Joe, I'm sure you understand that."

"Because I lied to you."

"Yes." Luke sits back down. "I've got to think about all this. I may not be able to work with you as I have."

Allison goes pale.

"What about this divorce deal? Did she actually go so far as to discuss it with a lawyer, to your knowledge?"

"Check it out if you don't believe me," Allison says. "Her lawyer was Walt Turcotte. He handled Glenna's side of the divorce when it finally happened. Ask him." He pauses. "It's a terrible thing to say, but Emma's death was a liberation for Glenna. A horrible way for it to happen, but she did get her freedom out of it."

Luke looks away. What's freedom from a bad marriage going for these days, he wonders? The price Glenna Lancaster paid was way too high for what she got in return.

Walt Turcotte, attorney-at-law, distinguished graduate of Stanford Law School, has for twenty years been the city's preeminent divorce attorney. He sits behind his large rosewood desk, smiling warily at Luke Garrison, a friend and boon companion in the good old days. "You're the second most unpopular man in this city right now," Turcotte quips, after they exchange greetings and sit down. He goes on, "Seriously, it's been too long a time, Luke. I'd assumed you'd resurface someday, but not under these auspices. Friend to friend—why the hell are you doing this?"

Luke gives Turcotte the short version. His fellow lawyer is underimpressed with the validity of the reasons, but accepts them at face value. "Around my second year in law school I made the decision not to moralize about my work," he tells Luke. "Everybody else saw the law as some kind of political tool, but to me it was the foundation that held up the building, solid and unswayable. I don't judge, and I try to hold my own biases in check." Pressing a button others might shy away from, he says, "Ralph Tucker was a victim of a fallible system that's better than any of the other fallible systems we've tried, so I could sleep with what happened."

"I thought I could, too," Luke says, "but it turned out I couldn't."

Turcotte leans back in his chair. "You want to talk to me about Glenna Lancaster?"

"Yes."

Turcotte thumbs open a file resting on the corner of his desk. "This is attorney-client privilege, of course."

"Of course."

"I talked to her this morning, after you called. She's okay about me talking to you about her looking into getting a divorce from Doug before Emma was killed. Which surprised me, since you're Joe Allison's lawyer, but it's her decision."

He doesn't know, Luke realizes with a start. That Glenna and Allison were lovers. He has to be wary here, it isn't his place to tell Turcotte about that. Turcotte would kick him out of his office if he knew about the affair.

"Maybe she doesn't think Allison did it," Luke says carefully. "They were close friends, according to him. I'm sure she wants her daughter's murder avenged, but not at the expense of the wrong man."

A cloud comes over Turcotte's face. "I doubt that. But she has agreed to let me brief you on some of her history. So shoot—what're you looking for?"

"Did Glenna Lancaster discuss divorce with you before Emma was kidnapped?" The affair is going to stay hidden, at least for now.

Turcotte nods. "Yes, she did."

"Seriously, or was it an exploratory thing?"

"It was serious. She wanted to nail his scalp to the wall. Given their financial situation, she would've scored mightily. She did anyway, when they finally split."

"Did she have a specific reason? Or reasons?"

Turcotte hesitates a moment before answering. "Adultery."

"Doug was involved with someone else?"

"Elses. Plural."

"Any names you could throw my way?"

Turcotte thinks about that request. "We're getting in over our heads here, Luke," he says, shaking his head. "I don't see how this relates to your defense strategy."

Luke wants this information, so he makes a decision. "If I tell you a deep, dark, juicy secret, will you tell me some of yours?"

"Depends on the quality of the information," Turcotte answers, intrigued.

"This is me and you, Walt. Strictest confidence."

Turcotte hesitates. "Okay."

"Doug Lancaster made me a substantial offer to turn down Joe Allison."

Turcotte gapes at him. "No way!"

"He did. In the interest of justice, of course." Luke leans back, having played his hole card. "Now, what're you going to give me in return?"

"What do you want?" Turcotte asks cautiously.

"Did Glenna have a P.I. on Doug's case?"

Turcotte nods. "Several."

"Did they come up with anything?" He leans closer to Turcotte. "Here's why I ask. If Doug Lancaster was screwing around, who knows what kinds of people could be attached to it? He's screwing some bimbo who knows he's richer than God and she's got a whacked-out boyfriend who thinks the daddy will pay big bucks for the baby, so the boyfriend goes in and snatches Emma and it turns to shit and somehow Joe Allison gets framed." He sits back. "Stranger things have happened. I'm going to turn over every single rock in California, if I think there's something under one of them."

Turcotte exhales, impressed at the passion of Luke's wild thinking. "Okay," he agrees. "I can help you. Not that it'll help your case, but I have information for you."

"Thanks. By the way," Luke says, remembering the other part of this expedition, "did Glenna Lancaster ever talk to you about someone *she* might be seeing? Since she didn't have her husband's attention as much as she wanted? Some secret love interest she was hatching?" He has to nail down whether or not Turcotte knows about Glenna and Joe, America's favorite clandestine couple.

Turcotte nods slowly. "There was someone."

"Do you know who?"

"She wouldn't tell me. Why?" he asks. "Do you think whoever it was might be connected? A parallel track to the Doug Lancaster theory?"

"No," Luke lies. "I was just wondering." When Turcotte finally finds out about this, it'll be the end of the friendship, one of the few he has left.

Turcotte picks up the file folder he's been pushing around his desk. "The detective reports Glenna Lancaster compiled. I want them back and I don't want anyone to know you have them. I don't want my reputation sullied, even with my client's permission." He finger-riffs through the reports. "Most of them didn't check out—Doug was good at covering his tracks." He hands the files across the desk.

Luke sticks them in his briefcase. "No one's going to know."

Turcotte walks him to the door. "Like I said, it's good to see you again. Take care of yourself. And don't be a martyr to the cause. It isn't worth it."

The files Glenna Lancaster's sleuths compiled are okay. They show a pattern of screwing around on Doug Lancaster's part that's steady and consistent over a period of years. But they go back several years—the most recent are more than a year old—and to Luke's practiced eye, the trails seem cold. One thing they do trigger in his mind, however, is that screwing around on his wife was the man's m.o. for a long time. According to these reports, almost every time Doug Lancaster was out of town he was seeing a lover, alongside whatever legitimate business he was attending to. So it seems logical that on the night Emma was abducted, when her father was out of town on business, he would be seeing someone too.

One thing is certain, Luke wants to know where Doug Lancaster was that night. Luke can't conceive of a man being involved in his own daughter's kidnapping and murder—that would be horrendous—but it's happened before. If Doug was catting around though, he'd have an alibi for his time that night. It would be ugly and messy and he'd lose sympathy points, but better that than the alternative.

He has another reason to check this out, too—the personal reason, the one that's been festering—Doug Lancaster's crude, insulting move to try to buy him off. The more he thinks about it, the more dismissive he realizes it was: the act of a superior to an inferior, a boss to an employee. King to serf is the best analogy, to be brutally honest.

He appreciates that the man lost the most precious thing in his life, that his life will be damaged forever. He'd feel for anyone in that situation, friend or foe. But the idea that he or any lawyer could be bought off a case with the stroke of a pen on a check is outrageous. And what makes this particularly outrageous is that Doug Lancaster thought—not thought, assumed—he'd go for it. That Luke Garrison has become such a loser in the eyes of this community.

The drive down the Pacific Coast Highway, especially from Oxnard to Malibu, is one of the great motorcycle runs in California. The ocean on one side, the Santa Monica mountains on the other, you pass beach after glorious beach of surfers, campers, hikers, volleyballers, the sun a golden mantle shining off the water, the air fresh, clean, bracing, smelling of salt and sea life, and the bodies stunning, women and men, California sun worshipers all buffed and sleek, moving on the sand, lying on it, swimming in the water. Golden beaches of the golden people of the Golden State.

On a motorcycle, like a vintage Triumph, you feel a part of the life you're riding through, a piece of the completeness. Luke knows—he's done this route many times over the years. This, along with the ride up Highway 1 to Big Sur, is his favorite.

But some coward put his machine in the ground, and he hasn't gotten around to buying another one. He wants the right bike, and finding the right motorcycle takes time. Besides, he's still in mourning for the late, lamented Triumph. He can't desecrate its memory by replacing it so soon after its demise. So he's driving a rental Toyota. All the windows are down, he feels the air rushing by on his face, but it isn't the same thing.

The one benefit of being in a car instead of on a motorcycle is that on a motorcycle you're engaged in the ride one hundred percent; you have to be, or you can become a statistic lickety-split. In a car you can think, let your mind wander.

Which is what Luke's doing. He's evolving a hypothesis, which is a reason why he's driving down to L.A. this morning.

It's a risky scenario. Buying into it means believing, much more than he has previously, Joe Allison's assertion that he was framed by someone else, the real kidnapper/killer. And it involves doing something he's always detested—putting the victim on trial. Only a desperate defense attorney would be thinking along these lines. But as of this moment, he has nowhere else to go.

His hypothesis goes as follows:

1. The kidnapper and Emma Lancaster knew each other. (*And he wasn't Joe Allison. Unless Luke, Allison's lawyer, buys that, he's dead.*) She let him wrap her up in a blanket and carry her away without struggling. In fact, the abduction wasn't a kidnapping at all. *In Luke's mind, this point is unquestionable.*

2. Emma Lancaster was pregnant; *this much is in the record.* It stands to reason that whoever carried her away got her pregnant.

3. The gazebo was a fuck pad. A reasonable deduction is that Emma and her lover had some of their trysts there.

Here's where the big leap comes:

4. Emma's lover *didn't know* she was pregnant. She tells him that night. Maybe she's going to go public with it, bust him. He panics and kills her.

That's his number one scenario. He has a number two as well.

1. Again, Emma knew her "abductor," but he *wasn't* her lover.

2. Whoever carried her out of her bedroom knew Emma was pregnant.

3. The abductor was taking her to get an abortion, with "kidnapping" to explain her absence.

4. Something unexpected happened, with or without reference to her pregnancy. The "abductor" kills her, etc.

They both make sense, meaning they could have happened, although they seem pathetic stretches to Luke, thinking about them on his sunny drive down the coast. The idea that Emma was being taken to get an abortion is particularly messy, since she had friends sleeping over. But maybe the abortion had been planned, and the friends were an afterthought; too late *not* to go through with it.

That, however, is not the most serious problem. The real problem with these scenarios is that all the criteria could easily fit Joe Allison, literally her mother's lover.

In the first scenario, Joe Allison, despite his denial, could have been Emma Lancaster's lover too. Joe Allison could have knocked her up—the drugstore was out of pink rubbers one day, so he went bareback, with dismal results. He didn't know she was pregnant, that night she told him, and furthermore she was going to tell daddy, his boss. He freaked and killed her and did the rest.

Or, in a combination of the scenarios, he did know she was with child, took her to get rid of it, bad results, same bad ending.

And if scenario number two is real, it still could be Joe. Emma is too ashamed and frightened to tell her parents she's pregnant. She confides in Joe, who agrees to help her. Something terrible, beyond an abortion, happens, he panics, and so forth.

Her key ring was found in Joe Allison's car. Incontrovertible. The same brand of condoms found on the Lancaster property was found in his house, also without question. That he didn't use rubbers with Nicole, his woman, only makes things worse.

Allison and Emma knew each other. They spent time in each other's company. He was desirable, she was a fruit too ripe and tempting not to pluck. Nature took its course. Humbert and Lolita. A match made in tabloid heaven.

Was Emma Lancaster ever at Allison's house by herself, without her mother present? He has to get straight with Allison on that. He should have asked the Wilsons that question. He'll have to go back and do that.

Scenario number two presents its own set of problems for Allison. If he wasn't Emma's lover, then who was? Who would she know and trust well enough to let the mystery man carry her out of her bedroom with her friends present?

The list is frightening. Men who worked at the house? A minister? A sports coach?

Her father?

Doug Lancaster knows she's pregnant and is taking her to get an abortion? That feels completely wrong, and unnecessary. He wouldn't sneak her out of her bedroom while others are present, with the possibility of being seen, when they could go out of town, to L.A.

or San Francisco, have it done without fear of being discovered, come home, and no one's the wiser. And then he's going to hide the corpse of his own daughter miles away, letting her lie there and rot, rather than properly burying her? Only a complete monster could do that, and Doug, whatever else Luke thinks of him, is no monster. Is he?

He has to know where Doug was that night.

Palms is a working-class enclave in West Los Angeles, tucked between the tonier areas of Westwood, Cheviot Hills, and the movie studios in Culver City. An old section as far as L.A. goes, it's been stagnating for decades, not going up, not getting worse. A place to live and work, nothing special.

The restaurant, a hole-in-the-wall Mexican place, is on a side street in the seedier section of the area. It does just enough business to stay open.

The owner's brother, the man Luke drove down to see, is sitting at a table at the rear of the small room. The lunchtime crowd, whatever it was—people who work nearby and want a fast, cheap meal—has come and gone. No one's in front now except the owner's brother, who sits hunched over a Tecate in a can. From the way he's dressed—white shirt unbuttoned, the clip-on bow tie askew, black slacks, black shoes—he's the waiter. His thick black hair starts a couple inches above his eyebrows, flamboyantly styled with a generous helping of gel.

Luke introduces himself. "You're Ramon Huerta?" he asks, slipping into a chair opposite the man.

A slight nod. Sip of beer.

"Thanks for seeing me."

A shrug. *"De nada."* Huerta pauses, holds up his can questioningly.

"Sure. Appreciate it."

Huerta fishes a can out of the display refrigerator behind the counter. "Can you drink on duty?" he asks. He has a basic east L.A. Mexican accent of a native, not a wetback.

"On duty? I'm not a cop," Luke says. "You didn't think I was with the police, did you?"

Huerta shakes his head. "I meant on business. When you're doing business."

"No problem," Luke says, smiling. "I work for myself, make my own rules."

"Good for you, man." Huerta sips from his beer, almost with a daintiness, his pinky finger extended. "I don't work for myself. My brother, he's my employer now. I got to do it his way." The way he says it, his brother's way isn't fun.

"But it's better than working at Shutters, isn't it?" Shutters on the Beach is the fancy hotel on Ocean Avenue in Santa Monica where Doug Lancaster was staying the night Emma disappeared.

"Shutters paid better money," Huerta says, staring at Luke. "Especially with the tips. But I don't work there anymore." He frowns, saying that.

"You were fired?"

Huerta nods. He looks away, his beer can at his lips.

"How come?" If the guy has a record, this could be a wasted trip.

"They said I came on to one of the guests."

"You accosted a woman?" This isn't starting out well.

"A man," Huerta says with no inflection in his voice. He looks at Luke. "Do I look like a fag to you?" he asks with a challenge in his soft voice.

You could be, Luke thinks; so what? "No," he says. "You don't."

"I'm not," Huerta says belligerently. "The guest was drunk. He was angry because he said I didn't bring his car around fast enough. So they eighty-sixed me." Another shrug, another hit from his brew. "No more big tips." He looks around the tiny restaurant. "No tips, period."

"That's too bad."

"I got my application in at the Miramar, Holiday Inn, Hilton. Someone'll hire me on. Anything to get away from here," he says in a quieter voice, glancing over his shoulder towards the kitchen in the rear. "The hotels always need experienced parking lot attendants. I'm good at it. The people at Shutters are prejudiced, anyway," he adds, finishing his beer and crushing the can in his hand, a show of manliness for Luke's benefit. He gets up and fetches another for himself. Then he sits down again.

Prejudiced against Latino laborers? Luke thinks. They couldn't stay open a week with that attitude.

He gets down to business. "You were working the parking lot at Shutters the night Emma Lancaster was kidnapped?" he asks.

Huerta stares at him. Then he extends his hand, palm up.

Luke pulls out his wallet, plucks a crisp hundred-dollar bill from inside, lays it on the outstretched palm: the price Huerta quoted over the phone for speaking to him. The disgruntled waiter squints at it, making a show of holding it up to the light to make sure it's authentic. Satisfied, he folds it once and puts it in his shirt pocket. "Double shift," he confirms. "My regular shift was nights, but one of the guys called in sick, so I took his shift. The early morning shift."

"So you were there all through the night?" Luke hits on his beer. It's cold, the metallic taste from the can stings his throat going down. A good sting.

"From five that night till ten the next morning. Wore me out. I slept there in a caretaker's room, because I didn't have time to go home, sleep, change, come back for the five o'clock. But I made double overtime," Huerta boasts, remembering.

"But you were manning the parking lot all through the night," Luke says. "You didn't take any breaks?"

"To piss. Five minutes. I was out there the whole time. I didn't miss a thing," he declares.

"So you were there when Mr. Lancaster went out for the evening."

"Went out, came back, went out, came back. Went out."

"Do you remember when he came and went? The different times?"

"Went out at seven, came back at eleven. Closer to eleven-fifteen," he says with more precision.

"You're sure? This was over a year ago."

A forceful nod. "I'm sure. Mr. Lancaster stayed with us a lot. He was a big tipper. You remember the people who treat you good, everybody wants them. I made sure I was special nice to him, so he used to ask for me by name."

Great. Luke jots that down.

"I especially remember that time because it was on the TV practically every day," Huerta continues. "It stuck in my head."

Makes sense. "And the second time?"

"Left at one, about ten after one. I remember that clear because I was watching *Saturday Night Live* in our command post in the lobby by the front doors, and he called down to have his car ready right when the show was ending. Then he came down for it a few minutes later."

"You brought it around for him."

A nod.

"When did he come back after that?"

"A quarter after nine in the morning."

This is critical: "You're sure?"

"Positive," the former parking attendant says. "I remember looking at my watch, 'cause I was dragging my ass by then. He pulled up real fast, jumped out, told me not to garage it, because he was going to change clothes and leave again right away."

From one at night until nine that morning Doug Lancaster was not in his hotel room. Which is not the story he told the police. "Do you remember what he looked like?" he asks. "When he came back at nine o'clock?"

"Like he'd been rode hard and put up wet." Huerta smiles slyly.

Where was Doug Lancaster from one at night until nine in the morning? Luke grimaces inwardly at the thought of having to pursue that, but now he has to, he has no choice. "When did he come back for his car that third time?"

"Twenty, twenty-five minutes later."

"And how did he look then?"

"Better. He'd changed his clothes."

"Dressed for golf?"

Huerta thinks. "Could have been. He was casual."

Luke drinks the last of his beer, leaves the can on the table. "Thanks for your time," he says. "Appreciate it."

Huerta pats his shirt pocket where the hundred's nestled. "Anytime."

Luke gets up, shakes the man's hand. It's soft—he uses hand lotion. He walks to the door. As he's pushing it open, Huerta calls after him.

"Say hello to Mr. Lancaster for me," he calls out plaintively. "Tell him I miss him."

Riva has also been quietly snooping around, trying to ferret out information about Emma Lancaster. Pregnant at fourteen, that's heavy. But sophisticated young girls have been known to be promiscuous. Witness her coming on to Allison.

Questions abound. For instance, how much did her parents know? Riva's guessing that Emma's parents were in the dark about it. Most girls that age, especially girls from Emma's background, don't reveal their lives to their parents, and they're too scared of the parents' reaction. But they confide in friends, and friends tell other friends, and the word gets around the teenage underground. Sometimes a sympathetic teacher will find out, or a girl might even go to a teacher, for adult advice and support.

Emma's pregnancy isn't in the public record, won't be until the trial, although all kinds of rumors and stories have been floating around ever since the autopsy report came back. When the fact that she was pregnant becomes public knowledge, it will create a sensation in the courtroom. Not necessarily a positive for Luke's client.

It's a delicate matter, trying to uncover this kind of stuff. If she and Luke can find out who Emma was screwing, Joe Allison might walk out of jail. Was it one boy (or man), or more than one? Whoever it was, *someone* got Emma Lancaster pregnant—it was not an immaculate conception. The planter of his seed was almost certainly the actual killer. Which means that man or boy—*assuming* he wasn't Joe Allison—is still at large, somewhere out there. Probably still living in the area, watching the developments carefully, hopeful that this will play out all the way, that Joe Allison will be convicted and imprisoned for the crime.

Who was sleeping with Emma Lancaster? Everyone in law enforcement thinks it was Joe. His condoms matched the ones in the gazebo. That's damning evidence—convictions have been won with less evidence than that. It's so slam-dunk it seems futile to try and fight it.

But they have to, if they're going to have a prayer of winning this case. And she has to keep an open mind, and be optimistic, or she'll sabotage the man she loves.

If Emma Lancaster were alive now, she'd be finishing ninth grade. If she were still alive she would be going to Bolt School, a prestigious private boarding school in Summerland. She applied before she was murdered, and with her good grades and her parents' clout in the community, she would have been accepted. She would be one of the handful of day students, getting all the benefits of the school, but sleeping in her own bed at night instead of sharing a cramped dorm room. On weekends she would bring her boarder friends to her house, where her mother would fuss over them, feed them well.

If Emma were still alive her parents would get her a car on her sixteenth birthday. Nothing fancy, the style at Bolt is understated. An old Volvo, Jeep, or Honda, something slow and safe. She'd be chauffeuring her friends around, driving them into Santa Barbara on the weekends, taking them off campus to break up the monotony.

She would be popular; she always was, from kindergarten. Most kids don't date in ninth grade, they travel in packs, boys and girls combined. But she'd date some boys, too, juniors and seniors. She had already lost her virginity. She was way ahead of most of these bright, sheltered kids.

The hangout of choice for the kids Emma used to run with, those who now go to Bolt, is the doughnut shop in the Carpinteria Mall. Riva sits at a table near the back nursing a latte, away from the counter where customers line up to order their drinks. Teenagers drift in and out, more girls than boys, getting drinks, talking with each other in high, laughing tones, comparing stories, notebooks, gossip. It's easy to tell the Bolt kids from the locals.

These girls are women, Riva thinks, looking them over. Emma would be here with her friends. She'd be the center of attention, and she'd be enjoying it. The first blush of her emerging sexuality having passed, she'd be taking her life easier, not having to prove anything, including her womanhood.

Or she might be indiscriminately fucking her brains out. She'd started at a very early age. Well, I did too, Riva thinks. I was fifteen when I lost my cherry. As did other girls I knew.

By now it might be second nature to Emma: you liked a man or a boy, you slept with him. You just took better precautions.

The girl she's been waiting for walks into the shop. She's with friends, a group of other girls. They're Bolt girls—two are wearing Bolt sweatshirts. They all order mocha cappuccinos with extra whipped cream.

The girl sees Riva. Excusing herself from her friends, she comes over and sits down at Riva's table.

"Hi, Hillary," Riva says, her tone friendly, inviting.

"Hi, Miss Montoya," Hillary responds in greeting. She's at ease with Riva.

Hillary Lange was the girl who, along with Lisa Jaffe, was sleeping in Emma's bedroom the night Emma disappeared. She was Emma's best friend. They had grown up together, had gone to school together from kindergarten.

If any of Emma's friends knew about her secret life before she died, Riva guesses, it would be Hillary. She's been cultivating the girl for weeks: coming into the coffee shop, gradually introducing herself, accidentally running into Hillary at the Paseo Nuevo shopping mall in downtown Santa Barbara on the weekends. Hillary knows who Riva is, that she's involved in the murder trial. Riva has been careful not to spook the girl. After all, she is working for the man accused of murdering Hillary's best friend.

Curiosity is a powerful seducer, being in on a secret is another, and flattery rounds out the trio. Combined, they're hard to resist, especially when you're fifteen and the adult world is inviting you to join it in something special, which only you have entry to. Slowly, slowly, Riva has been drawing Hillary into her web, talking to her about school, about the case, marveling how sophisticated and cool Hillary is compared to other girls her age, gradually gaining her confidence. Hillary knows she shouldn't be talking to Riva about Emma; Riva's the enemy, she's working for that lawyer everyone hates, to get Emma's killer off. But the exclusiveness and deliciousness of the situation are too much for Hillary to resist; she knew about Emma's crazy, daring life, her forays into the world of sex with grown men.

"How's school going?" Riva asks.

"It's going. I've got a physics test tomorrow I'll be up all night studying for."

"Isn't that a lot of work for ninth grade?" Riva asks, coming on sympathetic. "I never stayed up all night studying in high school."

The girl shrugs. "Everyone will be. That's Bolt."

Riva glances around the room. A few of Hillary's friends are casting curious looks in their direction, but they aren't a focus of attention. The others don't know who she is. Riva knows that Hillary wants to keep this relationship to herself, her secret, private status.

"Can we talk about Emma?" Riva says, getting down to business, keeping her voice quiet.

"Sure." Hillary runs a finger around the rim of her cup. "What do you want to know?"

"Do you know who the man was that Emma was having sex with?"

They've gotten this far in previous conversations—that Emma was no virgin, that Hillary knew about it, that Riva has found out. But Riva hasn't told Hillary about the coroner's report.

Hillary shakes her head. "She'd never give me a name."

"Did she say it was an older man? Or was he, you know, one of your friends?"

"It was a man. The boys we know—knew—were way too slow for Emma."

"Did she say anything about him?" Riva asks, pushing gently.

"I think . . . I think she was a baby-sitter for his kids." She dabs a finger of whipped cream into her mouth, sucking on the finger.

All right! Not Joe. That's a big break, if it's true. "Do you know when it started? Emma and this man?"

"Near the beginning of eighth grade, I think. Maybe the summer before eighth grade started."

Emma would have been barely fourteen. She didn't waste any time. "Do you think that was the only one?" she asks carefully.

Hillary hesitates before speaking again. "There were more men than one," she confides.

"More than one?" Riva asks. Jesus. Little Emma got around. "Do you know how many?"

Hillary shakes her head. "I think only one other."

"Did she say anything about him?"

Another head shake. "He was handsome. He drove a really cool car."

Joe Allison's made-for-television handsome. And he drives a Porsche, by any definition a really cool car.

Still, this is progress. Emma had multiple lovers, and one of them is going to be easy to find.

"But Emma never told you who he was?" she still probes, very carefully.

"No. She never did."

Riva pushes her latte away—it's cold now. "Thanks for talking to me," she says sincerely.

"I'm not going to get Emma in trouble, am I?" Hillary asks, suddenly fretful.

She's dead, honey; she's way past any trouble you can bring. But she knows what the girl means. The memory, the idealized picture of what people thought Emma was. "No," she lies. "No one's ever going to know what we talked about."

"Thanks," Hillary says brightly, feeling relieved. "Emma was really a good person," she says earnestly, wanting Riva to believe her. "She just . . ."

"She was a great kid," Riva assures her. "And that's the way everyone's going to remember her."

Driving back up the coast, Luke thinks about what he's done today. Interviewing witnesses, gathering information—that's all part of the job, nothing he hasn't done a thousand times. He's much more involved now, of course. Once you're the D.A., or high up in the office, you're more an administrator than a litigator. You push papers around and make decisions. In that sense, this is more rewarding. It's hands-on, you're the man, it's your show.

That's not what he's thinking about. He's thinking about the law, his attitude towards it, how he's dealing with it. He didn't have an epiphany and start believing the world was any more of a corrupt place, that the jails are full of innocent people and he has to be one to stem the tide, none of that stuff. He knows that almost everyone who is in jail, should be, small-time drug busts being the only exception.

It's about methods, what *means* justify what *ends*. Yes, the old Luke Garrison would have paid an informant what amounted to a bribe. You have to, sometimes. No one will get hurt—no one who shouldn't—and the information might be helpful to Joe Allison, his client, which is his primary concern.

It's the *way* he did it. He never would have misrepresented himself, even by omission.

He acted the way he did for good reasons, which he can justify to himself. He doesn't want to alert the prosecution, and thus Doug Lancaster, that he's pursuing this line of investigation. He doesn't want to give Doug the chance to cover his tracks, should they need covering. Nor does he want to alert Ray Logan's office that he might be traveling down this particular road; he wants to hold that back until the last possible minute.

Those are proper, legitimate reasons to mask his activities. But he doesn't like the *means* by which he reached the end. It's beneath him; or if it isn't, it should be.

The other reason he acted the way he did is the animosity he's carrying towards Doug Lancaster. He's still smoldering over the attempted bribe. And although he told Riva he didn't think Doug was involved in the trashing of his motorcycle, deep down inside he thinks Doug was. And that angers him further.

But there's another, deeper reason he's determined to keep Doug Lancaster in the dark for as long as he can. The accepted rule of thumb in every prosecutor's office in the land is this: When a child is murdered, and there is no concrete evidence to the contrary, the presumption of guilt falls first upon the family. And most of the time, someone in the family did it.

He doesn't know where Doug was the night his daughter was taken from her room and subsequently murdered, or what he was doing. Given his history, he was probably shacking up with some woman. But as of now—and he's the only one who knows it, besides Doug—the man's time can't be accounted for. And he flat-out lied to the police about it, which casts even more suspicion on him.

But what if, on that awful night, Doug *wasn't* lying in some other woman's arms? Sometimes, if you're doing your job right, you have to think the unthinkable. Emma Lancaster was carried away from her bedroom without putting up a struggle. She *knew* her abductor, she went willingly. She was pregnant, very possibly by whoever carried her away.

Did Doug know his daughter was pregnant? According to the sheriff's files, he and Glenna were stunned when they found out she'd been sexually active. But what if Doug had known? How would he have reacted to that? Here's a husband so estranged from his wife that she's thinking of divorcing him, which means, almost certainly, that they aren't having sex with each other. His daughter is beautiful, precocious, she's becoming a woman before his eyes. Is she also becoming, in his eyes, a love object?

It's a scary, sobering thought. It would explain why Doug was so aggressive in running lawyers off Allison's defense, why he would try to bribe Luke with such an outrageous amount of money.

Think the unthinkable.

Back in the office at the end of the day, he and Riva compare notes. "Joe Allison was having an on-and-off affair with Glenna Lancaster," he tells her.

She stares at him. "What in God's name did you say?"

"Allison and Glenna Lancaster were clandestine lovers."

The information stuns her. "How do you know?"

"My client finally told me," Luke says, his voice heavy with angry sarcasm.

"That ruins your case." She slumps onto a couch. "Just when I was beginning to think you might have one."

"Yeah, I know." He sits next to her. "But that doesn't mean he killed Emma." He fills her in on the discussion he and Allison had, and Allison's reason why he wouldn't have been involved with Emma.

"That sounds like bullshit to me." She turns. "Where does this leave you now?"

He shakes his head. "I don't know."

Riva moves closer to Luke, their bodies touching. "What's next, then?"

"I don't know. I have to think about it. What do you have that'll brighten my day, besides your body naked in bed next to mine and a good bottle of champagne?"

She gives him a smooch. "We'll do that later." She sits back up. "Actually, I have some real information that, until you told me your own news, was lifting my spirits."

"What?" he asks impatiently.

"Hillary, Emma's best friend, thinks Emma was in a sexual relationship with at least *two* adult men. One was someone whose kids she baby-sat—"

"That should be easy enough to find out," Luke kicks in.

"—and the other was a good-looking stud who drove a cool car," she finished.

He groans. "Sounds like our close personal friend Joe Allison. Who was boffing her mother, but not her. So he says, the lying bastard."

She nods. "I thought the same thing as soon as she said it. About the description fitting Allison."

"Great!"

"But," Riva says, trying to find a sliver of brightness in that dark cloud, "Hillary *was told* the second man fit that description. I don't know anyone who ever actually *saw* Emma with a man who could be her lover."

"Yeah," Luke says dubiously. "But taking it all together, it isn't good. We need to find out who she was baby-sitting for." He pauses. "There is another man who fits the second one's description." He hesitates.

"Who?"

"Her father."

"You can't mean that. I know it's happened before, but still . . ."

He walks her through how he's arrived at this theory.

"You'd have to have actual proof to introduce that," she says, shaking her head at the idea. "You bring that into the mix without solid, concrete footing underneath you and any jury in the world will cut you to ribbons."

"Where was Doug?" he challenges her.

"Like you said, in bed with another woman."

"He'll have to expose himself with that," he says. "Which will be damned embarrassing, and cast doubts on his credibility. It's a lousy alibi to give a jury."

She stares at him with uneasiness. "You're hoping he can't, aren't you? You're hoping he has no alibi for those eight hours."

He nods. "Yep, I am." He shrugs. "Anyway, even if Doug has a mistress alibi, my other idea still holds, that he might have gotten involved with a woman who set this up behind his back. That is not so implausible. In fact, if Joe Allison weren't a suspect, I'd say it was the most likely explanation."

Riva shakes her head, the look on her face dubious at best.

He brings up his other point. "And what about Glenna? She admitted to her lawyer that she was seeing someone. Now we know it was Joe Allison. But what if she had another stud horse in her pocket, a backup for when Joe wasn't available? Hey," he says, "if she and Allison were screwing, what's to say she wasn't doing others? Why stop with one?" He's pacing around the room. "The father's screwing around, the mother's screwing around, the fourteen-year-old daughter's screwing around, and she's pregnant. This trial's going to be a frigging three-ring circus!"

"I wish there were another way to do this," she says. "I wish you didn't have to drag so many people through the mud. Especially Emma. She can't defend herself. She's going to come off as a cheap little whore, no matter what finally happens." She pauses. "I want you on the high road, Luke, not in the gutter."

He puts his hands on her shoulders. "So do I."

She puts her arms around him and lays her head on his chest. "I know this can get ugly and dirty—it already has. I'm hoping not too much of that mud will splatter on you."

He should've checked this out when he was in L.A. talking with Ramon Huerta, the car parker, but he didn't, he was too excited about what he'd heard from Huerta to think clearly and thoroughly, so he has to drive back down there again, to Shutters, the hotel where Doug had been that night.

He meets the detective outside the hotel, in the parking lot. Nolan

Buchanan was an investigator for the D.A.'s office when Luke was the boss. Ray Logan, insecure, felt Buchanan was a loyalist to Luke (which was true) and forced him into early retirement. There's no love lost between the two.

Luke fills Buchanan in on what's required.

"That's all? You could do this yourself, boss."

Luke knows he could, but if the ploy were discovered, he'd be in trouble. "I'll watch you from the other side of the lobby," he says.

Buchanan enters the hotel and strides confidently to the concierge desk. "I'd like to speak to the manager or assistant manager," he says, flashing his badge. Like cops in many jurisdictions, they get to keep a facsimile when they retire.

The woman scrutinizes the badge. She writes the name down. Without questioning him, she picks up the telephone on her mahogany desk and dials a number. Within minutes a tailored woman whose hair is pulled back in an efficient bun comes out of the elevators and approaches him. "I'm Noreen Strong, the assistant manager. How can I help you?"

"We're investigating a credit-card fraud ring that may have made calls from your hotel last year," Buchanan lies smoothly—he's had decades of practice. He gives her the date of the night Emma was abducted. "The calls would have been made between ten p.m. and two a.m." Luke has given him the times in question. No point wading through twenty-four hours of telephone calls.

It takes her a few minutes to retrieve the telephone logs from the basement files. Buchanan takes them to a quiet table in a corner of the lobby, where he sits and begins scanning the calls and the room numbers.

From across the room, Luke watches. His former investigator writes some numbers down, hands the logs back to the concierge, and skedaddles. Luke meets him outside. He hands over two hundred-dollar bills.

"You don't have to."

"You're a professional. When you work, you get paid."

"Easy money," Buchanan says. "Good luck, boss." He pockets the bills and walks away.

Sitting in his car, Luke looks over the information. Doug Lancaster made two phone calls that night. One was shortly after eleven, to his house. The other was logged in at 12:45 in the morning, to a 310 area code. The prefix is near the beach, the Palisades or Malibu.

Now he has a club: Doug Lancaster called someone shortly before one in the morning, then left his hotel and didn't return until after nine.

Riva has done more checking. Emma Lancaster had been a babysitter for five families. She'd been doing it for a little over a year before she died. She was thirteen when she started, but she had an air of maturity and authority about her, and adults felt comfortable entrusting their five- and six-year-olds to her care for a couple of hours in the early evening while they took in a movie or went out to dinner. All the families she sat for had kids at the same school she went to, Elgin—they knew her and her parents. She didn't need the money, but even at thirteen she liked making some money of her own; from an early age she wanted to be independent.

Riva checks out the families. Two of them are single-parent, both mothers. In each of those cases, Doug or Glenna or one of their staff dropped Emma off and picked her up. In two of the other families, the mother always drove her home, for propriety's sake. Only in one of the families Emma sat for did the father transport her, not only bringing her home but often picking her up at the house as well. On a few occasions, he picked her up at school.

Riva drives to the man's business, *All Natural,* a well-regarded health food store and restaurant at the northern edge of the city's center. She browses for a few minutes, taking note of the large cheese display including sheep and goat cheeses from France and Italy, the impressive wine area featuring local and regional wines, the fresh organic fruits and vegetables (there are NO CHEMICALS signs scattered throughout the store), and the long meat counter at the rear, where only free-range meat and poultry, raised without pesticides in the feed, are sold.

A wine and cheese dinner would be nice. She buys half a dozen hunks of various cheeses, a bottle of locally produced syrah, and a head of romaine. "Is Mr. Fourchet around?" she asks the cashier as her groceries are being bagged. Mr. Fourchet is the father in question.

"He's in the back," the woman replies. "Would you like me to get him for you?"

"If you would." She walks to an uncrowded corner near the front door and waits.

A man comes out from the back near the butcher counter and walks up the aisle to the cashier, who says something to him and points to Riva. He strolls over to her. "Hi," he says, fixing her with an easy, practiced smile. "Is there something I can help you with?"

He looks like the kind of man who would own a store like this. Bearded, longish hair, triathlete-thin, wearing a short-sleeved denim shirt and wrinkled khakis, he was probably an organic farmer or something related before he became an entrepreneur.

"I'd like to talk to you about Emma Lancaster," she says.

The smile vanishes. He looks back over his shoulder, as if fearful someone might have heard her. "What about Emma?" he asks cautiously.

She was hoping to catch him off guard, and she did. "Can we go someplace private?"

Another nervous look-around. "Follow me."

Fourchet leads Riva back through the store to his office. It's a small, cluttered, utilitarian space. There's a desk with a computer screen and keyboard on it, a multiline telephone, a fax-copier. The only chair is an old, beat-up wooden one on casters behind his desk; against the other wall is a small futon couch covered with an Indian blanket. He moves around behind the desk, creating space between them. "How can I help you, Ms.—?"

"Montoya. I'm working for Joe Allison's lawyer."

He stares at her. "You are?" he says dumbly.

She nods briskly. "Why don't you sit down, Mr. Fourchet?"

He lowers himself into his chair, which wobbles unevenly. "What do you want to talk about?" he asks impatiently. "I talked to the police last year, when Emma disappeared."

"I want to know about Emma as a baby-sitter," she says.

He nods. "Well, you probably know she baby-sat our seven-year-old son occasionally, when my wife and I wanted to get out for a few hours." He pauses.

"Was she a good baby-sitter?" she asks, working her way in circuitously. "Never any problems with her?"

"No problems. She was very good," he says. "She was the only sitter Seth would tolerate."

"You liked her."

"We did." He nods vigorously. "We all did. She was a great kid."

"How did you feel when you heard what happened to her?"

Fourchet grimaces. "We were devastated, all of us."

It's time to up the ante. "Mr. Fourchet, could you tell me where you were the night Emma was kidnapped?"

No longer the friendly, accommodating storekeeper, he stares at her suspiciously. "Why are you asking this?"

"I've asked all the families Emma worked for." A small lie, which he'll never check on.

He sits upright. "I was in Paso Robles, with some of my produce growers."

"All night long."

"Yes. In fact, I was there from the day before she disappeared until the day after."

"The police asked you where you were because you used to drive her home from her baby-sitting some nights?" she asks.

"I guess so." His attempted nonchalance doesn't come off. "They questioned everyone who knew her. Hundreds of people."

"There were times when you were alone with her. Picking her up and driving her home."

He's squirming now. "Yes."

"Sometimes you even picked her up from school. Even when it was the afternoon and she wasn't going to sit for you until evening."

He starts to speak, his mouth a furry hole in the middle of his beard.

"You were seen," she tells him. Not exactly what Hillary told her, but close enough.

He nods unhappily. "It was more convenient sometimes to do that. Seth was always with us in the car," he affirms. "They went to the same school, Elgin. It's a private school in Montecito." He knows he's talking too much, but his mouth won't obey his brain.

She shakes her head. "Not always." She stares at him.

He jerks nervously at a sidelock.

"When did Emma stop baby-sitting for you?"

"About four months before she . . ." He doesn't finish.

"Before the kidnapping."

He nods.

"Why did you stop using her, if she was the only sitter your son liked?"

He turns away, fixing his look on a side wall. "My wife didn't want her to."

"Why not?" Riva asks. She feels the closeness of the windowless room, the stale air. She's claustrophobic, she would like to open the door, but she restrains herself. They're in a vacuum together that has to be kept sealed.

Another bad shrug. "I don't know. It was just . . ."

There's a silence. Riva waits for him to continue. When he doesn't, she hits him with the hard question. "Your wife thought you and Emma were getting into something, didn't she?"

Fourchet reddens. "My wife has a suspicious mind about that topic. It's from when we used to live on a commune and everyone was free and easy."

"Including adult men and teenage girls."

"It was a different situation." He's beginning to have a hard time getting his breath. He covers his face with his hands. She leans forward on the desk, bracing her weight on her hands.

"How old was Emma when you started sleeping with her, Mr. Fourchet?"

He begins sobbing soundlessly behind his hands.

"How old?" she asks again.

He moves his hands from his face, staring up at her with red eyes. His complexion is red and blotchy. "I don't know," he whispers. "Fourteen." He pauses. "Maybe not quite."

Riva rocks back onto her heels. Jesus. "Were you the first?"

His sigh is an Old Testament lamentation. "I think so."

"You're not sure?"

"Her hymen was broken," he says. "She said it was from riding horses."

"Did you believe her?"

He nods. "I did." He buries his head in his hands again.

Riva stares at him. She knows what Emma must have gone through. She was involved with a drug dealer, she's seen the dark side from several angles. But this is plumbing the depths. "Why would you do such a thing?" she can't help asking. "How could you be so craven as to seduce a thirteen-year-old girl?"

The first time was at his store. He and his wife had returned earlier than expected—they didn't like the movie—so Emma wasn't due home for another hour. The store wasn't far from his house, and he needed to check on his walk-in refrigerator, make sure it was running at the right temperature, he was worried about his meat. They had installed some new coils that afternoon, and he wanted to make sure the unit was working properly.

"It'll just be a few minutes," he told her. "You can wait in the car." She had her schoolbooks with her, she had been doing homework when they came home.

"Can I come with you?" she asked. "I've never been in your store."

They went in through the service entrance. He flipped on a few lights. The empty store glowed, light and dark areas casting long striped shadows on the walls.

"Take a look around," he said. "I won't be long." He had pulled the heavy refrigerator door open and gone inside.

The refrigerator was humming along smoothly. He walked along the rows where haunches of meat hung from hooks in the ceiling, running his hands along sides of beef, pork, lamb. Perfect.

"It's freezing in here."

He turned with a start. She had come in behind him; he hadn't heard her. "You shouldn't be in here," he said. "You hardly have anything on."

She was wearing a light top, shorts, and sandals. Her breath was coming out smoky, rimming her pretty young face. She looks like a Botticelli, he thought. Something otherworldly. The perfection of youth.

Her hand was on his forearm. He too was in short sleeves, but he was used to the cold, for brief periods.

"You're cold too," she said.

He felt the erection forming—suddenly, violently, rush of blood-gore. "Time to go," he said with forced lightness. "Your parents'll be waiting for you." He could feel goose bumps forming, and not from the coldness of the room.

"They're out," she said. "They won't be home till late. They're never home," she said. "I could be gone for a week and they wouldn't miss me." She shivered. "I really am cold."

He hustled her out of the cold room, shouldering the heavy door shut. "I'm still cold," she said as they stood in the rear of the store, where it was dark. Her face was close to his. He could smell her breath. It smelled like peppermint chewing gum.

"The only one who cares about me is our housekeeper, Maria," she told him in a soft, wistful voice. "You care about me more than my parents do. A lot more." And then she kissed him—a woman's kiss, full on the mouth.

She was too beautiful, too impossible to resist. He kissed her back. When the kiss ended, she said, "You're a cool guy, Mr. Fourchet." She giggled. "I mean cool, not cold."

They kissed again, his hand going to her breast under the light shirt. She was braless. Her small breasts hardened at his touch.

They'd done it on the couch in his office. Once they got started she was all over him, scratching, biting, screaming. She bit down hard on his shoulder when he started to enter her, clawing at his back.

His office, after hours, had been their assignation spot of choice, but they went to motels and other places as well. Never in his house, or in hers. A few times, when he brought her home and there was no one around, they did it in the gazebo at the back of her property. There were chaise cushions there, but sometimes they did it on the bare wood floor.

They made love as often as they could, until his wife pulled the plug. After that, he'd seen her at school occasionally, when he went to pick up his son, but they were never together again.

"How did she react when you told her you couldn't see her anymore?" Riva asks. Her head is swimming.

"It was like nothing had ever happened," he says. "There was no feeling at all, no sadness."

"What about you?"

"I missed her," he admits. "That was an out-of-this-world experience—which I'll never do again," he adds hastily.

"Does your wife know?"

"She has no proof, but . . ." He lets the rest go unsaid.

"Did you use contraception?" she asks him.

He lowers his head. "Not that first time. I wasn't prepared. But every time after," he says firmly. "Christ, I was in terrible trouble already, I wasn't going to chance getting her pregnant." He's shaking, from the rekindling of memory and the fear of being exposed.

Riva picks up her bag of groceries from where she's set it on the floor. It feels heavy, cumbersome. She isn't going to eat this cheese tonight. "How many months after you and Emma stopped your affair was she murdered?" she asks, hitting hard on the word "murdered." She hates saying "affair" to describe the relationship this man had with Emma. It was a betrayal.

"Four." He gets up. "I've got to go."

Four months not screwing her, and he has a solid alibi. This man wasn't the father of Emma's never-to-be-born child. And he wasn't the killer. He was a way station, a launching pad. But she isn't going to let him know she thinks that. He doesn't know Emma was pregnant, that the killer could have been the man who knocked her up. He mustn't be told that.

She walks to the door. "If I were you, Mr. Fourchet, I wouldn't tell anyone we had this conversation," she says, her voice a dire warning.

He nods, eager to agree. "We've never talked."

The clinic is crowded: women, mostly, several in various stages of pregnancy, but there are men too. To Riva's untrained eye, the majority of the men look like they're in various HIV-positive stages, with the look in their eyes of abandonment before death. Some of them wear surgical masks to ward off infectious contact that could come from anything on the street. Riva read in one of the local papers that the only AIDS hospice had closed, because there were fewer people now with full-blown AIDS—the medicine combinations being administered to combat AIDS are giving HIV-positive people a chance to live longer and healthier lives. These men, obviously, are beyond that.

The Free Clinic is on the east side of town, sandwiched between a doughnut shop and a cut-rate tire store. It was a house in a previous incarnation, a two-story small-scale bungalow of no particular charm. Now it's a city/county/state-run agency, funded by taxpayer dollars and voluntary donations. Some of the city's wealthy philanthropists contribute money and sit on the board. For the past few years the building has been slowly going to seed, in need of a fresh coat of paint, its creaky porch floor dangerously rotting. The old house, like some of the patients it serves, is slowly dying: men about to lose their lives in the world, and girls fearful of bringing new ones into it, who need to find out if they're pregnant but don't want their families to know, or do know about their pregnancies and haven't yet decided when they're going to have their abortion. The clinic maintains a confidentiality policy, so most of the unwed girls in town, especially the underage ones, come here for their testing and counseling.

The rest of the clients are people, families mostly, who don't have health insurance and can't afford regular doctors and managed-care facilities. Children sit on their mothers' laps waiting to have ears examined, throats swabbed.

Riva lost her way coming over, making her late for her appointment, so she has to wait to see the doctor. She sits on one of the plastic-coated kitchen chairs leafing through an old *National Geographic*. A little boy across from her, perched on his mother's lap, smiles at her. She smiles back. He turns away, suddenly shy.

A Birkenstock-shod female aide calls Riva's number. Riva follows her into a small office that looks like it used to be a kitchen pantry. "The doctor'll be in in a minute," the aide says. She leaves Riva alone in the room.

Finding this doctor and making the connection was an incredible stroke of luck. Riva hopes the doctor will be able to help her.

The doctor, a Latina in her thirties, comes in and closes the door behind her. "It's nice to meet you," she says warmly but warily. "My brother says you're good people."

"It's nice to meet you, too."

The doctor's brother had been in trouble with the law up where Riva and Luke live. A drug charge, selling to an undercover DEA cop. Luke was the man's attorney, and through a combination of good lawyering and bad police work—the buy and arrest resulted from a sting that didn't play by the rules—he had gotten his client off, sentence suspended. Now Riva, having learned that the man's sister is a doctor at the Free Clinic, is calling in her chits.

"What you're asking," the doctor says, "is against our rules."

"I know."

The doctor stares at her, torn. Then she makes a tortured decision. "What do you want to know? Maybe there's some way I can help you without violating my oath."

"Did Emma Lancaster come here for a pregnancy test?"

The doctor looks away. "I can't tell you that," she says.

This is going to require some finessing. "Okay. Let me ask you this. If Emma Lancaster thought she was pregnant and wanted to find out without her parents knowing, is this where she could come? Is this where girls like her would come?"

The doctor nods. "Yes."

"And if she was pregnant, you would tell her?"

"Yes."

"And offer her counseling?"

"Yes."

"Do you give her options? Adoption, keeping the baby, abortion?"

Another yes.

"In the case of a girl like Emma—young, from a family that will freak out if they find out, whatever—is the usual choice to have an abortion?"

The doctor hesitates. "The girl makes that choice. We never make it for her. We give her all the options, and what the pros and cons of each one are."

"If she chooses to have an abortion, is it performed in the clinic?"

"It depends on how long she's been pregnant. We only do first trimester procedures. Anything beyond that, we refer her to an outside physician who makes arrangements to have it done at a hospital."

"So if Emma Lancaster was pregnant and wanted to have an

abortion, and wanted it done here because she was afraid that going to a doctor would mean her parents would find out, she would have to make the decision within the first three months of her pregnancy."

"Yes."

Riva thinks about how to finesse this last part. "You can't tell me specifically that Emma Lancaster came here to be tested for pregnancy."

The doctor nods. "No, I can't tell you that."

"Would you tell me if she *hadn't* come here to see you?"

"If she hadn't been my patient, I'd tell you that, sure."

"So you won't tell me she wasn't your patient."

The doctor thinks. "I won't tell you that, no."

"And you won't tell me that you didn't counsel her on having an abortion."

"I won't tell you that, that's correct."

"So if she had been your patient, and had tested positive for pregnancy, and had wanted an abortion, and wanted it performed here, you would have told her that for you to do that, the abortion would have to be done within the first thirteen weeks."

"Yes. That's what I would have told her."

According to the coroner's report, Emma Lancaster was about three months pregnant when she died. If she had been planning on having an abortion done here, with this doctor she trusted not to tell anyone, especially her parents, she would have had to have it done almost immediately.

"One last question," Riva says. "You're *not* saying Emma Lancaster was *not* your patient and she *didn't* come to you to do an abortion."

The doctor nods solemnly. "Yes. I'm *not* saying that."

It's the end of the day. Luke and Riva meet in the office to exchange information. Outside in the corridors, students are getting ready for evening classes to start. In the past few weeks, as his presence has become more commonplace, a few of the bolder ones have tried to initiate conversation. Politely but firmly he's rebuffed them—they can't help him, they'd only be a distraction. And he's paranoid that one or more might be a plant, either by Doug Lancaster or Ray Logan, to find out what he knows and where he's going. He's friendly, but he keeps his own counsel. Riva follows his course, although she's gregarious by nature and would like to make some friends here.

She fills him in on her visit to the clinic.

Luke smiles at her in appreciation. "You're an incredible sleuth, Riva, the way you get people to talk to you, to open up. I'd be lost without you."

"I'm glad you've figured that out," she says, feeling almost shy at his praise.

All the new information has energized Luke. "This is one dysfunctional family," he declares. "I've seen some pretty amazing cases in my day, but the Lancasters take the prize."

"But does their behavior make a difference to your case? Directly," she asks, playing the devil's advocate.

"How much more evidence do you need before you think there's something rotten at the core of this?" he grouses.

"I don't know," she says. "It's not my decision, you're his lawyer. I'm worried that all this muck will ooze to the surface, and it'll turn out that none of it is relevant to this case, and all these people, including this dead girl, will be crucified." She's much calmer than he is. "And I dispute that they're dysfunctional. It's only sex. Men and women having extramarital sex. In our society, that's not dysfunctional, it's normal."

"And a thirteen-year-old girl?"

"Not so uncommon, either."

"It's a lethal combination," he says doggedly.

"But is it the best way for you to defend Joe Allison?"

He takes a beer out of the small cube refrigerator, twists the top off, hits on it. "It's the best one I have until a better one comes along."

Neither has eaten all day; they're both famished. "I'm tired of ordering in," Riva says. "I want a good meal in a good restaurant with a good bottle of wine and good service." She walks around the office, turning off the computers and the lights. "Take me to the best place in town." She gives him a supportive hug. "You can't cloister yourself forever, Luke."

It's true he's been avoiding public contact. It's a small town, wherever you go you're going to run into someone who knows you. He hasn't wanted to deal with the negative vibes, the smirking looks and sniping behind-the-hand remarks.

"Okay," he says, relenting. She's right—he has to be in the world. Hiding from your demons is the coward's way.

It's late, but they luck out and get a last-minute cancellation at Downey's, one of the city's premier restaurants. A quick trip home, fast shower and spiff up, then the drive back down the hill in the old truck. "The brakes're getting mushy," he comments as he navigates a hairpin turn. "We need to take it to Midas."

They find a parking spot on the street a block away. Walking arm in arm with Riva along State Street, mingling easily into the early-evening pedestrian gumbo, he ruminates on all the nice things he likes about this little city. The old, stylish, unforced Spanish architecture, the ease of moving around, the friendships he used to have, the quality of life—sophisticated enough for his taste, but unhurried. He misses it more than he'd realized.

The restaurant is one white-washed room separated into sections by waist-high partitions. Candles and fresh-cut flowers are on each table, and California landscapes by local painters adorn the walls. The place is only three-quarters full, but all the tables not yet in use have "reserved" signs on them—the chef-owner is nationally renowned.

The maitre d' leads them to a table in the back. Luke didn't realize he'd been apprehensive until he'd walked the gauntlet from the door to their table and taken his seat, his back to the room. Riva has the good seat; looking over his shoulder, she can survey the entire scene. He's happy to have it this way.

"Care for a cocktail?" The waitress, a young, smiling woman wearing the restaurant's uniform of starched white blouse and black skirt, stands poised over them.

"Champagne," Riva says, before Luke can voice a choice. "Two glasses."

The waitress hands them menus. "Take your time," she says. "If you need anything explained, let me know." She goes to get their drinks.

Luke lays his menu aside, smiling at Riva across the table. He's enjoying her attention, reaching under the table and stroking her ankle as it teases his thigh. "As long as you're running the show, you can order for me."

"No *problema,* big boy." She scans the menu. "Everything looks yummy. How hungry are you?"

"I could eat . . ." He grins lasciviously at her.

"Don't say it," she says, grinning back, her foot moving further up his leg.

"Good evening, Dr. Tenley." The maitre d's voice drifts back to them through the low-pitched fog of dinner conversation.

"Hello, Wilber," a woman's voice says in greeting.

Luke hears the voice. He tenses.

"We have your table ready." The maitre d's voice again.

"Thank you." Again, the woman's voice.

The waitress places two flutes of pale champagne in front of them, tightly clustered bubbles rising up the center of the slender glasses. Riva raises hers in toast. "To our fun evening," she says. "All night long."

He's transfixed, the glass sitting untouched in front of him.

She looks at him, perplexed. "Luke?"

"Luke?" From behind them, a woman's questioning voice. The voice that had greeted the maitre d'.

Glacially, he turns. The woman, her stomach now so distended he can see her protruding belly button through the fabric of her maternity dress, is standing a few feet behind their table.

"Hello, Polly," he says, his mouth going dry. He lumbers to his feet.

"Hello, Luke." Her dark blond hair is cut shorter than when they were together, above her shoulders—trouble-free hair, mommy hair. Green eyes, Irish porcelain complexion now mottled red from the nervousness of this unexpected encounter. Behind her a few paces, her husband, the man Luke saw her with at the beachfront when he first came back to town, hovers awkwardly, a half smile on his face, not knowing how he's supposed to be reacting, what his place in this is.

"You look . . . good," she says. "Different."

"You too. You look very different. I mean good. Both," he fumbles, feeling ridiculous. He forces a smile, glancing at her protruding tummy.

She smiles back. "D-Day's approaching," she says lightly.

"You have a son, too, don't you?" he says. Riva has gotten up from her chair and is standing at his shoulder. She reaches out and takes his hand and squeezes. He squeezes back.

Polly nods. "Eighteen months old." She rubs her stomach. "They'll be a year and a half apart."

"You moved fast," he says, wishing he hadn't said that, wanting to bite his tongue off.

She looks him in the eyes. "I wasn't getting any younger."

Her husband is standing next to her now. She turns and smiles at him. Turning back, she says, "Luke, this is Grant, my husband. Grant Tenley." To her husband she says, "This is Luke Garrison . . ." She hesitates.

"Hello," Luke says, extending his hand. The man reaches out and shakes it. His grip is firm.

"Grant's a surgeon. At Cottage," she adds, as if naming the best hospital in town confers added prestige on him. "We're a two-doctor family," she says, smiling.

"I know," Luke replies. He knows more about the new husband than he wants to.

There's a moment's awkwardness, then he pulls Riva forward. "Polly, I'd like to introduce you to my—"

In the nanosecond that elapses, his brain flashes wilder than the speed of light: *Lover-mate-significant other-friend-associate-partner-mistress-companion . . .*

Screeching halt.

"—my woman. Riva Montoya."

Her hand is gripping his fiercely. Then she releases it. She holds her hand out to Polly. "Nice to meet you. Congratulations."

Polly shakes Riva's hand. Polly's is moist. "Thanks, I guess," she says modestly, a slight blush playing on her neck.

"When are you due?" Riva asks, woman to woman.

"Any day now, I hope." Polly laughs, a nervous-friendly laugh. "I feel like a monster cow, all I want to do is spit this out."

"I'll bet. Boy or girl?" Riva asks. "Do you know?"

Polly nods. "Another boy. At my age you do an amnio."

Luke, watching the byplay between the two women, is surprised at his calm.

"Do you have children?" Polly asks Riva.

"Not yet," Riva answers, without a trace of guile.

"Someday." Luke hears the word coming out of his mouth. It takes him by surprise, but it doesn't feel wrong.

Riva stares at him, struggling to contain her astonishment. This time he takes her hand.

"That's . . . I hope you do," Polly says to him.

He smiles at her. Man, she really is large. Do they all get this big? But she's still pretty. Still Polly.

He doesn't love her. That's why he's so calm, why words about a future with someone else come so easily, so effortlessly.

What a wonderful revelation! He feels like the weight of the world has been suddenly lifted off his shoulders. And he also realizes how, subconsciously, he's been burdening himself with the memory of their relationship, and his fantasies about it. Which is what they were, he now knows. Fantasies. Wishes. Historical rewritings. But not the real thing.

Standing here with her and Riva, he knows he doesn't love her anymore, knows he's really happy Riva is standing here with him. Goddamn, he's lucky she stuck with him through all his shit.

"Well . . ." Polly says. The awkwardness is returning now. As much from her as from him.

Luke leans over and kisses her on the cheek. Then he touches her belly. "Good luck," he says.

"Thank you."

It's over. The couples retreat to their respective tables.

"Would you like to change seats?" Riva asks, glancing at Polly and her husband over his shoulder. She doesn't know what's happened, exactly, but she knows something has, and that it's good for her. For them.

He shakes his head. "I'm comfortable where I am." Reaching across the table and taking her hand, he adds, "Very comfortable." He lifts his still-bubbling glass of champagne. "To a fun evening," he says, repeating her earlier toast. "To a wonderful life."

She has tears in her eyes. "I hate it when I get sentimental like this."

He reaches across the table and dabs gently at her eyes with his napkin. "Don't worry about it. It's sexy."

"You find the weirdest things sexy." She's forcing a smile through her tears.

"You," he tells her. "What I find sexy is you."

They lie in bed, naked, under one thin sheet. The windows are open, the breeze coming up the mountain off the ocean ruffles the curtains, stirs the sheet. Long, languid kisses, touches. He feels a glow coming off both their bodies, a heat passing back and forth. His tongue caresses her dark nipples and she moans softly, sliding in rhythm to his touch.

"I'll be right back," she whispers, tonguing his ear. She starts to push the sheet aside so she can get up and go into the bathroom, to put in her diaphragm.

"Stay." He pushes her back down onto the mattress. The mattress is moist, their bodies are moist and salty.

Her eyes, dark, large, stare at him with intensity. "Are you sure?"

"*I* am. Are you?"

"You're not reacting to tonight?" she asks.

"I *am* reacting to tonight. That's why I want to. With you."

She pulls his face to hers and kisses him fiercely, kisses him with a freedom that comes with love and the assurance, finally, of being loved, and knowing they're going someplace new and where it will take them she doesn't know or care but she wants to go there, she wants to go there because he wants to, because he's able to.

The private detective, who's from Houston and has a well-earned national reputation—his fees match those of top lawyers, and he has clients lined up months in advance—has been in Santa Barbara for three weeks. Doug Lancaster hired him because he's the best in the business, and because he isn't from Santa Barbara or anyplace close. This detective, Paul Bowie by name, is known for getting results without leaving any footprints. When his job is done he's gone, and his quarry is none the wiser.

Doug meets with Bowie in a private cabana at the Coral Casino, a swanky exclusive beachfront swim club across Channel Drive from the Biltmore Hotel. The media mogul has just swum a mile in the pool; he tries to swim thirty to forty minutes every other day, in the pool or the ocean, as part of his workout regimen. Bowie has information for Doug. It's contained in an oversized manila envelope. They wait to discuss business while the white-jacketed waiter serves them lunch. Bowie hands Doug the envelope. Doug opens it, slides out the contents.

There's a written report, and photographs, eight-by-ten color glossies.

The photographs were taken with a long lens. They show Luke Garrison with Huerta, the car attendant from the Santa Monica hotel; Riva with Hillary, Emma's friend; Luke and Nicole Rogers in the entranceway of her law firm; Luke talking to the old couple who were Joe Allison's landlords; Luke's trashed motorcycle.

Luke Garrison's been covering the waterfront, Doug can see that at a glance.

Bowie picks up the report. It's about twenty pages thick. "He's interviewed the police, whose work was sloppy, because they were under the gun. Nothing should come of it, but he might make some noise. And he has the phone number of the, uh, lady you're seeing down there in Malibu. He hasn't contacted her yet, because the phone's registered in her husband's name—a business acquaintance of yours, if I'm not mistaken."

"You're not," Doug says curtly.

"Yeah. Well, like I said, he hasn't pursued that angle yet, but if he does, you'll be embarrassed."

"I can handle that. I want to know what Garrison knows that could put Allison's conviction in doubt."

"Your daughter's pregnancy." He shakes his report, holding on to a corner. "That's in the record, in the autopsy report."

Doug looks stricken. "That was supposed to be sealed," he says. He lays the pictures down, increasingly annoyed. "Ray Logan was supposed to keep a lid on that."

Bowie, in turn, is getting annoyed with his client's naivete—a man of this caliber should be hipper. "There's no way Logan could do that," he tells Doug. "It's part of the record. The defense has the right to see everything in the record, sealed or not. Anyway," he continues, "the prosecutor's going to use that at trial, you've always known that. It's the most important part of his case."

"They're going to crucify my daughter. Desecrate her memory." Doug grips his iced tea so hard, Bowie's fearful he's going to shatter the glass. Taking a deep breath, he collects himself. "But why would Emma's being pregnant help Garrison help Allison? It should sink them, shouldn't it?"

Bowie leans forward, tapping his large fingers on Doug's knee. "I hate to be the one who breaks this to you, Mr. Lancaster, but sheltering you from the truth isn't what you're paying me for." He wolfs down the last of his fries. "Your daughter was not the sweet little girl you're remembering. Rumors are starting to fly around town that she was involved with more than the one guy who got her pregnant."

"What do you mean?" Doug asks slowly, his voice chilly.

"Your daughter Emma was screwing around *before* she met the stud who knocked her up," the man says bluntly.

"How could she have been?" Doug blurts out, his voice rising. Conscious of his surroundings—the cabana's walls are made of canvas—he lowers his pitch. "We would have known!"

Bowie's philosophical about Doug's behavior. He's seen worse. He's also used to the scorn and anger that comes with the information he dispenses; he's the messenger, the blame falls on him. "It happens, Mr. Lancaster," he says calmly. "You're going to have to come to grips with the fact that her history is going to be part of the trial."

Doug composes himself. He slips the pictures and report into the manila envelope. "Thanks for your effort. Have your office send me a bill." He opens the cabana door-flap, escorts Bowie out. People are scattered about the sides of the pool, reading in deck chairs and reclining on chaise longues, mostly middle-aged women but a few lookers, Bowie notices appreciatively, young housewives and teenage daughters.

"I'm sorry I was the bearer of the bad news about your daughter, Mr. Lancaster," he says. "But you needed to know."

Doug, a father aggrieved, stares at him. "I didn't want to. I didn't want anyone to."

The call comes to the office late, when Luke's wrapping his work up after a long day. Classes are finished for the evening, the building is dark; down the hall, through his open door, he can hear the vacuuming of the cleaning crew. He still has material to read, but he'll take it back to the house, even though it's Friday night.

He picks up the phone.

"Luke Garrison, please." A woman's voice, an efficient secretary. His own part-time secretary leaves on the stroke of five; this is a high-powered executive secretary who works at her boss's beck and call and is paid well to do so.

Hedging, he asks, "Who's calling?"

Too late to duck the call—she's already made the connection, as soon as she heard his voice.

Doug Lancaster comes on the line. "Luke? Luke Garrison?"

He doesn't need this now. Not this late at night, or any night, or any day for that matter. "Yeah?" he mutters.

"Can we talk?"

Luke sighs. "Go ahead, Doug. But make it short. I've had a long day and I have work yet to do."

"Not over the phone. I want to talk to you face to face."

Luke holds the speaker away from his ear for a moment, contemplating. Then he brings it up again. "We're on opposite sides of a legal action, you know that." Suddenly paranoid, he asks, "Are you taping this call, by any chance?"

"No, of course not," comes the immediate, irate answer. Almost too immediate, Luke thinks.

"What about your secretary? Is she listening in? Taking notes?"

"No one's listening in, or taking notes, or anything else," Doug tells him.

Was that a click Luke heard, someone replacing an extension phone on the cradle? "Okay," he says. "But you did hear me, right? If you want to talk with me, have your attorney or Ray Logan's office contact me so we can set this up through official channels. Now, good night, Doug. Have a pleasant weekend."

"Wait!" The plea comes so fast he doesn't have time to move the receiver from his ear.

A long sigh. "What? We can't talk, don't try to force this." A thought comes to him—start taping your calls, for your own protection.

"The autopsy report," Doug says hurriedly. He can't not keep talking. "My daughter was not a tramp." The man's voice is rising, he's definitely losing it.

Luke says nothing. But he can't bring himself to hang up, either. His morbid curiosity about where this is going overwhelms his better judgment.

"She was a sweet, young, wonderful girl." Doug isn't yelling—it's almost as if he's pleading. "And you can't drag her through the mud. You can't drag this girl's reputation through the gutter for everyone to see."

The voice breaks; he's almost crying, Luke realizes.

"I don't care what the D.A. says or does, or what he has to do. *You* don't have to, Luke. You don't have to destroy the little that's left of her. She's dead, man. Isn't that enough? What more do you and your pedophile client want?"

There's a click on the line. Luke's day is over.

Leisurely cruising west out of town in the old glasspack pick-up, heading up Highway 101. The truck's handling is harsher than normal—he needs to get the brakes and shocks attended to. He drives slowly, giving himself plenty of space between the truck and other traffic on the road.

It's Sunday morning, crack of dawn. Up at 4:30 and on the road by five. At this hour on a weekend there's little traffic. He drives past the oil terminus at Gaviota, which operates 24 hours a day and looks, with all the polished metal and running lights and tubing, like a docking station out in space, turns off 101 at the state beach, and heads south towards the ocean. His excitement grows as he nears his destination—he hasn't surfed Hollister Ranch for over three years.

He's alone. Riva flew up north yesterday to check on her business and look in on her house, she won't be back until late Monday night. The trial is coming up in less than a month, and knowing all too well that he'll be working eighteen-hour days, seven days a week, he's allowing himself a day off.

Hollister Ranch is one of the legendary California surfing spots. Originally a huge oceanfront ranch, it was subdivided generations back into 100-acre parcels; up to a dozen people can share ownership in a lot. Most of the parcel-holders don't live there—they have the property so they can use the beach. Unless you own a parcel, or are the guest of an owner, you can't get on the beach—it's private, patrolled by security. If an intruder is caught, he's unceremoniously booted out or arrested.

The beauty of surfing Hollister, aside from the waves, is the exclusivity—you aren't jaw to asshole with other surfers out in the water. And everything's pristine, a piece of the world as it used to be in the good old days.

Luke has owned a parcel for years. It's the only thing in Santa Barbara county he held onto. About the only smart thing he did in that period of his life.

He leaves the county hardtop and drives a short distance down an access road. There's a guarded gate, attended around the clock. He shows the attendant his ID. The gate swings open. He gets back in the truck and drives through, the gate closing automatically behind him.

He rides along a winding road that parallels the ocean, crossing the railroad tracks, where he parks his truck next to some nondescript sedans, a vintage '49 Ford woodie station wagon, and another truck almost as old and beat up as his. There are also newer cars, mostly SUVs, Explorers, Range Rovers, Toyota Land Cruisers. Peeling off his T-shirt and shorts, he pulls on his wetsuit, grabs his board from the truck bed, his Igloo cooler and his daypack with his towel and other necessities from the front seat, and walks towards the ocean.

Standing at the water's edge, he looks out to sea. The waves are good—four to seven feet, long, regular lines. Out in the water he sees half a dozen other surfers—from this distance it looks like four men and two women—spread out over a couple hundred yards. Hard-core wave riders—he was up before the sun and yet there are people already in the water ahead of him. He remembers when he was younger, just beginning to surf here, sleeping on the beach so he could roll out of his bag and hit the water before the sun was up.

A big wave starts to form a hundred feet out from where the surfers are lined up. Two of them, about twenty yards from each other, start paddling furiously, getting into position. The wave picks up momentum, then it's cresting, and the surfers are straining to catch it, and they do, they rise to their feet. They catch it clean, dropping and turning with the wave as it breaks towards shore, both of them riding all the way in to the beach.

Luke's seen enough—he needs to be out there in the water, pronto. He tosses his board into the surf and starts paddling out, pushing his way past the breakers. He hasn't surfed for a few months, not since that time at Rincon, and he can feel the muscles straining in his chest and arms. He'll be sore tomorrow, a good sore.

He gets past the shorebreak into open water, leisurely paddles out to where it looks like he can catch some waves without crowding anyone else, setting up at the high end of the point, twenty-five yards from the nearest surfer. A few of them closest to him glance over as he paddles out, reserving judgment—they'll see how he does, but unless he messes up, he gets the benefit of the doubt. This isn't cutthroat, like down south in parts of L.A. and Orange counties, where surf gangs establish territories, breaking boards and heads if a stranger, or anyone they don't want there, which is everyone except them, tries to surf.

He takes it easy at first; conservative maneuvers, nothing audacious. The regulars watch him a few times until they see he knows what he's doing, then they ignore him, which is fine with him. He wants to surf, be in the water, be left alone.

Often, in times past, there would be people his age, or older, out in the lineup, but today he's the oldest by a good decade.

He's a "pops." He never thought he'd see that day.

He surfs until the sun peaks, midday. Hungry, he rides in, carries his board ashore, props it up in the sand to give himself some shade, peels his suit down to his waist, and eats his lunch, a couple of tuna-fish sandwiches he picked up at a Von's deli, a bag of jalapeño chips, a lemon Snapple. He's in good shape for an old guy who doesn't work out as much as he should—lean torso, flat stomach, swimmer's muscles across his back and triceps. But he's already sore in his muscles, he'll have to marshall his strength if he wants to make it through to the end of the day.

He rests for about an hour, then goes back out again. It's not the best time of the day to ride, the surf is flattening in the midday tide, and the sun is hot on the water. He doesn't care. This is his last time to be out on the ocean for months, he's going to milk every minute, until it's too dark to see.

Slowly, then gradually faster, the day slips away. A few other diehards hang on until near the end, but finally, as the sun is dipping into the ocean, a huge fuchsia meltdown, he's the only one out there.

Then, like a window blind being abruptly drawn, it's dark. There's enough residual light left, along with some splotchy moonlight, for him to ride in one last time, which is all he has in him anyway. He's bone-weary, but it's been a great day. He's drained, happily wrung out. A long hot shower, the stinging needles massaging his body, then dinner, a good bottle of wine, and he'll be asleep before his head hits the pillow, dreaming of waves and Riva's warmth.

A big wave is breaking behind him. A good one to ride home on. He sees the foam on the lip, phosphorescent in the moonlight. He paddles in rhythm, feeling the speed of the wave, then he's on his feet on his board, riding one last time.

It's a big wave, long, it's going to be a long ride, one of the best of the day, he's tucking in, almost getting under the curl, his legs are still steady and strong. He rides forward, crouching down on the nose of his board, the power and speed exhilarating.

He takes a quick hop-step back as he nears the shoulder, and as he does the board shatters under him, right where his foot had been an instant before, it explodes into thousands of shards like it had hit a land mine, one second he's balancing on a nine-foot surfboard and the next second he's going under, and then he hears the sound, the delayed sound of the rifle firing, carrying across the water from the shore. Echoing. The water explodes two inches from his body, and then he hears another delayed sound.

Someone's out there in the dark, trying to kill him.

Treading water, he looks towards the shore, over a hundred yards away. There's nothing there, it's all black. Past the beach he can see the outline of the low bluffs, a dark blotch against the night-time sky. Someone is up there with a rifle. The rifle has an infra-red night scope, the shots were too close to be that accurate with a regular scope in this non-light, which means that even though there isn't much moon, he can be seen clearly, he can't hide in the dark water.

Another explosion hits a few feet from him. The shooter's good, he's honing in. Taking a deep breath, he dives under and starts swimming in what he thinks is a sideways direction, not directly towards the beach.

He swims underwater as long as he can, and then comes up for air, and less than a second later, there's another shot, right by him again, he's being tracked with that night scope, the motion of his swimming can be detected, even if his actual body can't be seen. Treading water for a moment, his lungs burning, he goes under again on a diagonal as yet another shot explodes the water, right where he was. One second's more hesitation and the bullet would have hit him. Even a nonlethal shot will kill him, he'll never make it to shore if he's wounded.

He can't stay out here long, he's too tired, too muscle-fatigued. The lactic acid buildup will kick in and he'll freeze up, unable to move his muscles well enough to swim strongly. And the water feels much colder because he's tired, even with his wetsuit on he feels the chill. He won't be able to stay underwater as long as he'd like, because he needs the air, he has to come up for it, already his lungs are starting to feel as if they're catching fire. When he comes up the rifle will find him, the shooter knows what he's doing, it's a matter of time. How long the shooter will stay up there, firing down at him, before he worries about someone hearing the shots, is the only question.

He has to get to shore, before the fatigue and the cold make it too hard to swim fast enough and move around enough to have any chance at all of dodging the sniper. He has to take the chance that he can swim in without getting hit, at least not fatally, then make a run for it once he gets to the beach and finds safety under the edge of the bluff. His cell phone is in his daypack. If he can make it to temporary safety under the bluff, he can call 911. He knows his chances aren't good, they're terrible, but if he stays out here in the middle of the water he's a duck in a shooting arcade.

He swims underwater towards the beach, making as little motion as possible. He sculls his hands along his body and tries to pretend he's a dolphin, a natural swimming machine.

His muscles, particularly his chest, triceps, and stomach, feel like they've been attacked by a sledgehammer. The dark black–green water is getting colder—he feels his strength rapidly ebbing away. His lungs are bursting. He has to come up.

He surfaces, gasping instant breath, then immediately down again, the water directly over his head catching the bullet, a few quick sideways strokes then up for real air this time, gulping it down, taking the chance he has a second or two, the shooter didn't anticipate that move, he breathes in, out, deep breath in and dive, and immediately another shot, exactly where he was.

Zigzagging his way through the water, forcing himself to push through the pain, he gets closer to shore, each time when he emerges to gasp for breath knowing that the closer he comes to whoever wants to kill him, the easier it will be. Maybe the shooter will run out of bullets—about the only realistic chance he has.

He's almost to shore now and somehow the shooter hasn't been able to hit him. A miracle.

Except it's no miracle, he realizes with dread. It's deliberate. Every single bullet that's been fired has hit within six inches or less of its target: him. You don't consistently miss by that little bit unless you want to. This shooter isn't someone who can't quite find his target—just the opposite. This is a marksman who knows exactly what he's doing.

The problem, Luke realizes, is what if the shooter misses by that little bit, and hits me? I'm dead, that's the problem.

He's still moving while his mind races, he's in knee deep water now and he's running, immediately diving to the ground and rolling, the shot this time catching the water less than five inches from his body, the bastard's toying with him, he's up again running through the surf, it feels like he's running in slow motion, then he's onto the shore, another dive to the sand, this time sideways, the bullet hitting an inch, literally, from his head, kicking sand into his face, he can feel the power of the explosion, then he's up and running for the safety of the bluff, where the hunter can't get to him, accidentally or deliberately, not from up there, and as he's running, zigging and zagging, another shot rings out, now he's close enough to the shooter that the sound and the impact come simultaneously, and he feels the burn in his left side above his hip, the pain immediate and excruciating, a hot poker-slash.

He goes down.

Don't stay down, don't stay down, now that you're hit the shooter has to finish you off, he's crawling on his hands and knees, as slow as a turtle, it feels like, instinctively rolling again, by some miracle, this one major—a true act of God—the next shot, which he knows was meant to hit him doesn't—it misses.

And then he's under the bluff, protected enough that the shooter doesn't have a shot.

He's safe. Until the shooter comes down to the beach to finish him off.

He puts his hand to his side. It comes away red, sticky. But the gods are with him today, the shot didn't hit bone or anything vital. An inch lower and it would have hit his hip, would have shattered it, he would be unable to move.

He would have been lying there, writhing in agony and fear when whoever wants to kill him walked down and blew him away.

He claws open his daypack and gets the cell phone out—*dear God and all the gods of all the religions, I know I have sinned, enough for a hundred lifetimes, but please don't be out of range, or blocked by this bluff*—and he gets the police operator, truly the gods are with him today, he screams at her, where he is, what happened, hearing his voice carrying up in the wind, and on the bluff above him he hears a door slam, a car motor starting up, the screeching of tires on dirt, the sound of the car fading.

He collapses to his hands and knees, vomits up his lunch, and starts to shake uncontrollably.

The security patrol, the paramedics, and the highway patrol arrive almost simultaneously. The lead security man, an old surfer who isn't used to this kind of violence, is twitching with apology when he discovers who the victim is. "We were on the other end of the ranch, we run a skeleton crew on Sunday."

Luke waves the man off. "I'm not blaming anybody," he grunts, feeling the pain of the wound, now a dull, throbbing ache, which the paramedic is dressing. "But I do want you to get your people out here and try to find out who did it." He turns to the cop, who earlier took his statement. "You, too. Or call the sheriff's office, if it's their jurisdiction." He knows it is, he wants this cop to know he knows.

"We're handling it," the trooper says flatly. He also knows who Luke Garrison is, and he couldn't give a shit less.

"We're ready to take you to the hospital," the paramedic tells him, finishing his patch job. "Any preference?"

"Cottage. Have someone drive my truck down there," he charges the private officer, flipping the keys to the man. "And the rest of my stuff," he says. He's carrying his clothes and daypack with him.

"It'll be taken care of," the security cop promises.

The state trooper's been on the horn. "Someone from the sheriff's office will meet you at the hospital, to interview you. I'm going to go up top and take a look, see how many spent shells I can find," he says, letting Luke know he's on the job.

"If you run a metal detector over the sand," Luke says, pointing back to where he was hit, "you should find some bullets, too."

"I'll pass that on to the sheriff's department," is the reply.

Taking one last look at the bloody patch he left on the sand, he climbs into the paramedic's van and lies down on the bench.

"You are one lucky fella," the emergency room doctor comments as he patches Luke up. "One inch lower, shattered hip. One inch to the left, bye-bye kidney."

"Yeah, I'm lucky," Luke says without irony. He's alive, therefore he's lucky.

It's a relatively clean in-and-out. There's minor muscle damage, and he's going to be sore for a few days—his torso will be black and blue. The doctor inserts a drain and gives Luke a tetanus shot and some antibiotics. "Do you have your own physician?" he asks.

"Not anymore here." He winces as the doctor probes.

"Come back tomorrow and I'll check this," the doctor says, meaning the drain. "We want to make sure this is clear." He starts bandaging the wound.

Luke's already talked to Riva; he called her as soon as the wound was examined and the doctor was satisfied it wasn't life-threatening. She freaked out, predictably.

"You're getting off this case!" she screamed at him.

"Calm down," he told her, surprised by his own placidity over the phone. In that paramedic's van on the way to the hospital he had trembled for a long time.

Inwardly, he was still shaking.

"It's too late to get a flight tonight. I'll come back tomorrow morning, as early as I can."

"Stay there and finish what you have to do," he'd said. "It's over now."

She was adamant over the phone. He was not risking his life for a client.

Which was all well and good. He shouldn't. But there is another facet to this, and it's monumental. Joe Allison didn't take that shot at him—Joe Allison's in jail. Someone else has a huge investment in this, so huge he is willing to commit murder. And the understanding of that enrages him. He will, absolutely, not abandon this case.

Earlier, within minutes of his being admitted, the press showed up. A reporter and two-person camera crew from Doug Lancaster's television station (talk about irony), reporters and camera crews from other papers and stations. They're waiting outside, hoping for a statement.

The doctor finishes with his bandaging. "Do you feel all right to drive?" he asks. Luke's truck is parked outside, delivered to the door by a ranch security driver. The driver had a message from the security company: they wanted Luke to know they'd cover all his medical bills, they had already phoned the hospital to make the arrangements, and if there was anything else he needed, he shouldn't hesitate to call. Anything to forestall a lawsuit, he thinks. The corporate mentality.

He's stiff, but he can move around. Tomorrow's when it'll be bad. And the days after. "Yeah, I'll be okay to drive home," he assures the doctor. And have a drink. Several. "Can I take a shower?" He wonders if he should stay in the house tonight or check into a hotel.

"Uh-huh. The bandage'll hold. Try not to get it too wet." He hands Luke a packet of pills. "Take two of the antibiotics and one of these before you go to bed," he says. "That'll knock you out so you can sleep."

Luke struggles into his T-shirt. He feels sticky from the salt water, sand, blood. "Thanks for the help," he says, shaking the doc's hand.

"Glad to be of. You really are lucky. Count your blessings."

Luke signs the release forms and walks stiffly, slowly into the lobby. The reporters start to rush him. He puts up a hand to stop them. "I'm going to make a brief statement," he says, "and that's all. No questions, please." He stands as erect as he can, looking straight ahead. "Here's what happened. Someone shot at me while I was up at the Hollister Ranch beach, swimming and surfing. It was dark, I don't know who it was." He pauses. "I was hit, once, luckily a minor wound. The police have interviewed me, and hopefully they'll be able to shed some light on this."

He starts to push through the crowd. As they're making way, a reporter blurts out, "Do you think this was motivated by your defending Joe Allison, and is that going to be affected by your being shot at?"

He turns to the questioner. "What do you mean?"

"Might you not withdraw from this case because someone tried to shoot at you? Aren't the shooting and your client and your defense of him connected?"

"I don't know the reason I was shot at," he says, trying to stay calm, "so I haven't thought about that." A blatant lie. Of course that's the reason the sniper was trying to kill him, and he's thought of little else since. "Now please—I need to speak to the police, and I need to go home."

He and the sheriff's detective go into an empty examining room, where they have some privacy. Luke gives the man a statement, basically the same one he's already given where the shooting took place: he doesn't know who shot at him, he has no idea regarding who it might be specifically, he knows there are many people in the community, including the dead girl's parents, who don't want him on this case, it's pretty clear from his motorcycle being trashed, the hostility he's encountered, et cetera. Beyond that, he doesn't want to speculate.

The detective leaves. He's finally on his own. He starts for the exit door.

Ray Logan, huffing like a locomotive, comes rushing in, almost colliding with Luke. Logan's wearing a Big Dog golf shirt and Bermuda shorts—the first time Luke's ever seen him not in long pants. A glance at his former assistant's spindly, milk white legs explains why.

"I just heard," Logan says breathlessly. "Are you all right? I guess you are," he adds, "if you're walking out of here on your own."

"It was only a flesh wound," Luke hears himself saying, almost laughing at the absurdity of it. He feels like John Wayne, or Clint Eastwood.

"Have you talked to the police yet?"

"Twice, once out there, then here. I just finished giving my statement."

"This is horrible," Logan says. "Sheriff Williams is outraged. We all are."

"So do something about it." He's angry, tired, frightened. He feels an overwhelming lassitude coming over him. He wants out of here.

"We're going to, believe me. But before you go, can we talk for a minute?" Logan is flushed, anxious.

"I'm beat, Ray. Getting shot takes the starch out of you."

"Just for a minute?" The man is almost begging.

They walk into a small empty lounge off the main desk area. Slowly and stiffly Luke sits on an orange Naugahyde bench. Why do hospitals go for the ugliest colors? he wonders as Logan sits catty-corner from him. To remind you that you're in a house of pain?

"What do you want, Ray?" He doesn't bother to cover his impatience. He was just shot, almost killed. He should be allowed his space. So he can shake in private.

"First, let me say how appalled I am at this," Logan says. "I don't know who in the world would do something like this."

Luke starts to laugh, but it hurts too much, so he stuffs it as best he can. Jesus, this hurts, it throbs. He wants to get out of here, go home and take those pain pills. "I can think of a few people who would love to see me out of the way, permanently. Starting with Doug Lancaster."

"You can't be serious." Logan is flushing red from the mention of it.

Luke tells him about the frenzied telephone call he had from Doug Lancaster Friday night. "There was an implied threat in that call. Almost an overt warning."

Logan whistles. "Damn. He shouldn't be calling you. He shouldn't have any contact with you."

"That's what I told him. But he wouldn't shut up, he went on and on about his daughter's reputation being tarnished. Like it isn't going to be, anyway."

Logan nods somberly. "I have to tell Doug to stay away from this."

There's an itch inside Luke to tell this pink-faced, jittery man sitting in front of him, this man who still seems cowed by his former boss, about the bribe Doug Lancaster laid on him. Logan would have a heart attack, and then he'd never get to go home. No, keep that for when it's really useful, such as when he's cross-examining Lancaster on the stand.

"Here's something you might not know," he says. "Doug Lancaster's whereabouts can't be accounted for between one and nine in the morning on the night Emma was taken from her room."

Logan's face darkens. "Yes," he says cautiously. "I'm aware of that—that rumor. I'm not sure that it's relevant. Or true."

Does he know something about it that I don't? Luke wonders. Does Doug have an alibi for those hours? He needs to check that out before he goes down a blind alley that could bite him in the ass. "Why?" he asks. "Do you know where he was?"

Logan composes himself. "You tell me," he challenges.

"So much for your feeling bad about tonight," Luke flares. "Is that why you came down here? To pump me while I'm feeling like shit? I ought to go to the judge and ask him to sanction you."

He starts to get up. A lightning flash of pain shoots up his left side. He steadies himself, one hand on the couch.

Logan's quick on his feet, assisting Luke. "No. That's not why I came down here. I apologize." He seems truly contrite. "I really was concerned about you."

"Okay." Luke deep-breathes, feeling the pain dull out. "I believe you. But I still think there's dirt around the Lancaster family. I know Doug wasn't in his room, and if you didn't, you'll find out. I also know the Lancasters own property up at Hollister, which would give him access. You might want to look into whether anyone saw him up there today. And check the state gun records, find out if Doug's into guns, especially rifles."

"What about tonight?" Logan asks. "Where are you staying?"

"My house. We've rented a bungalow up on Mountain Drive."

"Do you want protection? I could put a patrol car outside."

Luke thinks about that for a moment. Whoever came after him isn't going to do it in a public, crowded place. If he does try to kill Luke again, it'll be a sneak attack when Luke's alone.

"This sucks," he complains. "I can't go around for the rest of this pretrial and into the trial with a cop on my ass all the time."

"It's your choice. But I think you should, for a few days at least, while the sheriff's office investigates this."

Logan's right. "Okay, the house," he says grudgingly. "It's isolated up there, so okay. But not in public, I don't need to draw that kind of attention."

"Your call. I'll have an officer follow you up." He extends his hand. "We're on opposite sides now, Luke, but that doesn't mean I don't respect you."

He means that. Luke reads it in his eyes.

"You too, Ray." The man's stature just rose in his eyes. "You too."

They walk towards the exit. "I've got to ask you this, Luke," Logan says with a tone of apology. "The trial. Have you thought about withdrawing?"

"I've thought about it," he says. "Lying out there with a gunshot wound in my side, I thought about it plenty, after I knew I wasn't going to die tonight."

"So what do you think you're going to do?" Logan asks. "If you do withdraw it's completely uncontestable, I'd support it, and not because I'm afraid of going up against you. You're a great lawyer, but

I'm not worried about that. I've got a good case, and I'm going to prosecute the hell out of it."

"I'd expect nothing less, Ray."

"But if you are considering it," Logan continues, "you should decide as soon as possible, one way or the other. It would throw a huge monkey wrench into the process. We'd be set back six months, at least."

"Yes, I know." And what lawyer with a brain in his head would take Joe Allison on as a client now? Who's willing to risk his or her life on what's still, objectively looking at it, a loser case?

"I'll give it a day or two, Ray. No more. Then I'll let you know one way or the other. But I promise I won't leave you and everyone else dangling in the wind."

There's an unfamiliar car parked in front of the house as he pulls up, a late model Cadillac Seville, dark burgundy. One man is sitting in front, behind the wheel.

Luke coasts to a stop behind him and cuts the truck lights. He gets out carefully, spotting the police car coming up the hill behind him. He turns to the cops and makes a pointing motion with his hand towards the Cadillac, mouthing the words: "there's someone here." Then he waits, positioning himself behind the big boxy car, while the cops pull up alongside. They shine a light in the window, causing the driver, caught unawares, to throw his arm up as a shield.

Luke relaxes when he sees who it is. "It's okay," he calls out to the cops. "He's friendly." He walks up to the driver's side door and yanks it open. "What are you doing sitting here in the dark like a hit man?" he says to Judge De La Guerra.

Ferdinand looks up at him. "I was waiting for you. I heard about what happened. I came to see how you are."

"I'll survive. Come on in." He walks across the street to where the cops have parked. "A friend. He's harmless."

"That's okay," one of the cops says. "We'll be right here, in case someone who isn't shows up."

"Good deal. Thanks. You want anything?"

The passenger cop holds up a thermos. "We're in good shape.

Another unit'll relieve us at some point, but you're covered round the clock up here."

Inside, keeping the lights low, he pours three fingers of Conmemorativa tequila, the good stuff, into two glasses without asking, hands one to the judge. It's painful to sit down; it's painful to do anything. He needs more drinks, a hot shower, the pain pills of doom. "How'd you hear so fast?" he asks.

"On the radio."

Luke grunts. "It'll be on the tube later on. You can watch me look like a jackass." He raises his glass in toast. "To a goddamn fool, and the misguided do-gooder who led him into this mess. That should cover the two of us." He swallows the tequila down in one gulp, pours another stiff shot.

De La Guerra cradles his glass in his hands. "I'm sorry, Luke."

"Don't be. No one held a gun to my head."

"You had a new life. I should have let you live it."

Luke shakes his head. "I was hiding from my old life. Now I'm not anymore, so it's actually a good thing, someone wanting to kill me notwithstanding."

"But I'm worried about you now, really worried. Your life's in danger. That's more than I ever expected." He pauses. "Who do you think tried this?"

Luke downs his second portion. "Doug Lancaster," he says slowly, drawing out the syllables.

The color slowly begins leaving the judge's ruddy face. "That's a serious accusation, Luke."

"I know. And I'm damn serious about it, too."

He gives the judge all his reasons for suspecting Doug, beginning with the bribe, listing each new transgression in turn. Doug's unaccountability for eight hours on the night his daughter was murdered. His known infidelities, and his wife's knowledge of them. His warning Luke not to pursue Emma's pregnancy as a defense strategy. His ownership of property at Hollister Ranch.

The two sit in silence, holding their drinks.

"And there's something else," Luke says. He's on his third drink, none of which have been timid. The pain is coming on hard now; he needs to wrap this up, have the judge take his leave, and pop some potent relief.

"There's more?" the judge asks. "What more could there be, unless you have an actual confession?"

"You'd better hang on to your chair for this one." He'd laugh if it didn't hurt too much, a laugh at himself and his guest, two chumps. "Joe Allison was having an affair with Glenna Lancaster."

De La Guerra groans. He tosses his drink down. He'd like another, but he has to drive, and the road is narrow, winding, a treacherous passage even when you're sober.

"From almost the day he came to work at the station, over two years ago," Luke says, piling on the misery.

"Even after Emma was killed?"

Luke nods. "Before, after, during. Up until recently, from the way he dances around it. I don't know whether to believe anything he tells me anymore," he says in anger, "the way he walked me up the garden path. The prick."

The judge slumps in his chair. What Luke's telling him is intolerable. "You have to withdraw," he says, his voice quavering.

"That's what Riva wants."

"She's right. You have to quit this."

"For what reason? My client lying to me, or getting shot at?"

"Either. Both. Damn, Luke," the old man says, his voice almost breaking from the empathetic pain he's going through. "I am so sorry. About everything."

"All clients lie to their lawyers," Luke says. "It goes with the territory. I probably would have, too, if our positions were reversed. It doesn't mean he's Emma's killer. Maybe it means the opposite." He's parroting Allison's idea, but it's not completely far-fetched. "Getting shot at and having your only surfboard blown to smithereens, now that's different."

De La Guerra shakes his head. "No. You're giving him too much of the benefit of the doubt." He hesitates before going on. "And that doesn't matter, anyway." He leans forward—here comes the hardest part. "Remember what we talked about, when I first recruited you? Not about whether Joe Allison was guilty or not. I didn't know that, and frankly, I didn't care. I still don't. I don't know the man, I have no vested interest in him. My concern was that he have capable representation. That's all."

Luke shifts in his seat, trying to find a comfortable position. He can't. "Yes, I remember that," he says wearily. "You didn't want your beloved city getting a black eye by railroading someone onto death row lickety-split, like some cracker city in Arkansas or Louisiana." He pauses. "In fact, you would have preferred that I *not* get as deep into this as I have. Not upset the applecart, not expose the skeletons. A good competent job that would hold up to an appeal from whatever bleeding-heart civil-rights law organization gets involved in this after the conviction. That's what you wanted and no more. Didn't you?"

De La Guerra stares at Luke across the dark room. "Yes," he says. "That's what I wanted."

"That's what everyone wanted," Luke says. "Including me." Fuck it, he's going to have another drink. As many as he likes. He isn't going anywhere, and a man who's been wounded in combat deserves limitless amounts of drink on his survival day. He helps himself, sipping from the glass as he puts down the bottle.

"The problem with that," he continues, "is it never works that way, Freddie. You can't defend a man for any crime, especially one as final as murder, like you put together a jigsaw puzzle. This piece here, this piece there, they all fit, it's over. They don't all fit, they never all fit. Even when a jury comes in with a verdict, when the convicted man pays his penalty, it isn't over. It's never over. Not one like this." He pauses. "You and I know that. That's why we're here."

The ghosts of the past, never laid to rest. De La Guerra peers into his tequila. "You're going to stay with this," he says with infinite sadness.

Luke shakes his head. "I don't know yet, and that's the truth. For damn sure I'm not going to get killed over it. But I'm not going to let some coward hiding out there in the dark run me out of town, either. I did that once, to myself. This time, if and when I leave, it'll be my way, with my head held high."

"What are you going to do?" De La Guerra asks. "If you stay on this." It's time to go; he has to go.

"Try to find out where Doug Lancaster was that night, if that's possible. If he doesn't have an alibi, start building a bonfire under him." He's rekindled his rage, thinking about what almost happened to him tonight. "If Doug is the bastard who tried to kill me—and I can't think of anyone else who is so set against me that he would try something that reckless and insane—then he's psychotic and could have become enraged enough to kill even his daughter. And if he did, I'm going to find that out." He shooters his drink—truly the last one for tonight. The pain, the damage to his body, and the tension have hit him like an axe blow across the back. It's time to go to sleep.

"Someone out there tried to murder me," he says, pointing amorphously to the world outside. "I'm not going to walk away from that, Joe Allison or no. Whether I stay on as Allison's lawyer or not, I'm going to find out who it was, and why."

Riva doesn't take Luke's advice to stay up north until her business is completed. She arrives back in Santa Barbara early in the morning, having driven her rental car all night, nonstop.

"Why aren't you packed yet?" she demands as soon as she walks in the door.

"Calm down," he mumbles, his mouth full of mushy cotton, shielding his face from the sudden onslaught of the morning sun shining through the bedroom window curtains as she pulls them all the way open, blasting him in the face.

"I'm serious," she says. "We're getting out of here today, so start packing." She's in a no-nonsense mood. She's throwing drawers open, flinging clothes out of them onto the bed and floor, grabbing handfuls of his hangered pants and shirts and laying them on a chair.

Groggy from the tequila, the pills, and the pain, he staggers out of bed and crabs into the bathroom, straddling the toilet for a long piss, then splashes water on his face. The water helps, but not much, especially when he sees what he looks like. His entire upper body is black, blue, and several nauseating shades of yellow.

He turns away from the mirror. He needs rest, and Riva won't give him any, not until they're gone from these parts. Cupping his hands under the faucet, he drinks deeply, thirstier than he realized, finally bloated enough to stop.

He comes out of the bathroom. Riva is still throwing stuff all over the room. She screams when she sees his technicolor body. "Oh my God! Oh Jesus Christ!"

"Stop," he tells her. "It's not that bad. It looks worse than it is, really."

"You're insane!" she yells. "Look at you!"

She won't stop screaming, so he grabs her by the arms, hard enough to stop her. "What's your problem?" she asks. "Besides terminal dumbness?"

"Calm down," he tells her for a second time. "Just chill out a minute. Come on." An arm flung over her shoulders, he walks/pushes her into the living room, where she flops on the sofa, staring up at him.

He lowers himself next to her. He can feel the pain coursing throughout his body, moving up and down, around and around. A hard, dull ache, like a monster toothache. "I can't just up and go."

"Why not?" Riva says, now feeling calmer.

Why not? Good question. "Because . . ." He has to lean forward, try to. Otherwise the pain will take over and he'll let himself fall into it and he won't have the strength to do anything except wallow in it, and he can't do that, not now, he has work to do. He has to deal with her, get himself together, and go into town to start taking care of business, however that turns out.

"Because I'm Allison's lawyer," he begins explaining. "You can't leave a defense without the court's permission, no matter the circumstances. I have to make a motion for withdrawal with cause, and Judge Ewing has to approve it."

"What if you were dead?" she says, her voice rising. "Would you have to make a motion to withdraw?"

"Well, I'm not dead."

"All right, then. Get dressed. We're going down to the courthouse so you can make your stupid motion and we can get out of here. Come on." She grabs his arm and starts to drag him to his feet.

"Ahhh!" His left side feels like it's on fire.

She lets go of him, jumping back from his cry. "Sorry. I didn't realize—"

"That I'd been shot? I thought that was the whole point of all this." The pain is making him surly. He doesn't want to be, not with her. She's the focus of his life now. They have a good thing going and he wants to make sure it keeps going, but—shit, that hurts!

"It's okay," he says. "I know you're trying to help." He stares at her. "I can't leave. Not yet."

"Why not?" She's tough, but she's near tears.

"Somebody tried to kill me. I have to find out who." He pulls her to him; it hurts like hell, but he doesn't care, not enough to let go. "Walking away from this, that's not going to solve the problem. I can run from this, but I can't hide from it. So I might as well stay here, where at least I've got protection." He looks into her eyes. "I came back for a reason, Riva. I didn't even know what it was. I thought I knew, but that was surface stuff. Polly. Important, but not what it is. Not deep down."

She buries her head in his chest. "I'm scared. We've got it going finally, and then this."

He holds her tight. "I'm scared too, Riva. I'm scared too."

Riva drives him to the hospital. The doctor checks him out—he's coming along okay. Then she drops him off at the jail.

Once again, he sits in the interview room with Joe Allison, bringing him up to date. Allison is visibly shaken, not knowing what to say. Then it dawns on him. "Does this mean you aren't going to be my lawyer anymore?"

If it wouldn't hurt so much, Luke would kick some sense into this narcissistic shit's ass. "How many times are you going to ask me that? Am I supposed to get myself killed over you?" he fires back. "Is that all you can think about? Yourself?"

Allison slumps. "No. I'm sorry. I didn't mean that. You shouldn't have to be subjected to something like that. You have a perfect right to get out of this if you want to."

Luke stares at his client. "I'm not dropping out."

Allison looks up, startled. "You're staying on?"

"I have no choice."

Allison doesn't know how to react. All he manages to say is "Thanks."

Luke shakes his head. "I'm not staying on for you, so don't thank me." Off Allison's perplexed look: "I'm not going to get into the particulars, it's none of your business and it doesn't matter, but I was driven out of this town once. I did it to myself, and I've been unhappy with myself ever since." He leans in. "I'm not going to be driven out of town again, for you or anyone else." He eases back. His body's throbbing. "One important thing," he says. "Listen up now. You listening?"

Allison nods.

"No more lies from you, by commission or omission or any other excuse. If there's anything else out there I should know about, I want you to tell me—right now."

Allison nods. "There's nothing else, I promise."

Luke rises. "All right, then. Let's keep going on like we have been."

Behind Allison, the door leading back to the jail interior swings open. A guard awaits his exit back to his cell. "Thanks," he says softly to Luke.

Luke shakes off the thanks. "I'm doing this for me, Joe. You're incidental to it now. But I'm still here, and that's all you need to be concerned with."

Sheriff Williams has left four messages on Luke's phone service, asking him to call. He will. But first, he decides, he'll talk to the press.

He stands in front of the courthouse across the street from the jail, recently remodeled and enlarged, where Joe Allison, now the most notorious person they've ever incarcerated, is being held in his solitary cell. Luke has positioned himself so that the lenses of the television cameras will capture both the courthouse and the jail: the ornate, almost rococo building where justice, however one interprets that, is dispensed, and the practical building where the police do their work and the people who are deemed criminals are locked up until said justice is dispensed and are then, almost all of the time, sent somewhere worse.

Luke is dressed for the occasion, with Riva's help struggling into a white shirt, string tie, sport coat. He talks about the attack on him. "It was a cold, premeditated attempt to kill me, Luke Garrison, a specific person. Whoever was shooting at me wasn't doing it because he doesn't like the way I put ketchup on my fries. He was shooting at me because I'm representing Joe Allison, a man accused of a heinous kidnapping and murder, a man this city wants to bury. We all know what that's about, I don't have to elaborate on it."

He looks off to the side. Riva's standing there watching intently, her face a troubled mix of confusion, worry, love. He stares at her for a moment, then turns back to the cameras.

"There is a good reason that someone would want to eliminate me. It's that Mr. Allison is *not* the murderer, and whoever did kidnap and murder Emma Lancaster, who's still at large in the community, knows that I might uncover material that could not only undermine a guilty verdict on Mr. Allison but implicate *him*, the real killer."

He pauses for a moment. "I have one job. To make sure an innocent man does not get convicted. I am not withdrawing from this case, despite the concerns of my friends and even of some of my foes. Now, more than ever, I'm determined to see this through to the finish."

He turns and walks away, without a whisper of a smile.

His meeting with Sheriff Williams and Ray Logan is tense, as he knew it would be. Indeed, he'd have been disappointed if it wasn't. They meet in Williams's office, a standard-issue corner room, the walls festooned with plaques and pictures, awards and encomiums. The sheriff sits behind his desk. Luke has the seat opposite. Logan's off to the side. He's a party to the show, not a participant. The door is closed. The sheriff has instructed his secretary to hold all his calls, without exception.

Luke feels the tension. That's okay—that's what he wants.

"That was a nice performance you gave out there," the sheriff remarks dryly. He and Luke go back a long way. They worked closely together for more than a decade, when Luke was an assistant DA, the rising star in the office, and then after that, when he won the election and became the boss. They were a good team. Now they're opponents, and it doesn't wear well.

"Somebody put a bullet in my side, Bob, in case you've forgotten," Luke replies. In a funny way he's in the catbird seat, for the present at least. They have to take him seriously now, and they have to treat him well. "I assume you're trying to find out who it was."

Williams's reply is serious indeed. "You don't have to assume, Luke. We have a dozen detectives out in the field, trying to work some leads."

"I'm impressed." Then he asks the harder question: "Any hints on who you think it is?"

Williams fidgets in his chair. "Who do *you* think?" he counters.

"Doug Lancaster, who else?"

The name hangs in the air like stale cigar smoke in a closed room. Williams looks at Logan. "He's on the short list."

"Do you know where he was?"

"He says he was at home. We're checking it out."

"Like you checked out where he was the night his daughter was kidnapped?"

Williams looks uneasy.

Luke glances at Logan, who's sitting uncomfortably in his corner, then fixes his stare on the sheriff. "You didn't handle this right, Bob. In a crime like this, the immediate family is automatically under suspicion and you check the hell out of their alibis. That's a given, you and I did a hundred cases like that. But in this case, you didn't—or if you did, you didn't pursue it with any vigor. You let the Lancasters' position and power in the community cow you. You set it up so they'd be off the hook almost immediately."

"I resent that," Williams says angrily.

Luke has to stand. Sitting in one position is too painful. "I didn't say it was a whitewash, Bob. I'm saying it *looks* like it. The fact is that Doug Lancaster's whereabouts on the night his daughter was kidnapped can't be accounted for between one and nine in the morning. I know that, and I assume you do."

Williams looks over at Logan—how much of their hand should he show?

Logan answers. "We know he wasn't in his hotel, like he told us he was—which is a mark against him, I'll admit that."

"Do you know where he was?" Luke asks. "Some physical proof?"

Logan draws a breath. "No."

Luke thinks a moment. "He made a late-night call to a number in the Malibu area. Do you know about that?"

Logan nods. "Yes."

"Have you interviewed the party he called?"

Another nod. "He wasn't there."

"So the call didn't go through?" Luke asks, surprised. This feels weird. If the call wasn't connected, why would the hotel have a record of it? Of course, the phone would be connected to an answering service. Doug could have left a message.

Logan shrugs. "The man, whose name is Buchinsky, gave us a statement. I'll fax it over to you. He wasn't at his beach house the night in question. He wasn't even in the country, he was in France."

"So it's not an alibi for Lancaster. He wasn't there."

"No. But that in itself doesn't make him a suspect," Logan says doggedly.

"No," Luke agrees. "It doesn't." Then he asks, "Do you mind if I talk to Buchinsky?"

"Not at all," Logan says. "I'll call him and let him know you'll be in touch."

"I appreciate that, Ray." Being a crime victim yourself, especially of the crime of attempted murder, opens doors that would otherwise be locked.

"You know we're sorry you were a target," Logan says lamely.

Luke shakes his head. "Someone tried to kill me," he reminds his successor. "Someone is desperate to get me out of the way. Doug Lancaster has been trying to get me off this case from day one, way beyond a father's grief and desire to avenge his daughter's death. He tried to warn me, he tried to scare me, he threatened me." He still doesn't tell them about the bribe—that's too precious to waste now.

Williams and Logan both look somber. "I hear you," Williams says finally.

Logan turns to Williams. "What about protection?" He's Mr. Efficient now.

"Around the clock," Williams says without hesitation. Before Luke can utter a word of protest, his big ham-hand goes up like a traffic cop's. "Someone out there did try to kill you. I'm not going to let them have another shot. I have a job to do, just like you do, and taking care of the citizens is it."

It's a reassuring feeling, although Luke won't give Williams the satisfaction of telling him. Riva will appreciate it. She's going along with his decision, but she's unhappy and scared about it. This will give her some comfort.

"Okay," he answers. "But only at the house, around my lady. I can't conduct my case properly if your men are always watching me. I have witnesses to interview, some of whom I don't want you to know I'm interviewing. But I won't let myself be alone like that again."

Williams nods sourly. "I wish you were on the right side on this one," he says.

"I am." He pats the sheriff on the shoulder. "We're all on the side of justice, Bob."

What can be good about someone trying to kill you? Simple answer: They have to take you seriously now. Joe Allison might be guilty as charged, and the odds are he's going to be convicted no matter what you do. But someone wants you off this case so badly they will kill you to get you off—which makes what you're doing legitimate, and makes your opponents nervous.

There will be plenty of publicity about this. It's already started. You keep it going, fan the flames. Give interviews, hold press conferences, demand to know why the authorities haven't caught your would-be murderer. Are they part of a conspiracy to push this entire thing under the rug, cover it up? Is there a cover-up, and if so, what are they covering up? Could the cover-up be about some doubt on their part now about Joe Allison's guilt? That maybe they're not a hundred percent sure anymore but can't admit it, because they have too much invested in this to back down?

Joe Allison isn't as guilty as he was the day before yesterday. Now, because someone was desperate and crazy enough to try to kill his lawyer, Allison has a chance. He may be found guilty in the end, but for now he's more like he should be, a man innocent until proven guilty. Beyond a reasonable doubt.

Someone tried to kill Luke Garrison, Joe Allison's lawyer. And everything changes.

Except no one tried to kill me.

He's been pounding his brains over that since he got home from the hospital and his subsequent discussion with Ray Logan. What has been tearing up his mind is his certain knowledge that the getting hit was a fluke. It was a lucky one, in that he wasn't killed. But he wasn't supposed to be hit at all. He was supposed to be warned. Those were shots across the bow, calling cards, one last, ultimate warning: *I can knock you off, man, anytime I want. So back off. Now.*

But he isn't backing off. So he has to assume something else is coming, down the line. He has to be prepared for it, he has to be vigilant.

If he survives all this, Luke thinks as he pops another pain pill, getting shot will be worth it. But only the one time. He's willing to risk his career—he doesn't have enough of one left anymore to have that much to risk—but he isn't willing to risk his life again. Even if it was only a warning, once was enough. Because the next time, the shooter won't be aiming to miss.

Ted Buchinsky's interview with one of Logan's assistant D.A.'s is on Luke's desk when he arrives at his office. He reads through it. It was a short interview, only two pages. Buchinsky had seen Doug Lancaster the day before at his home in Beverly Hills, they had some business dealings, talked about continuing the discussion when he got back from Europe. He had flown out the afternoon before the night of the kidnapping, so he obviously wasn't around when Doug had called. End of interview, end of story.

Luke tosses the interview on his desk. Doug wasn't with the man.

He starts to go over some other material, then something clicks. He picks the pages up again, scans them. The telephone number on the interview, Buchinsky's house—it's a 310 area code, all right, but it's a Brentwood prefix, not a Malibu one. Doug hadn't called Brentwood, he'd called Malibu.

Pulling the hotel sheet out of his file, he checks the number Doug called that night. It's a different number from the one on the interview sheet.

He dials the Malibu number. The phone rings. One, two, three times. He doesn't want to leave a message. He starts to hang up.

"Hello?" A woman's voice on the other end of the line.

"Is this the Buchinsky beach residence?" he asks.

"Yes?"

It hits him. How could he have overlooked something so obvious? "Is this Mrs. Buchinsky?"

The woman opens the door. "Thanks for seeing me on short notice," he says as graciously as he can. She's wearing a cotton shirt over her two-piece Lycra bathing suit. "Luke Garrison." He offers his hand.

His name doesn't seem to register with her. "Helena Buchinsky." She shakes, a firm grip, gives him a good eyeballing. "You don't look like a D.A. type."

He smiles. "I don't? How's a D.A. type supposed to look?" What an accent! he thinks. It gives her an offbeat charm—not that her casual, natural voluptuousness isn't itself offbeat in the land of anorexic blondes with pumped-up breasts.

"Buttoned-down. Conventional." She stares at him again, smiling.

He's dressed pretty conventionally. Still, there's the goatee, the ponytail. Not regulation district attorney mufti.

She's liking what she sees, he thinks, feeling the flirtation, which comes as naturally to her as breathing. This is a woman who goes after what she likes, he bets himself. "The times they are a-changin'," he tells her.

"I'm all for that," she says. "Come on in."

She leads him through the house towards the covered sundeck out back. "You want a Coke or something?"

"If it's no trouble." He's walking stiffly; his body, still sore from the bullet intrusion, froze up on him during the ride down.

"No trouble at all." She veers off into the kitchen, comes back a moment later with two cold cans of Coca-Cola. Handing him one, she leads him out onto the deck.

They sit opposite each other in white Adirondack chairs. Everything in this house is white or off-white: the canvas-covered sofas, the wicker chairs, the bleached wood floors. An extension of the outdoors, of the sand and the sun. She runs a hand through her thick long hair, which has been recently highlighted, golden streaks running through the black. Her tanned, oiled legs are crossed, but not primly—he has a clear shot all the way up her thighs. She has a bikini wax.

He takes his eyes off her legs and looks at her face. Not elegant, but open. "Cheers," he says in toast, raising the sweating can.

"Cheers to you," she answers. She looks at him a moment, a questioning look on her face. Like she's onto him?

He didn't lie to her. He didn't tell her the whole truth, either. He didn't tell her he isn't a district attorney; he didn't correct her now, when she brought it up. She hadn't asked him point-blank, so he didn't have to lie or make up some convoluted answer.

He had called the number, told her he was given it by Ray Logan, the district attorney in the Emma Lancaster murder-kidnap case, that he was another lawyer working on the case (implying that he and Ray were working together, but not stating so directly), that they were interviewing everyone who knew any of the principals in preparation for the upcoming trial—such as her and her husband, who were acquaintances of Doug Lancaster. "And Glenna Lancaster," she had told him during the call. "I've met her a couple of times. While they were still married."

He went on to say he needed more information, could he come down and talk to her briefly?

She said sure, and here he is.

"How long have you known Doug Lancaster?" he asks.

"Several years. He and my husband are both in the business."

The television and film business. To her, there is no other. Languidly, she recrosses her legs. They're fine, and she knows it, playing with him easily.

And how long have you been fucking your husband's friend? he thinks. Doug is a philanderer deluxe, and if you're not after the baby-fat stuff, this is as good as it gets.

Doug Lancaster was with her that night. He'd bet the farm on that. Doug knew the husband was out of town. He called—he could even have been returning her call—she told him to come on down, and he did, at a gallop.

Which he could never tell the police. The dead daughter's pregnant, that same night the father's out fucking a friend's wife, God knows what the mother's doing, she could be getting it on with the murder suspect. A nice picture to put in front of a jury.

Luke opens his notebook. "Doug Lancaster placed a call to this residence on the night of his daughter's kidnapping, at approximately one in the morning." He looks up at her.

Her composure isn't ruffled. "Yes, I recall that."

"You spoke to him?" That's a surprise, that she admits it so readily.

She nods. "I did."

"Could you tell me the gist of the conversation, how long it lasted, and so forth. Isn't that late, getting a call at one in the morning?"

She stares at him like he's from Mars, then breaks out laughing, a real belly laugh. "In this business you get phone calls around the clock. If Roseanne or Dustin or Jeffrey or Steven wants to talk to you, it doesn't matter what time it is. One o'clock's pretty reasonable."

"So you were up?"

She nods. "I'm a night owl. I don't need much sleep, I like to sit out on my deck here and watch the waves in the dark. It's wonderful." She smiles. "It's especially wonderful with a glass of Dom Pérignon nearby."

"I'm sure it is." He gets back on track. "What did you and Doug Lancaster talk about?"

"He wanted to talk to Ted."

"Your husband."

"Yes."

"And what did you tell Mr. Lancaster?"

"That Ted wasn't here."

"And that was it?"

"Pretty much." A swallow from the can, another crossing of the legs.

Is she waiting for me to make a move? "Did you and he talk at all?"

She smiles. "Oh, sure. We gossiped for a few minutes. He was upset that he'd forgotten Ted was leaving town—they had some unfinished business. I told him he'd have to wait until Ted returned."

"And that was it?" he asks.

She stares at him. "That was it," she says, as if challenging him to say otherwise.

"So to make sure I have this straight," he says. "Neither you nor your husband saw Doug Lancaster on the night his daughter was kidnapped. He made a short phone call to your house, you spoke to him briefly, and that was it."

She nods. "You've got that right."

"You didn't invite him to stop by for a nightcap on his way up the coast. Since you're a night owl and would be up." He smiles at her, his look drifting down to her legs now, deliberately, obviously.

Just as obviously, she yet again recrosses them, rubbing one against the other. "No," she says softly, "I didn't do that." She smiles back at him. "My husband wouldn't go for that, even with an old friend like Doug."

He feels reckless—he's been shot at, wounded. Right now, he's on a pass. "What if your husband didn't know?" he asks boldly. "Just a drink between friends, a glass of Dom Pérignon at two in the morning."

She shakes her head, a slow rotation, the smile still fixed, still languid. "Doug Lancaster wasn't here that night," she says smoothly. "Why?" she asks. "Did someone say he was? Did he?"

He closes his notebook. "No. I was just making sure." He gets up, trying not to show his stiffness. "Thanks for your time."

She walks him to the front door. As he's about to go, she puts a hand on his arm. "I saw you on television the other night," she says. "You're better looking in person. But of course, no one's going to look their best an hour after being shot and almost killed."

He almost laughs out loud—she's known all along. "Well, thanks for talking to me anyway," he says. Hell of a woman; he hopes Doug appreciates her. He doubts that he does.

"I have nothing to hide. Doug Lancaster wasn't here . . . that night. And that's all that matters, isn't it?" Her hand is still on his arm.

"Yes," he agrees. "As far as I'm concerned, that's all that matters."

* * *

Driving back up the coast again, Luke has one eye on the rearview mirror. His cell phone sits on the seat beside him, ready for a 911 call at the slightest provocation. He's jumpy, he admits it—he doesn't know if he's being followed, or what the deal is. If Doug Lancaster really is behind all this, which increasingly he thinks is the case, someone could be bird-dogging him right now, waiting for an empty stretch of road to try something.

It would be a risky business, a broad-daylight attack. Logan and Williams are on full alert now; if anything else happens to him their asses are in a sling. Hopefully they've spoken to Doug by now, told him to cool it, whether he was the assailant on the bluffs or not.

Going to see Helena Buchinsky was a calculated risk. She'll call Doug, he'll freak. But that's part of the plan, to ratchet the pressure up on him, see if he can be flushed out.

If he's the killer.

The situation is getting gnarly. Initially, Luke's looking into Doug Lancaster's whereabouts on the night of his daughter's kidnapping was a wild grasping at any straw blown up by the wind. Now, with Helena Buchinsky's flat denial of his being with her that night, the matter of where Doug was becomes a major issue, a powerful weapon for their defense.

She could be lying about Doug's not being with her, to protect herself and her marriage. If Doug does come under suspicion, and they were together, would she maintain her denial?

The converse, if there is one, is much more dire. What if Doug truly wasn't with her that night? Where the hell was he, then?

Doug Lancaster lives in Hope Ranch now, another of Santa Barbara's exclusive enclaves. It's closer to the station; on nice days, when he's feeling vigorous, he rides his mountain bike to work. Ever since his divorce from Glenna he's buried himself in his work, often going in before seven in the morning and staying until the eleven o'clock news wrapup. Right now, however, he's at home, awaiting his appointment.

Ray Logan drives his county-issue Buick Park Avenue through the tree-lined streets towards Doug's house. Seated next to him is his senior investigator, Arthur Lovett. Lovett's been the lead investigator in a good dozen murder cases. He was Luke Garrison's number-one man when Luke was the chief. He still likes and respects Luke, and knows that the feeling is mutual. The two men had a drink together when Luke first came back to town, a nice couple of hours spinning old war stories. Lovett was upset that Luke was doing this, but it wasn't his place to say that.

They're adversaries now, of course. But there won't be the kind of personal animosity between them that Luke and Ray Logan feel towards each other—the old king (even though he's still a young man), now deposed, versus the successor who is trying to fill those big shoes, carve out his own space, and fight the old image, all at the same time.

"What do you think?" Lovett asks now. His boss is tense, he can read the body language. Logan's gripping the steering wheel so hard his knuckles are actually white.

"I don't know" is Logan's honest reply. "You know me—I don't like surprises, and I'm starting to feel edgy, like one's coming. I don't want to find out that Doug Lancaster hasn't been a hundred percent straight with us." He navigates a turn up a narrow road that leads to the gated driveway.

"Have you talked to the woman?" Lovett asks. "Since she talked to Luke?"

"Ronnie talked to her." Ronnie White is a deputy D.A. who does much of Logan's personal assisting. "Her story is consistent from when we interviewed her a year ago. She and Doug weren't together that night."

Lovett thinks about that. "Then Doug is going to be on the hot seat. Luke Garrison's going to put him on it, and keep him there. This could turn out to be the Doug Lancaster trial instead of the Joe Allison trial." He runs a hand over his bald, sun-blotched pate. "I know how Luke thinks."

"Doug Lancaster doesn't have to prove where he was that night," Logan says pessimistically.

Lovett gives his boss a withering look. "Ray. Listen to yourself.

Maybe by the book he doesn't have to have a good alibi, but you don't want to have to face a jury during summation and not have that question answered. Do you?" he asks pointedly.

Logan shakes his head. "No." His grip tightens on the wheel again.

They announce themselves through the guard box. The gate swings open and they drive through, winding up a long eucalyptus-lined lane to Doug's house. Like his old house, this one has views that go on and on. "It used to be everything Doug Lancaster touched turned to gold," Logan comments as he parks in the circular driveway in front of Doug's opulent house.

"Not anymore, poor bastard," Lovett replies as he gets out. He looks out over the manicured yard to the ocean, a hundred yards below where they're standing. "He'd give all this up in a heartbeat to have his daughter back."

Logan turns to him. "I hope so," he says, almost in a whisper, as if he's afraid Doug might be listening in from some hidden outpost.

"You're really worried about this."

Logan nods gravely. "What's a prosecutor's worst nightmare?" he asks. He answers his own question: "To be trying the wrong man."

Lovett grimaces. "That's the second worst nightmare," he corrects his boss.

"What's worse?" Logan asks, his voice betraying his nervousness.

"To be trying the wrong man and have it blow up in your face."

Lancaster's new study is different from his old one. It's light and airy, devoid of ghosts. "How are you doing?" Doug asks. "We're going to trial in a few weeks," he says, immediately taking control of the meeting they called. "Are we ready?"

"We're doing fine, Mr. Lancaster," Logan says staunchly. "We're as ready to go as we can be. At this point in time."

"Good." Doug glances at his watch, as if he's running late for an important meeting, more important than this one. "What is it you wanted to talk to me about?"

"Your whereabouts on the night your daughter was taken from her room," Lovett says, deliberately blunt. "For openers," he adds provocatively.

Doug stares at Lovett as if the man's slow on the uptake—a year slow. "In my hotel, in L.A.," he says, answering the question. "You know that," he continues, almost dismissively. He looks from one public servant to the other. Then the last part of Lovett's comment sinks in. "For openers *what*?"

Logan steels himself. This is going to be a bitch. "You weren't in your hotel that night, Mr. Lancaster." He isn't comfortable calling him Doug, not under these circumstances. "Not between one and nine in the morning." He recedes into his chair, as if trying to put as much distance between him and Doug Lancaster as possible.

Doug stares at him. "What are you talking about, Ray? Of course I was."

Another head shake, this one more emphatic. "No. You weren't. We have witnesses who saw you leave, and saw you return." He pauses. "Luke Garrison has already talked to them. He's ahead of us on some of this, which is outrageous, considering we're on the same side and he isn't."

Doug starts to flash an answer, catches himself, hesitates in mid-move out of his chair, settles back in. He looks from Logan to Lovett. They're staring at him with intensity. "I . . . I . . . that's not true."

Logan gets up and approaches Doug. This is going badly. He doesn't care who Doug Lancaster is or how powerful he is, he can't abide one of his key players lying to him. The whole case could unravel. "We *know* you weren't at the hotel, like you told the sheriff a year ago," he says, working to control his anger. "So let's have it—where were you? You have to give us something credible, or we are going to be in trouble. All of us."

Lancaster looks lost, shaking his head back and forth, like someone trying to will a bad dream away.

"You made a phone call to Ted and Helena Buchinsky right before one in the morning," Lovett says, boring in behind Logan. "You spoke to Helena Buchinsky."

Doug starts to protest. "No, I—"

"She spoke to you," Lovett says, cutting Doug off. "She's already told us she spoke to you, that she told you her husband was out of the country, which you had known but apparently forgotten." He looks over at his boss—they're on the same wavelength, so he goes for it. "What we'd like to know is, was the call intended for her, Mr. Lancaster, rather than her husband? Double-checking to make sure her husband was *out* of the country, so you could come on over and see her?"

Lancaster is startled by this aggressive and confrontational questioning. "No. I was trying to get him. I really did forget."

"So you weren't with her that night," Lovett continues. "Which she swears is the case. She says you weren't there."

"Well, then . . ."

Ray Logan's seething inside. They've been lied to, and they've been building a case based, in significant measure, on what's now proving to be false information. "Is Helena Buchinsky your mistress?" he asks bluntly.

Lancaster flies out of his chair. "What the hell!?"

Logan puts up a restraining hand. "You've had various affairs over the years, Doug." He uses the first name now, forget the deferential treatment. "So we have to assume—*and so will Luke Garrison,*" he emphasizes, "that you and this Buchinsky woman were—are—lovers, and that's where you were intending to go when you called her late that night."

Doug looks away. "I can't say she and I are . . . were . . . lovers." His voice is starting to take on a tone of desperation "Her husband is a close friend and business colleague. An accusation like that would be ruinous, disastrous."

"If you say so," Ray Logan responds. "But if you had been with her, you'd have an alibi. As things stand now, you don't. So once again. Where were you?"

Doug looks at them. "I . . . I can't tell you."

Logan can't believe what he just heard. "Mr. Lancaster." He's formal again. "This is serious. You have to tell us."

"I know it's serious. But I can't. I have a legitimate reason why." He looks at them almost beseechingly. "I'm not the one on trial. I'm the one who lost his child."

Logan feels impotent, manipulated. "It's your decision. But it's going to seriously cripple us."

Lovett horns in. "What about Sunday night?" he asks.

"Sunday night?" Doug asks, not connecting. Or, more likely,

faking it, Logan thinks darkly. This man is digging his own grave with this unfathomable behavior. "The night Luke Garrison was shot."

Lancaster stares at him in angry disbelief. "You can't think I had anything to do with that. How could you think that?"

Ray Logan eases out of his chair to get closer to this man who could be jeopardizing the case of his, Logan's, life. "We have to think of the possibility. Luke's going to, he's going to make a huge stink about it," he says as calmly as possible, ticking the salient points off on his fingers. "You're a property owner at the Hollister Ranch, so you have access, which is very important—the police have to assume that the shooter had easy access, in and out. Otherwise, it's too risky. Two, you own rifles, don't you?"

Lancaster stares hard at him. "Yes," he answers gruffly. "I own rifles, I own shotguns, I own pistols. So do millions of other people."

"Not many who have property at Hollister," Logan counters. "That's what's so troubling, Mr. Lancaster. Three," another finger raised, "and worst, you've been in contact with Luke, threatening him, God knows what." He's losing it, he can feel he's losing it, and he doesn't care, he can't help himself. "Why in the world did you do that?" he says heatedly, unable to keep his temper in check any longer. "Didn't I warn you *not* to have contact with him? Can't you see how that compromises us, and everything we're trying to do? For *you*!"

Doug slumps back into his chair. "I'm sorry. I don't mean to."

Logan's got to get out of here, the tension's overwhelming. "Okay," he says. "Sunday night." A longer pause than he would like—given Doug's attitude, he's fearful of asking this next question. "You can alibi yourself for then."

"I was here," Doug says.

"Not alone, I hope?"

Calmly: "Most of the time."

Logan looks over at Lovett. His investigator is shaking his head in shattered incredulity. "Can you produce someone—anyone—who will vouch for where you were between about eight and ten that night?"

"No, I can't. I was here, by myself. I was working."

Logan's starting to itch from anxiety. His shirt feels clammy on his back. "Where do you keep your rifles?"

Doug hesitates. "At the ranch."

"I'm going to send someone out from the sheriff's office to impound them temporarily. I hope you understand why."

"Do I have to go along with this? I'm not accused of anything . . . am I?"

Logan shares a look with Lovett. "No. But we can get authorization to search for them if you don't cooperate. Look," he says, "we're going to do it. With or without your assistance."

Doug looks unhappy at the prospect. With a show of resignation: "All right. If that's what you need. I'm beginning to feel like *I'm* on trial here."

"There are holes in your story, Mr. Lancaster," Lovett explains, taking the heat for his boss. "We need to fill them in. Call our office when you've located them and we'll pick them up. You'll get them back as soon as we run tests on them."

There's nothing more to be done here now. "We're leaving," Logan says. "Your mysterious whereabouts could come back to haunt us," he warns Doug.

Sitting in his chair, Doug looks like all the bones and organs have been sucked out of him, leaving a shell. "I didn't kill Emma," he says plaintively. "Never, never. And I didn't try to kill Luke Garrison, either." He looks up at them. "I admit I may have pushed too hard, regarding Luke. I felt it was something I had to do. But kill him? No."

Luke, sitting in his office as he reads over some transcripts for the umpteenth time, is frustrated. Doug Lancaster's whereabouts on the night of the shooting are unaccountable—Sheriff Williams personally called Luke to relay the information as soon as Ray Logan had met with him to recount his frustrating interview with Lancaster. The anger, disgust, and fear in the sheriff's voice came through loud and clear over the phone. Williams is still convinced Allison killed Emma, but he's not proud about the way he's handled the case, especially his kid-glove treatment of the Lancasters.

Over and over, Luke finds himself drawn to two anomalies in the growing mountain of information.

The first has to do with Emma Lancaster's key ring, the most damning piece of evidence against Allison. If Emma was being abducted, who would want it? She wouldn't be taking it, not if she was snatched against her will. The only reason she might have brought it with her would be if she was a willing participant, and needed to get back into the house later. Even then, that's a dubious premise, because she could come back in the same way she left, through the outside door to her bedroom. The key wasn't for that door, so it wouldn't have mattered. It would make a lot more sense that the key ring was lost or misplaced somewhere else. Conceivably it could have been in Allison's car, and when he found it he tossed it in his glove compartment and forgot about it. It's questionable whether he would have known it was Emma's, anyway.

The second piece that has always troubled him is the tissue of circumstances around Allison's initial stop-and-search. It's obvious by now that pulling him over on suspicion of drunk driving was contrived, as was the opened bottle of whiskey inside the car (how convenient), which prompted the search. Then the key chain buried inside his glove compartment under a pile of junk. And the condoms at his house, which his girlfriend asserts he doesn't use.

The arresting officer's testimony has too many what-ifs. Luke needs to explore it deeper. Without that dubious arrest, search, and seizure, the entire case would be dormant. Joe Allison would be in Los Angeles, climbing towards anchorman stardom; Luke and Riva would be up north, marking time with their lives; and the mystery of who killed Emma Lancaster would still be unsolved.

In a strange, seemingly inexplicable but fundamental way, he's glad this happened, even including the shooting that could have been fatal regardless of his perception of the incident. Something had to happen to break him out of the doldrums his life had been in. His demons had been running his life.

Now, one by one, he's shedding them.

* * *

Doug Lancaster owns one rifle, a Remington 700 .308, that matches the caliber of the weapon used for the assault on Luke Garrison. Sheriff Williams accompanies it to the state testing facility in Soledad, two hundred miles upstate.

"Not the same weapon," the head of the lab informs him, after the rifle is fired and they compare the bullets with the ones found at Hollister Ranch.

"You're sure."

"Positive."

"Thanks." A tremendous feeling of relief. If the shells had matched, the egg on their faces would have made an omelet the size of Rhode Island.

He calls down to Ray Logan, who's been hanging around his office, waiting for the results. Logan, while also relieved, still has doubts. "Lancaster could be holding out on us. He could've ditched the real rifle."

"He didn't do it, Ray," the sheriff says. He's holding on to his weakness for Lancaster. Or maybe what he represents. He isn't sure anymore.

"You have a vested interest in this," Logan reminds him. "We all do. But we can't go into this with blinders on. Lancaster's having no alibi for either night is giving me a case of the hives. I'm nervous as hell, I don't mind telling you."

"So am I," the sheriff agrees. "But put it in perspective, Ray," he counsels. Logan's still a relative tenderfoot. He, on the other hand, has been around the block a thousand times. "You know Doug Lancaster. He's a good guy at heart. Do you honestly think this man could have murdered his own daughter and then hidden her body like it was done? I can't buy that, regardless of whatever stupid things he's done. You don't know how you'd react to something like that. It could drive you crazy."

"Yeah," Logan concedes. He is relieved about the rifle tests.

"You know, the security up at the ranch is lax," the sheriff reminds his D.A. counterpart. "Anyone can get in and out of there. We can't assume that whoever shot at Luke is a parcel holder. It could be any asshole with a grudge. This could be something from Luke's past, an old-time wound that isn't healed. Luke Garrison put a lot of people in jail," he reminds Luke's successor. "There are scores of men out there who would like to see him dead."

"Maybe." Logan is not as sanguine as the sheriff. "But none of them ever tried to kill Luke until now."

"Luke's been missing in action for three years," Williams reminds him. "Now he's back, and he's high profile."

"I have a problem with the timing," Logan says doggedly. "Too coincidental."

"You might call Luke and give him the news," Williams says.

"I'd rather you do it. He and I are adversaries, in case you've forgotten."

The sheriff laughs to himself. "No, Ray. I haven't forgotten."

He hangs up. Chickenshit bastard, he thinks. We hand you an airtight case and you punch holes in it. Luke Garrison never would have done it that way. Luke Garrison would have run this one right into the end zone.

He misses Luke. But Luke has to go down.

Luke takes the news about the rifle testing with equanimity. If Doug was the shooter, he wouldn't have turned the weapon over to be used as evidence against him. "Did you take tire castings from up on the bluff?" he asks the sheriff.

"Yes, SOP. A standard truck tire, probably Goodyear, the kind used on a light truck or SUV. There's plenty of them out there. But we're working it. We're not taking this lightly, Luke. I mean that," Williams says.

"Good. I'm getting tired of seeing your boys every time I step out my door."

"They're there for your protection."

"I'm glad of that," Luke says. "But they remind me there's someone still out there who's trying to kill me. I wish whoever it is wasn't out there."

"We're doing our best. Something will turn up." A pause. "In the meantime, don't do anything rash. We want you alive. I still think of you as a friend, Luke, even if we're on opposite sides now." He hangs up.

A friend. What a crock. The man's scared I'm making headway, Luke thinks, that I'll upset his little red applecart. Luke has Joe Allison's life at stake, and his own as well, given he was shot at, but Williams has his career. Whether Luke Garrison wins or loses, his life will go on pretty much as it has for the last three years. If anything, it'll be better. He's back in the world, he's focused on his work, he's more at peace with himself than he has been for a long time. And he has a good woman at his side, which he's finally recognized and can deal with.

It seems stupid and, yes, callous, but the worst that can happen to him is that he loses the case. If he does, it'll be because Joe Allison is guilty. He's convinced of that. If Allison is innocent—if nothing freakishly dramatic, that he doesn't know about, comes up at trial to prove Allison's guilt—he, Luke Garrison, will get Allison off. He's that confident in his ability.

Williams and Logan, on the other hand, will lose their credibility. They will almost certainly lose their careers, which for both men define them. They will lose face, they will lose self.

He's already gone through that, and come out the other side. So in that fundamental regard, he has nothing to lose. Win or lose this particular case, his life has nowhere to go but up.

FOUR

Ferdinand De La Guerra and Luke Garrison. Two men. One of a certain age, one who sometimes feels he's aging too fast. Sitting in the living room of the old gentleman's house. It's a several decades-old Spanish colonial situated on a quiet, narrow lane in Mission Canyon, in the flats. It's a wonderful house, full of history, beautifully furnished with Mission-style furniture, the walls covered with early twentieth-century landscape paintings of the central coast, portraits of old land-grant ancestors stiffly posed, South American tapestries, ancient swords, guns, Spanish conquistador helmets. On some of the dark, burnished tables, there are small pieces of authentic pre-Columbian art: Aztec, Mayan. And one painting more contemporary, the centerpiece of the room, hung over the large stone fireplace: a Diego Rivera, a gift from the artist, personally, to the owner's father.

The house and its owner fit each other like kid leather gloves, Luke thinks. Aging but still elegant.

"You're going to be in trial in a few weeks. How do you feel?" The judge looks over at Luke as he poses the question. He pours two snifters of forty-year-old Spanish brandy. The aromas are overwhelming in the glasses, redolent of crushed flowers, wild berries, old succulent grapes. And beautiful women on dark candlelit nights when this house was overflowing with desire.

"Better," Luke says confidently. "Our odds are on the rise." He leans back in his chair, holding the liquid in his mouth, the flavors drifting into his head, heavenly fire.

"What about you?" The tone is anxious, trying not to be. "Aside from the case."

"I've got baby-sitters watching the dark corners, so I feel safe—safe enough. Whoever it was isn't going to come after me again, I don't think. Unless he's desperate or crazy, in which case—" Luke throws up his hands. "It's constricting, seeing a deputy over my shoulder every time I step out my front door." He points towards the door. "It's annoying as hell, especially to Riva. It reminds her of what happened."

De La Guerra smiles. "She's like me. She wishes you weren't on the case anymore."

Luke nods. "Like I said, if I let whoever did this run me off, he wins and I lose. And so does the law, which I care about, it's still my life."

"What about your life? How would you feel about losing that?"

"I wouldn't like it," Luke admits. "But I don't plan on that happening. Neither does our esteemed sheriff. He's tired of being embarrassed."

The judge shifts to the practical. "Has there been any progress? Do they have any leads?"

Luke shakes his head. "Not a one."

"You're still thinking it was Doug Lancaster."

Outside, an owl hoots in the darkness. Luke walks over to a floor-to-ceiling window. He looks out into the night, trying to see where the owl is perched, high up in a tall pine that sits at the edge of the property. "The owl a regular?" he asks. "What kind is it, you know?"

"It comes and goes," De La Guerra replies from his comfortable leather chair. "A great horned," he says to the second part of Luke's question. "They're pretty common around here." He sips from his drink. "You didn't answer my question."

"Owls are good hunters," Luke says ruminatively. "Sit there dead still for hours, then they swoop down silent with that great wingspan and take their prey before the poor rabbit or mouse knows what hit him. Reminds me of some situations I've seen lately." He turns back into the room. "It's what I think, yes. Who else is a better candidate?" He picks up the decanter holding the brandy. "May I?"

"Go ahead." The old man warms his glass in his hands. "No one, but that doesn't mean it's him. It seems far-fetched to me that he would go after you personally."

"You mean he'd bring in a hired gun?" He pours a small amount of the fiery potion. A little goes a long way with this stuff. He hasn't been drinking much lately. He wants to be sure his wits are about him, not dulled and slowed by alcohol.

"That's a more likely scenario, don't you think?"

"I guess so. Yeah," he says, thinking more about that. "Doug wouldn't directly get his hands dirty." He smells the brandy nose as it drifts out of the snifter. "Which is more scary, really. It could be anyone walking around, someone I wouldn't have a clue as to who he is. He could be watching me right now, and I wouldn't know it."

His old mentor nods ponderously. "Yes. That's my point."

Luke sits down again, heavily. "Shit."

"You need to think this through, Luke. That's what I've been trying to tell you."

Luke looks out into the darkness again. "I've got to be really careful," he agrees. He looks over at De La Guerra. "Don't talk like this around Riva, all right? She's freaked out enough as it is."

"She has to be thinking about it," the judge tells Luke. "You have to realize she's protecting you by keeping quiet about her fears."

Luke sits back. "She's really been good for me," he says. He's never commented on her before like that, not to someone else.

"She loves you."

Luke nods. "I'm lucky."

"You don't appreciate how lucky you are."

"I'm beginning to." He glances at his watch. "I'd better be moseying. Thanks for the good stuff." He sips the dregs from his glass.

"Thank you for the company," De La Guerra says. "This old house needs company. I'm not much good company for it anymore."

Luke feels a pang. "I'll come around more."

"And bring your lady. I promise I won't mention what we've been talking about."

"I will. Don't bother getting up, I'll let myself out." He walks to the front door. "Thanks for the advice."

De La Guerra smiles as he shakes his head. "I can't give advice anymore," he says. "I haven't figured my own life out yet, let alone anyone else's." He pauses. "Be careful. That's all I ask."

The assault on Luke has achieved a certain notoriety. The tabloid television shows—*Hard Copy*, *Inside Edition*, *Geraldo*—ran stories on it within a week of when it happened, and some have followed up.

Lying in bed with Riva, Luke watches himself being interviewed by a vacuous woman. The interview is a week old, a syndicated program. He and the interviewer are standing outside the courthouse, where he had gone to file a subpoena for some documents. "How do you feel about someone trying to kill you?" she asks him, teeth flashing through a frozen smile.

"Like anyone else would," he says, looking in the vague direction of the camera over her shoulder. "Angry. Worried."

"What a genius," Riva comments, watching with him.

"Are you satisfied with the job the police are doing in trying to solve your case?" asks the interviewer. It was obvious to him, all during the interview, that she was trying to make eye contact with him. He evaded her overtures.

Luke chose his next words carefully. He has the sheriff on the run, psychologically speaking. He doesn't want to upset that balance. "They're trying hard," he says to the camera. "A hit-and-run shooting, that's a tough crime to solve."

"Which you should know, since you were the district attorney here," she throws in.

"I used to be," he answers.

The only story about him that's been negative was done by Lancaster's station. The new station manager, Tim Talbot, read an editorial a couple of weeks ago on the six o'clock news. Referring to the shooting, he described Luke as "an out-of-county lawyer who specializes in defending drug dealers," and "a man with an obvious aversion and hostility to authority." There was scant reference to Luke's being the former county district attorney. Talbot questioned out loud what Luke was doing on private property, as if by being there he was committing a criminal act of his own.

On the screen, the woman interviewer throws Luke a curve: an intelligent question. "What happens if the police catch the person who tried to kill you, either before or during Joe Allison's trial? Won't that have a big effect on it?"

He's been asking himself that very question ever since he started thinking clearly after the shooting. He hasn't come up with an answer, because he's been avoiding it. Now he has to. "It would depend on who the person was," he answers.

Riva, in bed, sits up, looks over at him.

"If it was someone connected to Joe Allison's case, as opposed to . . ." She stumbles momentarily over her script.

"Someone not connected?" he finishes for her.

"Yes, that's what I meant," she says, recovering quickly. She's smiling gamely, but it's obvious to her that he won't be taking her out for drinks later this afternoon.

On the television set he shrugs. "We'll cross that bridge when we come to it." He smiles back, an unencouraging smile.

That's the end of that interview. He flicks the set off with the remote.

"What did you really want to say?" Riva asks him, referring to the last set of questions.

"Were my evasive tactics that obvious?"

"Yep, to me. I know you."

"You know the answer to that." He turns to her, leaning on his elbow. In the moonlight he can see the outline of her breasts through her thin nightgown. They're gorgeous; in this light they seem larger, fuller. He wants to nuzzle them. "If it's someone connected, like Doug, all hell breaks loose. We'd have a mistrial. If not, it won't amount to much."

She slides her body closer to his. "When *are* they going to catch him?" she asks.

He looks at her. "Maybe never."

"Do you really think that?" Her face is frightened.

He nods. "If whoever it was doesn't try to do it again, the police may never find out. There are no solid clues, no witnesses, no one's come forth with a tip. That's the way these things are usually solved, somebody ratting out somebody else. That hasn't happened yet." He strokes her slender back. "If that's the case, it's fine. It means no more harm will come. I'm hoping that's the case," he says. "I'm not looking for revenge. I'll be content if it fades away."

"But don't you want to know who did it?" she persists. "*I* want to know who tried to take you away from me."

He draws her to him. "No one's going to take me away from you."

She snuggles closer. "Is that a promise?"

Outside, a sheriff's deputy in a car is watching over them. In here, he has to protect her from her fear that some madman might take him away.

"Yes," he says, feeling the night closing in on them. "That's a promise."

A week and a half to go. Luke mock-trials with some men and women from the public defender's office that he's asked to help him. It's an awkward session; they were used to being on opposite sides from each other, when he not only kicked their asses with regularity but enjoyed it. And they are miffed that he was chosen because Allison and certain powers-that-be in the community wanted a high-profile lawyer. So their participation is less than wholehearted.

Still, it goes okay—not terrific, but not a catastrophe, either. He works at what he thinks will be the most important issues, for his side and his opponents. The way he conducts his case will be largely reactive: how witnesses for the prosecution spin their stories, what new or unexpected information comes up, how he can use it to his advantage. Judge De La Guerra observes, occasionally making a note.

The session lasts most of the day. By the time they're finished, a grudging bond has developed between him and the other lawyers. He's on their side now, and he's good. And he's genuinely appreciative of their help. When it's over, they all walk down the street to the Paradise Bar & Grill, where he buys a couple of rounds. Then the others leave, and he and De La Guerra are alone.

"What do you think?" Luke asks. He feels the session was worthwhile. Nothing jumped up that he hadn't anticipated.

"It's going to be an ugly situation," De La Guerra observes, "what with all the family laundry being aired in public. You never know if that will help you, by making them look bad, or hurt, by making the jurors feel you're taking advantage of a family's suffering. It'll depend on your jury," he advises sagely. "You can't necessarily win with the right jury, but you can easily lose with the wrong one."

"I know. Given the notoriety of the case, and the passions that have been aroused, I feel like I'm starting with a strike against me. Maybe two," he says somberly.

"Do you have a profile of your ideal juror?" the judge asks. "Are you using a jury consultant?"

"No, I'm not using a consultant. I know what we need." When he was the prosecutor they often used consultants, and although they were helpful, eventually he didn't use them much. He's been doing this a long time; he has a good feel for how jurors react. "The key will be seating people who are appalled at the Lancasters' lifestyle. Think about it—father, mother, teenage daughter, all having illicit affairs. My hunch is that Glenna, especially, might catch a lot of it. A woman who was sleeping with a man while she was grieving, and he turns out to be the accused. What a bad taste *that* leaves in the mouth."

De La Guerra taps Luke on the forearm. "In light of which," he says, "I think Emma's being pregnant makes your job harder, not easier. If she hadn't been, that whole side of the story wouldn't exist. No one would have ever known she was having sex, and it wouldn't have added this bad element."

Luke nods. "He knocked her up, she was going to bust him one way or the other, he had to kill her. I know Logan's going to hammer that." Darkly: "He should. I would."

One week to go. Luke and Allison confab in the jail. Luke has been stopping in every day for the past two weeks, more to touch base with his client and bolster his spirits than to glean any new information—there is none, that he can figure out. He discusses his strategy with Allison, not for input, but so that his client will know where they're heading and feel like he's part of his own defense.

It's evening, around nine o'clock. Luke prefers seeing Allison late, after he's finished his work for the day, when the jail is quiet. Riva's back at the house, patiently waiting dinner on him. They haven't seen much of each other these past few weeks. He's up early, poring over his material. A little time in the morning before taking off (the sheriff's deputy dutifully following his truck down the hill), passing each other in the office, late-night dinner, always in the house. They haven't been out for weeks.

He's started to compose his opening statement; he'll finish it the day after jury selection is completed. He wants to give himself some flexibility, not so much in the content of his remarks as in how he delivers them. It will depend partially on what the prosecution says, since they'll go first, and more important on the makeup of the jury, and how well he succeeds in seating people he thinks he can reach. He's realistic about his prospects for an outright acquittal, given the sentiment against Allison. But a hung jury, one or two hardy souls who have the *cojones* to withstand the pressure from the majority, is not a totally unreasonable expectation.

He and Allison sit across the table from each other in the putrid room. "How're you holding up?" he asks his client, who doesn't look bad, just dulled, institutionally anesthetized.

The prisoner shrugs. "I'm coping—one long day at a time. But I hate it," he says in a surge of anger. Then he slumps back, emotionally exhausted. "I'll sure be glad when the trial starts. At least I'll have someplace to go to, instead of sitting in that shitty little cell." He cracks his knuckles, another nervous gesture he's developed since his arrest. "How're we doing?"

"Okay," Luke says. He voices an idea he's been kicking around in his mind for the past few weeks. "When you and Emma got together, did she ever talk about *one* man in particular. Or a boy? Someone she might have been romantically involved with?"

Allison shakes his head. "No. She never talked about that." He smiles. "She wanted to hear about my love life, though."

Luke nods. "Do you think she might have had any suspicion that you and her mother were getting it on?"

Allison starts to answer no, then stops and thinks. "I don't think so, but I can't say for sure." Continuing, he says, "I don't think she thought of Glenna with any man, except Doug. To Emma, Glenna was like any other mother, a pain in the butt who got on her case too much, even though Glenna gave Emma a lot of liberty for a kid her age. Her mother having sex appeal? Emma wouldn't have thought that way."

"Why not?" Luke counters. "Kids will talk to outsiders about problems before they talk to their mothers or fathers. Especially when the parent is part of the problem."

When he was a young assistant D.A., way back when, he worked juvenile cases for a few years. It was a sobering experience. Kids he had never met, who had been in his presence for five minutes, would say things to him they would never tell their parents.

He remembers back to one situation that he handled as a deputy D.A. A seventeen-year-old girl confessed to her mother that she'd been sexually abused by the mother's boyfriend for four years. The mother hadn't known, hadn't had a clue. She tried to kill the boyfriend. He'd had to prosecute her. He had lost that case, one of the few he had lost. It had been a happy loss.

Allison ponders that stark notion. "I guess I can't say *no* for sure," he admits. "I do know she had strong suspicions about her father. That he was fooling around behind Glenna's back." What he's said registers in the silence that follows. "I should talk," he says ruefully.

"She talked about that? Doug stepping out on his marriage?"

Allison nods. "Not straight out, but by strong innuendo. She would say things like 'He's gone to L.A. again, and Mom's here alone.' Stuff like that. She'd have an edge in her voice."

"Do you have any idea whether or not she ever confronted him?"

The prisoner snorts. "Are you serious? A daughter confronting a father as formidable as Doug Lancaster? He was a great guy to work for, don't get me wrong, but you don't fuck with the alpha dog. I can't imagine anyone throwing something like that in his face, especially his own daughter, who idolized him even when she was angry with him." He pauses. "Is my affair with Glenna going to come out into the open?"

Luke raises an eyebrow—how did we jump to this? The subject is obviously on Allison's mind. "I don't know yet. It makes her look bad, but it makes you look bad too. I'll have to see how that one unfolds."

"I still care about her," Allison says. "She's been hurt a lot already. I'd hate to see her get hurt anymore, if she doesn't have to."

"That's not your concern, Joe. You take care of you. And I take care of you. Glenna Lancaster has to take care of herself."

"I hope it doesn't have to come out. It's not about who killed Emma."

"You don't know that," Luke admonished him sharply. "I'm a professional at this, so let me do my job, okay?" Fucking civilians. "Everything and anything that involves that family is fair game, and I'll use any of it if it helps me help you. So again—forget about her. Your only concern is you. Tattoo that on your forehead, so you see it every morning when you look in the mirror." He rises. "I'll check in with you tomorrow. Stay calm. We're getting somewhere. It isn't hopeless."

"Ladies and gentlemen of the jury. Good afternoon." He pauses. "My name is Luke Garrison. I am the attorney for the defendant, Joe Allison." He hesitates. "Good morning, ladies and gentlemen. My name is Luke Garrison, and I am Joe Allison's lawyer. Joe Allison being the defendant in this case." Another hesitation. "Shit."

Riva, watching him from the kitchen while preparing a seafood salad for dinner, breaks out laughing. "What are you doing?"

"Royally fucking up my opening statement." He's standing in the middle of the living room, a fistful of four-by-six cards in hand.

"You're rehearsing it?" she asks, astonished. "You've done hundreds of these. You ought to know how by now."

"I *do* know how," he says, feeling defensive. "But this is different. It's here, and it's huge, and I'm sitting on the other side of the aisle from where I always used to sit. Talk about life in a fishbowl. I feel like I'm going to be standing naked in front of the courthouse at high noon."

"In that case, pull in your gut," she chides him. "You're sagging, lover."

He pinches his waist. "What're you talking about? I'm in great shape. For a seventy-year-old man."

She laughs again. "You're in great shape, period. Great enough for me."

He tosses the note cards onto the coffee table. "I know how to do this. The more I rehearse, the worse it's going to get. Wooden and predictable. I know what I'm going to say." He comes into the kitchen. "You're cooking," he comments. He's so wrapped up in his own cocoon he's unconscious of everything going on around him.

"Making a salad hardly qualifies as cooking. I'm giving takeout the night off." She turns to him. "We used to have a real life. Drinks on the porch, dinner with candles, back rubs. And sex. We don't have much sex these days."

"I'm too busy for sex," he grouses. It's true; it's been longer than a week. "Besides, I was too sore from my wound."

She puts down the salad utensils, wipes her hands on a dish towel. "Your wound has healed. And you can't be that busy, not twenty-four hours a day. You left that rat-race life. Or have you forgotten?"

He takes her face in his hands, stares at her. God, how he's come to love this face. "No. I haven't forgotten."

Their lovemaking is almost dreamlike in its near quiescence. She takes the lead, making sure she avoids touching hard the place on his side where he was shot. There is a small scar-hole in his side, a battle wound that will be a reminder for the rest of his life.

Lying together, she lightly traces her finger around the scar tissue, which is redder than the rest of him and protruding, a ridgeline etched in hair. "What does it feel like now?" she asks.

"It doesn't. There is no feeling." All the nerves were desensitized. "Like rubber, would be the closest description." He can imagine, in a small way, what it would feel like to be paralyzed and have that nonfeeling all over. The loss of connection to yourself. It almost happened.

They eat their dinner on the balcony. In the down-below distance are the lights of the city, the harbor, the offshore oil rigs: an earthly firmament. "Are you nervous?" she asks. She's never seen him nervous, not about work. But he's never cared about it before like this, either.

He nods. "I've got to be great."

"You will be."

"We're both on trial. Allison and me."

"You'll be great," she reiterates.

He puts down his fork. "I can't lose this." His throat is starting to tighten, he almost feels like he's going to have a panic attack. Like he felt months ago, when he saw Polly with her pregnant belly and her husband and child down by the harbor.

She stares at him. "Don't talk like that."

"I can't lose this. It's hit me. *I cannot lose this case*. Shit!"

"Luke." Her appetite's gone. She might as well throw her plate over the edge for the coyotes. "That's not what this is about. Winning or losing."

He shakes his head in disagreement. "No. It is."

"It isn't, goddamn it!" She's practically shouting. "You knew coming into this that the odds were against you. Overwhelmingly. You did it as a favor, you did it for the money, you did it to show them you weren't afraid to be here, you did it to get over your ex-wife, you did it for a gazillion reasons, *but you did not do it because you thought you could win!* So knock off the bullshitting yourself! This is about you coming back to your world, not this case. No one expects you to win this."

He stares at her across the table. "That's why I have to."

Her nerves are fraying, too. She's been feeling weird for the past few weeks, her appetite's been irregular, sometimes she's starving, other times the idea of food is repellent. And she isn't sleeping soundly. From his shooting, she's sure that's what it is. "Luke, you don't have to win," she says, finding calmness within herself. Forcing it. "You've already won."

"I shouldn't have done this. I knew I shouldn't have. I let goddamn Freddie De La Guerra shame me into it." The anxiety's flowing from him like spring runoff.

"Then you should've quit when whoever it was tried to kill you.

That was the time. Everybody in the world wanted you to, then. Now it's too late," she says in resignation. "The pity of it."

"That's not it." He won't take off the hair shirt. "It's the case itself. I should have stayed away, like I wanted to."

"Uh-uh." She shakes her head. "You didn't want to."

"I didn't want to come back with a loser," he answers back.

She comes over, takes his hand, leads him to the balcony railing. "Look down there. What do you see?"

"A bunch of lights. What I see every night."

"You are so freaking stubborn," she rails at him. "People travel here from all over the world to see this and all you see is a bunch of lights?"

He turns to her. "Okay. What do I see?" He starts to smile, despite himself.

"*Your* city, Luke. The city you used to own. And will own again. Which has nothing to do with winning or losing. You've already done that, just by being here." She puts her arm around his waist, leans her head on his shoulder.

He puts his free arm around her, drawing her closer. Man, does she know how to make it work for him. His corporeal body, his entire essence, suddenly and wonderfully feels lighter. Almost giddy with relief, he sings: " 'Have I told you lately that I love you?' " He always wanted to be able to sing like Joe Cocker. He doesn't come close.

"No. You haven't."

"I love you."

"I love you, too."

Below them, the lights of the city. Above them, the stars.

"Are you done feeling sorry for yourself now?" she asks. "Can we put that bullshit to bed?"

He smiles. "Yeah," he promises her. "Over and done with."

"Let's go to bed." She takes his hand as she leads him inside, back to the bedroom.

Joe Allison's job in L.A. was scheduled to begin two weeks after he left KNSB. He was going to take the time off between jobs to move and settle into his new apartment down south, in Santa

Monica. Those plans were scuttled when he was arrested, charged, and delivered to the Santa Barbara jail's maximum security section. So the guest house he rented from the Wilsons sits unoccupied, in the same condition as it was on the day he was taken into custody.

Now, a couple of days before the trial is to begin, Luke's there. He hasn't set foot here since his meeting with the Wilsons. They were going to put Allison's belongings in storage and rent the place out to someone new—guest houses are at a premium in the city, they would have found a new tenant in a day—but one of Luke's first acts when he came on board was to quash that. He doesn't want the place disturbed, in case there is anything there he might need later, for information or background. He's been sending in the monthly rent check, fifteen hundred dollars, from the legal retainer. It assures him unlimited access.

Who had motive to kill Emma? Whoever knocked her up, surely, that's a hell of a motive. But that can't be the focus of his attention. He was hired to defend a man accused of murder, not to be a detective looking for everyone who had sex with a fourteen-year-old nymphet. She could have been banging the high school fullback, or had a one-time episode with anyone, man or youth. And the prosecution's case is contradictory on that issue: they're saying condoms found in Allison's place are the same brand and type as those found in the gazebo, ergo he's the man, but if he was using rubbers, how did he knock her up? Back to the theory that he got careless, etcetera. A dog chasing its tail and never quite catching it.

Still, the theory of her impregnator being her killer is better than any other, except for the one he's been developing—by incessant investigation—of her father's porous timeline. If Doug Lancaster had found out that his daughter, his only child, barely in puberty, was pregnant, and had gotten into a fight with her about it, rage could have taken over. It was a common enough scenario when he was the D.A., and he knows it still is.

But there's a major problem with that theory, one the prosecution would surely raise, should this line of attack come into play: why does her own father spirit her out of her bedroom at three or four in the morning, with two of her friends sleeping in the same room? He can be alone with her at any time.

Again, you're dealing with rage, irrationality. Doug Lancaster works up to it, the anger building. Maybe, despite his declaration to the sheriff that he hadn't known she was pregnant, he had. Maybe he had found out within a few days prior to the abduction, or that very day. His mind is blown. He has to confront her, to find out if it's true, and who the person is. He wants to kill him. Even if she "loves" him, whatever that means to a fourteen-year-old, even if it's the nicest boy in the world, Doug Lancaster wants to kill him. More important, he wants to know who violated her.

He can't stop himself. He drives ninety miles in the middle of the night, sneaks onto his own property, goes into her room to confront her. And sees two other girls sleeping there. He has to get her out of there. And then something tragic happens.

One thing Luke knows. He knew it from his first day on the job as a deputy D.A. almost two decades ago. Rage, in its uncontrollableness, is the biggest reason (outside of alcohol, and the two often go hand in hand) that people kill, rape, maim. And there is a great amount of rage around here. Someone directed it at him, and could have killed him. And someone directed it at Emma Lancaster, and killed her. If it wasn't Joe Allison, the killer is one and the same. And he's still out there, waiting.

There's one line Luke has not allowed himself to cross. But now, with the trial looming, he has to. It goes like this:

Doug Lancaster abducted his own daughter. And then he killed her. Because he had been in an incestuous relationship with her, and when she found out she was pregnant she couldn't handle it anymore. She was going to blow the whistle on him.

It's a disgusting, brutal thought, but he has to think it now. This is the way it could have happened.

Think the unthinkable.

The guest house is musty, hot, dark, the windows closed, the curtains and blinds drawn. He pulls the blinds on the front windows and opens them, feeling a rush of air.

It's an attractive little place, nicely furnished. Glenna Lancaster brought a personal touch that fits Joe Allison. It's spare; the house is modified Mission-style, which lends itself to simplicity and lack of clutter.

A cleaning crew came in to straighten things up, some time ago. Nothing since. Luke runs a finger along a thin row of dust on a bookshelf. It isn't bad—a couple of hours of elbow grease and you could move in right now.

He has a copy of the original search warrant with him, as well as a description of what was removed by the sheriff's search party led by Detective Sterling, and where each item was found. The condoms and the running shoes. Later they came back with another warrant, but didn't find anything else incriminating.

The pink condoms were in the bathroom, in the medicine cabinet over the sink, bottom shelf. He goes in there, opens the cabinet. Shaving gel, twin-blade disposable razor, roll-on antiperspirant, Dr. Scholl's foot powder, aftershave lotion from Caswell Massey in New York, scissors, tweezers, nail clippers, dental floss. The scissors, tweezers, clippers, and floss are on the bottom shelf, where the condoms were also found. It's a crowded shelf, although orderly, even with the box of condoms gone. He looks at the evidence list. There were two three-packs of condoms, half a box. If Allison was using that brand with Glenna, then Allison and she were getting it on hot and heavy, more than Allison copped to—which is a good assumption. You don't buy rubbers by the dozen if you're only going to use a couple.

He can tell one thing about Joe Allison from looking at his medicine cabinet—the guy's a neatness freak. Everything is lined up just so, nothing pushing anything out of the way. No spillage. If a box of contraceptives had been on that bottom shelf, it would have crowded everything. A neatness freak wouldn't have put them there.

Think, man, think. Allison wouldn't have them there at all. His girlfriend was here all the time, she stayed over. She would have occasion to use the medicine cabinet, it's right over the sink.

Luke can imagine the scene:

"Honey, could you come in here a second?" This being Nicole, fresh from her shower. She's gone into the cabinet for foot powder or deodorant—and there they would be. "Where did these come from?"

Allison would reply, "Oh, I use them when I'm fucking the wife of the man I work for. For some kinky reason, pink turns her on."

That explosion Luke hears in his brain is the crash and burn of Allison's relationship with Nicole. No way! If Allison was careful enough to never have Nicole around when he was with Glenna, is he careless enough to leave incriminating evidence in plain sight, where his girlfriend would find it?

It doesn't fit. Not even loosely.

Allison keeps his shoes in his clothes closet. He has several pairs, arranged by style and color. Dress loafers, dress laceups, running shoes, basketball shoes, beach thongs. Each category separated from the others by a wooden divider. On the rods above, suits, sports coats, slacks, jeans, shirts. All in categories, the formal stuff he wears in front of the camera in one space, his casual stuff in another. Several items are still in their plastic bags fresh from the cleaners.

Allison had someone come in and arrange his closet, one of those outfits that maximize space. And he was assiduous about maintaining the order.

Luke scans the police report again. Where were the shoes found?

Stuffed in a laundry bag that had been shoved under the bed. There's no mention of what laundry was in the bag.

He squats down and looks under the bed. Nothing is there, only a thin layer of dust. He makes a mental note to have the cleaning crew in again, to keep the place from becoming an allergy incubator.

Back to Allison's closet. In one corner, a hamper. He lifts the lid—a few items to be washed, all darks.

There's a small service porch off the kitchen, in back. A washer and dryer are situated against the wall. Luke opens the washer lid. It's empty. Then the door to the dryer.

A load of whites. That have been sitting there for almost six months.

So here's another nagging question, a series of them: If Allison had left the incriminating running shoes under his bed, in a laundry bag, mightn't there be others under the bed as well? Had he been out running earlier that day and left them there, to be moved later to their rightful spot in the closet?

But why in a laundry bag? Under the bed? From the look

of things, the man didn't use a laundry bag, he threw his stuff in a hamper. He had no need for a laundry bag. He had his own washer and dryer.

Allison has steadfastly maintained that the shoes were lost before the kidnapping, a year earlier. Standing in the man's bedroom, Luke is forced to believe him.

The trial starts tomorrow. There will be a bunch of preliminary stuff, motions and so forth, and then they'll get into picking the jury, and that will take time, a lot of it.

All of that is to come. Tonight is to live, to be alive. He's grateful to be alive, he's come too close to not being. He appreciates what he has, more than he ever did. It's a revelation, a good one.

He takes Riva to The Bistro, a new, small restaurant tucked away on a quiet lane in Montecito. He's calm—she's the one with the pre-trial jitters.

"How do you feel?" she asks, sipping some water. He'll allow himself one more drink, a glass of wine with dinner. He wants to be supersharp tomorrow morning.

"Okay. *Qué sera, sera,* or whatever."

"How can you be so calm?" she asks. "I don't know how I'm going to sleep tonight."

He smiles. "I've been doing this all my life. It's all the other stuff that gets me nervous."

"Like waiting for it to start?"

"Yes, that. And other things. Look," he says, "the shooting is in the past. I'm here. I'm a survivor. I'm stronger than ever. And because all that crap happened to me, I met you, and that's been the best thing in my life in years. So let's celebrate tonight."

She smiles. "I'll drink to that. And your case." Her smile to him has an almost Mona Lisa quality, a hidden contentment. Like she knows secrets he doesn't. "You're going to win," she asserts. "When it's all over, you're going to be the last man standing, Luke."

* * *

They lie in bed. The midnight hour chimed long ago.

"Are you asleep?" she whispers, knowing without looking that he isn't.

"No. Are you?"

She laughs without making a sound. Her hand goes to his thigh.

He's enjoying the touch. He never sleeps much the night before the show begins. He isn't lying in bed awake with worry, but with anticipation. This is what he does, what he lives for. "What are you thinking?" he asks.

He isn't completely here with her; he's in the courtroom, making his opening statement. He hears the sounds resonating in his head. It's like playing air guitar in front of your bedroom mirror and the next second you're on stage at the Rose Bowl and a hundred thousand maniacs are going out of their minds because of you.

"I'll tell you later," she says. "This isn't the time."

He turns on his side, looks at her. "Why can't you tell me now?"

"Because you're starting the trial tomorrow and you don't need any more distractions than you already have."

He touches her face. "Now I'm really curious. Come on, tell me. Whatever it is, it won't distract me. I could use a distraction, to tell you the truth."

"I've been waiting for the right moment," she says, clearly procrastinating, "but there isn't one."

He takes her hand in his. "What?" he says, not really here, his mind still racing with courtroom anticipation. Jokingly, he says, "You're going to tell me you're pregnant, is that it?" *Ladies and gentlemen of the jury . . .*

"Yes."

He isn't in the courtroom anymore. He's here, in bed, with her. Long after midnight, when all the world is asleep, except for them. And maybe Joe Allison and Ray Logan and a few others. "You are?" His voice is a mixture of disbelief, awe, surprise, shock. "Pregnant? You're pregnant?"

"From the night I didn't use the diaphragm." She hesitates. "The night you didn't let me."

"This is—this is—*whoa!*"

She exhales, as if she's been holding her breath for weeks. "God,

I've been worrying about this—the timing—you're about to start the trial, that's where all your energy and thought should be," she's almost stammering, the words are racing so fast out of her mouth, "when you have a kid, things are different—"

"Riva." He squeezes her hand. "Slow down."

She sits up. In the moonlight her figure looks like something out of a perfect Botticelli etching. "Do you want to have this baby?" she asks.

He feels a shock through his body. "Yes."

"You *want* to, you're not just going to tolerate it, go along with it."

"I want to," he says. "I do." He pulls her to him, cradling her, cuddling her, holding her. "We have a life, Riva. This is proof."

"Is the prosecution ready?"

Ray Logan stands. "We are, Your Honor."

"Is the defense ready?"

Luke stands, buttoning his coat, touching Allison lightly on the shoulder, for reassurance. Allison's all spiffed up for his court appearance—freshly pressed suit, crisp white shirt, rep tie. He's had a haircut by his own barber, who went into the jail to do the work. He even got a manicure, to smooth out his bitten cuticles.

"Your Honor, the defense is ready."

Judge Ewing nods to both men. "The case of the People versus Joseph B. Allison will commence. Before I bring the first group of jury candidates in, do you have any motions?" He looks at the prosecution table, where Ray Logan sits. Accompanying him are two assistant D.A.'s, his jury consultant, and an executive assistant. Seated in the row behind them are more members of his staff, paralegals, detectives from his office (Lovett prominent among them), Sheriff Williams, and other establishment heavies.

Ewing swings his look over to Luke. "Mr. Garrison?"

Luke stands tall. "Yes, Your Honor, we do."

Logan's head jerks at this unexpected development.

Luke picks up a manila folder that is on the table in front of him. "We have recently discovered a key piece of evidence that the prosecution has been withholding from us, Your Honor," he says gravely. "It casts tremendous doubt on the entire validity of the initial search and seizure of Mr. Allison's car on the night he was arrested, and thus on the entire legal underpinning of the prosecution's case. We ask that you examine this and then declare the search of Mr. Allison's car to have been illegal, pursuant to the California penal code, section 1538.5, and that any and all evidence discovered as a result of that search and any subsequent events be inadmissible at trial."

"Your Honor—" Logan begins.

Ewing puts up a hand for the prosecutor to be silent. "You already filed an Information on this issue, Mr. Garrison," the judge says sternly. "It was not accepted. Why are you attempting to revisit it now?"

"Because, as I just said, Your Honor, new evidence has come to light which we did not know existed, and which should have been given to us as part of discovery. It was not." He brandishes the file in his hand, then drops it with a thud on the table. "In addition, Your Honor, an attempt was recently made on my life, which you may be aware of."

"Of course I am," the judge replies.

"It follows logically that whoever tried to kill me had a motive," Luke asserts. "The motive possibly being that whoever it was doesn't want me on this case. That person might be afraid that in the course of my defense of Mr. Allison, I might simultaneously uncover exculpatory evidence that not only will exonerate my client but point the finger in the direction of Emma Lancaster's real killer."

A buzz goes up in the courtroom. Ewing's mouth sets in a hard line. "In my chambers, gentlemen." He gets up and marches off the bench. Logan, following, sidles by Luke. "What are you trying to pull?" he hisses. "This is the worst kind of showboating."

Luke wiggles the folder that he's holding. "Let's see," he replies. "Let's let the judge decide. In case you've forgotten, Ray, you're not the judge." A pause for effect. "And you sure as hell ain't the jury, either."

Judge Ewing looks up from the pages he's just read. "When did you physically take possession of this?" he asks Luke.

"Three days ago, Your Honor."

"When did you find out about it?"

"Earlier that same day."

Ewing looks at Logan. "Why wasn't this turned over to the defense at the proper time?" he demands. "Why are we having these eleventh hour shenanigans? Good God, this isn't the eleventh hour," he fumes, "we're technically in trial."

"I didn't know about this, Your Honor," Logan says, red-faced. "This is the first I've heard or known of this document's existence." Luke has given him a copy, which he read while the judge read his.

Ewing regards Luke's successor with a baleful eye. "I find that hard to believe."

"It's the truth, I swear it. I don't like being surprised any more than you do," Logan says.

Ewing drums his fingers on his desk. "I'm going to have to sleep on this," he says after some time thinking about it, which both lawyers sweat out. "And the linkage between the shooting of you, Mr. Garrison, and this trial. I'll render my decision in the morning."

Until then, everything's in limbo.

Back in the courtroom, barely 10:30 A.M. The trial's adjourned for the day. The confused members of the jury pool, who were expecting to be on hold all day long, are released until tomorrow morning.

Luke sits at the defense table with his client. The deputy sheriff who will accompany Allison back to the jail hovers impatiently nearby. "We fired our first shot across their bow," Luke tells Allison, "and the first juror hasn't been impanelled yet."

"That's good, I take it?" Allison asks optimistically. As for anyone caught in the jaws of the system, especially for those who "don't belong," for whom it's an unending maze of fear, confusion, and misguided hope, every small "victory" magnifies in importance.

"Yeah," Luke reassures him. "We're on the attack now, and they're on the defensive. Hopefully, that's how it's going to go the entire trial." He scoops his papers into his briefcase. "See you *mañana.* Keep the faith."

* * *

Sheriff Williams and Ray Logan meet in Logan's office. Logan's beyond being upset; he's enraged. And he's worried, because things are happening that he should know about and doesn't. Williams may be the senior member of this law-enforcement team by longevity, but Ray Logan is the prosecutor who has to conduct the trial and get a conviction in the highest-profile trial in the county in a decade. And right out of the box he discovers there might be an obstruction of justice emanating from the sheriff's office.

"I feel like an asshole," he bitches. "How come Luke Garrison knows about this phone call to the police dispatcher and I don't?"

"It didn't seem important," Williams answers. It was a mistake on his department's part, a bad mistake. They had all been so damned excited to have a bona fide suspect in the Emma Lancaster kidnap-murder that specific details were disregarded. "It still doesn't," he maintains.

"It was important enough for Ewing to send everyone home so he could study it," Logan counters hotly. "And that's only half the point, Sheriff." He occasionally uses Williams's first name, Bob, but only when they're comfortable together, which is definitely not the case now. "I have to know everything, and I have to know it up front. It's like the way you handled the parents. You virtually granted them immunity before my office even spoke to them. Now we can't pursue any of the shit that's built up around Doug Lancaster, like *where the fuck was he*, for example."

Williams nods. He hates conflict, especially with his own people. Logan and he are partners, joined at the hip; the success or failure of this trail will reflect on both of them, for good or ill. But he also knows that in the long run the small stuff is forgotten. Jurors look at the big picture, the key evidence. The rest is shoe polish.

"No superior court judge in the country would rule against the police on something like this," he Dutch-uncles Logan. "They'd be run out of town on a rail."

Logan forces himself to take a deep breath and calm down. "That's not the point, any one or two specific details. I can't be operating in the dark. What Luke brought up, that's not going to derail us—I hope. But somewhere down the line, he could find something critical that we've overlooked." He steeples his fingers, thinking. "I'm going to have one of my assistants go over every inch of this, all your procedures, everything. Let's make sure we haven't overlooked anything else."

"That's fine by me," Williams agrees. "I don't want to blow this conviction on a technicality."

Logan says, "Good." A moment's thought, then he goes on. "What's happening with Garrison's shooting? Anything? Any leads?"

Williams shakes his head. "Nothing. It's frustrating."

Logan's tight-lipped. "It looks like we're stonewalling. Punishing him."

"No." Williams is adamant. "I want to know who it was, more than anyone." He pauses. "You know, Luke's on the other side now, but he and I made a lot of cases together. The man's a standup guy. I don't like the idea of some vigilante madman out there trying to take him out."

"No more surprises, okay?" Logan stands, concluding the meeting.

"All we can do is our best," the sheriff says.

The call comes to the house at 10:30 that night. "I hope I'm not waking you up," Judge Ewing says to Luke, "but I assumed you'd want to know as soon as I made my decision. It's a three-way call. Ray Logan's on the other line, listening."

"I haven't been to bed this early since grade school," Luke tells the judge. "And I do want to hear, of course."

"I'm denying your motion."

The receiver feels hot in his hand. He was expecting this; he couldn't get his hopes up so high as to think Ewing would, in essence, throw the case out. But still, it's an empty feeling in his gut.

He finds his voice. "Well, thanks for calling so promptly, Judge."

"It was a close call," Ewing says, both defending his decision and assuaging Luke's feelings. "But it isn't conclusive. In a situation like this, there has to be no doubt. You understand."

"Yes, I do."

"I'll announce it tomorrow morning, before we begin jury selection," Ewing says. "You can file an exception, of course."

"I'll think about that." The guy's almost telling him out loud to protest. Let a higher court reverse, if they see fit. He must have spent some troubled time figuring out how to play this, Luke thinks. He wonders what Logan's thinking, listening to this.

He didn't expect to win. Outside of that, this is as good as he can get. Not a victory, but a notch on the wall.

"I'll see you in the courtroom tomorrow," Ewing says, signing off. There's a momentary silence. "Good luck, Luke." The phone goes dead.

"That was Judge Ewing," Luke tells Riva, who's been listening to his end of the conversation. "He turned us down."

She's in her nightgown. Her hair is up, her face is clean of makeup. She looks young, innocent, he thinks, gazing at her as she's curled up on the couch. She looks beautiful. She isn't showing yet, but she will, soon. He's looking forward to it. "You should be going to sleep," he says. "You need your rest."

"I'm fine." She smiles. "You're going to take care of me now?"

"Of course. I'm the father of our child." *Our child.* The words have a magical ring to them. "Do you think we should . . ." The magnitude of it hits him all at once.

"We should what?" she asks.

"You know." He can't say it. He never thought he'd ever say it again, or even think it.

"What?" She's smiling at him, her face screwed up in a question.

He feels like a prime doofus. "Get married," he stammers.

Her jaw drops. "Get married? Are you serious?" She sits up.

He comes over, sits next to her. "Well, I don't know. Isn't that what people do when they get pregnant?"

She stares at him. "What for?"

"So the kid won't be a bastard. So . . ." He's at a loss.

"Nobody cares about that," she says. "What do you think, my father's going to lay a shotgun upside your noggin?"

"I've never even met your father. We've never even talked about him."

"And we never will." Her smile has faded.

"You've never mentioned your parents. I don't even know if they're alive," he says.

"My mother died when I was young," she informs him. "My father might as well have. I haven't seen him in years, since I was old enough to get away."

He looks at her. "You've never talked about any brothers or sisters, either."

"I don't have any. My life started at seventeen, Luke," she says with finality, closing the subject. "Before that, that was another life."

"Okay." Maybe later. He isn't going to push it now. He reaches his arm out. She nestles against his body. "I'm your family. Me and Bubba here," he says, patting her stomach. It's just beginning to protrude—now that he knows, he can feel the difference.

"If that's what you want." She seems shy suddenly.

"It's what I want, Riva." He pulls her closer. "It's going to make all this so much better."

Eight in the morning. The courtroom is empty except for the principals. The court clerk hands copies of Judge Ewing's decision to the prosecution and defense tables. Luke already went over to the jail at six to deliver the news.

"Don't be down about this," he told his client. "The judge had no choice. We got what I wanted."

"What was that?"

"Their attention."

"In the motion under section 1538.5, the court denies defendant's motion," Ewing says in a flat voice. "However," he continues, turning his look to Logan's table, a look of *I don't like being fucked with*: "I am strongly admonishing the prosecution regarding the withholding of evidence. Any more such incidents and the court will hold you in contempt. Do I make myself clear?"

Ray Logan gets up, the color in his face rising. "Yes, Your Honor. This was not intentional, I assure you. We have no intention of—"

Ewing swings his gavel hard, silencing Logan. "Intentional or not, I don't care," he says sternly. He's giving Luke everything he can short of a victory. "Don't do it."

"Yes, Your Honor." Logan stands in place like a chagrined schoolboy.

Ewing turns to the clerk. "Bring in the first group."

The jury selection process is excruciatingly slow. Glaciers move faster. Because of technicalities and legal objections from both sides, more than half the candidates have to be privately examined in Judge Ewing's chambers, and that slows things down even more.

More than anything, what makes selection go so slowly is that this is a capital crime, which means the death penalty is an option. And that means that the jury has to be death-penalty qualified. Every potential juror has to be asked, in specific detail, about his or her attitudes about capital punishment, for or against. Any jury candidate who stipulates that he can't vote to send anyone, regardless of the circumstances of a crime, to his or her death, is automatically excluded from the jury pool.

When Luke was on the other side, he loved picking these juries, because anyone who's willing to approve of a death sentence is more likely to convict; it's human nature, and the statistics bear it out. A defense lawyer already has one strike against him going in on a death-penalty case, Luke always figured.

Now he's that defense lawyer. So he has to fight like hell to find jurors who can convict, but aren't knee-jerk about it. A tough proposition. By the end of the first week, only five jurors have been accepted, while one hundred nine were rejected. Luke's had to use only four of his twenty peremptory challenges; the prosecution's used six. So many people have been disqualified for cause by Judge Ewing that the process starts to become a joke in the corridors outside—the trial that will never take place because of the jury that will never be impaneled.

Friday is the court's dark day. On Thursday afternoon, during the midafternoon recess, Ewing, clearly frustrated by the lack of progress, meets with the lawyers in his chambers. "We're moving too slowly," he says, showing his irritation. "It's partly my doing, although you guys are taking way too much time with some of these jurors. Come Monday, I'm going to start moving things through faster, so if there are any potential jurors still on the current list that you really think you don't want, save your objections for them. I don't want to bring in another two hundred prospective jurors—there aren't any. The jury's going to come from this group, and I won't keep trying to get jurors that both sides think are perfect."

True to his word, Judge Ewing is brisk to the point of curtness on Monday morning. Five more jurors are selected Monday, and two on Tuesday makes twelve. Ewing wants at least four alternates, to be extra careful, although the most jurors he's ever lost on a panel are three. This isn't going to be an O. J. deal, with jurors dropping like flies for any trivial reason. This train is going to run on time.

Three alternates come on board Wednesday, and by the time Ewing recesses at the end of the day on Thursday two more are set. Twelve jurors, five alternates. More than enough.

It's a multiethnic jury, six men, six women. Seven anglos, three Latinos, one black, one Chinese-American. Luke isn't crazy about this jury. If he were prosecuting this case instead of defending it, he'd be happy with the group—but there are a few members he thinks he can work. It'll be interesting to see how they react when they discover the myriad sexual transgressions the family members were involved in. If they can stomach those and still see the forest for the trees, which is that a girl was kidnapped and then murdered, forget her sexual history, then he and his client are in trouble.

The show starts on Monday. In the morning Ray Logan will give his opening statement. Then, barring any unforeseen complications, it'll be his turn on stage, for the first time in this county in more than three years. And wearing a different hat.

Luke always gets to the courthouse before anyone else. He prides himself on that. It's been a ritual since he started litigating as an assistant D.A. Today, though, as he walks down the long tile hallway towards the courtroom, he sees, from a distance, that others have beaten him to the draw.

The inside of the building is dim—the lights have not yet been turned on, only slivers of predawn sunlight filter through the high windows. Three people are huddled in a corner, faces furtively turned inward towards the wall, as if by not looking out they won't be seen. Although they are in darkness, he immediately recognizes them: Ray Logan and Doug and Glenna Lancaster.

They are unaware that someone else has intruded on their private rendezvous. He stops and watches for a moment; then silently, carefully, he moves against the wall, melding into the dark, cool bulk as much as he can, straining to hear them. Even from far away, at least forty yards—the hallway is as long as a football field—it's clear to Luke that they are having a strenuous argument.

The voices drift down towards him, inchoately echoing off the walls of the cavernous corridor, a natural echo chamber. The words are muffled, but the intent is clear—the Lancasters don't want Logan to introduce Emma's sexual history. Logan keeps shaking his head, shifting back and forth from foot to foot, Doug Lancaster leaning in towards him, haranguing him, Glenna standing back from both of them, her body rigid.

This must be mighty important, Luke thinks, if Doug and Glenna are in each other's proximity. They avoid each other at all costs.

She knows, Luke realizes. He should have figured she would—it was naive of him to believe otherwise. She was Emma's mother.

Now that he thinks about it, they would have been the main proponents for sealing the coroner's report in the first place. And now, two hours before the coroner is to take the stand, they're still trying to protect their daughter's image. And their own. A cynical attitude to take, but a truthful one.

One last harangue from Doug and then Logan turns to him, says something that Luke can't make out, and walks away. Doug starts to go after him, almost lunging at him, but Glenna grabs him by the biceps and restrains him.

Luke watches the divorced couple staring at each other. Not a word is spoken. Then Doug spins on his heel and strides off in the opposite direction from Ray Logan.

Glenna Lancaster is alone. A lonely figure in a large, barren space. She starts to weep, her shoulders shaking from the sobbing. Luke watches, a fly on the wall, mortifyingly embarrassed at being an intruder on her excruciating sadness, but locked in place with no means of escape. The sounds of her sobs drift down to him, the lamentation of a mother in perpetual grieving for her lost child.

"Ladies and gentlemen of the jury . . ."

Ray Logan is standing in front of the jury, beginning his opening statement. All eyes are on him, and he knows it. Especially the eyes of Luke Garrison, the man he used to report to.

He's nervous, going up against Luke. He would be nervous anyway, it comes with the territory. It's like standing on the first tee of the U.S. Open in front of a gallery of a thousand spectators and starting your backswing for the first drive of the day. All you want to do is make contact and not kill anybody or, worse, whiff it. Once you've taken that first swing, the butterflies start to go away.

"My name is Ray Logan. I am the district attorney for Santa Barbara County."

And right on cue, the calmness begins to come over him. He's feeling better already—saying the words "district attorney" make him feel good, give him a sense of achievement.

Courtroom Number 1 is the legendary mural courtroom, where the history of California, from the Spanish conquistadors to the Depression migrants, is depicted on the walls and ceiling, like an antinativist Sistine Chapel. This courtroom is rarely used anymore, reserved for special cases. And now it's packed, every seat taken. You have to have a pass to get in. Much of the space is taken up by reporters from newspapers and television stations. The rest is family members, friends, public people like politicians, and others with juice.

Doug and Glenna Lancaster are present. They're both sitting on the prosecutor's side of the aisle, but apart from each other. Doug is in the second row directly behind Ray Logan's chair, while Glenna is in the back, looking like a wraith. She's all in black, including a scarf tied over her head, like a woman in mourning, which she still is, more so now that this trial is beginning and her life and her daughter's life are going to be exposed. She is wearing no makeup, no jewelry.

Lancaster is dressed conservatively, in a dark business suit. For the briefest of moments, when he first entered the courtroom and walked down the aisle to his seat, his eyes locked with Luke's. There was pure hatred in them. This man, Luke thought, wants me dead.

Under normal circumstances, neither Doug nor Glenna would be allowed in the courtroom: they're potential witnesses. Logan has both on his witness list, and Doug is on Luke's as well. Tearing up Lancaster's non-alibi is going to be a cornerstone of his defense. Logan, however, had beseeched the court that they be granted exceptions to the rule, in the interest of compassion.

"It's their daughter who was murdered, they've already suffered terribly," he passionately argued in the judge's chambers. "Not allowing them to observe the trial would be cruel and inhumane."

It was Luke's call; and to both Ewing's and Logan's surprise, he acquiesced. Having Doug Lancaster in the courtroom will mean that Lancaster will learn, from Luke's opening statement, what Luke is planning to do; but Lancaster is going to find out anyway—Logan will be briefing him daily. To exclude the grieving parents will be bad public relations. He and his client already have enough negative publicity.

He also has a more practical motive. He hopes that as the trial progresses Doug Lancaster will become increasingly agitated, to the point where he might do something stupid, something that will play into the defense's hands. Knowing Doug Lancaster as Luke does, this isn't a far-fetched notion.

One person isn't here: Nicole Rogers. She may be a witness later on—both he and Logan have her on their witness lists—but that isn't why she's absent. Luke talked to her days ago about coming, to offer moral support, and she turned him down flat. She and Joe weren't going on anyway, and she wants no part of this. "I thought I knew him," she told Luke over the phone. "It's terrible to think you know someone intimately, and suddenly you don't know a damn thing about them." Luke knew then that, despite her former assertion, she thinks his client is guilty.

Logan's voice rings strong in the vaulted-ceilinged room. "You have been chosen to make a momentous decision. To decide whether or not Joe Allison, the accused in this case, kidnapped and murdered Emma Lancaster, a fourteen-year-old girl." He turns and points.

"That dark-haired man seated at the defense table, next to his lawyer, is Joe Allison."

Luke has anticipated this, and worked with Allison in the jail. About returning looks, not being vague or ambiguous in demeanor, staring straight ahead. And keeping his cool.

Allison is doing that. He's doing okay. He holds eye contact with the jury members who are looking at him. Not with aggression or evasiveness. A firm, clear look. A man who has nothing to hide.

Riva, sitting in the row behind Luke and Allison, also stares at the jury, and at Logan. She is going to be here much of the time, and she is going to stare daggers at Logan's back.

In a deliberately dismissive manner, Logan drops his hand, turns back to the jury. "You are going to be given a lot of information that is not directly related to this case. It's peripheral information—information about people's personalities, their foibles, their imperfections. My associates and I will share some of this with you, not to confuse you, but to set the background, and to show you the difference between the *truth*, as it applies to *this case and this case only*, and innuendos the defense is going to allude to, to try and confuse you from the issue at hand, the only issue you are here to consider—did Joe Allison kidnap and murder Emma Lancaster?"

He pauses to let that settle in. Then he continues. "We are going to show you proof that Mr. Allison *did* kidnap and murder Emma Lancaster. Real, tangible proof. Not theories. Not conjecture. Not 'what-if's.' We're not going to try to dazzle you with smoke and mirrors. We are going to show you *motive*, we are going to show you *opportunity*, we are going to show you *physical evidence* that connects Joe Allison and Emma Lancaster on the night of her abduction, and before then."

He's doing good, Luke thinks—short, sweet, concise, hard-hitting. He learned good lessons from me.

"Joe Allison was found with certain pieces of evidence in his possession that only Emma's murderer could have possessed. Certain things that belonged to Emma Lancaster, certain pieces of evidence that place him at the crime scene on the night in question, certain pieces of evidence that will show the extraordinarily strong link between Joe Allison, an adult man, an employee of Emma Lancaster's father, and the victim, Emma, a fourteen-year-old girl who was in the eighth grade." Another pause. "A fourteen-year-old girl, ladies and gentlemen. Barely a teenager. Still wearing braces."

He stops for a moment and walks to his table. One of the other lawyers hands him a large manila envelope. He walks back to the jury box and opens it, taking out the sixteen-by-twenty-inch picture inside and holding it up so the jurors can get a good look at it. "This is Emma Lancaster, ladies and gentlemen of the jury. A few weeks before she was abducted from her bedroom in the dead of night, and subsequently murdered. And then hidden away in a terrible, lonely place, while her frantic parents and thousands of volunteer citizens searched for her in vain until, more than a week later, her body was accidentally discovered."

An easel has been set up at the corner of the jury box. He places the color photograph, a typical school yearbook picture, on the easel. She looks even younger than she was, about the age of her First Communion.

The jurors all turn and look at it. A few then turn and look over at Joe Allison. Doug Lancaster does, too. Venomously.

It's a moment to catch, Luke thinks. He swivels in his chair, a glance at Glenna Lancaster sitting ten rows behind him on the other side. She is dry-eyed, but her skin is flushed, and he can see, even from this distance, that her breathing is ragged. She is scrupulously avoiding looking in Joe Allison's direction.

"That was Emma Lancaster before she died," Logan says. His aides hand him a second envelope. He pulls the black and white enlargement out, looks at it, grimaces. From where Luke's sitting, it's an honest grimace.

"And this was Emma Lancaster the week *after* she died." Logan turns the photograph around, so the jury can see it for themselves.

There is a collective gasp. One of the woman jurors cries out audibly, her hand flying to her mouth. Logan holds up the picture a moment longer.

It's one of the first police photographs that was taken of Emma when her body was found buried on the trail. It's a grisly sight. Her body is swollen, her clothes have been ripped.

Luke glances at Emma's father. The man is looking down at his feet, not acknowledging the picture of his dead child that's being displayed. He's shaking. *If he was involved, Luke thinks, he's paying a heavy price for it now.*

Logan mercifully puts the picture in its envelope. "I'm sorry to have subjected you to that, ladies and gentlemen," he says to the twelve jurors, most of whom look like they want to throw up, "but you had to see it. You had to know. How this beautiful girl"—he points to the cherubic photo on the easel—"became the victim of a heinous crime.

"We don't know why, exactly, Joe Allison took Emma Lancaster from her bed, where she was fast asleep, took her outside, and killed her in cold blood," Logan says. "But we have a good idea. I'll explain that to you in a moment. Before I do, let me caution you: you will not like everything you hear—in this tempestuous age, none of us lives in a vacuum, including the Lancaster family—but you will understand it, how it relates to your own lives, and the lives of your children and grandchildren."

He pauses to let the jury catch up with him; they have to be wondering, *what is he talking about?*

"The reason might have been anger, mixed with fear. Or it might have been passion gone haywire," Logan goes on. "Yes, there was passion in this. Passion between a young girl with a crush on a handsome male celebrity, and the male celebrity who used that advantage for his own narcissistic ends. And that will connect with the anger and the fear, also. Especially the fear."

Now the jurors are really paying attention. Logan's going to tease them a bit more before he brings out the hard evidence—Emma's pregnancy, the condoms found in the gazebo, the same condoms found in Allison's house. Luke's ready for the other shoe to drop.

"Or it could have been an accident," Logan says. "Not the killing—that was premeditated, without question. That is why we are going to ask for the death penalty in this case—because Emma Lancaster's murder was clearly premeditated. But before that, who knows?" He pauses, grasps the railing of the jury box in both hands, leans forward, the bar bracing him. "Not Emma Lancaster—she isn't here anymore to tell us. But ladies and gentlemen, in a way she *is* telling us. By the evidence she left behind, and the style in which she left it. And ladies and gentlemen, I am here to tell you that, by the time this trial is over, Emma Lancaster will have spoken to you loudly and clearly. She will have spoken to you from her grave. And she will tell you, and you will believe beyond a reasonable doubt, that Joe Allison murdered her. And here is the clearest, most compelling thing she is going to tell you." He pauses; even for him, presenting this is difficult. Then he says it: "She was pregnant."

The jurors are a classic tableau of human reaction to surprise and disbelief: shock, fear, horror. One man keeps shaking his head back and forth, a hand over his mouth to cover the self-conscious kind of smirk that comes on people when they see some terrible tragedy, like a ten-car crash or a train wreck.

Luke sits quietly in his chair at the defense table while the maelstrom swirls around him, and thinks: it's all changed. Months go by, people form opinions about this girl, her death, her family, her community, which for a while was the entire community, everyone was linked to everyone else through their connection to Emma Lancaster, a girl almost none of them had known. And their collective searching for her and mourning her when she was found, and their grief in the days after, and their frustration and impotence when her killer somehow vanished, out of their grasp; and then their relief—not happiness, it's too somber a thing and it took too long to resolve, more than a year, to bring any kind of happiness to conclusion—but there was relief. It was finished. Her murderer had been caught. Life could go on, with a pattern, a rhythm that everyone can attach to, everyone can know.

And now, with one sentence, those patterns and rhythms have been broken.

Logan continues.

"It would follow—I think any reasonable person will make this assumption—that whoever impregnated her had good cause to kill her. Because if he was ever discovered, he would be ruined. He would go to jail, for a long time."

He takes Emma's photo off the easel. Holding it with both hands, he walks the length of the jury box, making sure each juror takes a close, hard look at it.

"Listen to the voice of this poor victim, this helpless girl, this wonderful daughter who will never brighten her parents' lives again.

Who will never dance at her senior prom, never marry, never have children of her own. Listen to Emma Lancaster speaking to you from the grave, ladies and gentlemen—and you will hear her telling you, 'Joe Allison killed me.' It will be a young voice, a sweet voice, a clear voice. And it will tell you that there is only one verdict you can find in this case. A verdict of murder in the first degree."

He steps back from the jury box, so they can all see him clearly. "There is no real justice that can be administered here," he says in a low voice. "Nothing you do will bring Emma Lancaster back to life. The best you can do is make sure her murderer is not allowed to pursue his life. The *best* you can do, and the thing you *must* do, is to find Joseph Allison guilty of murder with aggravating circumstances." Then, and only then, will the spirit of Emma Lancaster begin to find rest. Then, and only then, will it finally be at peace."

Luke stands in front of the defense table, facing the jury across the room. Over the lunch break he's changed shirts. He's wearing the exact same style he had on at the beginning of the day, but it's crisp. Most of these people remember him from before. He doesn't want to disappoint them. Not even sartorially.

"Good afternoon," he begins. He's in laser mode—there are no butterflies in his stomach, as he knew there were in Ray Logan's. That was pretrial, before he was shot at, before he found out about Riva's pregnancy. After those things, this is another day at work. Important, yes, but not life-shattering.

"My name is Luke Garrison. I represent the defendant in this case, the man sitting at this table." He turns and sweeps his arm towards Allison. "His name is Joseph Allison. Joe. An easy name to remember. Many of you do remember him, of course, as our city's leading television anchorman until recently. When he gave you the news, you believed him. You felt you could trust him." He pauses, taking time to look each juror in the eye for a brief moment. "Ladies and gentlemen of the jury, by the time this trial is over, you will know that you can trust Joe again."

He walks towards the jury box. Halfway there, he stops. He's in the center of the front section of the room, the action arena where the spectator's railing divides the room between the players and the watchers—between the bench, where Judge Ewing sits, the prosecutor's table, and the defendant's table. The midday sun, filtering in through the high windows that are pocked with bird shit, insect mash, and dust, radiates emotional and psychological isolation.

He turns and looks directly at Ray Logan, staring at him with intensity. Logan, startled, looks away. Then he looks back defiantly, as if to say to Luke, *You can't cow me, that was from surprise, that's all.*

Still staring at Logan, Luke says, "I used to be him." He points at Logan, who's fighting not to squirm. Pivoting back to the jury, he goes on, "I was the district attorney in this county for ten years. Some of you might remember that. Ray Logan worked under me then. He was one of my chief assistant D.A.'s. Let me tell you, he was really good. He won a lot of tough cases for the people of this county."

He pauses to let the jurors think on that. "And the other D.A.'s sitting with Mr. Logan—they worked for me, too, worked *with* me. We were a great team. I have no reason to doubt that they still are. With or without me."

His voice is finding its cadence, like that of a good country preacher. When he was starting out, he studied famous preachers, men like Martin Luther King and Billy Graham. He doesn't "preach" in the courtroom, it isn't who he is and this isn't the place for it, but he likes the undercurrent of the rhythms, the musicality of their voices, the repetition of key words and phrases, the leaning on certain words to give them importance beyond their corporeal meanings.

"These are good people," he says. "They believe in the law, in justice. They try to be fair, as fair as they can be. And they don't like to make mistakes, because they do try to be fair, and because they know that their mistakes can come back to haunt them. Like one of mine did to me."

The jurors are paying rapt attention—this is not your normal opening statement. "Prosecutors and police departments don't make that many mistakes, ladies and gentlemen. Especially not in Santa Barbara. They do a good job, they're thorough. When they bring charges against a suspect, they usually have the goods. And of course, they always think they do. At least initially.

"But, ladies and gentlemen of the jury," he says, his voice rising with the emotion of what he's doing—not getting loud, but more intense, fuller, coming from his entire body, his entire being—"sometimes they do make mistakes. We all do—we're all human. And when they do, my friends, they can be tragic. Which is the case here, where Joe Allison, truly an innocent man, is being tried for a crime he didn't commit. A crime he *couldn't* have committed."

There's an undercurrent in the large room. Ewing starts to pick up his gavel to silence it, but thinks better of it. All that would do is call attention to something that's organic and not really consciously noticeable, except it's coming from everyone, everywhere. He lays the gavel down. The undercurrent fades away as Luke stands in the middle of the floor, waiting to go on.

"There is a bit of physical evidence against my client," he says. "I grant you that. But it's flimsy, folks. It's so contrived. It was found so conveniently. Way too conveniently. And even the police procedures that 'uncovered' this evidence, if that's the right word—stumbled onto it is closer to the truth—even those very procedures are suspect."

Logan starts to rise in his place to protest, but Ewing waves him to sit down. "This is opening, Counselor," he says before Logan can open his mouth in protest. "It's supposed to be informative, just as yours was."

Logan falls back into his chair. Without missing a beat, Luke goes on. "Let me give you one example of how contrived the state's evidence is. The police found an incredible piece of evidence in Mr. Allison's car—a key chain that belonged to Emma Lancaster, that was missing the next day, when her mother first realized she had disappeared. *It's one of the most important pieces of evidence they have against Mr. Allison,*" he says, emphasizing its importance. "And they're going to claim that Mr. Allison, who they allege was her kidnapper, took it with him when he abducted Emma. Now let me ask you this, ladies and gentlemen: Why would a kidnapper take her keys? If you're going to abduct someone, you don't stop to look around for things like keys. There are two other girls in that bedroom. You want to get out of there as fast as you can." He shakes his head at the ridiculousness of it. "And Emma certainly wouldn't have taken them," he continues. "Somebody's kidnapping her but she somehow manages to take her keys with her? And if she was leaving voluntarily, which the evidence is clearly going to show, she still wouldn't have taken them, because she would have returned to her room through the same patio door." He sweeps the jury box with his eyes. "You're all intelligent people. Does that make sense to you? It sure doesn't to me.

"But there's more to this, my friends. Much more. We're going to show you, we're going to *prove* to you, that many of the people closest to Emma Lancaster should be suspects in this, but never were." A strategic pause. "Now, the prosecution knows about all this. They've known about it for months, but they've never pursued any leads about it. They have Joe Allison in their jail, and that's all they care about. They want a conviction, regardless of whether or not justice is served. Because the pressure to get one is too strong to resist."

Now he moves, a deliberate pacing, a caged tiger, back and forth in front of the jury box. "Here are some of the things the prosecution *doesn't* want you to know about, because it looks bad for them, for their case. They don't want you to know that Emma Lancaster's father was missing when his daughter was abducted. But did they ever pursue that?" He looks past the prosecution table to Doug Lancaster, sitting two rows back, directly behind Ray Logan. Doug is glaring wildly at him. He stares back before turning away. "No, they did not, even though immediate family are always—*always,* ladies and gentlemen, unless there is concrete, irrefutable proof to the contrary, like eyewitnesses—the initial suspects. Because we know that in the majority of murders like this one, a member of the family did it. But the authorities didn't investigate Doug Lancaster fully. They interviewed him, took him at his word that he was innocent, and let it go."

The murmur is loud again. The courtroom is electric. Luke stops and looks at Sheriff Williams, who's staring straight ahead passively, not moving a muscle in his face.

Pacing again. "You're going to hear things about all the principals in this case that will chill you, ladies and gentlemen. I have no desire to throw mud on Emma Lancaster's reputation, or her parents'. They've already suffered enough. But that does not mean, and I want you all to hear this and remember it, *that does not mean* that Joe Allison has to be found guilty of the crime of murder because we're all feeling sympathy for the Lancasters, even though they're no longer a family. They're parents, they'll always be parents. And they're never going to get their daughter back, regardless of whether we execute Joe Allison or a dozen Joe Allisons."

He stops again. Composes himself for the jury's sake, although inside he feels great. Walking over to the jury box, he rests his hands against the railing. A few avert their gazes, a few smile nervously. "This is not an ordinary trial for me," he tells them. "This is personal—very personal. A couple of months ago, someone tried to kill me. Maybe you know about that, it was on television and in the newspapers. Right now, every day and night, a sheriff's deputy stands watch over me. The sheriff's office is working hard to find out who tried to kill me, but so far they haven't been able to."

They are with him now, they are drawing breath when he is drawing breath.

"Maybe the attempt on my life had nothing to do with my taking on Mr. Allison's defense. In a way, that would be preferable to believing that it did. But think about it, ladies and gentlemen—doesn't it seem awfully coincidental to you that someone randomly tries to kill the lawyer for the most despised criminal in recent county history right before the trial starts, when that lawyer—me—is starting to find cracks in the prosecution's case? Isn't that pressing the old 'coincidence' envelope pretty far?"

He turns away from the jury for a second, making eye contact with Riva. Her eyes are bright—she nods an emphatic yes.

"When you hear all the facts emerge in this case, you're going to find yourself in a maze more complex than anything you could imagine. Alice in Wonderland couldn't find her way out of the labyrinth you're going to find yourselves ensnared in. But there's one thing you are going to know: the state will *not* have proved their case beyond a reasonable doubt."

He shakes his head emphatically. "They won't have proved it at all. Maybe, if we're all lucky, something will emerge from this that will point us in the direction of the real killer, Emma Lancaster's true murderer. That would be wonderful. But that's not the purpose of this trial, ladies and gentlemen of this jury. The purpose of this trial, the only purpose, is to decide whether the state has proven Joe Allison guilty beyond a reasonable doubt. That means very, very clearly." His voice drops theatrically low. "I know, friends. Because I used to have to do it. And I also know that in this case my former assistants . . . and colleagues . . . in the Santa Barbara County district attorney's office cannot do that. Because they have no compelling evidence. All they have is the desire to find someone, anyone, guilty."

His final pause. He feels the perspiration forming under his crisp new shirt. He's glad he changed at lunch.

"Desire isn't enough. Wanting to do the right thing isn't enough. Exorcising a demon from the community isn't enough. You have to have the facts, and you have to have the truth. And the prosecution has neither."

He paces back and forth in front of the twelve jurors.

"No one has ever come forward and said he or she saw Joe Allison at the Lancasters' house on the night Emma Lancaster was taken from her room. No one could have—he wasn't there. And no murder weapon has ever been found. Those are key elements in this trial. No eyewitnesses, no murder weapon."

He walks back to the defense table, goes behind it, places a safeguarding hand on Joe Allison's shoulder. "This man did not murder Emma Lancaster, ladies and gentlemen. Her true killer, possibly the person who tried to kill me, is still at large, somewhere out there"—he points through the windows towards the distant mountains as, involuntarily, all eyes follow his arm, even Ray Logan's, Doug and Glenna Lancaster's, even Judge Ewing's—"hiding, waiting. But he is out there. Because Joe Allison did not murder Emma Lancaster, and you are going to know that, in your guts, in your hearts, in your souls. And when all this is over, when all the testimony has been given, and the talking is done, you will come to the only conclusion you can: that Joe Allison is innocent of the crime with which he has been charged."

The shooter stands on a ridge across the canyon from the house, sighting it through a high-powered telescopic lens attached to a rifle like the one that shot at Luke at Hollister. It is night, but the lens has infrared, it can see as clearly when it's dark out as when it's light. Through the living room windows, Luke Garrison and the woman are in clear view, moving about.

The lens pans off the house to the street next to it. The sheriff's car is parked there, a deputy inside.

Garrison can't be taken out here. It's too risky. Sometimes, when he comes out on the deck, he's an easy target. But the chances of being caught are too great.

When it happens, it will have to be someplace else. When the police aren't around. Last time it could have been done. If the shooter had wanted Garrison dead, he'd be dead.

He should have quit the case, the damn fool. Anyone else would have. That's what the shooter had counted on. Now it has to happen. He's begun clouding the issues, raising doubt in some stupid juror's mind.

The shooter puts the rifle back in its case and locks it in the trunk of the car. One last look at the house, then the car starts up and drives away. There will be a time when Luke finds himself alone. That's when it will happen.

FIVE

"Call Lisa Jaffe."

She's let in a side door from a private room where she's been waiting with her mother. She knows where to go. She crosses the well and takes her place in the witness chair, standing with her right hand raised high, left hand on the Bible, swearing to tell the truth.

Lisa is a different person from the young girl who awoke groggy and confused that night. That was a year and a half ago. She's changed, too, from when Luke interviewed her a few months ago. She was fourteen on the night Emma was taken away. Now she's a month from turning sixteen, and suddenly, overnight it seems, she's a woman. A young woman, less timid. Grown into her body, an attractive young woman's body—high breasts, rounded behind, hips jutting from her waist.

The prosecutors have done what they can to turn back the hands of time and young her down. She's dressed more appropriately for a preadolescent than a girl her age; she has no makeup on, not even lip gloss. The attempt is to get her to look close to what she looked like then, when she hadn't even started menstruating.

Ray Logan walks her through the events of that night, and of the following morning. Her narrative is clear and straight: She saw a figure carrying Emma out of the bedroom. She believed it was a man. It wasn't a dream, a hallucination, an imagining. It happened. She saw it. Emma not being in the house the next morning, when she woke up, confirmed that.

She's a good witness. She doesn't try to impress, or embellish. She doesn't cry, either, but looking at her, you know she's holding on bravely, that the tears, even after a year and a half, are just below the surface.

Logan concludes his examination. Luke takes the podium.

"Hello, Lisa," he says. He smiles at her. He doesn't want her to be scared of him—he doesn't want the jury, or the people in the courtroom, to think that he's a bully, right out of the box.

She blinks. "Hello," she says back, her voice low, but audible. She has been coached—as all the witnesses are coached—to present a certain picture, a persona that works. So far, she's done fine. But that was with the people who are on her side. She's afraid of Luke, intimidated by him. He knows that. Logan's people have cautioned her to be careful about what she says when responding to Luke's questions. Don't say anything more than necessary, they've impressed upon her. Don't volunteer anything. Still, she's scared she will. She can't help it. All this is new to her.

"This won't take long, Lisa," Luke tells her. "I only have a few questions."

She nods, but her body retains its rigid wariness.

"On the night of Emma Lancaster's alleged kidnapping, when you first woke up—"

Logan is on his feet. "Objection, Your Honor."

Ewing looks at him. "Yes, Counselor?"

Logan is already beet red, and they're only on the first cross-examination. He's in for a sweaty time, even when he's doing well, Luke thinks. "The use of the word 'alleged' is prejudicial, Your Honor," Logan says. "That Emma Lancaster—"

"A kidnapping is a forcible taking of a person against his or her will," Luke butts in. "There's been no proof offered that Emma Lancaster was forcibly abducted," he claims. "The witness's own testimony would indicate the contrary."

Ewing thinks but a moment. "Overruled."

One witness, one victory. It's on the record now that Emma Lancaster may not have been kidnapped. If he can push that through, the death-penalty part of the indictment against Joe Allison will be substantially weakened.

Luke continues, keeping his voice low, even, as calm and reassuring as he can. "It was dark in the bedroom, wasn't it? Almost pitch black?"

"There was some moonlight," Lisa says.

"But no lights were on, inside or outside."

"No."

"You saw a man."

"Yes."

"Holding something?"

"Yes."

"But it didn't look like a body. You didn't immediately think 'there's a man in here who is holding a body,' did you?"

She hesitates, glances at her mother, who is sitting directly behind Ray Logan. Luke glances in that direction—Susan Jaffe is fighting her own body, trying to help her daughter without being apparent about it. "No," Lisa answers. "I didn't think that."

"And at the time, you didn't look over at the beds Emma and the other girl were sleeping in, to see if either was out of her bed, did you?"

"No," Lisa answers quietly.

The court reporter signals to the judge. "You'll have to speak up a little bit," Judge Ewing tells Lisa, leaning over from his perch. "So that the court reporter can hear your answers."

She nods, her tongue nervously licking her dry lips. "No," she says again.

From the podium, Luke nods. "You didn't see this person's face?"

"No."

"And you didn't see him come in, either, did you?"

"No."

"Had you been outside that evening?" he asks her. "After you came back to Emma's house. You and Emma and Hillary?"

"Yes," she answers.

"What were you doing out there?"

She looks at her mother with a frightened expression. After a moment, when she's still silent, Ewing leans towards her again. "Answer the question, please," he instructs her.

"We were . . . smoking."

"You were smoking cigarettes?" Luke asks, clarifying the situation.

"Yes." She steals a look at her mother, whose lips are tight, straight-lined.

"Did you smoke anything else?" Luke goes on.

She stares at him.

"Did you smoke any marijuana?" he asks.

She reddens, feeling a surge of shame. "I didn't," she says in barely a whisper.

Ewing leans down yet again. "You will have to talk louder," he tells her. "The court reporter and the members of the jury can't hear you. I'm sitting right next to you and I can barely hear you."

"I didn't smoke any marijuana," she says, more loudly. "I don't do any drugs. I took a vow, at school."

"That's good," Luke praises her. "What about Emma? Did she smoke marijuana that night?"

The miserable girl looks down at her shoes, a style she hasn't worn in two years. She wishes the district attorney had let her dress the way she wanted, like a grown-up instead of like a little seventh-grader. She's always been behind the other girls in development; now that she's finally growing into womanhood, pretending to be that young again feels lame. But they told her she had to, to help out Emma the most.

"Yes," she admits.

"Emma Lancaster smoked marijuana that night," he repeats. "Were there other occasions when you saw or knew about Emma doing drugs?"

"Objection, Your Honor." Logan's on his feet again. "Irrelevant to the questions at hand, and calls for hearsay on the witness's part."

Ewing is ready with his answer. "The witness may answer as to whether she has any firsthand knowledge of drug use by Emma Lancaster," he says. "But not secondhand."

"Thank you, Your Honor," Luke says. To Lisa, he asks again, "Did you personally ever see Emma Lancaster doing drugs? Marijuana or anything else?"

The girl nods.

"You have to say your answer," Luke reminds her gently.

"Yes," she says clearly.

"Did she ever tell you where she got drugs?"

Before Logan can object, she answers: "Her mother."

Logan is livid. More because he's too late to stop her answer than to the question itself. He still cries out, "Objection!"

"Sustained." Ewing pounds his gavel. He turns to the jury. "You will disregard the last question and answer," he instructs them.

Fat chance of that, Luke thinks. Another little victory for him. He turns and looks towards the rear of the courtroom, where Glenna Lancaster is sitting in the middle of a row. She is dressed in her usual black, and is staring straight ahead, her face devoid of expression.

He continues with his cross-examination. "Okay. You came home . . . what time did you get to Emma's house?"

"I don't know exactly." She's losing the veneer of composure she had struggled so hard to learn. "Around eleven."

"Well before midnight?"

She thinks. "Yes."

He nods, as if the two of them are working in tandem here. "You got to Emma's house around eleven, and you talked and watched TV for a while, then you went outside and smoked. Right?"

She nods. "Yes," she remembers to say.

"When you went out to smoke, where did you go?"

"To the back of the lawn."

"To the gazebo?"

Another nod. "Yes."

"Did you go into the gazebo? Up the stairs and in?"

"Yes," again.

"Did Emma say anything about why she wanted to go all the way across the lawn and up into the gazebo?" he asks.

Lisa nods. "She said it was the party room. Where you came when you wanted to do things you didn't want people to know about, or see you doing."

"And then you came back to the house, to her bedroom, and went to sleep."

"Yes."

"Do you remember what time that was?"

She shakes her head. "No."

"Well after midnight, though."

"Yes. It was really late. I was really tired."

"And then the three of you went to bed. To sleep."

She answers, "Yes."

"And you didn't wake up until you saw this other presence in the room."

"Yes," she says. She's less nervous now. He isn't trying to scare her, like the district attorney warned her he would. He's pretty cool, she thinks, the ponytail and the beard. Too bad her mother doesn't have him as a boyfriend. He'd be neat to hang around with.

"We're in Emma's bedroom now, and you've just wakened up, and you see what looks like a man standing there with a bundle in his hands. With me so far?" he asks her.

"Yes." She's almost eager to answer now.

"His back was to you?"

"Yes."

"So you only saw the back of his head, not his face."

"No. I mean yes, that's what I saw," she stammers.

"It's okay. We understand what you're saying. You're doing fine," he says soothingly. "We're almost finished."

"Thank you." She hopes she isn't blushing too much, but she can feel the heat rising up her neck into her cheeks.

"Okay. You didn't see him come in, and you didn't see his face. Was the door leading outside unlocked?" he asks her. "Do you remember if Emma locked it back up when you and the others came back inside?"

She thinks for a minute, her forehead scrunching up. "I think she did," she finally says.

"But you're not certain."

"No." She wishes she were certain. She thinks that's what he'd like to hear.

"Well," Luke says, "we all know the door wasn't forced. So either it was left unlocked, or someone let him in. Like Emma."

Again, Logan's standing and objecting. "Absolutely without foundation," he rails.

Ewing nods in agreement. "Stick to verifiable facts, Counselor," he admonishes Luke. "The objection is sustained."

Luke continues. "This person in the room, whose face you didn't see. I want us to be completely clear on that," he says, turning to the jury. "You never saw this person's face. You definitely never saw the face of the defendant."

"No," she says. "I never saw his face."

"Or any face. You didn't see a face."

"Yes, sir." She's starting to get scared of him again. "That's right."

"Okay, good." He pauses, sips some water. On the witness stand, Lisa does the same. "You didn't actually see what was wrapped up in that blanket, did you?"

"No."

"It might not have been Emma at all."

At the prosecution table, Logan starts to stand and make an objection, then thinks better of it and sits back down.

"I guess." Lisa shrugs.

"You saw this person walk out with a bundle, a blanket in his arms, it could have been a person, it could have been Emma, but it could have been something else, right, Lisa?"

The questions are coming faster now. She feels like a strong wind is pushing her back in her chair. "Yes."

"Emma could still have been in her bed, couldn't she?"

Another shrug. "I guess."

"And you didn't think, at the time, that this person, this man who you saw for a few seconds, leaving a completely dark room with something that looked like a bundle in his arms, you did not think that he had Emma in his arms until almost noon of the next day. Even when you and Hillary woke up, and Emma wasn't there, and you went into the kitchen, even then you didn't think someone had taken Emma out of the room. Is that right?"

She feels that wind, blowing at her like a sundowner. "Yes," she says. She's just drunk some water, but her throat feels completely dry, like she's eaten a handful of sand.

"It was only when everyone realized Emma was missing that it occurred to you that what you had seen earlier—which at the time felt like a dream—might have been someone in the room taking Emma out. Without a struggle," he adds. "Whatever was in the blanket, Emma or anything or anyone, wasn't trying to get away."

"Yes," she answers to the whole thing.

"No further questions, Your Honor." He smiles at Lisa. "Thank you," he tells her, remaining at the podium.

Ewing looks to the prosecution table. "Redirect?" he asks.

Logan rises. "No, Your Honor. The People are finished with this witness."

The judge turns to Lisa. "You may step down," he says with a smile. Sitting in the witness chair is tough on anyone; for kids, it's especially traumatic. "You're finished," he adds, making sure she knows her ordeal, after a year and a half, is behind her.

It's finally over! she thinks. She feels light-headed from that knowledge. Hurriedly she stumbles from the stand and rushes out of the courtroom, her beleaguered mother hot on her heels.

Ewing turns to Logan. "Call your next witness, Counselor."

As Logan starts to instruct the clerk, Luke interrupts the proceedings. Rising in place: "I have a motion, Your Honor."

Ewing, surprised, turns to him. Regaining his composure, he barks, "In my chambers."

He strides from the bench, exiting the door behind him. Luke, a copy of the California Penal Code in hand, follows. Ray Logan, caught unawares, hustles to catch up.

Ewing closes the door to his small office. "What is it?" he asks Luke, clearly irritated.

"I move to dismiss the kidnapping section of the indictment against my client under sections 207 and 278 of the California penal code, Your Honor," Luke says matter-of-factly. "The testimony of the prosecution's own witness clearly shows that Emma Lancaster was *not* taken from her bedroom by force. If she was taken by the unknown man in the room, as described by Miss Jaffe—and that has not been proven, I wish to point out—it was in no way forcible. If Emma Lancaster did indeed leave her bedroom with anyone, and again I want to be very clear that that allegation hasn't been proven at all, she did so freely. There was no struggle. The state's witness was very clear on that point." He hands the book to the judge, who reluctantly takes it.

Ray Logan weighs in, his voice conveying his clear, heartfelt anger and irritation. "One witness's testimony doesn't prove or disprove anything. We have other witnesses who will add to this, and anyway, proof or the absence of it is up to the jury to decide."

Ewing nods. "I have to agree with you," he concurs. He knows, though, that when it's all finished, he's going to have to revisit this—Luke Garrison will force him to, and properly so, even if the prospect of it ticks him off royally. He turns to Luke. "Motion denied. The charges as brought will stand."

Luke didn't think he'd win with this first thrust, but he's set the lance. Down the road, it'll come up again. And again.

This trial's going to go longer than expected, Ewing realizes. Luke Garrison isn't going to give a rote defense, no way. He's going to give it everything he's got, and he's going to show colors and tactics he never showed when he was running the show. Guerrilla lawyering, if that's what it takes.

He admires Luke Garrison, always has. But the guy has changed, and not a little, a lot. Any courtroom is always theater, real or potential. Ewing is a decorous man, prudent, cautious. He believes in the tried and true way of doing things, in his life and in his courtroom. If this trial turns into theater of the absurd, will there still be a place for justice, as he knows and has always defined it? Or will "let the best man win" be all that counts?

The lead detective who followed the three sets of footprints made by Emma, Lisa, and Hillary, and found the marijuana, used condoms, and other evidence in the gazebo, takes the stand and gives his spiel.

Luke cross-examines. The man is unflappable. Luke knows him from back then—this witness isn't going to give anything away.

"You didn't arrive on the scene until late in the afternoon of Emma Lancaster's disappearance, did you?" he starts out. "Several hours after she was reported missing, is that true?"

"Yes," comes the laconic reply.

"Several people had been on the scene by then? The investigating officer, other policemen, family members, and so forth? Particularly by the time you and your partner tracked these footprints you've alluded to, from the bedroom to the gazebo and back to the bedroom."

"That's correct," the detective admits.

"You can't tell with any certainty when they were made, or who made them, can you, Detective?" Luke quizzes him.

"No, we can't. And about the time, it was within twenty-four hours. More precisely than that, we can't tell."

"So they could have been much earlier," Luke goes on. "They could have been made the afternoon before, or the early evening, say around four or five o'clock."

"They could have. It's unlikely, though. They would've started fading."

Luke ignores the latter part of the answer. "So instead of being made around midnight, as the testimony of the previous witness has suggested, they could have been made six or seven hours earlier?"

"It's possible," the detective gives him. "But given the depth of the prints, the later time is much more likely."

"In fact," Luke says, "they could have been made a few hours before you arrived on the scene. Isn't that also true?"

The detective frowns. "I guess it is. I hadn't given that any thought."

"Hadn't given it any thought, Detective? By the time you found these footprints you had already heard about the conversation that Lisa Jaffe had with Detective Garcia, right? You knew what she had told him."

The detective shifts in the chair. He's a tall man, angular, thin, the large Adam's apple in his throat bobbing up and down every time he speaks. "I knew what the girl had told Detective Garcia," he acknowledges.

"So you had a certain preconceived attitude as far as the time frame went, didn't you? About when those footprints were made, and by whom."

The detective cops halfheartedly to Luke's assessment. "I might have."

"So you can't be positive when the footprints were made, except you think they were made sometime in the twenty-four-hour period preceding your discovery of them," Luke summarizes. "And so many people had been there, walking around on that wet grass, that anyone could have made them, not necessarily the three girls in question. Emma's mother and a couple of her friends, for example, sneaking out to smoke a joint."

"Objection!" Logan screams.

Ewing has already pounded his gavel. "Sustained! Refrain from making such outrageous, unsubstantiated statements," he warns Luke.

"Yes, sir. Sorry." He doesn't even feign contriteness. "I'm merely reiterating the claim made by the previous witness about Mrs. Lancaster's conduct, which went unchallenged."

"That's nonsense," Ewing tells him sharply. "Knock off that kind of wild reaching in my courtroom."

Luke nods. "Yes, sir." He turns back to the witness. "Any three people could have made those footprints, isn't that true? At any time within your twenty-four-hour window."

The detective nods tightly. "Yes," he admits. "What you've said is possible. Not true," he adds bitingly, "but possible." He can't help going against his taciturn grain and putting a button on his remarks: "In theory only."

That's it for day one of the witness parade. Luke, with Riva at his side, pushes by the mass of reporters congregating outside the courthouse doors and in the grassy area in front of the imposing stone building. In response to the questions thrown at him, the microphones thrust in his face, the print reporters trying to block his path, he gives an impromptu interview as he keeps walking. "I didn't see any particular surprises in any of today's testimony. . . . Both of the state's witnesses reversed themselves, I think everyone saw that. . . . I could comment further on whether there was a kidnapping at all, but I have a motion pending that speaks to that. . . ." And so on. Then they're at the old truck, parked in a no-parking zone. Luke swipes the parking ticket from his windshield and stuffs it in his pocket—an acceptable price to pay to get in and out of the maelstrom as quickly as possible. Later, after dinner, when it's quiet, he'll fall by the jail and see Allison, let him know how he thinks they're doing, keep the man's spirits up.

Today was easy, nothing much happened. Tomorrow is going to be another story.

Sheriff Williams is a fine, strong witness. Juries love to believe guys like him. He sits straight and tall in the witness chair, and his answers to the prosecution's questions are firm and authoritative, giving no grounds for doubting him.

"Did you question the accused during your initial investigation?" Logan asks.

"We questioned everyone who had ever known the victim," Williams replies firmly. "Hundreds of people, thousands. Intensive interrogations. Including the accused, who we questioned within two days after the victim's body was found. At the time we didn't have reason to suspect him, although there were factors, such as acquaintanceship with the deceased, and access to the property and the layout, that we noted in our report. But the truth is, the accused wasn't a suspect at that time, and I'd be lying if I said otherwise."

Logan is quiet. Gathering steam, Williams continues, "Our department, by itself, put in twenty-five thousand man-hours investigating this crime, more than three times any other crime investigation in the history of Santa Barbara County. To give you one example of how exhaustive our effort was, someone from our department or the city police force personally questioned every single student from her school, every one of their parents. It was the most thorough investigation I've ever worked on, or even heard of."

PR, Luke thinks. To make the department look good, since it was by sheer luck they stumbled onto Joe as a suspect. He likes the way they constantly refer to Allison as "the accused." Not "Allison" or even "the defendant" but—twice in fifteen seconds—"the accused," a word that implies "guilty." *J'accuse.*

"Go on," Logan says, continuing his minuet with the sheriff.

"We enlisted the help of the highway patrol, the state's sexual predator computer bank, several neighboring sheriff's and police departments. We even consulted with the FBI, despite the crime not being an interstate situation.

"But we had run out of the normal range of possibilities," he admits. "The case was still alive, of course—we had a detective on it full-time right up until the night the accused was arrested—but we had run into a stone wall. The killer had managed to cover his tracks, for the time being. But we never quit trying." He turns to the jury. "We would have caught Joe Allison, sooner or later. It happened to be on that particular night, but we were never going to let go of this until we had Emma Lancaster's murderer in custody."

Williams is forced to overstate the situation, given the circumstances. The importance of this case, not only legally but politically and socially, has damaged everyone involved in it, dulled their normal caution and professionalism. The case was dormant. Doug and Glenna Lancaster had been told—warned, really—not to keep their hopes alive. Luke also knows that Williams, since Allison's arrest, has developed suspicions about this case on his own. Doug Lancaster's lying about where he was on the night of the disappearance, and his intransigence about coming forth with any kind of credible alibi, has eroded the sheriff's confidence in Emma's father. Doug's arrogant stonewalling has drawn suspicion to him. The distrust is deep in Ray Logan's gut too, Luke knows, although Ray will never admit it publicly. But he must be gobbling Tums by the handful.

The real root of Williams's skepticism, even more than Doug's nonalibi and lying about it, is the attempt by someone to kill Luke at Hollister Ranch.

Logan walks Williams through the night of Allison's arrest, from the time he was brought into the jail. Williams accounts for his role in the gathering of evidence against—yes, once again—"the accused." Luke feels like jumping up and screaming, "He's got a name! He's innocent until proven guilty beyond a reasonable doubt!" But he stays calm.

Ray Logan's direct questioning of Sheriff Williams takes three-quarters of the day. By the time Luke gets up to start his cross, it's after three. He looks over at the jury. They believe Williams, whatever he says. And they've been listening to him for hours in the name of law, order, and justice. They want to be done for the day.

Luke takes his time anyway. Screw the jurors and their impatience. Juries get antsy about the second day, that's been his experience.

Thinking they might be stuck in here for months, listening to a ton of boring testimony.

"Good afternoon, Sheriff." He stands at the podium. Relaxed, smiling. One old friend quizzing another. On opposite sides now, yes, but still old friends, the reservoir of experience, shared investigations, and convictions too deep not to acknowledge, if only tacitly.

"Afternoon, Counselor."

"Joe Allison was never a real suspect, was he?" Luke asks, plunging right in. "He didn't fit any profile at all. You never thought twice about him, all the time you and your men were spending those twenty-five thousand hours hunting down whoever killed Emma Lancaster. This man sitting here—Joe—was as clean as a hound dog's chewing bone, isn't that right, Sheriff?"

"We didn't have him under suspicion," Williams acknowledges.

"You never had him under any kind of surveillance, did you?"

"No."

"If his car hadn't been stopped that night, six months ago, on a fluke, you have to admit it was a random, lucky coincidence, you wouldn't be thinking of him as a suspect, would you? Even though you told the jury here"—he turns and looks at the jurors before readdressing the witness—"that sooner or later you knew you were going to find out who killed Emma. You were going to find and arrest her killer, even if he didn't live around here anymore and there wouldn't be any evidence against him for you to get your hands on. Isn't that right, Sheriff Williams?"

"We would have found him," Williams responds evenly. "If he had moved to the moon, we would have found him."

"On the moon," Luke says, not keeping some sarcasm from his tone. "Okay. Whatever." He continues: "Was my client ever read his Miranda rights once he was under suspicion? Out in the field or in the jailhouse?"

"He was read his rights in the field," the sheriff answers.

"About being a murder suspect, or that he might have to go up on a DUI, which is only a misdemeanor, not a felony?"

"He was read his rights," Williams doggedly reiterates. "He wasn't a suspect when he was brought into the jail."

"Then why did you question him about the murder? You had Emma Lancaster's key ring. You must have been suspicious, at least."

"Some," the sheriff parries. He knows exactly how far he can go without casting doubt that he violated Miranda. "Law enforcement is permitted a certain leeway. You know that better than me, from when you had a different job description, Mr. Garrison."

This is true, Luke thinks, admiring the man's control. You know how far you can bend the law without breaking it. "But sooner or later, during Mr. Allison's police interrogation, where he was held without advice of a lawyer, and wasn't informed of the extremely serious charges against him, sooner or later you suspected him enough of somehow being involved in Emma Lancaster's death that you persuaded a judge to issue a warrant to search his apartment. Once you'd gone that far, weren't you then obligated to read him his rights?"

"Yes, of course," Williams answers. He's maddeningly calm, and stonewalling for all he's worth.

"When did you inform him of his rights?" Luke asks. "There's nothing in the record that states you Mirandized Mr. Allison."

"I did it at the same time my detectives came back from his apartment."

"Isn't that too late? *After* you found some dubious evidence that suggested his involvement with Emma Lancaster's disappearance and subsequent murder?"

"It happened that way," Williams says with no apology or trace of guilt in his voice. "These things happen fast, they're spontaneous, all over the place. You do the best you can. We did, that night and in every single element of this case. And the evidence isn't dubious," he adds.

Luke wants to make a motion about this, but this is the wrong time and the wrong witness. For now, with a sheriff who is the most popular politician in the county, he'll furrow out as many inconsistencies and disregardings of the law as he can.

"Going back to the day that Emma Lancaster was reported missing, and you and your people were at the house beginning your investigation—there were dozens and dozens of footprints all over that backyard, weren't there? All those police snooping around, trying to find clues. And the Lancasters' personal staff, also trying to help. There had to have been dozens of different footprints and shoe prints all over that backyard, weren't there?"

"There were some, yes," Williams agrees.

"Some leading from the vicinity of the bedroom to the gazebo in question, I would guess."

"I'm sure there were. My people were doing all kinds of different things. I was with the worried parents for the most part, trying to find out as much as I could from them."

"But the particular shoe prints," Luke goes on, "you singled them out. Of all the different shoe prints found in that backyard that night, they were the only ones you took castings of." He pauses for a moment, to make sure the jury realizes there's some significance to his questioning. "Isn't that true, Sheriff?"

Williams nods readily. "That is absolutely true," he says, projecting his reply in the jury's direction.

"Why did you pick that particular shoe print? What was so special and unique about that shoe, except that a year later it would happen to turn up in Mr. Allison's home, a rather fortuitous coincidence, wouldn't you say?"

Williams leans forward, almost on the balls of his feet even though he's sitting, like a boxer ready to throw a knockout punch. "We were lucky to find them, of course," he agrees easily. "But luck had nothing to do with our reason for taking impressions of those shoe prints and not others."

"And why is that?" Luke asks.

Williams turns to face the jury. "Because that shoe had made a significantly deeper imprint in the grass and dirt than any other shoe," he tells the jurors. "It was worn either by an extremely heavy man, a man who would have weighed three hundred pounds or more"—here he stops for a moment, takes a drink of water, wipes his lips—"or by someone carrying something, or someone, who was heavy. Like a person. And then, of course, when we found the identical shoe print at the site where the victim's remains were discovered, we knew we had made the correct assumption—that whoever was wearing that shoe kidnapped, and subsequently murdered, Emma Lancaster."

The sky just fell. Williams had set his trap, and Luke, the dumb-schmuck prey, had stepped right in it.

Bad lawyering. Pathetic. He should have seen that one coming. Now he's got to get the hell off the stage, as fast as he can.

"No further questions, Your Honor," he says in a low, mortified voice.

Dinner will be the usual—order-in pizza while he hunkers down, going over everything he knows about tomorrow's witnesses from his interviews and profiles and personal knowledge. It's going to be a long night. All of them are.

"Do we have any Cokes?" Riva is scrounging around in the pantry.

"I don't know," Luke answers distractedly. He's in the living room, his paperwork spread out on the coffee table, the floor, the couch. He couldn't care less about what they have to eat or drink.

"There's nothing to drink in this house except wine and beer," she says in exasperation, coming into the room. She checks her watch. "The pizza guy won't be here for twenty minutes, they always take forty-five minimum. I'm going to run down to Von's and grab some drinks." Being pregnant, she isn't drinking wine. "Do you want anything?" She's grabbing the keys off the front hallway table.

"Do we have juice for the morning? And maybe some yogurt? You'll still be asleep when I leave." Ewing's courtroom opens for business at eight in the morning, but he's out the door at six. "And remind me to set the coffee timer tonight for five-thirty."

She gives him a quick peck on the cheek. "I'll be right back." The door shuts with a loud thunk.

The deputy sheriff on duty, sitting in his patrol car, stirs to attention as he sees the figure come out of the house and head towards the old truck. He starts to turn the ignition on, then he realizes it's the woman, not the man. His job is to watchdog the man. He leans back in his seat, relaxed.

Riva slowly backs the truck out of the driveway, checking for oncoming traffic. She pops the clutch and wrestles the gearshift into first, waving to the ever-present sentry. Luke's being protected—she feels safer, knowing that.

The road, sloping downhill all the way to town, is twisty and narrow, barely wide enough for two vehicles to pass each other. It's a dark night, foggy too, and there are no streetlights on Mountain Drive. The only light comes from her own headlights. One hand on the wheel, she rubs her belly. She's just beginning to show—you can't see it when she has clothes on, only a tiny bit when she's naked—but she can already feel the life inside her.

No one knows. Only she and Luke.

The radio is tuned to public broadcasting, nighttime jazz. She taps a finger on the gearshift lever as Miles Davis percolates out of the old speakers. A couple of cars pass her on her way down the hill. She slows to make sure there's room to go by, edging slightly to the right, but not very much—the road drops off sharply here, and there are no guardrails. This old, pot-holed mountain road that's barely five minutes from the center of Montecito is charming, but it's a bitch to drive.

Another car is coming towards her. She can't see it yet, the road is too twisty here, it's around the next curve, but she can see the headlights cutting through the fog. It seems to be coming fast, considering the bad visibility. She slows down, edging towards the right side of the road, making sure the other car has enough room.

Then the other car is out of the curve and coming in her direction, about a hundred yards down the road. It has high headlights, too, another truck or SUV. Every other car around here is a four-wheel-drive of some kind, it's become the housewives' station wagon. It's moving at a good clip, faster than it ought to be going, she thinks again. People get these four-wheel-drive contraptions and they think their off-road capability makes them invincible.

The other vehicle is slowing some, seeing her headlights, but it's still going too fast for her taste. Now it's almost upon her, and it isn't giving enough ground, it's too far over the center line, she can't get by, and then suddenly, without thinking of the consequences, the other hits the high beams, they shine right into her eyes, blinding her, she isn't expecting that, it feels like two searchlights suddenly turned full onto her.

She slows more, staying to the right. The oncoming vehicle comes abreast of her, and as its headlights slide by she begins to swing back towards the center of the road.

Then she realizes what's happening and she screams to herself: *You're not giving me enough room!*

The Range Rover, seemingly oblivious to the danger, almost brushes against the side of the truck. She stands on the brakes as hard as she can and fights the steering wheel, straining to hold her course.

Somehow, she hangs on. The other vehicle powers by her, lost in a cloud of fog and dust.

She pulls over at the first wide spot on the road. She's shaking. Was that deliberate? she thinks. Someone thinking it was Luke driving the truck?

It takes her five minutes to calm down enough to drive into town. Even in the safety of the supermarket, her purchases in her basket, she's still shaking.

She takes a different, longer route back to the house. No cars in sight.

It was an accident. Some road-raged crazo oblivious to anything else on the road. As she heads into the last section before their place, she glances up the ravine towards the house. It's easy to spot—the only one with the lights on, blazing in the darkness. Almost everyone else around here seems to have gone to bed.

For a moment, on the other side of the deep barranca that separates the two sides of the canyon, two or three hundred yards from their house as the crow flies, a flashlight comes on, probing—a distant neighbor looking for a cat that won't come in. Coyotes are all around this area. They don't fear humans—they'll come into your yard and take your pet cat or small dog or even—it's rare but it did happen a couple of years back—a toddler. The mother heard the baby screaming and managed to save her, but it was a reminder that you're living close to nature up here, and you have to be careful.

She continues on to their house, where the cops are keeping them safe, tomorrow morning's yogurt for the father of her yet-to-be-born child resting on the seat next to her.

* * *

Doug Lancaster is in the courtroom. He isn't in his normal seat, directly behind the prosecution table. Today he's sitting in the very last row, in the seat closest to the door—insurance in case he feels compelled to bolt. Glenna is absent. Luke, scanning the audience as he awaits Judge Ewing's entrance, knew she wouldn't appear for this testimony, not after what he had witnessed in the corridor.

"All rise, the Honorable Prescott Ewing presiding." The bailiff sings out the ancient courtroom salutation. Everyone stands as Ewing sweeps in through the private door from his chambers directly behind the bench. Sitting, he wastes no time. "Call your next witness," he tells Ray Logan.

"Call Dr. Peter Manachi," Logan says.

The coroner takes the stand, the oath is administered.

"Good morning, Dr. Manachi," Logan says.

"Good morning." The coroner sits erect in the wooden captain's chair, lord of all he surveys. He's testified in thousands of trials, they're all the same to him. He gives his results, fends off questions from the defense that in any way cast aspersions on him or his staff or their findings, and goes back to his lab in the pathology department of Cottage Hospital, of which he is the head. He's hardly ever challenged on points that are substantive, and on the rare occasion when the veracity of his conclusions is called into question, he always has a decisive, black and white answer that brings any further doubt to a screeching halt.

The interrogation begins. "Will you describe for the jury the condition of the murder victim, Emma Lancaster, when you first saw her?"

"I will," Dr. Manachi says. He has his report in his hand, reads from it. "The victim was a Caucasian female, approximately fourteen years of age. She had been wearing a flannel nightgown. She had been dead for some time, at least five days, more likely a week. There was gross swelling and discoloration of her abdominal area and gross swelling also of her extremities. Decaying of the flesh had commenced on various parts of her body." He flips the first page, continues. "There was a significant indentation of her right temple, in the soft area almost directly above her right ear. This was black from occluded blood. And there were the usual atrophic conditions associated with a corpse that has been unattended for this period of time. Do you wish me to elaborate?"

"No, that won't be necessary," Logan says quickly. Blood and guts turn juries off, even when the victim is good evidence for you. He wants to skim over this part of his examination. He doesn't want to overload the jurors with any more than the bare necessities.

Luke is watching the jury keenly. They're attentive, all twelve of them. This is going to be a tough day all around—for the prosecution initially, and then for him and Joe Allison. Much of the jurors' collective attitude is going to be formed today. That may change, move around, ebb and flow, as future witnesses and contradictory evidence come forth. But opinions formed today will last for the rest of the trial, and have a powerful effect on the outcome.

Logan moves on. "Were you able to determine the cause of death?"

"Yes," Dr. Manachi says authoritatively. "The victim was killed by a single blow to the right temple. The impact caused a rupture of the blood vessels in the right side of the brain, creating massive trauma."

"Can you speculate as to how soon the victim died after this occurred?" Logan asks.

Manachi nods. "Instantaneously. A blow of this force causes almost as much damage as a bullet. The brain would have gone into spasm and ceased to function."

Luke is impassive as he listens. He's heard testimony like this, much of it from Manachi, dozens of times. The jury, though, hasn't. The shock and anguish they're feeling about how Emma died is clearly registered on their faces. Stealing a glance over his shoulder, he spots Doug Lancaster in his back-row seat. The man's face is splotchy red; he looks like he's holding himself back from vomiting, or breaking down.

Where were you that night? Luke thinks for the umpteenth time. Are you feeling pain? Guilt? Both?

Logan asks his next question. "Could you speculate as to the type of weapon or object that was used?"

"It wasn't a sharp object, like a knife or a tool," Manachi says. "More likely a hammer, a brick, a two-by-four. Something with weight and a certain massiveness to it. It was a very hard blow to have caused the amount of damage that was inflicted."

Logan nods. "All right. I think we've covered this sufficiently." He walks from the podium back to the prosecution table, picks up a manila folder, walks to the witness stand, takes some pages out of the envelope, and hands them to his witness. "Would you examine these, Dr. Manachi?"

Manachi leafs through the six-page report.

"Can you tell the jury what this is, Doctor?"

"This is an autopsy report. A standard form used throughout the state of California."

"Did you prepare this report?" Logan asks.

"With the assistance of my staff, yes," the doctor replies.

"Request to be placed in evidence, Your Honor," Logan intones. "Counsel for defense and the court have copies."

Ewing nods. "This will be marked as People's exhibit fifteen," he states, looking at his evidence chart.

Logan hands it to the clerk, who marks it and places it on the evidence table.

Luke knows what it says. It's the hand grenade from which Logan pulled the pin during his opening remarks.

Crossing back to his questioning spot, Logan says, "Was there anything in your report that goes beyond what you've told us? Any special injuries, abnormal circumstances surrounding the death, anything out of the ordinary?"

Manachi looks at Logan, then at the jury. "Yes, there was," he says gravely.

Here we go, Luke thinks.

"What was that, Dr. Manachi?" Logan asks. "What did you find upon your examination of this victim that you felt was unusual, considering the death and how it was caused."

"She had been sexually penetrated."

Although Logan had introduced this in his opening remarks, a gasp still comes from everyone in the courtroom, powerful in its intensity.

"Was she raped?" That's the logical question to ask. A fourteen-year-old girl is abducted, raped, murdered. It's even worse than people thought, but it's understandable.

Dr. Manachi shakes his head. "No, she wasn't raped."

Logan has to play this out. He is the liaison between the facts and the jury that will judge guilt or innocence based on those facts, and the emotions that arise from them. "I don't understand," he says.

"Penetration and rape are two separate and distinct acts," Manachi says carefully. "Rape is not consensual."

Now the gasp is a murmur, a buzzing, people speaking in whispers.

"Are you telling us that Emma Lancaster had consensual sex with her killer?" Logan asks, his voice ringing with incredulity.

"Yes."

More buzz, a swarming. Ewing thinks to gavel it down, but he can't, it has a life force of its own. He could only stop it by clearing the courtroom, and that would cause worse problems.

"What leads you to believe that, Doctor?" Logan asks. "She had been dead for a week or more. With her body decaying as it was, how can you tell if sexual penetration is consensual or rape?"

"The extent to which the tissues are damaged, and so forth," Manachi says. "But there was the reason, the physical condition that our autopsy revealed, that indicated that forcible entry had not occurred. She was pregnant, as you have already told this courtroom. That indicates an ongoing history of sexual activity, which would lead a reasonable person to believe that the sexual encounter, as well as other sexual encounters, was consensual." He pauses. "But as I said, the evidence points in that direction as well."

Even though Logan had already lobbed this grenade into the arena, talking about it now, and so dispassionately, causes a collective stopping of breath. Luke, as much as anyone else, feels the importance of what this means.

Logan waits a moment for the hubbub to subside, then continues questioning the coroner. "Was there sperm present in the victim's vaginal cavity?"

"We couldn't tell."

"But you're convinced that she'd had sex shortly before death. *Could* contraception have been used?"

"Yes."

The condoms in the gazebo, the condoms in Allison's house. It doesn't take a genius to make that connection, Luke thinks.

"Once more about the method of killing, to make sure we all understand you correctly, Dr. Manachi. It was one blow, strongly delivered, from an object such as a hammer or brick?"

"That is correct."

And with that, the prosecution's direct examination of perhaps their most important witness, certainly their most attention-grabbing one, is over.

Luke notices that Doug Lancaster isn't in the courtroom when he begins his cross-examination. He isn't surprised.

"Good afternoon, Doctor."

"Good afternoon, Luke—" He catches himself. "Mr. Garrison. I'm sorry."

"That's okay," Luke says. "We've carried a lot of water together, you and me. But you'll forgive me if I don't call you Peter."

The doctor smiles.

Luke glances at his notes. "Did you make your determination that there was sexual activity before or after you performed the autopsy, Dr. Manachi?"

Manachi thinks for a moment. "After," he answers.

"You're sure it wasn't before? No one called your office and told you that the victim was pregnant? Or might be pregnant?"

The doctor has to think about that. "Not to my knowledge."

"You're positive."

"I suppose it's possible," Manachi temporizes, "but I don't recall getting such a call."

Luke shifts gears. "You speculated as to what kind of weapon was used. Hammer, brick, two-by-four were examples you gave."

"Yes."

"She wasn't shot, knifed, anything like that?"

"No," the doctor says. "Absolutely not."

"Would you conclude, then, Doctor, from your long and expert experience in the field, that this killing was accidental or, at least, spur-of-the-moment? Considering the type of object you're claiming had to have been used?"

Logan, immediately on his feet, calls out, "Objection! Leading the witness, Your Honor."

"This is cross-examination, Your Honor," Luke says sharply. "That's the point."

Ewing nods in agreement. "Overruled."

Shaking his head in disgruntlement, Logan sits down.

Luke repeats his question. "Is it your opinion that the killing of Emma Lancaster was either accidental or unpremeditated?"

Manachi looks up at the ceiling, exhales slowly, squares his shoulders. "Given the nature of the fatal injury, that was probably what happened. Not definitely—you could plan to kill someone using an object such as those—but it's more logical, when a killing occurs as this one did, that it's a spur-of-the-moment thing and the killer used whatever was handy."

Luke pauses to let that sink in. Again, a strong admission to have on the record. Little Lisa Jaffe took forcible abduction off the table. Now the coroner, the most expert witness the state is going to offer on this matter, has proclaimed the killing *not* to have been premeditated: *not* first-degree murder.

Ray Logan steals a look at the jury. They're listening with interest, but the importance of the point seems to have escaped them. Luke will remind them during final arguments, of course, but for now the shock of the coronor's recitation of Emma Lancaster's pregnancy has dulled their critical antennae to anything else.

"A few more questions, Dr. Manachi," he says, gathering his notes. "The object that caused Emma Lancaster's death. You said it was a blunt object, like a hammer."

"Yes."

"Could it have been something other than a hammer? Say a golf club? Like a three-wood, or a five-iron? A golf club is a blunt object."

Manachi considers. "That's an interesting angle. I'd have to say yes. A golf club could certainly be the murder weapon. The arc of the swing would generate tremendous force."

Luke smiles. Peter Manachi, M.D., the county's leading authority on cause of death, has now gone on record as declaring that a golf club is a weapon that could have killed Emma. Before this trial is over, Luke is going to hammer the point home. Everyone will know who the golfer is among the close circle that had sure access to the Lancaster estate and could have taken Emma out of her bedroom without a struggle from her and then—in the heat of passion, argument, or anger—killed her.

"Thank you, Doctor." Taking his leave of the podium: "I have no further questions for this witness, Your Honor."

The reference to a golf club as the possible murder weapon, that bothers Logan. It pushes Doug Lancaster deeper into the center of the story. Sooner or later he's going to have to face that and figure out how to defuse it, if he can. Otherwise, it's going to be the elephant in the parlor—no one's talking about it, but you can't help but notice it.

Logan knows that Luke expects him to follow a certain chronological line, going from the autopsy report to a year later when Joe Allison was arrested, but he throws a curve: another young girl, a friend of Emma's who wasn't there that night but in whom Emma often confided.

"Deanna, thank you for coming here today to help us out."

"That's okay, Mr. Logan. Emma was one of my best friends. Whatever I can do to help, I want to."

Her name: Deanna Dalton. A pretty girl, more sophisticated-looking than Lisa Jaffe. The kind of girl who would have been in Emma's fast-life crowd, as much as a fourteen-year-old from a sheltering family could have a "fast life." She sits straight-backed in the witness chair. Disdaining normal courtroom protocol for someone her age, Deanna makes no concessions to youthful innocence—she has on an adult-style dress, makeup, heels, sheer pantyhose. Girls her age don't wear hose, Luke thinks as he watches her on the witness stand, unless they want to be seen and known as someone who does. A girl who wants the world to think she's grown up. On her left ankle there's a small tattoo. From where Luke sits it looks like a beetle. Each earlobe is pierced with four or five earrings.

Logan quickly establishes Deanna's relationship with Emma: same schools from third grade, same interests—they both rode horses, played tennis, sang in the school chorus. They were very close friends. Emma told Deanna things she didn't tell other girls. She definitely told her things she would never tell her mother.

Pointing across the room to Allison, sitting alongside Luke at the defense table, Logan says, "Do you recognize that man, the one with the dark hair?" he asks.

She nods. "Yes, sir."

"How do you recognize him, Deanna?"

"He used to pick Emma up at school."

"What grade was that?" he asks.

"Eighth grade," she answers. "The last year Emma . . ." she hesitates.

He waits her out patiently, not prompting her.

"The last year until she was killed," Deanna finishes awkwardly.

Logan nods gravely, as if the statement requires a moment of silence in respect for the memory of Emma Lancaster. "How often did Joe Allison pick Emma up?" he then asks, after an appropriate pause.

"I don't remember. There wasn't any particular pattern. He'd be there after school sometimes, waiting for her out on the street."

"Not in the school parking lot? He wouldn't wait for her there?"

She shakes her head. "That would've been weird. Like, he wasn't her parent or anything.'"

"How did Emma get home otherwise?" Logan asks.

"The usual," she answers. "Sometimes her mom would pick her up, sometimes one of the people who worked for her mom. If Emma didn't want them to come, she'd tell her mom she had a ride. Or she would tell her she was going with me, or some other friend. Her mom didn't seem to pick up on who all was giving her rides. Emma said she didn't care, because her mom wanted her to be a free agent. Her mom's one of those real forward-thinking moms."

Luke, glancing back into the crowd, spots Glenna, who has returned to the courtroom now that Dr. Manachi has finished testifying. She's looking straight forward, her face expressionless. An iron maiden, Luke thinks. She'd have to be, to get through this ordeal.

"Was the accused, Joe Allison, easy for you to recognize? When you saw him waiting for her?"

"Sure."

"Why is that?" Logan asks.

" 'Cause he drove a really cool car," she says brightly.

Smiles break out in pockets of the courtroom, including some in the jury box.

"Do you remember what kind of car it was?"

A vigorous nod. "It was a Beemer convertible. A Z-3. Gunmetal blue, with tan leather interior."

"That is a cool car," Logan agrees. He leans casually on the lectern, as if this is a natural conversation in some ordinary setting, instead of testimony in a murder trial. "Did Emma ever say anything about Joe Allison to you, or to anyone else? Did she ever talk about him? Either when he was outside your school waiting for her, or when he wasn't around?"

"Uh-huh." Her low-heeled shoe has slipped partially off her foot. She jangles it from the ends of her toes. She's only been on the stand for a few minutes and already she's getting jittery, her attention span starting to slip.

Deanna's inability to focus is fine with Logan—he's about done with his examination. Luke can have her with her mind wandering. "What did she say?" he asks.

"She'd joke around. She'd say, 'There's my boyfriend, come to pick me up.' "

"She called him her boyfriend?"

"Yeah. I mean, it was, you know—a joke."

"But did you think she liked him?"

"Oh, yeah! She liked him, for sure. He's a neat older guy, he's on TV, he drives a cool car," the girl rhapsodizes.

Luke steals a look at his client. Allison is looking down at the table, his head shaking imperceptibly, almost an involuntary reflex.

Logan continues, asking his witness, "So even though Emma talked about Joe Allison as her boyfriend in a joking manner, it felt to you like maybe she really believed it, too?"

"Objection, Your Honor." Luke's on his feet. "That's a leading question. Calls for speculation."

"Sustained," Ewing agrees. "Rephrase your question, Counselor," he instructs Logan.

Closing the file folder in which his notes are gathered, Logan asks Deanna, "Did Emma ever tell you that the defendant, Joe Allison, was her boyfriend, or that she was in some way involved with him beyond liking him, and his being someone who worked for her father?"

She nods her head, furrowing her brow as if to say are-you-kidding-me? "Oh, yeah."

"What did she say?" Logan asks.

"She said he was her main man. That was the way she called him: 'my main man.' She said he wasn't anything like the jerk boys in school."

"What did she say he was like?" Logan asks, turning to the jury to make sure they're paying attention. He sees, with satisfaction, that a few are even taking notes.

"She said he was a real man. Not a boy, a real man. She, like, emphasized that. Him being a 'real man.' "

"Those were her exact words?" he says.

A final nod. "A real man."

Luke wants Deanna off the stand and out of the jurors' minds, so he only asks her a few specific questions.

"Did you ever get the impression that Emma didn't want people to know about Mr. Allison picking her up after school?" he asks her. He's treating this casually, to the point that he isn't standing at the podium, he's questioning her from his seat.

She squinches her eyes up, opens them. "No."

"Did she ever say to you, 'I don't want my parents to know about this'?"

"No," again.

"She was open and aboveboard about her being with Mr. Allison."

"Uh-huh. Everybody saw him. Saw them leave together."

"So you didn't think she was sneaking around with him."

"No." The girl shakes her head. "She had a crush on him. Like, you know, she was fourteen."

"Did you, like, have a crush on him, too, Deanna?" Luke asks, smiling at her.

She blushes. A quick eye-shift towards Allison, sitting stoically at the defense table next to Luke, then down at her shoes. "Uh-huh," she murmurs.

"And some of the other girls. Did they have crushes on him?"

Another muttered uh-huh.

Judge Ewing's clerk catches his eye. The judge leans down to Deanna. "Please speak up a bit, Miss Dalton. We're having a hard time hearing you."

"Yes," she says, in a low but clearly audible voice.

"So wasn't their being together like, you know, a fantasy trip on Emma's part, rather than anything real going on between them?"

"I don't know," she says. "I mean, once they left school together, I don't know what they did. She'd hint around that something was going on, but it was, like, maybe trying to be adult, you know what I mean?"

Looking miserable, Dr. Janet Lopez, the doctor from the Free Clinic who was consulted by Emma about her pregnancy, takes the oath and sits in the witness chair. She's a reluctant witness for the prosecution, but not a hostile one.

Riva got the call the night before. Ray Logan had been playing hardball with the doctor, threatening to subpoena records and bring pressure on the clinic. The clinic, being a nonprofit organization, depends on the support of the community, especially rich people with social consciences. But even though their supporters are progressive, this case has violated their sense of propriety; their normal broad-minded attitudes have been suspended. In other words, the doctor had told Riva, if she didn't testify, some of the clinic's strongest supporters, many of them friends of Glenna Lancaster, might abandon them. The capper came when Glenna, who is now responsible for making these decisions, since her daughter is dead, personally told the doctor to come forward with whatever information she had.

Riva had commiserated with her. She was doing the right thing. A young girl was murdered. If the doctor's testimony can shed light on who did it, then she shouldn't think she's violating her dead patient's trust.

She's testifying under duress, so Logan gets right to it. "Did Emma Lancaster come to your clinic for a pregnancy test?" he asks.

"Yes, she did," Dr. Lopez answers.

"And did you administer one?"

"Yes, we did."

"And what were the results?" he asks.

"They were positive. She was pregnant."

Logan nods. The jury is paying close attention to this testimony. "Were you able to determine where she was in the pregnancy? How long had she been pregnant, Doctor?"

"About eleven weeks," is the answer.

"She was three months pregnant," he states, setting it in the time frame he wants the jury to be aware of.

"Almost three months," she corrects him. "She was about two weeks shy of three months."

"Did she look pregnant to you?" he asks. "Was she showing visibly?"

Dr. Lopez nods. "She was just beginning to. Her breasts were swelling, and there was some distension of her belly. If you didn't know it, her looks wouldn't strike you that she was."

"If she had not been killed," Logan says, "how soon would her condition have become noticeable to the casual observer?"

"Within a month."

He nods. "Okay, let's go on. When you told her she was pregnant," Logan continues, "what was her reaction?"

"She was concerned, but—" She stops.

"But what?" he prompts her.

"But not as much as I would have thought," she tells him.

"Why do you think that is?" he asks.

Dr. Lopez thinks for a moment. "She was a very composed girl, especially for someone her age. She seemed to take the news pretty much in stride."

"Did she ask you if you could perform an abortion on her?" He looks at the jury after he asks the question. They're poised and listening, every one of them.

"She asked what her options were," the doctor answers deliberately.

"Her options. Such as having the baby and giving it up for adoption, for instance?"

"That is one option I presented to her."

"What were the others?"

"Terminating the pregnancy was also an option she was informed of."

"Having an abortion," Logan says plainly.

"Yes."

"Do you perform abortions in your clinic, Dr. Lopez?"

"We do abortions, yes." She's visibly ill at ease.

"What conditions do you place on performing abortions at your clinic, Doctor?"

She rearranges herself in the chair. "The patient has to be in good general health," she states. "She has to be fully informed, and conscious of the ramifications of her decision." She pauses. "She cannot be pregnant beyond the first trimester," the doctor concludes.

"What about age? Are there any age restrictions on performing an abortion on a patient?" he asks.

She demurs. "No. There are no age restrictions. As long as the patient is healthy, and knows what she wants, there aren't any age restrictions." She stops.

"No matter how young a patient might be?"

"Age is not a restriction," she repeats.

"So you—your clinic—would perform an abortion on a fourteen-year-old girl if she was healthy and wanted one, wouldn't you?" He's coming on stronger than he wanted to, despite his desire to stay cool. He takes a deep breath, forces himself to relax, be friendly towards her. She is his witness, he doesn't want her clamming up on him.

"Yes, we would." She takes a beat. "We have."

He nods. "And when you perform these abortions, do you tell the girl's parents?"

She shakes her head emphatically. "Not unless the patient wants us to. Everything we do is in complete confidentiality."

"A fourteen-year-old girl can have an abortion in your clinic and you don't tell her parents?" Logan asks, seemingly disbelieving.

Luke is on his feet. "Objection, Your Honor!" he calls out sharply.

"Counsel is well aware of the law in this case. He's pandering to the jury, inflaming the issue."

"Your Honor—"

Ewing guns Logan down. "Sustained," he says sharply. He turns to the jury. "Parental consent is not obligatory for termination of pregnancy in the state of California," he explains to them. "The prosecution knows that," he says, glaring at Logan. He pauses for a moment, then explains his action and amplifies their understanding of the law, something he rarely does. "Many young, pregnant girls come from abusive situations," he explains. "If these unfortunate girls, already in distress, were compelled by law to inform their parents of their pregnancy, an unfortunate situation could be made even worse. This problem has gone back and forth in our courts, and the supreme court of the state has ruled this way, and that's the law." He leans forward, towards the jury box. "You are to forget that you heard that question," he tells the twelve men and women. "Strike it from your minds. It has nothing to do with this trial, or your deliberations." Turning away to Logan, "You may proceed," he says coldly—he's pissed off and he wants Logan to know it, and he wants everyone in the courtroom to know it. "But no more inciting questions like that one, or I'll hold you in contempt. Are we in agreement?"

"We are, Your Honor," Logan says quickly. "I certainly didn't mean to incite the court."

"Then don't" is the brusque reply.

In subtle ways, Luke thinks, this judge wants me to do well. Ewing isn't trying to tip the scales, but he doesn't want Luke to be streamrollered, either. All the good he'd done in the past, doing the county's work, is, in an unknown, unfathomable, but real way, a force in this trial.

Logan has turned his focus to the stand again. "Three months is the end of the first trimester, isn't it, Dr. Lopez?"

"Yes, it is."

"So if Emma Lancaster had wanted to have an abortion in your clinic, she would have had to do it right away, from the time you told her."

Dr. Lopez nods. "Two weeks, that was the timeline."

"So it was urgent that she make her mind up in a hurry," he says.

"Emma had already made her mind up. She was going to have an abortion."

Luke surveys the jurors. They're listening intently. Some look like they are not drawing breath.

Logan shakes his head slowly, up and down. "She was going to have an abortion," he repeats. "Was she going to tell her parents?" he asks. "Did she discuss that with you?"

"We discussed it," the doctor admits. She looks at him squarely. "She wasn't going to tell them."

All eyes seem to pivot to the same direction: towards Doug Lancaster, now again sitting a few rows from the front of the prosecution side of the aisle, and Glenna Lancaster, all the way in the last row.

Doug's head is buried in his hands, his shoulders slumped over. Hampshire, his lawyer, has a comforting arm around Doug's shoulders, which are shaking visibly. If he's making a sound, he's muffling it with his fist and sleeve.

Glenna is completely still. Eyes ahead, staring in the direction of the witness, but not seeing her. Not seeing anything specifically, it feels like. Just being there. Her body present, her mind who knows where?

They shouldn't be here, Luke thinks. Especially Glenna, the mother. But she cannot do otherwise. She comes because this is all there is to her life now, and even pain, as tormenting as it might be, is better than nothingness.

Logan continues with his questioning. "When was Emma planning on having the abortion?" he asks.

"The following Friday. She was going to come to the clinic after school and have it performed that afternoon. That way, she'd have the weekend to recover."

"Did she say how she was going to get there? Or more important, how she was going to get home afterwards? You wouldn't let her leave without a proper escort, would you?"

Lopez nods in agreement. "No, we wouldn't." She pauses. "I told her I'd drive her home, if she couldn't get anyone else she could trust."

"It wasn't going to be her mother. Or father. I want to be clear on that."

She agrees. "It wasn't. She did not want them to know."

Logan pauses for a moment. "Did she ever tell you who the father was, Dr. Lopez? Of her unborn child?"

A vigorous shaking of the head, the woman's dark, wavy curls rustling up in the air. "No. She never said a man's name."

"Did she make any reference to him at all? Who it might be?"

If the courtroom was quiet before, now it's dead still. Dr. Lopez answers carefully. "She didn't say anything . . . precisely. The closest she came to anything about who he was . . . um . . . he may have been an adult. An older man. But I got that indirectly, so I'm not sure."

"Was she going to tell him? The father? Did she say anything about that?"

A slow nod. "Yes. She was going to tell him."

"But she hadn't yet."

"She'd just found out herself," the doctor points out.

"Yes, right. So she had just found out she was pregnant, and she wanted to tell the father that she was pregnant and that she was going to have an abortion. Is that correct?"

Another nod. "Yes."

"Before or after?" he asks. "Do you know if she was going to tell him about being pregnant before or after the abortion was performed in your clinic?"

That's a cheap shot, Luke thinks. He's the only one in the courtroom who feels that way, though.

"She was going to tell him before the procedure was done."

"I see." Logan looks away from her, towards the defense table. The jury, which had been pivoting their looks back and forth between him and the witness, like spectators at a tennis match, follow his look directly to Joe Allison.

The D.A. turns back to the doctor. "How soon before Emma Lancaster was abducted from her bedroom did you tell her about her test being positive for pregnancy?" he inquires.

"One day," she answers. "She found out she was pregnant the day before the night of her disappearance."

Logan somberly walks away from the lectern. "No further questions of this witness at this time, Your Honor," he says in a heavy, battle-weary voice.

* * *

"You stated that Emma Lancaster found out she was pregnant the day before she disappeared from her bedroom, is that correct?" Luke asks.

"Yes," the doctor says. "That's right."

"But before that," he says, "did she think she might be pregnant? Did *you* think she might be pregnant?"

"When she walked into my office, I thought she was pregnant," Dr. Lopez responds.

"Why did you think that?"

"From how she looked. I've seen thousands of pregnant women, that's what I do." A moment's pause. "I think Emma knew she was pregnant. She wouldn't have come to see me otherwise. If she thought she was merely sick, she would have gone to her own doctor. Her family doctor."

"Right," he agrees. "You say she alluded to an older man. She didn't say she was pregnant by an older man, did she?"

"Not directly, no."

"Did she say she was having an affair with an older man?"

"Not directly," she says again.

"Then what brought you to the conclusion that it was an older man who was the father?" he asks questioningly.

"I can't put my finger on anything precise," she admits. "It was the tone of how she talked about him."

"So she never said, directly or indirectly, that she was having an affair with an older man, and—make that or—that the father of her child was an older man."

"No."

The assistant housemaid's command of English is okay, but her Salvadoran accent is thick, and she's scared. She is wearing what is obviously her best dress, an elaborate lavender-tinted chiffon concoction with puffed sleeves that she'd originally worn to her cousin's wedding. Her shoes are black suede, with ankle-busting heels, and she bought a new pair of stockings for this appearance. She knows she's overdressed, but she can't afford another fancy outfit. A short woman, her flat facial features suggesting indigenous Central American Indian stock, she sits cowering in the witness chair, her legs too short to reach the ground.

Logan has a court interpreter standing by, in case she freezes up on her English. "Good day, Ms. Rodriguez," he says solicitously. Her name is Lupe Rodriguez.

"Hello, mister," she answers back nervously. Not yet twenty-five, she's been a long time in the U.S., long enough to have gotten her green card, found a husband, and given birth to two children. But even though she's legal through and through, she still has the wetback's intense fear of gringo authority.

"Is it all right for us to talk in English, or would you prefer Spanish?" he asks. When he interviewed her, he'd had a woman interpreter along, but she was only needed a few times, fortunately. He hopes the witness can handle this in English. If every question has to be translated for her, then translated back into English, it won't go as well as straight English. Jurors bore easily, and some will be distrustful or resentful of a "foreigner," even though women like her have been an integral part of the California fabric for several generations. Still, there is a caste system in place in the community, and she's close to the bottom.

"English," she answers stoutly. She looks like a little bird on a wire, a sparrow perched on a roadside telephone pole. "I speak English okay, mister."

Good—so far. "Were you employed at the Lancaster household last year, including during the time when Emma Lancaster was taken from her bedroom?"

"Objection, Your Honor," Luke shouts. "We don't know if she was taken or left voluntarily."

"Sustained."

Logan starts over. "Did you work for the Lancasters at the time Emma disappeared from her bedroom?"

"Yes."

"What was your job?"

"I cleaned the house. I did laundry. I did dishes. Whatever the head housekeeper told me to do." Her attitude towards her work is bright, expressed in her tone of voice—this wasn't drudge work for her, it was a chance to make money for her family and live in a beautiful household. A chance to see what is possible in America.

"Would you describe for the court, please, what happened during the day and evening of the night that Emma Lancaster—disappeared—from her bedroom? Anything that might be important to this case that you know about firsthand?"

Luke looks through the notes of the prosecution's interview with this witness. There are no formal notes—all that's indicated is that she was interviewed. It was one of the last interviews done, he notes, only a couple of weeks ago. He had been too busy tying up other elements to seek her out and interview her himself. He hopes that wasn't a mistake.

"Mr. Allison called the house."

"By Mr. Allison, you mean the man who is sitting at the defense table." He points to Joe.

"Yes, sir, mister."

"How did you know it was Mr. Allison who called?"

"Because he said it was him. I know his voice. And also, he was on television every day. We would watch him on the news."

"So there is no doubt in your mind that Joe Allison, the defendant in this case, was the man who made the phone call."

"Yes, mister. It was him."

What the fuck is this? Luke thinks. He turns and looks at Allison. Allison catches the look, turns away.

"What's this about?" Luke whispers.

Allison shrugs.

"Did you call her?" Luke asks.

His client nods.

He turns away in disgust from Allison, staring across the chamber to the witness stand.

"What time was that call?" Logan asks.

"Four o'clock in the afternoon."

"Do you normally answer the telephone?"

"If there is no one else around. Of if I am close to it. Mrs. Lancaster didn't care who answered, as long as someone did."

"So you answered the telephone and Mr. Allison identified himself."

"Yes." Her head bobs up and down like a carousel horse. "He said his name, and he asked to speak to Emma."

"What did you tell him?"

"That she was not there."

"And what did he say?"

"He was upset. I could hear his voice was upset."

"Objection," Luke says. "Conjecture on the witness's part."

Ewing shakes his head. "I think the average person knows when someone's upset by the tone of their voice. Overruled."

"Thank you, Your Honor." Logan smiles. "What did Mr. Allison say, Ms. Rodriguez?"

"That he needed to talk to her."

"And what did you tell him?"

"That she wasn't there."

"Then what did he say?"

"When would she be there?"

"And you answered?"

"That I didn't know. I said, do you want me to tell her that you called if I see her?"

"And he said?"

"No. He said no, don't tell her. Don't tell anybody."

"He told you not to tell anybody that he had called?"

"Yes, mister. He told me not to tell anybody."

"Okay." He pauses a moment, picks up another sheet of paper, looks at it briefly. "Now, did Mr. Allison make another telephone call to the house that day?"

"Yes, mister."

Luke looks to Allison again. You moron, he thinks, what were you doing to yourself? What are you doing to *me*?

"What time was that?"

"About nine o'clock at night."

"Nine o'clock on the night she was—she disappeared from her room."

"Yes."

"What did he sound like this time?"

Luke starts to make another objection, but he stops himself. The judge has set the pattern for this witness. All he'll do is draw further attention to an already bad situation. Sometimes the best thing to do is nothing.

"He sound real concerned. Real worried. Nervous."

"What did he ask this time?"

"Where was Emma."

"And what did you tell him, the second time he called the house that day within five hours."

"She ain't home, mister. She's out with frien's. She won't be home till later."

"Did he say anything then?"

"It sounded like he say a curse word . . . but I'm not sure."

Logan nods. "Did he say anything else? Ask anything else?"

"What time later."

"Did you tell him? Did you even know?"

"I tell him midnight, 'cause that's her curfew, she got to be back by then, or her mama would be unhappy lady. She always was home by her curfew," she adds.

"Then what did he say?"

"He don't say nothing. He just hang up."

Logan smiles broadly at her. "Thank you, Ms. Rodriguez, for coming down here and helping out today." Turning to Luke, with a sweeping arm extended towards her, and a beatific smile on his happy face: "Your witness."

Luke and Allison powwow in the small attorney-client room adjacent to the courtroom. Before cross-examining the maid, Luke has requested a fifteen-minute recess.

He is beside himself with rage. "What's your goddamn excuse this time, ace?"

Allison is trembling from Luke's wrath. "I don't have one. I didn't think it was important."

"Wrong! Everything is important. Everything. I told you that a million times. *I* decide what's important." He slumps into the other battered metal chair. "What were these phone calls about, Joe?"

Some of the rage he feels is self-imposed: he should have interviewed the woman. She was one of dozens of family employees on the prosecution's potential witness list. He didn't have the time to get to all of them, and he didn't think one of them would come up with a bombshell like this.

Allison stammers as he tries to answer Luke's scathing question. "She . . . she had left several messages on my machine, earlier in the day. That she needed to talk to someone, and I was the only one she could trust. That's why I called."

Suspiciously: "Did she say why?"

"No. She just—needed to talk to someone, an adult. The message—messages—on the machine sounded like she was scared and needed some comfort."

"So good old Joe was going to comfort sweet little Emma. Who he was picking up after school and cruising around with. A very pretty picture, my friend."

Allison shakes his head. "That's not it, Luke. Her parents knew I was picking her up. They asked me to, some of the time. I'd drop her at home or take her up to the station. There was nothing more to that. You know that."

"I don't know what I know," Luke tells him, "because you still haven't told me everything, and that leaves me up shit creek. I have to know *everything*, even if you think it's inconsequential." He takes a deep, calming breath. "All right—go on about the telephone calls."

"I didn't leave a message because I was afraid her mother might find out she was trying to call me and not like it. Emma didn't talk about certain things to Glenna, and that ticked Glenna off."

"Yeah," Luke says, the sarcasm dripping onto the floor, "especially if her daughter's confiding in the guy who's fucking her."

"That's not why," Allison protests. "They were totally separate issues. Emma was outgrowing her parents, and they were having a hard time dealing with it, especially Glenna. It wasn't about Glenna and me."

"All right," Luke says. "Now what about the second call, the one at night? You knew her mother might be there. Why take a chance on calling then?"

"Because between the time I called in the afternoon and that one,

Emma called me again and left another message. It sounded desperate. She was practically begging me to get in touch with her." He exhales heavily, a man carrying too much of the world's burdens. "I was trying to help, that's all."

"Did the two of you ever connect?" Luke asks.

Allison shakes his head. "No. I never got to speak with her. And that's the God's honest truth."

Whether this is true or not, Luke thinks pessimistically, who in his right mind would ever believe this? And even if they didn't talk, why was she calling him? Because she had found out she was pregnant, and he was the father, and she needed to tell him? That's what Logan's going to tell the jury to think. At this point in the trial, they'd be crazy not to.

The deputy monitoring them sticks his head in the door. "Time."

Luke accompanies Allison back into the courtroom. Ray Logan's already there, dancing about on his toes, he's so pumped. He ought to be, Luke thinks, he's doing great. His client can't lie to him, or withhold information. His client, speaking from the grave, is telling a compelling story. Far more believable than theirs.

Again, another short cross-examination. Luke can't impugn the woman's testimony regarding who had called. The best he can do is soften the impact. "Do you know if Mr. Allison called the Lancaster house on a regular basis?" he asks her.

She nods her head vigorously, her shiny, wavy hair floating off her shoulders like a zephyr-blown handkerchief. "Yes, sir, mister. He call all the time."

"Who did he call? Did he call Mr. Lancaster?"

"Oh, yes, sir."

"And Mrs. Lancaster?"

"Yes, sir."

"And Emma Lancaster?"

"Yes, sir. He call all of them."

"So Mr. Allison's calling the house and speaking to Mr. Lancaster, or Mrs. Lancaster, or Emma Lancaster, was a common occurrence?"

"Common . . ." She stumbles over "occurrence."

"The calls happened all the time," he simplifies. "For all of them."

"All the time." She smiles with relief, now that she understands. "Mr. Lancaster, Mrs. Lancaster, Emma. He call them, they call him. All the time."

Evening. The sunset, as they watch it from the deck of their rented aerie, is blossoming with hibiscuslike brilliance across the ocean to the far end of the horizon: the sun dying as they watch it, liquefying into tentacles.

"Look at this sky and count your blessings."

He does as she tells him. Her, their unborn child. Those are blessings. Tonight, the sheer beauty of it, certainly a blessing.

Despite his surroundings, though, he can't shake his funk. This trial is not a blessing. Today wasn't good. The maid nailed them. On the very same day of her disappearance, Allison had been frantically trying to connect with Emma.

"You can't win them all, baby," Riva says softly, putting her cheek next to his. "Not every witness."

He sits up. "Well, that's one I certainly missed. I should've talked to her earlier. I messed up good."

"Luke, you're too hard on yourself."

"I'm trying to think of the consequences. Allison claims he didn't know why she was calling, but what if the reverse is true, that he did know and was freaked out by the news? Knocking up his boss's fourteen-year-old daughter—nothing but catastrophe there. He got her pregnant, she found out, something was going to happen. Either she tells the world who did it—him—or she wants him to help her go through the abortion process, or something equally dangerous. Dangerous not only for her life but for his career. At that moment, Joe Allison wouldn't have given a shit about Emma Lancaster's condition, or any danger she could be in. His ass is what he would have been worried about. So what do you do? You get rid of the evidence against you. You kill it."

"You have good material of your own," Riva reminds him.

"Especially about Doug Lancaster. And other things, too. Your day to present your side is coming. You have to stay with the big picture, and your theme. Isn't that what you keep telling me?"

"I know all that," he acknowledges grudgingly. He's on one of those down trips where you don't want to be reminded of the good side, it's like you want only the dark side, you wallow in it, almost, as if it's your deserved fate. "But I keep getting tripped up by my own client," he says. "That scares me."

And now the sun dies in the sky and there is only a pale thin ribbon of yellow to commemorate its passage. Overhead the dense, fast-moving clouds, heavily moonlit, seem even brighter now, a night-blooming celestial cloak.

She turns to him. "Do you want to know what I think?"

His elbows leaning on the protective redwood railing, he says, "Yes, of course." Then, "Am I going to like this? I'm not looking to get kicked anymore, not for what's left of this day."

"Maybe I shouldn't."

Sighing, he says, "Tell me. You always do. You're my lodestar, you have to."

"He did it."

His stomach contracts violently. This hurts worse than the bullet he took.

"Not killed her," Riva says, reading him, knowing he didn't want to hear this, that he's been avoiding confronting it. But he has to hear it, he isn't the judge or the jury, he's the lawyer. His job isn't about innocence or guilt, it's about defending his client as well as he can. If that's the truth, he has to know it, take it in, deal with it. "He got her pregnant."

As his stomach loosens, his heart starts pounding. "Is that what you believe?"

"Yes." She waits before adding the rest. "Don't you?" She reaches over and takes his hand.

"I don't know. Maybe." He nods confirmation. "Yes, he could have. At least he could've been sleeping with her. There could be someone else out there who was, too, besides the health-store guy. Someone we've never uncovered."

"Yes," she agrees, "but does that matter? The prosecution's entire case is based on that synergy—whoever got her pregnant killed her. But that's not your case. Keep your focus on your case, Luke."

"My case is Doug Lancaster. I don't know what else I have. And that could blow up in my face so easily, the martyred father. The jury could hate me and Allison before I even got to present that. I could be talking to the air."

"They'll listen. You'll make them. It's a good case, especially in raising reasonable doubt. Or unreasonable doubt." She moves close to him, nuzzling his cheek with her lips. "There's still a long way to go."

He holds her, feeling her body against his, the stomach starting to show now. "It's the lying that's bothering me. Every time I turn around, I find out something new about Allison, and it's never good, it's always bad. Either he's unconscious, which is hard to believe, or he's hiding key things from me, which is easy to believe. That's what's bugging me, babe. I've got a client who isn't straight with me. And the way it always goes—I can go back over hundreds of cases—when your client is doing that, he's guilty. Of something."

"Then you need to confront him again."

He shakes his head. "It's too late now. Whatever happened, happened. This is the hand I've been dealt, and I can't throw in my cards. Whatever it is, I've got to play it."

Officer Caramba, his uniform pressed to knife-blade sharpness, his hair freshly cut Marine-DI-style, sits in the witness chair like a tin soldier. He stares directly at Ray Logan. He does not look at the jury, nor does he look over at Joe Allison and his lawyer, the turncoat former district attorney. He is crisp, he is concise, he is coiled tight as a steel spring. Last night, for several hours, he went over his recitation with Ray Logan and Logan's staff. Sheriff Williams was also present, even though Williams isn't his chief, as he's a city cop. Williams, though, is the ranking peace officer on this case. Once the initial arrest was made, his department led the investigation and found the evidence in Allison's house. But he, Caramba, a city police officer, made the initial arrest. He got the ball rolling. Without him, there is no case. The city police force wants some of the glory, too. He's their poster boy. It's important that he do a good job today. That's what he's going to do. And he's not going to let ponytail over there break him down.

Using maps, photographs, and other visual aids, Logan walks Caramba through his arrest of Joe Allison. Following Allison down Coast Village Road late at night, observing him driving erratically, finding him flushed and not totally coherent, then discovering the open bottle in the car, and subsequently finding the key ring belonging to Emma Lancaster in the suspect's glove compartment, which, Caramba is quick to point out, the suspect himself had opened.

It's a good tight presentation. The kind a cop who's on the ball gives in a trial. Then Luke takes over. He opens the officer's file on the podium. There are only a few sheets of paper inside, primarily his notes from their interview, which he had scrawled down afterwards to make sure his memory stayed fresh.

"Good morning, Officer."

Caramba nods, but doesn't say anything.

"You stopped Mr. Allison because his driving was erratic, is that right?"

"That's right."

"How long did you observe Mr. Allison before you pulled him over, Officer?"

"Thirty or forty seconds."

Luke frowns. He looks at his notes. "When I interviewed you, you told me fifteen seconds. Ten or fifteen seconds."

"More or less," the cop says.

"Let's get this straight, how long did you follow my client? Ten seconds, or forty? Which is it?"

"Closer to forty."

"Are you sure?"

"I'm sure."

The guy's lying. Is the jury scoping that out? He looks over at them, but he can't read them. "Whatever it was," Luke throws away, "ten seconds or thirty, it was a short period of time."

"Forty," Caramba corrects him. "Not ten, not thirty. It was long enough for me to make my decision," he says firmly. "It's what I'm trained to do. If we followed every DUI suspect for too long, you could have a fatality, and that's a lot worse than not following someone long enough. If I'm wrong," he says, repeating what he'd told Luke in their interview, "I apologize and they go on their way. Most law-abiding citizens are appreciative of that."

"Not every law-abiding citizen is agreeable to being stopped on a hunch, Officer," Luke says argumentatively. He glares at Caramba. Caramba glares back at him, but doesn't respond in kind.

Luke continues. "After you stopped my client, and began questioning him, did you ask him to step out of his car?"

"Not at that time."

"Okay, so he's sitting in his car, talking to you, you're checking out his driver's license and registration, I presume—"

"He was having a hard time finding his registration," Caramba interjects. "That was another reason I started suspecting him. He seemed flustered about that."

"I see." He waits a moment, then asks, "Did he find his registration, Officer?"

"Yes, he did."

"Where did he find it?"

"In his glove compartment."

"Which is where people normally keep them. Did it check out? The license and registration?"

"I didn't get that far."

"Why not?"

"Because at that point in time I saw the open bottle in his car, so I was going in a different direction then."

"And how was it that you saw this open bottle, Officer? On a dark night, with the driver sitting in his car with the doors closed."

"I saw it when he opened his car door. I could see onto the floorboards in the back, behind his front seat."

Luke thinks a moment. "Why did he open his car door? Did you ask him to?"

"I did," the officer answers in a flat monotone.

"For what purpose?"

"So I could administer a field sobriety test."

Luke steps back. This is what he's been working to. "So at that point you gave my client a field sobriety test?" He makes a show of rummaging through the few remaining sheets of paper in the officer's folder.

"No."

Luke looks up. "Why not?" he asks, as if surprised.

"Because of the open bottle," the cop says patiently. He doesn't want to get into a pissing contest with this lawyer, who knows all the ins and outs from his time being the D.A.

"You found an open bottle and you didn't give him a sobriety test?" Luke puts on a good show of being puzzled. "Why wouldn't you do that? Isn't an open bottle further indication that he might have been driving under the influence?"

"Yes, it would be," Caramba admits. "And I was going to."

"So why didn't you?"

"Because now I was suspicious."

"Suspicious? Of what?"

"That maybe there were other things in his car that could be illegal."

Luke stops to think about that. He looks at the jury; they too are wondering about why this police officer acted as he did. "That doesn't make sense," Luke says.

Caramba bristles, but holds his temper in check. "Everything I did was perfectly legal," he says in his defense.

"I didn't say what you did wasn't legal," Luke corrects him. "I said it didn't make sense. If you think a man has been driving while drunk, shouldn't you test him to find out if he is? If he isn't, you let him go, isn't that what you just told us?"

The officer shakes his head. "Not in this case. Once that open bottle was found, that made it a different story."

"You're splitting hairs on me here, man," Luke says in an annoyed tone. He wants people, especially the jurors, to know that he's annoyed with a sworn peace officer who's pulling legalese to avoid answering questions. "You stop someone you think might be driving drunk, you find an open bottle of whiskey in his car, and then you don't test him. You go rummaging around in his glove box instead. What were you looking for, another open bottle? You already had one, one's enough, more doesn't matter."

"I was looking for whatever I could find."

"Really? Like what? Drugs? Guns? Or some piece of planted evidence that would tie my client to an unsolved murder!"

"Objection!" Logan is on his feet, on his toes, foaming, his hand shooting up into the air like a student desperate for the teacher to call on him. "This is totally inflammatory and irrelevant!"

Ewing hits the gavel. "Sustained." To Luke, he says in a harsh, tight voice, "You're about this far from contempt, Mr. Garrison." He's holding his thumb and forefinger half an inch apart. "No more questions like that, do you understand me?"

Luke's teeth are grinding. "Sidebar, Your Honor."

He and Logan stand at the side of the judge's bench, out of the jury's hearing. Luke fights to keep himself under control. "I understand you, Your Honor, but this goes to the heart of my argument about this evidence," he says passionately. Gesturing across the bench at Caramba, he says, "This officer stopped the defendant on a possible DUI. He was obligated to give him sobriety tests to find out if he was over the limit. The law is clear on that. If he wasn't drunk, there was no reason to search his car, regardless of whether there was an open bottle in it or not. Both of those offenses are misdemeanors. That's all they are. He signs a ticket, agreeing to appear in court, you send him on his way—assuming he's sober." Forging on, he says, "But this officer decided to go on a fishing expedition, instead of following standard, established procedure. In fact," Luke continues, his forcefulness picking up steam, "the defendant was *never* given a sobriety test in the field, and he was *never* informed that he was a suspect in a murder case. All he ever thought or was told was that he had been arrested for possible drunk driving, which he was never tested for. That is a fundamental violation of his rights under the Fourth Amendment. All the evidence gathered against my client is illegal, and I submit that it should not be allowed into evidence."

"Your Honor—" Logan begins.

Ewing has already started to get up. "The court will recess for one hour," he declares. "Opposing counsel will meet me in chambers."

* * *

Ewing, the Federal and state Penal Codes open on his desk, is leafing through the search and seizure sections. He looks up at Logan. "What do you think?" he asks the D.A. "He's your witness."

"The officer acted properly within the law, Your Honor," Logan insists. "He stops a man who's driving erratically, he sees there's an open bottle in the car, that not only grants him the right to search the rest of the car that isn't locked, it's dangerous for him not to. What if there *is* a gun hidden under the seat, and the driver decides to use it? He knows there's an outstanding charge against him and he doesn't want to come in. Bingo, one dead police officer."

Ewing is listening sympathetically.

"Once the officer found the key ring in Allison's car, the case moved beyond a simple DUI," Logan continues. "You don't waste time testing someone who might be a murder suspect. You bring him in for questioning as fast as you can."

Ewing nods. "That sounds reasonable to me," he says to Luke.

Luke shakes his head. "I disagree. The man produced his license and registration. He's out of the car. How can he get his hands on a gun *inside* his glove compartment if he's *outside* his car? The procedure is to check out his license and registration, find out if there are any outstanding warrants on him, field-test him for sobriety. If he fails, you cite him for drunk driving and having an open bottle in his car—they go together, it's a good bust. But if he passes, you take the bottle, write up a ticket, send him on his merry way, *because he isn't drunk*. Anyway," he adds, "it's a lot more complicated than simple DUI and having an open bottle, because of the subsequent investigation at the jail." He takes the sheets of paper from the folder he's been carrying, hands them to Ewing. "And this."

Ewing looks at them. He's already seen them, as has Logan. "Yes," he says heavily. "This does have bearing on the events and how they transpired." He ponders Luke's request a moment more. "At this point, I'm not going to rule on your point," he tells Luke. "Meaning I'm unofficially denying it, but if subsequent testimony or evidence, such as this"—he brandishes the pages Luke gave him—"is found to be relevant, I'll revisit the issue."

* * *

"Officer Caramba." Luke's at the podium again, the pages he's just shown Ewing spread out in front of him. "You were parked on Coast Village Road, the defendant drove by you, you started following him, you suspected him of driving under the influence, you pulled him over. Is that essentially the way it happened?"

The policeman nods. "That's how it happened," he attests.

"Was he speeding?"

"I didn't follow him long enough to check that out. That wasn't why I went after him."

"It was the erratic nature of his driving."

"Yes. I've already said that."

"He was weaving all over the road?"

"He was not driving in a straight line."

"But was he out of control, as you followed him, or just weaving a little, momentarily?"

"He crossed the double yellow line," Caramba says, not wavering in his story. "We've had fatalities on that stretch of road. Our watchword is to be overly cautious. A saved life is worth any amount of extra caution."

"Agreed," Luke responds. "But one crossing of the yellow line, when he isn't speeding? He could have been looking down at his radio for a minute, or been otherwise distracted. Shouldn't you have followed him longer, to make sure?"

"It's a judgment call. In my judgment, his driving warranted my pulling him over."

"To give him a field sobriety test you never gave him," Luke says with heavy sarcasm. Before Logan can object, Luke puts up a hand. "Only kidding, Officer. You were going by the book."

"Yes, I was." The policeman's mouth is set in a tight, thin line.

Luke turns to the bench. "Your Honor, at this point, I would like to place three documents in evidence." He's holding the papers he brandished in the judge's chambers.

Ewing nods. "So ordered."

The documents are marked for identification.

Luke hands one copy of the pages to the clerk, who moves them into evidence. Holding a second copy, Luke approaches the stand.

Handing the three pages to Officer Caramba, he asks him to look them over.

"Do you recognize these?" Luke asks. "All of them?"

Caramba looks at them carefully. "Yes."

"The first one is your hand-written report of you detaining Mr. Allison on Coast Village Road, is that correct?"

"Yes."

"And the other two are police logs of telephone conversations, aren't they? This one"—he taps the page the officer is holding in his right hand— "is between the dispatcher and officers in the field, and this second one is between the police switchboard and outside callers. Is that correct?"

Caramba makes a show of studying them. "That's what they look like."

"Have you ever seen these pages before? Besides the one you wrote yourself."

"Yes."

"When did you first see these pages, Officer?"

Caramba stares at them. "A month or six weeks ago. I don't recall exactly."

"That doesn't matter," Luke says dismissively. "Who showed them to you? Someone from the D.A.'s office? An assistant D.A., someone from that office?"

"Yes."

"Okay." He moves in close to the officer. The cop is wearing Canoe, and too much of it. He hasn't smelled Canoe on a man since college. Moving upwind ever so slightly, he points to a specific spot on one page, then the other. "I'd like you to look at two entries, Officer. But before you do that," he backtracks, "do you notice the dates, listed on the top of each page?"

The officer looks at the tops of the pages. "Yes, I see them."

"They're the same date, on both pages, is that correct?"

A nod. "Yes."

"One page lists outside calls coming in, the other page is dispatcher calls to and from the field. Is that correct?"

"Yes."

"The date on both these pages—this is the night that Mr. Allison was arrested, isn't it? The night you stopped him for suspicion of a DUI."

Another tight nod. "Yes."

"With your permission, Your Honor, I'd like to give a copy of these pages to each member of the jury, so they can follow along with us."

Ewing nods. "So ordered."

Luke hands the clerk two stacks of pages. She crosses to the jury box and crisply hands them out, one of each, to the twelve men and women, returning to her seat in front of the bench. Luke waits a minute for the jurors to look them over, then goes on.

"On the switchboard sheet, we have a call from an anonymous citizen. Correct?"

Caramba's nod is one inch. "Yes," he answers in a pinched voice.

"This stellar citizen—the log doesn't say male or female, and the caller doesn't ID him- or herself—has seen someone driving a car towards the vicinity of Coast Village Road, a few minutes after midnight. Anonymous stellar citizen tells the switchboard operator that the driver of the car appears to be intoxicated, is that correct?"

Looking at the sheet, Caramba answers, "Yes."

"This wonderful person was aware enough to record the make, model, color, and license plate of the car in question, is that also correct? On a dark, cloudy night."

"Yes."

Luke now holds up the second sheet. "Now this is the record for that same time frame—shortly after midnight, the night Mr. Allison was detained by you—of calls made by the central dispatcher in the police department to officers in the field. Which at that time included you. Is that also correct, Officer Caramba?"

Caramba nods, almost imperceptibly.

"Please answer vocally," Ewing reminds him.

Like sucking a lemon: "Yes."

"According to the time code on these pages, that call was broadcast less than a minute after the anonymous tip was called in to the switchboard, wasn't it?"

"Yes."

"You were the responding officer. You were, fortunately and coincidentally, smack dab in the path the driver was taking."

"Uh-huh."

Luke turns to the jury box. "That's a yes." Turning back to the witness, he now says, "So when Mr. Allison came into view, driving down Coast Village Road—at an acceptable rate of speed, I might add, you've testified that he wasn't speeding—you were waiting for him. You were primed to go after him, regardless of how his driving appeared to you objectively. You were going to pull him over, and then figure it out."

Caramba shakes his head in denial. "He was weaving on the road. I would have pulled him over if I hadn't gotten the call."

"I'm sure you would have, being the wonderful policeman that you are—" Luke says.

"Objection!"

"—the protector of society—"

"Objection, damn it!" Logan, on his feet, is pounding on his table with his fist.

"Sustained!" comes the judicial lion's roar. "Stop attacking this witness like this, Mr. Garrison!"

Luke steps back. "Sorry about that, Your Honor. But there's a point where the truth gets bent so badly and recklessly that a reasonable man and conscientious lawyer would be derelict if he didn't call attention to it."

"Objection!"

"Sustained!"

Luke puts up both hands in a gesture of supplication. Almost backing away, he declares, "I'm sorry. I won't do this again—with this witness, who I'm done with." He looks at Caramba. "I'm done with *you*—for now." Then rudely turning his back on the man, he says to Judge Ewing, "I am now, again—"

Ewing interrupts him. Looking down from his perch, he tells Caramba, "The witness is excused."

Stiffly, the police officer gets up, walks down from the stand, and strides out of the room. The judge turns to Luke, then to Logan. "Approach the bench." They stand at the judge's post. Luke speaks quietly so the jury won't hear.

"I am again asking the court, given this clear evidence that Officer Caramba did not stop the defendant because he looked like he was driving under the influence, but because of an anonymous telephone call that smells suspiciously like a setup to me—"

"Objection!" Logan says immediately.

"Sustained. Please save your editorializing for your summation, Mr. Garrison."

"Given the circumstances surrounding the initial search and seizure of Mr. Allison and his vehicle, I ask that any and all material and information gathered from said search and seizure be declared inadmissible in this trial."

Ewing stares at Luke even as Logan once again strenuously objects. Then he shakes his head. "No. I'm not going to do that."

Luke nods. This is the only ruling Ewing can make. For him to do otherwise would be grounds for a mistrial. No superior court judge in this world would have the guts to do that. Judges live in the real world. But Luke's deflated, nevertheless.

"Receiving a tip is not grounds for dismissal of an otherwise legal search and seizure," Ewing tells Luke, almost apologetically.

Luke knows the judge is in turmoil over this. The judge knows he's making a good case.

Judge Ewing turns and checks the ornate wall clock situated high behind his head. "We'll break for lunch until one-thirty," he notifies the assemblage. To Ray Logan: "Have your next witness prepared to take the stand."

Logan's direct of Detective Terry Jackson is meat and potatoes. Jackson ingratiates himself with the jury, which makes him a good witness. Luke, watching the examination, can see that the jury likes the man, and believes him. Logan doesn't tarry on anything, so in a little more than an hour, not much longer than the actual interrogation itself took, he's turning Jackson over to Luke.

Luke strides to the podium. He has the transcript of Allison's interrogation in his hand. "Good afternoon, Detective Jackson," he says, friendly today. "How're you doing today? You're looking good. Fit."

"Thank you." Jackson smiles. "You're looking good your own self."

"I'm hangin' in," Luke says. He opens the folder containing the transcript. "When did you read my client his Miranda rights?"

"I didn't," Jackson says without missing a beat. "He was read his rights in the field, by the arresting officer."

Luke shakes his head. "No, he was not. He was read his rights—as regarding a misdemeanor DUI, not a felony death-penalty murder charge."

"That's not my department," Jackson says with ease. "The man had been arrested in the field, he'd been sitting in a jail cell, me and him talked. I asked him did he want a lawyer, he said no. It's right there in your transcript you're carrying around in your hand."

Luke gives Jackson a skeptical eye. "Terry. That's not how it was."

"It sure was," the detective comes back with vigor. "Read it, man, it's in the transcript. And the name is Jackson. Mister."

Luke leafs through a few pages of transcript until he finds the one he's looking for. For obvious reasons, the district attorney didn't place the transcript in evidence—so Luke did, before he began his cross-examination. He wants the jury to have it in their hands when they go into the jury room to deliberate.

"You tell him he shouldn't be in there?"

Jackson nods.

"He was suspected of murder. Why did you tell a suspect facing a murder charge he shouldn't be in jail?" Luke asks. "That doesn't sound like good police procedure to me, and everyone knows you're a good detective."

Jackson smiles and shakes his head. "Hardly anyone knows who I am, let alone if I'm good at my job or not. But thanks for the plug," he says, almost laughing. "I'm gonna hit my boss up for a raise."

"Emma Lancaster's key chain was found in his glove compartment. Doesn't that automatically make him a suspect?"

"Of course not," the cop says. "She could've tossed it in there herself and forgot about it," he says.

Same old same old. "So he was just in there on a DUI charge and you were shooting the breeze with him until his time period for sobering up expired and he could leave."

Jackson shrugs, but he doesn't respond directly, because he knows what's coming.

"Except you told him he couldn't leave until the morning."

"It was three, four by that time," Jackson says. "Morning was right around the corner."

"Right." You're lying through your teeth. "So he wasn't a suspect until his shoes showed up, the shoes that had the sole print found out at the Lancaster house that afternoon after Emma disappeared, and later where her body was discovered. It wasn't until they showed up from his house that you decided he was a suspect after all. Is that right?"

"That's right," the detective says deadpan. "One built on the other."

"And that's when you told him he was a suspect in the Emma Lancaster kidnapping-murder case."

"That's when he was notified."

"And read his Miranda rights as they pertained to that charge."

"That's—" Jackson catches himself. "He already had been."

Luke shakes his head. "You just said he wasn't a suspect until the shoes turned up to buttress the key chain. So he couldn't have been read his rights, because there was no reason to, since he wasn't a suspect."

Jackson shrugs. "That's how it happened, Luke. Excuse me—*Mister* Garrison. We got the killer we'd been looking for, and we did it by the book."

Luke spins to Ewing—he's furious. "This man's not the jury. He is not allowed to render an opinion on the guilt or innocence of my client. This testimony is outrageous and has to be struck."

Ewing nods. "The witness will refrain from stating anything other than known, observable facts." He swivels around, facing the jury over Jackson's head. "You are to completely ignore that last set of remarks. They are not going to be part of the record, and you should erase them from your minds," he says forcefully.

Now royally steamed, Luke continues: "When Mr. Allison was in the jail, Detective Jackson, when was he given a sobriety test?"

Jackson shrugs. "I don't know."

"But he was given one, right?"

Another shrug. "I said I don't know. I don't do them."

Luke paces around in the well for a moment, coming closer to the jury box. "We've got a conundrum here, I think, don't you, Detective?"

"We got a *what*?" He smiles over at the jury. Their faces coming back to him are blank.

"A problem that doesn't seem to have a solution."

Jackson doesn't respond. He can see Ray Logan giving him the palms down sign, to cool it.

"Because you didn't know if Mr. Allison was drunk or sober."

"He was sober."

"How do you know?" Luke asks. This guy's starting to talk too much. It's a common disease among witnesses, particularly witnesses who have been around the block a time or three.

"I could tell looking at him. And they wouldn't have let me talk to him if he wasn't sober, it's against regulations."

"Ah!" Luke smiles. "Exactly my point. You can't interrogate someone who's intoxicated. But he was never given a test for that, so you didn't know. No one knew."

Once again, he turns to Judge Ewing. "Have I made my point now, Your Honor? If he's intoxicated, the police are not allowed to question him. And if he is sober, they have no grounds to hold him, unless they inform him that he's a suspect in a crime, read him his rights pertaining to that crime, let him bring in his lawyer, and so on. Either he shouldn't have been there in the first place, or he shouldn't have been interrogated. One or the other." He stares up at Ewing, challenging the judge to dispute him this time. "I move, once again, to strike all evidence taken from Mr. Allison's car, house, and anywhere else, under the search and seizure applications of the law."

Ewing has been preparing for this for weeks—it's cost him sleep, trying to figure out what to do. He can't let this trial die on a so-called technicality, no matter how compelling and fundamentally right it might be. He has his ruling on his bench, right in front of him. It's a beautiful job of finessing, a major-league curve ball. "Regardless of whether the defendant was legally intoxicated at the time of his arrest," he reads, "by the time he was questioned by Detective Jackson, the effects of any intoxication, as commonly understood under the four-hour sobering-up period, would have worn off sufficiently that he could be interrogated and understand what was going on." He looks up. "Motion to strike is denied."

Luke knew all along that Ewing wouldn't end this trial on an interpretation of law—the man would be run out of town on a rail. But to basically endorse trashing the Miranda rule, that comes close to flouting the law.

The ruling makes something crystal clear to him, which he's known, floating around in the back of his brain, but he hasn't allowed to surface, because it's a bitch to face: He's not going to win this fight on points. He has to win by a knockout. He has to find somebody else, other than Joe Allison, who is carrying so much guilt on his shoulders that no jury will dare convict Allison.

He's got his man. Doug Lancaster. He has to play every single card he has to make Doug look guilty—maybe not of this crime, he can't prove Doug did it, but of everything else. Bribery. Threats. Lying to the police. Deflect the thrust from his client to Doug, as was done down in L.A. when O. J. Simpson's defense team managed to make the trial a referendum on crooked cops instead of the prosecution of a wife-killer.

Not the way he prefers to work, but he has one job—to get Joe Allison off. By whatever legal means he can.

Maria Gonzalez takes the stand. She's poised, she's prepared. She stands tall, taking the oath. She's testifying in a court of law in the United States of America, her chosen country. She takes this very seriously.

Logan elicits who she is, how long she worked for the Lancasters, her relationship with Emma, and so forth. Then Logan asks the question that gets to the heart of his case, and it's stunning. "What did you see that night? Late that night, the night Emma Lancaster was taken from her room? Describe for the people in this court what you saw, Mrs. Gonzalez."

She adjusts her seat, shifting so that she is sitting absolutely straight. Eyes straight ahead, her voice crisp and clear, she tells her story:

She had worked late cleaning up after Mrs. Lancaster's party and was going to spend the night in the house, go home first thing in the morning. Sunday morning, her day off, she would be home before her own children woke up and she would get them all ready and they would go to church and have a family day.

The telephone rang in her room in the middle of the night. She had her own telephone, so that her family could call her and not disturb the Lancasters. It was one of the perks they gave her, because she was so good at her job.

Her youngest was sick. A terrible ear infection. He suffered often from them. Her husband was trying, but he couldn't cope. The baby was screaming. She had to come home, she had to take care of her own children.

She got dressed, she let herself out of her room in the servants' section. It was a nice room, very well furnished. Like Emma's room, it opened onto the backyard. There was a patio outside the door, which she could walk along to the side of the property, where she had her own car parked in the courtyard.

As she began walking to her car, worrying about her baby, she saw a figure moving across the lawn, away from the rear, towards the front of the property, near where she had her own car parked. It was a tallish figure, wearing a baseball-style hat with a swoosh on the front and a thigh-length windbreaker.

Whoever he was—she felt sure it was a man—he wasn't supposed to be there. She moved into the shadows against the wall as she watched him.

He passed by her on his way, about ten yards from her at the nearest distance. The moon was low but plenty full, casting enough light for anyone to see.

As the man reached the gate that led out of the backyard, he turned one time, looking back into the property. In the general direction of the gazebo at the far end. And when he turned to look, she saw his face for a quick moment.

If she had never seen this man, she wouldn't have been able to know who he was, have him imprinted in her brain, she wouldn't have been able, only a few days ago, to find the courage to come to the police and tell them what she saw that night. She wouldn't have been able to tell them that she saw Joe Allison in the backyard that night, if she hadn't seen him hundreds of times before. But she had seen him hundreds of times before, and that's how she knew it was him. Joe Allison. Walking across the backyard of the Lancaster estate at three o'clock in the morning.

Everyone in the courtroom sits in stunned silence. Ray Logan is motionless at the podium. Even the sheriff's deputies, the toughest cases, are standing and staring in disbelief. No one moves, not even the hard-boiled reporters, who should be ready to bolt, even they sit glued to their chairs.

Luke is stunned beyond imagining. Where in the world did this come from? And why didn't he know? He looks at Allison, sitting a foot from him, their shoulders almost touching. Allison is staring straight ahead, eyes unblinking, body rigid.

He did it. The bastard actually did it. I should've known all the time, the way he held everything back. The cynical, murdering fuck has taken Luke Garrison down—his lawyer, the man who had come back here to defend him, leaving himself open to every kind of wound imaginable and suffering most of them, leaving him dead now in this trial, a dead skunk in the middle of the road, stinking to high hell.

"Ah, you bastard." The words come out in a whispered exhalation. "You fucking bastard."

"I didn't kill her."

"Oh, fuck you." He slumps in his chair. He feels like he's dying.

"I didn't kill her."

From a far distance, as out of a chilly fog, the sepulchral, now maddening voice of Ray Logan: "Your witness."

Before the cross-examination begins, the lawyers and Judge Ewing meet in chambers. Maria Gonzalez is also in attendance, under judge's orders. Anticipating Luke's objection, Logan weighs in, starting to explain almost before the door is closed behind them.

"She just came to us with this," he tells Judge Ewing and Luke.

Luke has left Allison back in the courtroom—he doesn't want the man to stink up the small chambers, and he wants to put some space, if only for a few minutes, between them. To make sure that he doesn't lean over and try to strangle the sonofabitch to death with his bare hands. "Two days ago."

"This is outrageous," Luke fumes. "There is no excuse in the world why I didn't have this."

Ewing nods. "Why have you withheld this?" he asks the former maid sternly.

Her head is down. She doesn't respond.

"She didn't withhold it deliberately, Your Honor, and neither did we." Logan's got the goods and he's protecting her. "We didn't know." He looks down at the woman. "No one had asked her if she had seen anything like that, and she was too scared to come forward."

"I can't believe what I'm hearing," Luke says in disgust. "Judge, he can't do that."

Again, Ewing denies him. "Witnesses come forward at the last minute," he tells Luke. "It happens. It happened when you were the district attorney, if I may refresh your memory. You interviewed her months ago, didn't you? Why didn't you think to ask her if she had seen anything that night? If you had, Luke, we wouldn't be here now."

"So what do I do now?" Luke asks plaintively.

"Defend your client," the judge tells him. "As you have been doing, all along."

"Mrs. Gonzalez."

She's on the stand again. Luke, now ready to start his cross, has just had a harrowing, acrimonious half hour with Joe Allison, his client.

"Tell me you didn't do it," he said. "Tell me that wasn't you she saw. Please don't tell me that was really you there, that night. Don't tell me that, please."

Allison couldn't lie anymore. "I was there that night," he admitted, as Luke paced the small room, his gut exploding. "And it was me who took her out of the room." He looked at Luke, shaking his head. "I should've told you. But if I had, you'd be off the case. So I shut up." As forcefully as he did on the first day they met, he adds, "But I did not kill her."

I had dropped Nicole off, gone home, done some reading, gone to bed. Dead to the world, the telephone rang. Grabbing it, groggy, falling over myself, sprawled out on the bed. "Hello?" I said. A croak, like a bronchitic frog. Clearing my voice, "Hello," again.

"Joe." It was a soft voice, a whisper.

"Emma?" I knew the voice, knew it well.

"I've been trying to get in touch with you." She sounded whiny, as was often the case, but with a fear-edge I hadn't heard before. She was always so tough and in control, amazingly so, especially for someone her age.

"I've called you, too. We keep missing each other. Where are you?"

"At home. In my room. I need to see you."

I was half asleep and I didn't like the sound of this, she had never called me late like this before, usually Nicole was staying with me and I didn't want other women or, in Emma's case, girls, calling me here, Nicole would get suspicious in a heartbeat.

"Is your girlfriend there?"

I should have lied. If I had said yes, all this would be so different. I wasn't awake enough yet to figure that out, to lie, which she would have expected, not the lying but that Nicole was there, in my bed next to me, either asleep, or awake listening, wanting to know who in the world calls at two-thirty in the morning.

"No," I answered honestly. "I'm alone."

"I need to see you."

I was up now, sitting on the edge of the bed, drinking from the glass of water I kept on the night stand next to the bed, my mouth was dry from sleeping open-mouthed and from the wine earlier. "All right. Meet me at . . . Starbucks, over by Von's. I'll meet you there tomorrow morning. Around ten." I wanted to sleep in. "Can you get someone to drop you off without making a big deal out of it?"

"Now. I need to see you now. Right now."

"Right now?" I looked at my alarm clock. A quarter to three, almost? No, how could I?

"Go back to sleep, Emma. Ten o'clock tomorrow morning."

"Now, Joe. Right away."

I think I said, "Is something wrong?"

"I'll tell you when I see you." Still whispering, as if afraid someone might be listening in.

She instructed me to come around to the back of the house, to the back doors to her bedroom. She would leave the doors unlocked, the alarm off. But I had to come now, as soon as possible.

So I did. Who knew what she'd do if I didn't? I threw on a pair of jeans, T-shirt, windbreaker, baseball hat pulled down low over my eyes. I didn't think anyone would see me, but I wasn't taking any chances.

I parked at the edge of the property, where my car couldn't be spotted by the local security people, in case they were cruising in the neighborhood, entered the gate at the side, and went around to the back. I knew her door. I had been in and out of it before.

I turned the knob. It was unlocked, like she'd said it would be. I pushed the door open, and entered Emma's bedroom.

She was awake. She was sitting on her bed, Indian-style, with a blanket from her bed wrapped around her thin shoulders. It was dark out, but I could see her in the moonlight, sitting there in her nightgown under the blanket, looking up at me.

Then I froze. There were other girls in the room! Two other girls, one in the spare bed, the other on the floor. Both asleep, but what did they know? Had they been awake when she had called me? Was this some kind of perverted teenage-girl game?

She beckoned me to her with a crooked finger. When I was right upon her, close enough to reach out and touch her, she raised her mouth to my ear and said, "They've been asleep the whole time." Then she lifted her arms to me, wanting me to pick her up, carry her out of there.

I did. I carried her away, closing the door behind us.

I carried her across the lawn, all the way down to the gazebo. We had rendezvoused there before. It was a good place to go and not be seen. The grass was wet, I slipped carrying her.

"I'm pregnant." We were sitting on the floor, on her blanket. She had a stub of cigarette in her hand she had scrounged from somewhere in the debris on the floor, and was taking a couple of hits off it.

I rocked back on my heels. Oh, Jesus. This can't be.

"I found out today. Three months, almost."

"Emma . . ." I didn't know what to say. I was scared out of my mind.

"Remember when I told you that I'd missed my period? But that I wasn't worried, because I had missed other ones, lots of girls do for the first couple of years?"

"Emma . . ." I was starting to sound like a broken record.

"Well," she said, "I was wrong." She laughed, a high, breathy laugh. "Was I ever wrong."

"Are you—?" I was going to say "sure," but I knew that was the wrong thing, the worst thing I could say.

"I'm going to have an abortion."

"Emma, wait—"

"I have to do it now. I can't wait. If I wait, the clinic won't do it, it'll be too late, then I'd have to go to a private doctor." She squinted at me through the haze of the smoke from her butt. "If I don't do it right away, my mother could find out. Or my dad." She shook her head. "They'd kill me." Then she stared at me, stared right through me. "And they'd kill you. My father, for sure."

I knew that was true. "Emma," I said, "are you . . . ?" I didn't know where to begin. What should I say? What should I do?

"You're the father," she told me. In case I tried to weasel out of acknowledging that. "I'm not fucking anyone else."

I stood over her. Wanting to jump off the edge, fifteen feet to the ground. Hide. Vanish into the earth, forever. "When are you going to . . . have it done?"

"Next Friday. That'll give me the weekend to recuperate. The doctor said I should be okay to go to school on Monday."

"Do you want me to come with you? Bring you home?" I didn't want to, of course, but I had to offer.

"Fuck, no! Like, why not just tell them you're the daddy?" She shook her head. "I can do this. They'll help me." Then she looked up at me. "No one's ever going to know. That I was pregnant, or that you were the father. Or that we had ever done it at all."

I squatted down next to her. She was pregnant. I was the father. We had always used condoms, except the very first time, when she took me by surprise. Three months ago. One mistake, and you pay for the rest of your lives.

That had been the problem. I couldn't say no. She had seduced me, believe it, as cleverly as any woman of any age.

Which is what she did now. "I'm going to have an abortion, we might as well."

Off came her nightgown and there she was, naked, and I couldn't help myself, it had already been done, anything that could be, and I knew it would be the last time, and we made love in the gazebo, at the back of her parents' property.

"You'd better be getting back," I said, after I put my clothes back on, and she had pulled her nightgown back over herself. "In case . . ."

"Screw them," she said. She meant her friends. "They won't wake up, and so what if they do?" She was fishing around the floor under the soda bottles and beer cans and candy wrappers, coming up with another half-smoked Marlboro. "You leave," she said. "I want to stay out here by myself for a little while."

I was hesitant to leave her, but she shooed me away. "I needed to tell you right away. Now that I have, I'm okay. Go ahead. Go home."

I didn't need further convincing. I went down the steps and across the lawn, my head held low, looking back at the gazebo one last time as I left the property.

Luke leans against the wall of the cubicle, listening in enraged disbelief. He was there, he allowed her to seduce him right after she told him he's the father of her baby, but he didn't kill her? Nobody in the world would believe that.

"Don't you think that having sex with her that night was kind of stupid, under the circumstances?" he asks, for lack of something more intelligent to say.

Allison shuts his eyes. "Of course it was stupid, it was insane. But I did it." He's slumped over. "I deserve to be punished, I admit that. But not for killing her, because I didn't."

Where do you go now? "I sure as hell won't be putting you on the stand. That's one problem you've solved for me." He thinks for a moment. There is one detail in the maid's story that doesn't fit. He'll attack that, maybe drive a small wedge into this monolith. Even so,

Allison was there. He took her out of the room, exactly like Lisa Jaffe had described it. The jury isn't going to hear anything else.

"One question."

Allison looks up. "What?" he asks dully. His voice, his ticket to ride, is gone, a tremulous, congealed porridge. An old man's voice. The voice he'll have for the rest of his life, which won't be a problem, he won't have any need for a good voice.

"What kind of shoes were you wearing? Were you wearing the running shoes? And don't lie to me," Luke says, "you've blown it completely now, so tell me the truth, one time. I deserve that at least."

Allison shakes his head. "I told you, I'd lost them. I was wearing deck shoes, Timberlands. That's why I was sliding around when I was carrying her out there, the shoes I was wearing had no traction."

"You lost them, but then they were found in your closet, a year later." He puts up a hand as Allison starts to protest. "I know, I know. They were planted. You don't have to sing that song again. I know it by heart."

"They were," his client says doggedly. "Whether you believe me or not."

"That doesn't matter anymore," Luke says. "It's the rest of the world that has to believe you." He looks up as the deputy monitoring them sticks an inquisitive head in the door. "Or not."

"Mrs. Gonzalez." He stands at the lectern, feeling like a fool, like the man who has no clothes on and has been found out. "You saw Mr. Allison, the accused, walking across the lawn that night. Is that correct?"

"Yes."

"You're positive it was him."

"Yes." There is no equivocation in her voice. "I'm positive."

"He was by himself?"

"Yes."

"Emma Lancaster was not with him? Walking with him, or being carried by him?"

She nods. "He was by himself."

"Walking *away* from the house. You saw him leave the property, didn't you?"

"Yes."

A small wedge. The only one he has. He reinforces it one more time. "He was alone when he left the property. You could clearly see he wasn't carrying anything."

"Yes. He was alone."

"No further questions, Your Honor."

Ray Logan rises. "May it please the court, Your Honor."

Ewing nods.

"The prosecution rests."

The press corps, lying in wait on the courthouse steps, is bloodthirsty. They're all pushing and jostling against each other, microphones on long extended booms thrust in the air like tribal lances, on-air reporters elbowing and kneeing their way towards their preferred spots.

Ray Logan stands in front of a battery of microphones. He looks confident. He isn't gloating, the case isn't over yet, but the housekeeper's shattering testimony has allowed him, for the first time in months, to relax.

After the platitudinous questions—"How do you feel about your case," et cetera—he fields the one he knew was coming. "How do you reconcile the maid's saying she saw Allison leaving alone with your contention that he kidnapped and killed her?"

"I'm glad you asked that." If the question hadn't been asked, he would have introduced it himself, to clear the air of any lingering doubts. "My theory is that he didn't want to carry her across the lawn to his car without having something to wrap her in, something more substantial than the thin blanket he took from her bed. He didn't want to be seen carrying her body, not that he expected to be seen at that time of the night. Or maybe he was queasy about her dead body touching his, and wanted to cover it in something, a tarp or something he had in his car. It doesn't matter. The fact is, he did carry her away. And we know that because we found his shoe print where he hid her body. The identical shoe print we found at the Lancaster house. The same shoe print that we found on the shoe that was at his house, *which was his shoe*," he says emphatically. "A clearer trail of evidence than that, I've never seen."

He fields a few more questions, then he bails out. A maxim to follow—get out while the getting is good. And the getting today, for the prosecution, was very good.

Doug and Glenna Lancaster, exiting separately, are both swarmed upon by the media mob. They both decline comment, their lawyers and others shielding them from the rapacious horde. They duck into their chauffeur-driven cars and are whisked away.

Luke doesn't duck the press. He wants to, but he won't. That's admitting defeat, which he will not do in public. He's as courteous and cooperative as he can be, under the circumstances. Don't let them think you're flustered or feel defeated. Make as if you have a solid case of your own, and that when you present it, the field will tilt back the other way.

He looks out towards the television cameras. "I know what you're going to ask. Mrs. Gonzalez said she saw Joe Allison at the house that night. But did she, really? It was night, it was dark, she was distracted over her child's illness. And she's had eighteen months to think about it, and be bombarded by news accounts of Joe Allison, whose face has been plastered all over the newspapers and on the tube. So finally, his face fits the man she saw that night." He shakes his head. "Doesn't this sound really fishy to you?" He pauses, then goes on. "Don't rush to judgment. I'm saying this to you, the press, and to the public out there. Wait until I've put on my case—then we'll see who's more convincing. And whether the prosecution has established Joe Allison's guilt beyond a reasonable doubt." He pauses, dramatically—this is, after all, a performance. "Or even at all."

His two-step shuffle for public consumption will buy him a very brief amount of time to stave off the execution. Privately, in the comfort of the rental cottage, he's consumed with despair, feeling boxed in on all sides.

"I was right after all," Riva says, commiserating. "And I didn't want to be."

Luke grimaces. "You were, and I was wrong."

All Luke can think about is that he came back for this—to be taken in completely. He had gone in thinking Joe Allison was guilty, then gradually, bit by bit, he ferreted out enough of what he thought was real stuff to create reasonable doubt in his own mind; on top of which, he'd been shot at himself. More than enough incidence and evidence to have brought him around to believing Allison.

Judge De La Guerra has come over to their house to have dinner with them. "Do you want some advice?" De La Guerra asks. He feels responsible: he put this into motion.

"From the man who tracked me down and guilt-tripped me into taking this corpse of a case?" Luke asks in self-disgust. "Sure, why not?"

"Put your case on as if Allison is telling the truth."

"I second that," Riva weighs in.

Luke moans. "Thank you for your brilliant insight and support."

"Why not?" Riva demands, planting herself in front of him, getting in his face. "I told you I thought he had slept with her, but not killed her. Why couldn't that be true? What about Doug Lancaster, Luke? We still don't know where Doug Lancaster was that night, and the fact that he's still not telling points in his direction. What if he found out she was pregnant and that Joe was the father? He discovers it that day and he can't wait one day more, he has to come home and confront Joe, right now, in the middle of the night. And he sees Joe with Emma, he was following him or whatever—"

"Or whatever," Luke mutters to himself.

"Let me finish. Doug sees them together, gets into a fight with Emma over it, and in a blind rage he kills her. Accidentally, of course, he loves her, but it happens all the time, you know that better than me, you've seen it, you've prosecuted it. And then he panics, as anyone would, who's going to believe him that it was an accident? And he's still going to do time, for second-degree murder or manslaughter or something. So he hides her, and then it builds, and he's trapped, and here we are today."

Luke is shaking his head all through this. "Are you done?" he asks.

"Yes, I'm done." She's exhausted from this outcry, pregnancy tires her out so quickly.

"Where did the key ring come from? The shoes? The rubbers?"

"Doug could have planted them. They were together that night."

More head shaking. "No. And I'll tell you why. Doug wouldn't have waited a year to do that. It's too long. Too much could go wrong. And he keeps Allison on at the station? No way. The man's a daily reminder of Emma, of what he did to her, his only child." He sets his glass down on the table. "I can't buy it. I wish I could, but I can't."

Ferdinand De La Guerra struggles out of his chair, comes over and puts a fatherly arm on Luke's shoulder. "You have a case to put on. A defense. What are you going to do?"

"Other than plead him guilty and throw him on the mercy of the court?"

"That's not an option."

Luke pours himself a drink. Swirling it around in his glass, he thinks for a moment. He feels paralyzed.

"What are you going to do, Luke?" Riva chimes in. "You have to stand up in court tomorrow and do something."

"I'm going to defend my client. The best I can. I don't know how good that best is going to be now."

"It'll be good," she encourages him. "It's you." She says it again: "It will be good. It's got to be."

He works late, preparing. When he gets into bed, he slides silently in next to Riva, who is sleeping on her side, is turned away from him, her back lifting and lowering rhythmically, little spittle bubbles foaming in the corner of her lips. He can't sleep a lick, tossing and turning, getting up around three and lying on the living room couch, trying to catch some shuteye, but still unable to—he's too keyed up, vibrating with anticipation. And apprehension, flop-sweat anxiety, an emotion he hasn't felt on a case in years, decades. Finally, giving up, he shaves, showers, dresses, gathers his material together, and drives into town. He packs two spare shirts in his briefcase.

It isn't even six o'clock, a few minutes till. The streets are empty, flat, nothing moving, no breeze, the leaves on the palm trees outside the courthouse limp, lifeless. Dark becoming dawn, sky gray, color starting to seep into the sky in the east. Slowly. Coming down

Anapamu Street, heading towards State, a city street-cleaner crawls along the curb, its dry brushes pushing the accumulation of the day's and night's debris—newspaper scraps, cardboard coffee cups, cigarette butts, all the shit that streets accumulate—up against the curb where the vacuum attachment sucks it up.

He parks in the city lot catty-corner from the courthouse, leaning up against his car, reading the front page of the *News-Press.* He's on it, they're the main story. There are two pictures, both in color. One is of District Attorney Ray Logan holding his impromptu press conference, the other of Maria Gonzalez standing in the lobby directly outside the courtroom, looking dazed.

The lights go on inside the coffee shop at the corner of Anacapa and Anapamu. He's the first customer, he has to wait a few minutes for the coffee to brew. Then, double latte and bagel with cream cheese in hand, he crosses the street, goes into the courthouse, and enters the arena. His office. That's how he used to refer to the courthouse and all the courtrooms. They were his office, where he conducted his business. He sits in the last row, eating his bagel and cream cheese, sipping his coffee, looking around. A rich room, leather benches, high vaulted ceiling. The county spared no expense building it after the '25 earthquake.

He thinks about Joe Allison, his client, and all the jerking around Allison's done to him. The bitch is that he has to keep on defending the guy, he has no choice, the lawyer doesn't make moral judgments, he's bound by the rules and codes of his profession regardless of who the client is or what he did.

All the avenues that had managed, miraculously, in some divine fool's luck, not to intersect, have now come together in a massive snarl: Emma Lancaster and her secret pubescent sexual life; Doug Lancaster and his mistress who can't alibi him (or won't) and his bribe attempt and God knows what else, including attempted murder, still one of the unfathomable, unsolvable biggies; Glenna Lancaster with her affair with Allison, mostly unreciprocated by him, if you read between the lines.

No winners, not one victory in any of this. Only losers. Especially him.

* * *

Sheriff Williams is now his witness. An unusual way to start a defense, with one of the other side's own, but Williams is going to set the table for his theme—that someone other than Joe Allison had more reason, motive, and opportunity to kill Emma Lancaster.

"Your Honor, I would like to examine this witness as an adverse witness," he requests of the court before starting his direct examination. "Since he was the prosecution's witness already."

"Objection, Your Honor." Logan is on his feet immediately. This is going to be the pattern, Luke knows; trench warfare all the way down the line, witness by witness, question by question. "Sheriff Williams is appearing voluntarily for the defense."

Judge Ewing nods at that remark, but then says, "Since the sheriff was a member of the prosecution team that arrested the defendant and is bringing charges in this case, it must be assumed that he is biased in their favor. The objection is overruled."

Okay, Luke thinks. At least I'm going to be able to get to the meat of things—whatever meat is left on these bones. "Good morning, Sheriff," he begins. Without waiting for the perfunctory reply, he continues, "How long have you been the sheriff of Santa Barbara County?"

"Eighteen years," Williams answers. "I'm in my fifth term."

"You're popular with the voters."

"I guess I am."

"They know you're strong on law enforcement, fair, honest, decent." Rattling off his opening remarks like BB's from a pellet gun.

"I hope they do. I think I am."

"They know when you investigate a crime, particularly a major crime like a murder, you do so thoroughly, forcefully, and objectively. You don't pull punches, and you don't play favorites."

"Those are my objectives," Williams answers, his voice bland, flat, but sincere. "That and to solve it."

"Is that how you investigated the abduction and murder of Emma Lancaster, Sheriff?" Luke asks.

Without missing a beat, Williams answers, "To the best of my ability."

"Which is considerable—your ability," Luke replies. "I'll attest to that personally," he says, yet again reminding the jury that he used to be the district attorney, that he has a long-established working relationship with the sheriff.

"Thank you," Williams says dryly.

Luke hesitates a moment, pivoting around to look at the gallery behind him. Doug Lancaster is again in his usual seat, one row behind the prosecution table. Turning back to Williams, he fires his first volley. "But how come you didn't investigate Doug Lancaster thoroughly?" he asks. "Emma's father."

"Objection!" Logan calls out, jumping to his feet. "We've covered this, *ad infinitum*."

"On the contrary, Your Honor—" Luke begins to rebut Logan. But before he can explain further why the question is valid, Ewing has pulled his microphone to him and is handling the matter for him.

"The objection is overruled," the judge says decisively. "This is a relevant area to be discussing, and I'm going to give defense counsel broad latitude to explore it."

Logan sits down, his face set in a grim mask. Behind him, Doug Lancaster, his own face looking as if cast in stone, stares hard at Luke, who returns the stare for a moment before turning back to the sheriff. Ewing's playing catch-up, Luke knows, big time. He's making amends for not excluding the evidence Luke wanted thrown out on Allison's search-and-seizure and DUI-testing situations.

Ewing leans down towards Williams. "Would you like the question reread to you, Sheriff?"

"No, thank you, that won't be necessary," Williams tells him. Turning to face Luke, he answers, "I investigated him to my satisfaction. To what I knew at the time, and to what degree I felt was proper and necessary."

Luke presses. "Did you investigate him as a person under suspicion? As someone who might be under suspicion, or should be? At the time of the abduction and the discovery of Emma Lancaster's body, did you counsel Doug Lancaster to be a suspect in the murder of his daughter?"

Williams exhales a hard breath, shifts his posture to a more upright position. "I did not consider Doug Lancaster to be a suspect in the murder of his daughter."

There's a buzzing in the room again. The jurors, Luke notes with satisfaction, are paying keen attention; some are taking notes. "Why didn't you consider him to be a suspect?" he asks.

"The circumstances didn't warrant it. Didn't seem to."

"Didn't *seem* to warrant considering the girl's father a suspect. Even though it's a given in law enforcement that frequently an immediate family member is, in fact, the perpetrator of such a crime. Isn't that right, Sheriff?"

The sheriff concedes the point: "Yes, that's true."

"Was the reason you didn't investigate deeper into Doug Lancaster as a suspect because of the terrible loss he had suffered? He and his wife had suffered?"

Williams nods. "That was a factor, I have to admit it. I'm human, like anyone else. The man was in pain. I wasn't going to push him deeper into more pain."

"From a human point of view, that's admirable," Luke says. "I'm sincere when I say that," he adds, "I don't want anyone thinking I'm being sarcastic. Losing a child—the grief can be unfathomable." He hesitates. "At the time of your initial investigation, did Mr. Lancaster have an alibi for the night of the abduction?"

"Yes."

"You checked it out."

"Yes."

Luke paces around a little bit. Then he comes back to the lectern again, takes a fast swallow of water, and continues. "Did there come a time when you began to have doubts about the truthfulness of Mr. Lancaster's story of where he had been that night?"

Williams coughs, clearing some phlegm. "Yes."

Behind him, Luke senses a commotion. He turns to see Doug Lancaster, his face florid with impotent anger, getting up from his place behind the prosecution table, which is also behind the lectern at which he's standing, rudely push his way along the crowded aisle—his seat is in the middle of the row—walk down the side aisle, and leave, the large leather-padded door swinging open and shut loudly.

Everyone has watched this. Judge, jury, press, the rest of the spectators. Not the best way to impress a jury with your innocence, your lack of involvement, Luke thinks. Watching Doug's exit, he sees Glenna Lancaster, wearing her usual stark black wardrobe sans makeup, sitting in her usual seat in the last row, last seat closest to the door. A good seat to be in, he thinks, if you decide to beat a hasty retreat. He also notices that she did not look at her ex-husband at all as he was leaving. Their eyes never made contact.

He presses ahead. He has momentum going for him, he wants to maintain it. "Would you explain for the jury, Sheriff Williams, when it was that you first started to think Mr. Lancaster had not told you the truth about where he had been on the night his daughter was taken from her room, and what he was doing at that time."

"A few months ago, I found out that on the night Emma Lancaster was taken from her bedroom, Mr. Lancaster—"

"Her father," Luke interrupts.

Williams ignores the sally. "I found out that he had left his hotel in Santa Monica at approximately one o'clock in the morning and apparently had not returned until approximately nine o'clock in the morning. That same morning."

Luke nods. Yes! he thinks, glancing over at the jury. They're with this. Continuing: "Is that what he told you, when you initially questioned him, later on the day of Emma's disappearance?"

"No."

"What did he tell you?"

"That he had been in his hotel all night long."

"So he lied to you."

A slow, ponderous, unhappy nod. "Yes."

"Have you . . . have you tried to find out where he was?" Luke asks.

"Yes."

"Were you able to?"

"No, I haven't," the sheriff answers.

"From your pursuit of all this," Luke goes on, "did you have any idea of where he might have been? Any theories based on material you've uncovered, information you've found out subsequently?"

"Yes, I had a theory." He glances over at Logan. Logan conspicuously looks away.

"What was it?"

"Objection, Your Honor," Logan says, snapping to. He has to stop this hemorrhaging.

"Sustained."

"Did you interview a woman you thought Mr. Lancaster might have gone to see during that time he wasn't at his hotel?" Luke asks.

"Yes." The answer is as curt and tight as Williams can make it.

Ray Logan, sitting at the prosecution table, thinks, here it comes, all that damn stonewalling of Doug's. One witness into the defense's presentation, and their Achilles heel is exposed to the world.

"I'm not going to ask you for her name," Luke says to Williams. "It's irrelevant to this discussion. What I am going to ask you is, did she provide Mr. Lancaster with an alibi for the missing hours?"

The sheriff shakes his head. "No, she did not."

Luke nods. He's killed three birds with one stone. The chief law enforcement officer in the county has stated, for the record, that Doug Lancaster was not where he said he was during the time his daughter was taken from her room by a man who they're claiming is Joe Allison (and who he knows, but they don't with total certainty, is in fact Joe). He's established that Lancaster lied about it to the police. And the strong implication is that either he was engaged in an adulterous relationship on the night his daughter was abducted, or he was there, on the scene, when Emma was taken—and, by inference, was the taker.

He finishes with a flourish. "So to this very day you do not know where Doug Lancaster, the father of Emma Lancaster, was, on the night that his daughter was taken from her room only to be found days later murdered."

The sheriff gives his weary answer. "No. I don't know where he was."

Riva was not in court today. She was out on her own. She tells Luke about her day when they get together that night at the office. He's been there for a while, prepping for tomorrow's witnesses.

First, she listens to him recount his day. She's heard about it secondhand, but she wants his take on it.

Luke grudgingly admits that he made some points. "See?" she yodels triumphantly. "It isn't over. Not by a long shot."

"Tomorrow's another day," he grouses, refusing to accept the glory of the present. He knows what his opposition doesn't about Joe Allison and Emma Lancaster, and he's sure, in his doom and gloom about it, that somewhere down the line it's going to jump up and bite him on the ass and pull them down, all the way down.

"It ain't over till the fat lady sings, dude," she chides him. She pats her growing belly. "And I'm not singing. Not for public consumption, anyway."

"So," he says. "You." She's been champing at the bit to lay her news on him. "What did you do today, anyway? I missed you in court. I like having you there. I need all the moral support I can get."

"One day won't hurt, I hope. Especially when you hear my news."

The way she says it, the inflection and timing, bring him up short. "Okay." He sits down. "Go."

"For the sake of argument," she begins, sitting down too, "let's say that Joe Allison told the truth about what happened that night. That he was with Emma, but when he left she was still alive. All right?"

"All right." It's a mighty stretch, one he can't make, but she has the floor.

"Who besides Doug has reason to kill Emma?"

He shakes his head. "I don't know. Nobody has *reason* to. Doug didn't have reason; that doesn't mean he didn't do it in a moment of passion, though."

"But what if it *wasn't* in a moment of passion?" She's excited, bouncing in her chair. "What if there was premeditation behind it?"

"Who in the world . . . ?"

"Who has a life with him, but then discovers he's cheating on her? With a fourteen-year-old, no less."

He's slow on the uptake, but it's starting to register. Then it hits him, and the name is coming out of his mouth, but she's too impatient, she can't wait, she's way too antsy.

"Nicole Rogers suspected Joe was screwing around on her, didn't she?"

Slowly, he answers: "Yes."

"And Allison did admit that he and Glenna Lancaster had slept together a few times. A mercy fuck on his part, it sounds like to me, pardon my French," she adds with a touch of woman-to-woman bitchiness. "So there you are. Nicole is jealous of Glenna, who helps Joe decorate his house, plays tennis with him or whatever jockstrap shit they did, goes to him when she's depressed about where her marriage is going."

"Except it wasn't Glenna," he says, finally in synch with her. "It was Emma who Nicole was pissed off at."

"Give that man a great big panda." She claps her hands in excitement.

Now he's with her. "That night, instead of taking Nicole home, Joe drops her off at her place. He told us she had stuff to do, but maybe it was the opposite. Maybe he was dumping her and going to get it on with Emma, down at the old gazebo."

She picks up his line. "Nicole is suspicious. It's been building. Maybe she's seen them together before, whatever. She follows him to the Lancasters' house, sees them together, sees him leave alone—"

"—waits for her to come back to her room, waylays her, kills her, takes the body!" he finishes. "And Joe and Nicole live happily ever after."

"Except, a year later he lowers the boom on Nicole, telling her she isn't part of his plans anymore, he's moving to the big time and leaving her in the dust in little Santa Barbara. Nicole flips," Riva picks up, getting more and more excited as the scenario unfolds. "It's so logical. She seeds the evidence, makes the call to the police, and it's done."

He's rocked by this. Thinking a moment, he says, "Slow down. Let's look at this." He starts considering all the pieces in the puzzle. "There's lots of holes in this, Riva. How would Nicole have gotten hold of the key ring? And what about the shoes? Where did the prints come from? And my Triumph was trashed while I was in her office, so she couldn't have done that."

Riva nods. "I agree there are holes, big ones, of course there are. But maybe there are explanations for them, acceptable explanations. For instance, maybe Nicole took them from his house and wore them, to frame him."

"Hmm," he grunts from his chest. "That's a big stretch, Riva. That presupposes she knew she was going to do something bad, before she even saw them together."

"Unless she had seen them together before, which she probably did, and thought that was where he was going after he dropped her off." Despite his shaking his head, she presses on. "And what if Emma had the keys on her? Maybe she was afraid she'd get locked out accidentally and wouldn't be able to get back in. So she had them on her, and Nicole scooped them up when she, you know, did it."

"That's a big maybe, too," he says.

"But it's possible," she presses.

"Yeah. It's possible."

"Your ride could've been somebody else altogether, somebody angry at you. Lots of people were, and they are now. All the incidents don't all have to fit together completely."

"No, they don't," he agrees. He's thinking, he's thinking—there's something else. "What about my shooting? Are you saying that's separate and apart, too?"

She smiles. Then she gets up out of her chair and sits in his lap. "Do you know how handsome you are when you're excited?" she teases him.

"I must be handsome as hell now, 'cause you've got me real excited," he says. "Come on, give, Tweety-bird. You've got that canary sitting in your mouth."

"Here's the kicker," she says. "What got me started down this path in the first place. Nicole Rogers was born in Idaho."

He looks up at her, sitting on him, his hand on her swelling belly, feeling it. Soon there will be life he can feel, kicking, movement. "So she was born in Idaho. We all have to be born somewhere."

"She was born on a ranch. Her father's a big-time rancher and oilman."

"So she was born rich. What does that have to do with the price of tamales in Tijuana?"

"She was shooting rifles, pistols, and shotguns from the time she was six."

"She was?" All of a sudden it's hard to speak, his voice feels caught in his throat.

Riva nods emphatically. "Yes, she was. And she got so good at it, by the time she was in high school she was a national champion. She almost qualified for the 'eighty-eight Olympics."

His heart is beating fast. "This is unbelievable."

She climbs off him. "I know," she says softly. She looks at him. "What are you going to do?"

He thinks for a moment. "I don't know."

"Should we go to the sheriff with this?"

"I don't know," he says again. "I'm on his shit list right now. And they've got their man, don't you understand? They don't want a fresh suspect. They want to try this case and get their conviction. If there's fallout later, they'll worry about it then."

"So you're not going to do anything?" she asks in a halting voice.

"I can't. I'm in the middle of a trial," he reminds her. "I don't have time for anything else."

"You have to do something," she says firmly.

"Listen to me. I can't."

"Then I will."

"You will what?" He's out of his chair, hovering over her. "What will you do, Riva?"

"I don't know, but—"

"You're not going to do anything. Do you hear me? You're a pregnant woman. You're carrying our child. You are going to take it easy and cheer me on in court and that is what you are going to do. You are *not* going to do anything that could get you into trouble. There's been enough of that already. Too much."

She takes one of his hands in both of hers. Her hands feel good—they're warm, soft. "I'm going to take care of you, okay? That's why I came down in the first place, Luke. To take care of you. Let me. I'm not going to get myself into any trouble. So don't worry."

Ramon Huerta, the parking attendant who told Luke (and subsequently, to their horror, the D.A.'s office) about Doug Lancaster's disappearance on the night Emma vanished, is sprawled languidly in the witness chair. He's dressed half cholo, half throwback zoot suiter—hair slicked back and heavily pomaded, white T-shirt, black pants belted halfway up to his armpits, black suit jacket.

This sonofabitch is stoned, Luke thinks with a mixed feeling of anger and awe at the jerk's audacity. He regards his witness with a wary eye. Rising to begin his direct questioning, Luke notices that Doug Lancaster is absent today. His guess is that Doug is going to be absent most of the time from here on in.

He guides Huerta through his story. Doug Lancaster left his hotel at one and seemed to be upset. Came back at nine, upset then too.

"I want to introduce this piece of evidence, Your Honor," Luke says, holding a plastic bag that has a parking claim-ticket inside it. "This is a parking-lot ticket from Shutters on the Beach, the hotel in Santa Monica where the witness worked."

"So ordered."

Luke walks the ticket over to Huerta, takes it out of its protective plastic, shows it to the witness. "Do you recognize this?"

Huerta gives it a cursory glance. "Yeah."

"What do these numbers mean?" He points to some numbers on the back that have been imprinted by an automatic toll machine.

"When you took the car out, when you brought it back."

"What do these numbers tell you?"

Huerta scans them. "The car went out at one-sixteen a.m., was returned nine-oh-nine a.m."

"And this?"

"The day."

"The exact same day Emma Lancaster was taken from her house," Luke says. "May I, Your Honor?" he asks, motioning in the direction of the jury.

Ewing nods his approval.

Luke crosses to the jury box, hands the ticket to juror number one. "This was Doug Lancaster's parking ticket at the Shutters hotel on the night in question," he informs them. "The hotel has vouched for it being genuine, and the prosecution has stipulated it." He looks over at Logan, who nods grimly. "That means they accept its authenticity. Please pass it amongst yourselves and look at it carefully."

The ticket makes the rounds of the jury box. Some of the jurors write down the details, the same jurors who have been taking other notes. It comes back to Luke, who places it in the plastic bag and walks it over to the clerk.

As the ticket is tagged, numbered, and placed on the evidence table, Luke takes his place at the podium again. "You were personally present when Mr. Lancaster took his car out at one in the morning, is that correct?" he asks his witness. "He came for it himself and drove it away himself, nobody else did, is that also true?"

"I got it for him myself. And he was the driver."

"And you were personally present when he returned it at nine in the morning, is that also correct?"

"Yes." Huerta's eyes are drooping; he looks so comfortable now he could fall asleep, right here in the courtroom. That wouldn't be good for the cause. Time to wrap this up.

"He drove it himself, no one else did it?"

"No. It was him. He was by himself both times," Huerta volunteers. "Nobody was with him. Both times."

"No further questions of this witness, Your Honor."

Ray Logan's method of dealing with this bad-news witness is to impugn his character. He gets Huerta to admit that he was fired for improper advances towards a guest, a charge Huerta vigorously challenges—not the charge itself, that's irrefutable, but the reason for it. He was a victim of the bosses. They're always ragging on men like him.

He comes across as a petty opportunist and pathetic whiner and malcontent, Luke knows. But his basic story holds up, bolstered by the claim ticket. Thank God they'd found that, that the hotel had kept it. Doug Lancaster, contrary to his sworn statement to the police—that he'd been in bed, in his hotel, all night long—had demonstrably been MIA for eight hours that night: the eight hours that are the most critical to this case.

Doug Lancaster has been caught flat-footed in a lie. The question the jury has to be thinking is, why did he lie?

Luke's still down on the case, and especially his client, but he feels a little better than he did on the day the prosecution rested theirs.

* * *

Like Doug Lancaster, Riva hasn't been in the courtroom. She has her own agenda—to find out, if she can, whether Nicole Rogers was, or could have been, the real killer.

Luke's a lawyer. He can't skirt the law. But she can. She gets in touch with one of her ex's ne'er-do-well acquaintances up north and puts her problem to him. He can fix her up easy, he says. Modern technology, even an area of it that in today's world of supercomputer capability is pretty low-grade, unglamorous, can work wonders, large and small. So by the end of the day, an illegal but highly effective Lo-Jack will have been secured to Nicole's Nissan Pathfinder. Wherever she goes, Riva will know and will be able to track her whereabouts.

This could include the plateau on the opposite side of the ravine from their house, which she is driving up to this morning. The light she saw that night, driving back from getting her groceries, it was surely nothing. But under the circumstances, why not check it out, eliminate one variable from the mix? Particularly after her near-fatal collision with what could have been Nicole's vehicle.

Her foray doesn't put her mind at ease. To the contrary: there's nothing there, no human habitation. The area is an overgrown bluff of scrub oak and underbrush that needs to be cut back before fire season starts. The nearest house is a good two hundred yards away. Too far away.

Awkwardly squatting in the rutted dirt—being pregnant makes every physical movement a chore—she finds some tire impressions. That could be important. She needs to see the impressions the police took of the tire tracks they'd found up at Hollister Ranch, when someone had tried to kill Luke. If by some incredible stroke of luck they match, then it's a whole new ballgame.

She doesn't want the police to know about any of this, not yet. Nor does she want Luke to know. He'd be worried, for her, and for himself too. He's under enough stress already. He doesn't need any more problems.

That near miss. That was meant for Luke. The other driver thought it was Luke in the old truck. It was meant either to scare him, like the shooting in the water, or to kill him. Either way, someone out there wants him out of the picture, and will do whatever's necessary to make that happen.

She promised Luke she was going to take care of him. To him that means being in the courtroom, silently cheering him on, standing behind him, being home with him for dinner. To her it means more. It could mean helping him solve his case. Or—more important, much more important—it could mean saving his life.

Hillary Lange, the other girl in the bedroom that night—the one who slept through the whole thing and who, a few months ago, dropped the dime on Riva that Emma had an affair with a man she baby-sat for—sits in the witness box. She's definitely jail bait, to Luke's eye. He recalls reading an article in the *New York Times* about how girls in modern industrial nations are reaching puberty earlier than ever, due to improved diet, lack of hard physical labor, other modern reasons.This girl sitting here, fifteen years old, is a good example. If you didn't know she was fifteen, you could easily peg her age at eighteen or nineteen. And get in a world of trouble as a result.

Like Huerta, his previous witness, Luke knows, she's unhappy to be here. Riva long ago promised her that she wouldn't be involved, that the information she passed along—about Emma being sexually involved with some man—was a secret between the two of them. Now here she sits, for the whole world to see.

She tried to resist the subpoena. Her parents had thrown a major fit over it, not just about her having to testify—though they didn't like that, not one bit—but even more about her betraying Emma, laundering dirty clothes in public, and by implication making not only Doug and Glenna Lancaster look like unconcerned, thoughtless parents, but them as well, and all of their friends who have teenage kids in similar situations.

"Did Emma tell you she'd had an affair with an adult man?" he asks her. "A sexual affair?" He has Riva's notes in front of him; the prosecution, as is their due, has a copy too. There are no secrets here for Hillary to protect, even though she wants to.

"Yes," she simpers.

"Did she tell you who he was?"

"The guy she baby-sat for." She has a bit of a Barbara Walters lisp in her voice.

He can see tomorrow's headline already. So pathetic, so tawdry, the whole blooming thing.

"Not a name?" he asks.

She shakes her head. "No. She'd never say a name."

"But for sure she was the man's baby-sitter. For his children," he presses.

"Yes. She hated his kid. She only kept doing it because . . ."

Luke doesn't press her. He stands calmly at the lectern, waiting for her to finish.

After several moments of no answer forthcoming, Judge Ewing leans down towards her. "Because what?" he gently prompts her.

She scrunches her face up in a torturous mask. "Because they were . . . getting it on." At least she'd remembered to say that, instead of "screwing" or "fucking."

"It wasn't Mr. Allison." He points to Joe. "She never said it was Mr. Allison."

She shakes her head. "It was the man who she baby-sat for." Looking over at Allison, she says, "He doesn't have any kids. She wasn't talking about him."

Luke wants to bring in one more witness before the close of day, one who will add yet another element of doubt as to who out there might have wanted Emma Lancaster dead, and had the motive, means, and opportunity to kill her.

David Essham owns Tri-County Gun and Supply, in Paso Robles. "Yes, I sold a rifle to a Nicole Rogers," he says in response to Luke's question. "A Browning 270." He has the sales slip in his hand, refers to it.

Luke, the gun-shop owner, Ray Logan, and Judge Ewing are meeting in the judge's chambers to decide if Essham is going to be allowed to take the stand. Logan is vehemently opposed, thus this conference.

"That's an accurate, high-powered rifle, isn't it?" Luke asks. "It could stop a man at two or three hundred yards?"

"Easy. Piece of cake for a good marksman."

"Do you know if she is a good marksman?" he asks.

Essham grins. "A regular Calamity Jane. I went out to the range with her—she wanted to test it, to make sure it was what she wanted. That woman could shoot a petal off a rose at a hundred yards."

Logan is shaking his head, but Ewing's paying attention. "When did you sell the Browning to Nicole Rogers?" he asks.

Essham recites the date, reading from his sales book. "That's interesting," Luke says, from the corner of his eye watching the D.A. steaming. "One week later, somebody tried to kill me using a rifle of that exact caliber," he reminds Judge Ewing. "And that rifle has never been recovered."

Logan's had it. "Your Honor," he protests strenuously, "this is clearly inadmissible. Defense counsel is trying to throw up as many smokescreens as he can to obfuscate the facts in this case. Nicole Rogers is not a defendant in this case, or an accessory. You have to put an end to these extraneous fishing expeditions."

Ewing doesn't immediately respond to Logan's plea. "Please step out of the room," he says to Essham.

When the gun dealer is gone, Ewing turns to Luke. "The D.A.'s right. This trial is about the guilt or innocence of your client, Joe Allison, not whether anyone in the county could have done it instead. I've given you plenty of leeway in your pursuit of Doug Lancaster's possible involvement, and I'll continue to"—he looks over at Logan to make sure Logan hears this—"but not others. The appropriate place for this information is with the sheriff's office, which could, and should, pursue this lead as regards your own shooting."

Essham won't be allowed to testify. It was a long shot, trying to get him in, but it was worth the try. At least both the judge and the district attorney know about it, and the information has to cause them both doubt, more doubt than they already have. But he wishes the jury could have it too.

The sheriff will have to deal with this information; he can't avoid it. What worries Luke, particularly in the short term, is that Nicole Rogers really could be the sniper, and what does that mean for his future safety? Nicole wouldn't try to take him out merely because she's angry at Joe; that's overkill. Either she thinks (or knows) Joe is guilty and doesn't want to see him walk, or she herself, as he postulated, is deeply involved. Maybe fatally, all the way to the bone.

Even without the gun-store owner's testimony, it's another solid day for the defense. The newspapers and television broadcasts say so. Earlier, in his cross-examination of Hillary Lange, Logan barely tried to discredit or break her down; there was no point. That Emma had slept with someone else didn't mean she didn't sleep with Joe Allison as well. In a sense, it buttresses his case, or so he claims when he addresses the press at the end of the day, in what is by now a daily ritual. She was sexually precocious, and Joe Allison had taken advantage of that.

That's the spin Logan tries to put on it. It works, but not really, because it wrecks the image of Emma Lancaster being some innocent young virgin who was seduced by a predatory adult. Young, yes, but not the rest.

The lack of innocence is important, and that's why Luke has decided, after agonizing over the decision, to put Fourchet, the health-food store owner, on the stand. The man's testimony is going to be grueling, painful. Emma's character and behavior will be scrutinized and picked over, not only more than it already has been, but more distastefully. This is the worst part of a job like this—dissecting a dead person's character in the open without her being able to defend herself. But he has to do it. He has to show that Emma was not a victim in her sexual experiences but a willing participant.

Fourchet, of course, was not about to come forward voluntarily. Luke had to issue a subpoena for him to appear, like most of his witnesses. The man called Luke at his office, tearful, hysterical. "Please don't make me do this," he begged. "Don't put me on the stand. My life is already in shambles. This will destroy me."

Luke couldn't care less. "No one made you sleep with this young girl," he reminded Fourchet. "You could have said no. That's what a man of character would have done. It's too bad that I'm going to have to put you and your family through this, but you made the choice. Now you're going to have to live with the consequences of it."

* * *

"Call Adrian Fourchet."

Luke stands at the podium waiting for the appearance of his reluctant witness. It's nine in the morning; Judge Ewing has just gaveled his court into session. Everyone is in the usual places. Doug Lancaster again is not present but Glenna Lancaster is, sitting in her back-row seat, still dressed somberly. Riva isn't here either. She begged off; she had interviewed Fourchet, and seeing him up on the stand would be too uncomfortable. Also, she has errands to run. She'll stop by at lunchtime.

The doors to the corridor through which Fourchet should be entering don't move. Ewing peers over the top of his desk at Luke. "Where's your witness, Counselor?"

Luke is at a loss. "I don't know, Your Honor. He knew when he was supposed to be here." He glances at his watch. "Maybe he went to the wrong courtroom."

There are six courtrooms in the building, all of them in session. It's a big building, people frequently lose their way. But he's pissed at himself for not making sure the man was here on time, even if it meant picking him up at his house and escorting him here personally.

Ewing turns to the chief deputy in charge of courtroom security. "Go find him. We've got to get going."

The deputy nods and exits into the long hallway. Luke takes the opportunity to walk over to the defense table and look at some notes that he hadn't brought up to the lectern with him. He glances at the clock on the wall: eight-fifteen. Fourchet should surely have been here by now.

Another few minutes tick by. Finally Ray Logan gets to his feet. "Your Honor, we can't wait all day for this witness. I move that he be struck from the roster."

"Objection, Your Honor," Luke says heatedly, looking up from the defense table. "This happens. This isn't—" His head turns to the side doorway, where the deputy is making a hurried entrance.

The deputy hustles to the bench. Ewing leans over, so that they can have a private conversation.

Shock and surprise are clear on the judge's face, which is reddening rapidly. "I'll have lawyers in my chambers. Now." He bangs his gavel, harder than he normally does. "We're standing in recess until further notice."

The woman, Luella Fourchet, a full-on earth-mother-commune type down to her Birkenstock sandals, stands in Ewing's small office. Wordlessly she hands the judge a legal-size envelope. He opens it, takes out a single folded page, and reads the letter, his expression turning to dismay as the contents sink in.

He looks up. "You have no witness," he tells Luke in an uncharacteristically shaky voice. "He's defied the court's subpoena." He turns to Fourchet's wife. "Do you know where your husband is?"

She shakes her head. "No. I found this on the kitchen table this morning. He didn't tell me anything." Head thrust up, she adds, "And even if he had, I wouldn't tell you. I'm not going to be a party to his ruination, even if what he did was wrong. I know what he did . . ."

She breaks down. She's sobbing, no sound coming, shoulders heaving, her hands covering her face.

They watch her. Nobody makes a move to touch her.

The soundless sobbing lessens, subsides. Looking up, eyes red and tear-filled, she says, "We were working through this, he and I. And now this—he couldn't take it. *I* can't take it." She looks at each man in turn, her eyes fierce in accusation, ending on Luke, staring through him. "He had nothing to do with that slutty girl's disappearance, and you know it, Mr. Garrison, but you want to ruin him anyway. You want to ruin me, us, our family." She swipes at her cheeks and nose with a tissue. "He isn't going to come here, no matter what. You can find him, because sooner or later he'll have to come back, but he isn't going to testify. You can put him in jail, or whatever you do. But he's never going to talk about this. Not here, not with anyone. Never."

She turns away, wanting to leave, wanting to get out of here, but Luke won't let her go.

"I'm sorry that you're going through grief," he says, his anger at the flash point, "but that's not *my* fault, and I'm not about to let you make me the fall guy." He's in her face, inches away.

"Luke." Ray Logan, alarmed at his behavior, moves towards them.

Luke waves him away. "Let me finish."

He stares into the woman's eyes. "Your husband did a vile thing. He had sexual intercourse with an underage girl. I don't care how old she looked, or how much he lied to you about how she vamped him, or anything. That was a crime, and he could go to jail for it—if Emma Lancaster were still alive to press charges."

Now it's Ewing who's distraught. "Stop that, Luke!" He's out from behind his desk, moving towards them.

Luke won't stop. "Your husband might not have *physically* killed Emma Lancaster, but he killed her soul. Him and everyone else who took advantage of her. She was too young to get it, don't *you* get it? She wasn't accountable!"

The lawyers and Ewing sit in the judge's chambers. It's a few minutes later. Luke has calmed down some, but he's still agitated. More important, he has to put somebody on the stand, now that his witness has flown the coop. "What's your ruling going to be on my bringing Sheriff Williams back on and bringing up the synergy between this case and the attempt on my life?" he asks the judge, looking over at Logan. "Are you going to oppose that? You've admitted to me there's a good possibility the two are joined."

"I don't think they're joined for the purposes of this case," Logan answers in rebuttal. "I would oppose that vigorously. You can't connect these two crimes, Your Honor," he argues to Ewing, "no matter how subjective or personal they might be."

Ewing ponders this. "I'm inclined to agree with the district attorney," he says to Luke. "Do you have any case law that can bolster this connection?"

"I'm researching it even as we speak," Luke scrambles immediately. "Can you give me until after lunch?"

Another look from judge to prosecutor. "I don't know, Your Honor," Logan says. "With all due respect, Luke, if you knew you were going to bring that up, you should have had your material in order already."

That's true. He can't argue it logically. "I don't have the staff I used to," he says pointedly. "I don't have twenty paralegals running down every case on their computers. Give me a break, Judge," he implores Ewing. "Just until this afternoon. If I can't please you by then, I'll pass it by."

"That's acceptable to me," the judge says. "Let's go back out there. We'll recess until after lunch. But then we're moving forward," he warns Luke, "one way or the other."

Back at his office at the law school. He has three of the best students helping him research his point. Two hours after they started, they haven't come up with anything strong enough for Luke to convince the judge to let the sheriff testify about his shooting being connected to Emma's murder.

He doesn't want to end his defense here. Not on a missing witness. It's a huge letdown. You want to end on a high note, something that the jury will remember vividly when they go into that stuffy little room to begin their deliberations.

He looks at his watch. A quarter to twelve. Court will reconvene at one-thirty. He has less than two hours. Not enough time.

His cell phone rings. Snatching it up: "Yes?" It's Riva; he figured it was her; only a few people in Santa Barbara have this number. He listens, then his face brightens in an ear-to-ear grin. "Are you serious? Where did you find her?" Then: "Yes! Get her up here, right away!"

The woman swears to tell the truth, so help her God.

A middle-aged woman. Plain-looking. The kind of working-class woman whose face tells you she's spent too much time on her feet, so that the soreness never leaves them. She's a waitress at a Carrow's family restaurant in Camarillo, off Highway 101, midway between Santa Barbara and Los Angeles.

As with Essham, the gun-store owner, Ray Logan has tried mightily to keep this witness off the stand. This time Judge Ewing is on the defense side. He's already opened the door to Doug Lancaster's actions and whereabouts being examined in open court; this witness's testimony clearly falls under those set of circumstances. Doug Lancaster is not present. Luke excluded him from attending today.

He establishes the date that Emma was found missing. "Were you working the morning shift that day, Mrs. De Wilde?" he asks her.

"Yes."

"From when to when?"

"I go on at six in the morning, when we open, finish at two. The other shift works two until ten, when we close." Even her voice is tired.

Walking to the witness stand, he takes an eight-by-ten color glossy out of a folder and hands it to her. "Did you see this man that morning, in your restaurant?"

She looks at the photograph. "Yes. I did."

"You're positive? There's no doubt in your mind?"

"Absolutely not. He was there."

He walks over to the jury box, holds the picture up for all to see: a head-shot photograph of Doug Lancaster. "This is the man," he repeats, talking to her, but looking at the jurors.

"Yes."

"When was he there? Do you recall the time?"

"Between seven-fifteen and eight, give or take ten minutes."

"How can you be sure of the time?"

"We take a five-minute break every two hours," she explains. "Like I said, I came on at six, so my break was at eight. He had left a few minutes before."

Luke nods sagely. "How can you be so certain you aren't mistaken about his identity?" he asks, turning back to her. "This happened over a year ago."

"I know that. But he was very upset. He was sitting in a booth at my station and he looked like somebody who had just gone through something terrible. I didn't know what, but I asked him if he was all right. I asked him twice."

"What was his answer?"

"That he wanted to be left alone."

"Did he have anything to eat?" Luke asks.

"He had black coffee. I refilled his cup twice."

"You're not an expert, of course," Luke says, "but did it look to you like he might have been up all night?"

"Objection!" Logan calls out. "Speculative, calls for an opinion."

"Overruled," Ewing says immediately, surprising both men. He instructs the woman to answer the question.

"People come in all the time that've been up all night," she says. "It's easy to spot. Their clothes are wrinkled, their hair isn't combed, they're yawning." She smiles. "You don't have to be a genius to know if someone's been up or not."

"Waitress's intuition," Luke says warmly. This is a good witness; hell, this is a great witness. "So your answer is . . . ?"

"The man in that picture looked to me like he had been up all night."

"Good," Luke says. He pauses for a moment, then continues. "Getting back to the identification. You said you know it was the man in the picture I just showed you because he had been visibly upset, and that drew your attention."

"Yes."

"But still, that was over a year ago. Over that long period of time, isn't it possible you could be mistaken? That the man you thought you saw wasn't really him, maybe it was someone who looked like him? Isn't that possible?"

She shakes her head. "But that's not why I know."

He smiles at her. "And why is that?"

"Because two days later I saw him on the television set. He was talking about how his daughter had been kidnapped. It was such a shock, seeing him. I was watching with my girlfriend, another waitress from work, this was on the six o'clock news, and I said to her, 'That man was in the restaurant two mornings ago. He was so upset then.' That's what I told her. And I thought, when I was watching him, that he was upset because she had disappeared."

"And it wasn't until later that you realized that he had been in your restaurant *before* she was discovered to be missing?" Luke asks, leading her on.

Her quiet "Yes" and Logan's earsplitting objection come simultaneously.

"Overruled!" Ewing comes back with equal force.

Jesus, Luke thinks, standing there, this could actually work. "Please answer the question again, so the jury can hear you clearly," he tells her.

"Yes," she says. "He was in the restaurant that morning."

It's getting towards the close of day. Ray Logan worked Mrs. De Wilde over vigorously, cajoling, bullying, threatening, but she stuck to her story: She had personally served Doug Lancaster in her restaurant on the morning his daughter went missing from her bedroom. As far as she is concerned, there is absolutely no doubt about that.

Judge Ewing excuses her. He looks down at his witness sheet, then up at the clock. "Do you have any more witnesses you plan on calling?" he asks Luke.

Luke shakes his head. He's done all he can do with what he has. He had thought, long and hard, about calling Doug Lancaster. Lancaster's non-whereabouts on the night his daughter was abducted, now buttressed by this witness, could go a long way towards establishing good reasonable doubt in the minds of the jurors. And he was itching to tear into Lancaster, for reasons both professional and personal.

He and Judge Freddie had debated the situation at length.

"Don't do it," De La Guerra had counseled, after they'd hashed the pros and cons over for half the night.

"He's a sitting duck," Luke had protested. "I can tear his ass up from here to Bakersfield."

"You *think* you can," the judge had retorted. "But are you positive, one hundred percent?"

"Meaning what?"

"What's the old adage, Luke? You don't ask a question if you don't know what the answer's going to be. Yes, he's been stonewalling and lying from day one, and you may nail him, nail him good. But he could be lying in the weeds, waiting for you to come at him with this, and then slam you with something unexpected."

It was too strong a point to ignore. In the end, he decided to err on the side of caution. He had this witness who had placed Doug within forty miles of his house a few hours after Emma had been kidnapped. He would use that in his closing statement, hammer it home. The father had lied, the father was close by. And there wouldn't be any surprises. The only other thing he could do that he hasn't is call Joe Allison to the stand, and hell will freeze over to the core of the earth before he does that.

"No, I don't." He pauses, then says the magic words: "Your Honor, pending rebuttal witnesses, the defense rests."

A collective sigh of relief wafts up to the ceiling. Ewing makes a couple of notes to himself. "Tomorrow being Friday, our dark day, we will recess this trial until eight o'clock Monday morning, at which time I will instruct the jury. Counsel for both sides should be prepared for closing arguments immediately following." One final whack of his gavel, and he sweeps out of the room.

Luke sits at the defense table, trying to make eye contact with the individual jurors as they're led from the room. Starting tonight, they'll be sequestered until they've reached a verdict.

Sitting next to him, Joe Allison leans in close. "You did great, Mr. Garrison. Thanks a lot."

Luke doesn't conceal what has become a growing distaste for the man. "Don't thank me," he says sourly. "It isn't over, not by a long shot."

The jail deputy leads Allison away. Luke remains sitting, waiting for the courtroom to empty out. He's drained; he doesn't want to face anyone this evening, especially the press. Finally, the chamber empty, he gathers his papers into his briefcase, rises wearily to his feet, and starts to leave.

One spectator still remains. Glenna Lancaster, in her ever-present black, is standing by the back door, watching him. Staring at him, no expression on her face.

A harpy, he thinks, in the classical sense, a guardian at the gate of her own private hell, standing watch over her daughter's fate. Trying to will him to go away, him and Joe Allison. Especially Joe. The man she had befriended, taken to her bed, who then turned his back on her and took up with her daughter (that Allison had never been serious about her is out of her ken), who, Luke knows she's convinced, abducted and killed her daughter.

He has to walk by her to get out. Well, no sense in postponing the inevitable. Trudging towards her, he looks at her, not aggressively, but warily, the way you eyeball a dangerous dog that's planted itself in the middle of the sidewalk, right in your path. Move, please, he thinks, turn and go.

She holds her ground. He passes by her, no more than three feet separating them as he reaches the high, heavy door.

He's going to have to say something; he can't brush by her without an acknowledgment. It would be unspeakably rude, even cruel.

"Glenna . . ."

She says nothing.

"I'm sorry." That's all he can come up with. *I'm sorry. For everything, for everything, for everything.*

SIX

Luke's preparation of his summation to the jury is going to take all his weekend time. He burrows himself in his office, reading over the transcripts, making notes, thinking about the angles. Maria Gonzalez seeing Allison on the property is deadly, a real bullet to the heart, especially when combined with the other evidence, which was killer stuff to begin with, but it's still not an absolute smoking gun. He might be able to plant some slim doubts in the jurors' minds about her credibility. No one actually saw Allison with her body, alive or dead, and no murder weapon has ever been found.

But the worst thing you can do is lie to yourself. The prosecution's case, looking at it with a cold, objective eye, forswearing emotion and passion, is almost bulletproof. There's motive: she was pregnant, she was going to blow the whistle on him. Opportunity: he was there, according to the eyewitness. And the strong circumstantial evidence—the key ring, the shoes, the condoms. Everything he's known, and everything he's learned, points in one straight line: a guilty verdict.

But he's got to keep plugging away. The rules don't change when you're losing.

Riva, antsy, is sleuthing on her own. It's way late in the day, but she doesn't have much else to do, and she has her own theory that she can't let go of—that Allison slept with Emma, knocked her up, but didn't kill her.

Nicole Rogers, of course, is on her mind. And with that suspicion, she's started pursuing another element. It's a hit-and-miss kind of investigation, what she's doing. She isn't a real detective with an established private investigator's tools at her disposal—networking, computer programs, contacts in and out of law enforcement. Although she has the smarts of one and the curiosity as well, she lacks the resources—plus, she's pregnant and is often, to her annoyance, tired, which makes her cranky; she's a woman of action, she doesn't like being tired, sapped of energy—and she has nothing tangible to go on. It's all intuition. The truth is out there, as her favorite television show proclaims. But where?

What's the old rule? Follow the money. Joe Allison is the money in this case. So recreate a couple of typical days in his life and follow him.

One problem: his place of employment, the television station, took a lot of his time, and she can't tread in those waters, so she tools around the periphery: where he worked out, where he hung out, ate, drank, socialized. The organizations he belonged to, his community work.

Kris & Jerry's is a popular upscale bar where many of the city's hipper young professionals gather. The habitués knew Joe Allison as a steady customer. The barman, a buffed UCSB grad student, recalls that one woman who drank with Allison on a couple of occasions was a bourbon drinker. Designer bourbon—Maker's Mark, she asked for it specifically. The bartender remembers her because rare is the California woman whose choice of alcohol is bourbon. He doesn't recall her name; he doesn't know if he was ever told. She was only with Allison those few times. "I had the idea they worked together. After work, people from the office having a drink together, the usual thing."

Maker's Mark bourbon. The same kind of bourbon, seal cracked, found in Joe Allison's car. Interesting coincidence.

* * *

The woman is a friend of Glenna's. She's receiving Riva in her Montecito home, a few blocks from where the Lancasters used to live.

"Glenna was in an agitated state. She was drinking. She drank more than she should have."

"You were with her?" Riva asks. "You have firsthand knowledge?"

"Yes. There were a few of us together, late that night."

"Did she say why she was upset?"

The woman frowns. "No. Something had come up, something that had thrown her for a loop." Riva's interviewee, talking with the strict proviso that this conversation is off the record, lights up a Virginia Slim, sucks in a nervous drag. "I should quit." Another vigorous puff. "I shouldn't be talking about this."

"Was it about a man?" Riva asks.

"I don't think so—not this time. Not this time, but there sure were others." The woman snorts derisively. "What we do to ourselves in the name of love. I've been in that position, I know."

"This agitated state. It happened the night Emma Lancaster was abducted?"

"The very same."

Damn, Riva's thinking, where was I with this a month, two months ago? She doesn't know if Luke's going to be happy that she uncovered this stuff or upset that she did it so late. Too late to help, really. He's rested his case. The reason this information hasn't been found out is that they didn't have the time or the manpower to do everything they wanted to do: they live in a finite world. And Luke has a client who never came clean, only shedding light on the truth when it was forced out of him.

If they lose the case, and this information might have made the difference, Joe Allison will have no one to blame but himself. He could've remembered if he drank bourbon with his lady friend, and how upset she truly was over his leaving town.

* * *

"Hello, Janet." They're friends now, she calls the woman by her first name.

"Hello, Riva."

"Are you nervous, Janet? Your knee's doing the two-step mambo."

Doctor Lopez's knee is bouncing up and down to a spasmodic rhythm. "I shouldn't have talked to you. I should never have talked to anyone. I should have preserved the patient-doctor confidentiality."

It's Sunday afternoon. The clinic is closed. Lopez has come in at Riva's urgent request.

"You had no choice. Her parents waived the confidentiality."

"I should have resisted them."

Riva commiserates with the woman. They're sisters in their ethnicity, in this time and place a strong bond. And she likes her, she likes someone who's trying to do the right thing. "In the end it would've been forced out of you, so don't beat yourself up about it, *hermana*."

The doctor shrugs. Like, who will ever know? "So what do you want to know now?" she asks wearily. "I've already testified, they're done with me."

"I want to know for me," Riva tells her. "Outside of courtrooms, juries, laws. For the truth of it, whatever that is. If there can be said to be some, here."

"So what is your question?"

"Who besides you would have known about Emma's being pregnant? Who *could* have known?"

Lopez ponders the question. "That's a hard one."

"Other people working here?"

"Maybe."

"Did you tell anyone?"

The doctor nods. "I told my colleague. Our other doctor, Sam Hablitt."

"Who else?"

"No one else. She came in one day, and the next day she'd been kidnapped."

"Okay. So you only told one other person."

Lopez stares at her. "Yes."

"Did you write anything down? Was there anything on paper?"

Lopez nods gravely. "I wrote it all down."

"So someone could have found it, and told someone else, or taken some action."

"No." Lopez shakes her head vehemently.

"Why not?"

"It's all in code. We never identify a patient by name. That way, the government or anyone else who's trying to pry into our private affairs is stymied. It's a huge privacy issue, particularly regarding AIDS patients and their employers and insurance companies, and we fight to maintain our autonomy and independence, tooth and nail." Angrily, she adds, "These so-called conservatives in Washington. They're always talking about less government, but when it comes to social programs that help poor or disadvantaged people, their pawprints are on everything. Anything to try and shut us down, the bastards!"

"I hear you," Riva says. "So here's my question: Who knows these codes? Or could get access to them?"

Luke, buried in work, his tension level mounting, regards Riva snappishly. "Just what I need—an overflowing new bowl of fresh distractions."

Sunday evening, Mountain Drive. The true beginning of the end starts tomorrow. He's fidgeting over a draft of his summation, staring intently at the screen of his laptop. As if the answer he's looking for will leap off it, of its own volition.

"Sorrrry," she comes back at him, miffed. "I thought you might be interested in this. Some of this, any of it." She skitters away. "I worked my buns off all weekend, tracking this down. Try to help someone, and see the thanks you get."

"I'm preparing my closing remarks, Riva. Only the most important summation I've ever made in my life." He's buying into his own hyperbole. "What am I supposed to do with all this?"

"Reopen the trial?" she asks hopefully.

He groans. "Reopening a trial's serious business. You can't waltz in there and say, 'Listen up, Judge, I found out some new stuff that you might want to look at. Let's stop everything and turn left ninety degrees.' No judge in the world would ever consider that."

"But this is important," she argues vehemently. "It could be vital."

"I agree. And if we'd known about it earlier, which I guess I should have, we might have found a way to use it—although it's highly circumstantial. To go back in now and try to reopen would be an admission of incompetency."

"You didn't have the time to check out everything under the sun, Luke," she reminds him. "Don't get down on yourself again. It's a luxury you don't have time for. You know you were never supposed to win, Luke. You were supposed to tank this. Make it look good and exit gracefully into the night."

His gut feels like he's been shot, all over again. "I know." He looks out into the night, the darkness of the canyon below them, the lights further down towards town, the oil-platform running lights out in the channel defining the horizon.

"Do you plan to do anything with my information?" she asks.

"I don't know. It supports my theory that at the least someone additional is involved." He sprawls out on the living room couch. "Under different circumstances I'd leak this to the press. But Doug Lancaster *is* the local press."

"What about you?" she asks, flopping down opposite him, head to toe, presenting him with her bare feet to rub.

"What about me what?" He takes one foot in his hands, begins kneading the instep and ball.

She luxuriates in the delectable, rough caress. "There's still someone out there who tried to kill you," she says, moving in slow, libidinous rhythm with her foot massage.

"I know," he replies somberly. Cocking his head towards the street: "My keepers are a constant reminder."

"Shouldn't you at least turn this over to the sheriff?" she asks breathily.

"Good idea." Abruptly he lets go her foot, gets up, goes over to the dining table, which he's using for a desk. "When I see him tomorrow." He sits down, begins assembling his papers, turning to the speech he's composing.

"I'm going to take a bath." She heaves up from the couch, pads into the bathroom.

He's locked into his final argument, but he isn't focused, not the way he needs to be. He's thinking about Riva, how she's so with him it's almost heartbreaking. He wishes he'd pursued this angle more, but you can't do everything. His job was to defend his client, not search out and identify every possible suspect. That's the police's job, and they weren't thorough enough.

Tomorrow he'll pass this on to Sheriff Williams. Maybe something will come of it. That's not his concern now. His sole task is to get Joe Allison an acquittal. Then, if by some miracle he pulls that off, he'll deal with everything else.

"Ladies and gentlemen of the jury . . ."

Ray Logan is the man of the hour. And he knows it. This is his chance to shine like he's never shone before. To stamp his seal on his office, make it his own, once and for all. Luke Garrison will be his accomplice in this task—not a willing one, but a player all the same. The king is dead, long live the king. He's even bought a new suit for the occasion, a dark blue Hugo Boss pinstripe, which hangs on him like a million bucks.

Everyone who needs to be here, is. Doug Lancaster's back in his customary seat in the first row behind the prosecution table. Doug is looking calm, much calmer than he's appeared since the trial began, calmer than he's been for months. Luke, glancing over at him as they all wait for Judge Ewing to make his entrance, marvels at the man's newly acquired self-control. Maybe he's accepted whatever's going to come, Luke thinks. Or he's convinced himself that the verdict, once these last speeches are made, will go his way.

Glenna, too, is in her usual seat. Last row, closest to the door.

He had planned on handing over Riva's newfound information to Sheriff Williams and taking a few minutes before the day officially started to explain and discuss it, particularly as it might apply to his own shooting, but Williams, who is customarily early, came in only a minute before the bailiff called the proceedings to order.

"All rise."

Judge Ewing, looking formidably magisterial, sweeps in with the hem of his robe trailing on the floor. He's had a fresh haircut over the weekend, and under the top of his judicial garment he's wearing a new tie, Luke notices, silver and navy blue silk. He looks like a judge; there's more than a passing resemblance to the late chief justice Warren Burger. Dignified, calm, in control.

"You may proceed," he directs Ray Logan straightaway.

"Ladies and gentlemen of the jury . . ."

Ray Logan is organized. He is on top of this. He is smooth, confident, friendly, tough. He doesn't talk down to the jurors, he doesn't patronize them, he doesn't bully or in any way intimidate them.

"The facts are incontrovertible. All you have to do is look at them. There was a young, impressionable girl who was befriended by an attractive older man. The man worked for her father, so she knew him as a friend for a long time, was comfortable with him, trusted him. And as she progressed from a twelve-year-old grade schooler with braces on her teeth to a fourteen-year-old almost-woman in bloom, and her beauty and sexuality became a tangible, alive thing, she could feel her own inner stirrings, and she aroused them in this man, who has no conscience. Did she enter into sexual congress with him willingly? Yes, in all probability she did. She had a crush on this local media star. Many girls her age had a similar crush. So when the opportunity arose, all too tragically and predictably, they became lovers.

"Which you do not do, ladies and gentlemen. Not if you are an adult person with any sense of morality, of right and wrong.

"She became pregnant. She was carrying their love child. Except this was no love child, this was a fetus from hell, an albatross growing in the womb. It would be a social disgrace for her and her family if it became known, though they could weather it, as a family. Maybe she'd have an abortion—she had looked into that. Or maybe not, maybe they'd send her away on some pretext, they have plenty of money, a few months going to school in France or Italy is a wonderful experience for a young girl. And the baby would be put up for adoption. No one would ever know. Emma would survive it and her life would go on. Remember that, ladies and gentlemen of the jury. Her life would go on.

"For Joe Allison, however, the scenario was very different. This was ruination for him. He had to stop this right now, "by whatever means necessary." That's a military phrase meaning you do what you have to do to get the job done and protect yourself.

"So that's what he did. He murdered her.

"Let's follow the facts together. Emma Lancaster had missed her last two periods. She went to a clinic where her parents wouldn't find out about her possible condition. The clinic confirmed that she was three months pregnant. That was Saturday afternoon. Immediately she tried to call Joe Allison, the father of her unborn child. They kept missing each other. Finally, after two in the morning, they connected.

"He came to the house immediately. He took her right out of her bedroom. A witness saw him do it. They went somewhere to talk about it, probably the gazebo on her parents' property where they had made love before. We know that because the contraceptives he had used there matched the ones found a year later in his house. But we're getting ahead of ourselves here.

"Something happened between them. Maybe she wasn't going to have an abortion after all. She was going to have the baby. And who was the father? People would want to know. Sooner or later, that would come out. Or maybe she was going to tell her father what was going on. Do you have any doubt what would have happened if she had done that? Joe Allison, up there in the gazebo with his fourteen-year-old pregnant mistress at three in the morning, had no doubts.

"There was only one way out for Joe Allison.

"We know he was there that night, ladies and gentlemen of the jury. Because a courageous woman, who initially entered this country illegally and has always been afraid of what might happen to her if she 'got involved,' overcame her fears and came forward. But that too would happen later.

"A year went by. For Douglas and Glenna Lancaster, a year of continuous, nonstop grieving. A year in which their lives fell apart. And during that year, their friend Joe Allison was by their side, giving comfort and support.

"And then a miracle. We admit it, folks. It wasn't dogged police work that solved this case, this horrible, unthinkable crime. We probably would have solved it sooner or later, but there are no assurances. We were blessed. Which proves there is a God after all, I firmly believe that.

"The miracle is that Joe Allison got stopped on that drunk-driving violation. Which led to the search—all done legally, ladies and gentlemen, there is not one shred of illegality in any of the police work done in connection with this case, so cast that out of your minds, it's a clever smokescreen to try to stop you from seeing the plain truth. But you're more clever than that technical, desperate ploy, you see right though it.

"Allison was pulled over legally. And in his car was the key ring that had vanished from Emma Lancaster's bedroom the year before, on the night of her murder. And when the police saw that, and then searched his house, all done legally, ladies and gentlemen, what did they find? The shoes that had made the prints found on the property and later, where the body was found. The shoes that made a deep imprint, because the wearer of them had been carrying a girl, a dead girl, who weighed more than a hundred pounds, so of course they would leave a significant imprint, they were bearing close to three hundred pounds. And that's why the shoes are so significant.

"But there's more. Condoms found in Joe Allison's domicile are the exact same kind found in the gazebo. He used them for his illicit affair, with fourteen-year-old Emma Lancaster! Except one time when, in the heat of passion, he forgot to use them—or one broke, who knows, who cares?"

Logan is coming to the end.

Luke, sitting next to Joe Allison at the defense table, is watching and listening intently. This is good, he thinks. This is straightforward, solid, utterly persuasive. His adversary has even hit the bullseye on information he doesn't know firsthand, like how Allison knocked her up. He's got a jury that wants to convict, if they're given a reason to and instructions on how. And Ray Logan has done that. Done it beautifully.

"There is one issue that was raised by the defense that I want to get rid of right now. That is the idea that someone else committed this brutal crime. The defense has recklessly implied that it could be

Emma's father, who loved her with a love only a father can have for a child." Logan turns back and looks at Luke, sitting attentively at the defense table. "That didn't happen, ladies and gentlemen of the jury." His voice is heavy with contempt and disdain. "It's vile, and you know it." He pauses. "You know it." Said almost wistfully, his voice, saying those three words, dropping to a whisper, looking out in the room, finding Doug Lancaster, making eye contact.

Logan is finishing, the final punching up. "You have everything you need for conviction, ladies and gentlemen, short of a videotape of the murder. I literally mean that. The accused was there—two witnesses saw him. That in itself is enough to convict, more than enough. But look at what else you have to take into the jury room with you, when you begin your deliberations. Emma's key ring, missing from that day. Joe Allison's shoes, that made the distinctive print found at the murder site and where her body was found. And the condoms found in his house that are the same ones found in the gazebo.

"We have motive, ladies and gentlemen. We have opportunity. And we have evidence. We have everything a jury would ever want to do the right thing.

"Joe Allison, a man who has absolutely no morals, had a sexual relationship with the fourteen-year-old daughter of his friend and employer. He made her pregnant. He killed her to shut her up, and hid her body. And then, to sink the rapier in even deeper, he pretended to be a grieving friend, a source of comfort and support. How do you think Emma's parents felt when they found out that this man, who they thought was their friend—Doug Lancaster took Joe Allison out to dinner on the very night Allison was arrested and charged with his daughter's murder—how do you think they felt when they found out that he was the one who seduced her, impregnated her, murdered her, and abandoned her to a lonely grave? Imagine yourself in their shoes, folks. It's devastating beyond my ability to deal with, I can tell you that."

Logan pauses for a deep breath. He's almost home. "Your task is clear. It is to find Joe Allison guilty of first-degree murder and kidnapping, and to sentence him to death at the hand of the state. Any verdict less than that will be a gross miscarriage of justice, a betrayal of Emma Lancaster's life, and a denial of her death.

"Don't do that. Don't deny her. I implore you. Her parents and all the people of the state of California implore you. Do not deny her death. If you do, you deny her life, deny that she ever existed. And she lived, ladies and gentlemen. Not for long, but she lived. She should be living still. Her murderer is. And if you let him go on living while she lies dead, you will be doing yourselves and all of us a terrible injustice."

He turns and points a wrath-of-God finger at the defense table, homing in on Joe Allison.

"He killed her." His voice is ablaze. "The laws of this state stipulate that when one human being murders another human being, wantonly and with malice, he should pay for that crime . . . *with his life.* Make this man pay the ultimate price, ladies and gentlemen. Because he made Emma Lancaster pay it."

Well, Luke thinks, that was good. On a scale of one to ten, he'd give it an eight, eight and a half. It's the best Luke's ever seen Logan perform. Ray had to rise to the occasion, to prove that he is now "the man." And he did, damn well.

He *almost* pulled it off. But this afternoon, after the jury has come back from lunch, well fed and rested, they're going to hear the real thing.

The courtroom is empty. Luke alone is left in the big fancy chamber, to sit at his desk—the defense table—and review his speech one more time. Nothing Ray Logan said will change it, except to emphasize the issue Ray himself brought up—that not only *could* someone else have killed Emma, there is a surfeit of evidence to disprove, or at the least cast tremendous doubt on, Joe Allison's having done so.

Was Allison there? Yes. But they don't know that. No one knows that except him and Riva and the housekeeper Maria Gonzalez—Maria who owes her very existence to the Lancasters, Maria who saw Joe Allison at the house that night but didn't come forward for more than a year? Who are we kidding, folks?

He's ready. He wishes lunch was over, so he could jump into the saddle.

"Luke. Get out here! Right now!" Riva is running into the far doorway, calling to him from all the way back there.

Jumping from his chair, not knowing why but animated by the alarm in her voice, he rushes down the aisle and follows her outside into a sunlit noon where Doug Lancaster, standing on the sunken lawn outside the building, surrounded by news crews, is about to hold a press conference. The video people are setting their cameras in place—Doug's station has the best position, of course—while the audio guys are testing their microphones, slipping different wind baffles and types of mikes on and off their booms, talking into the microphones to the recordists in the trucks parked along Anacapa and Anapamu streets.

What's going on? Luke thinks. Looking around, he smells a setup.

He sees Ray Logan, standing to one side just out of the massed cameras' vision, and next to him, the sheriff. The two men have taken identical stoic military-style postures, which look good to the camera in case they're caught on screen; from where Luke is standing, in the shadow of the arched entrance forty yards away, he can see that beyond the for-show, impassive facade they're presenting to the world, their inner emotions are far different. But what that means, exactly, he doesn't know. He does know that this isn't good for him.

Logan senses Luke's presence and looks over to where Luke's standing on the stairs, behind where the microphones have been set, looking down at the event, at Doug Lancaster's back. He makes eye contact with Luke, then nudges the sheriff, who looks in Luke's direction also. Williams's face is a tight mask, his eyes crinkling against the sun.

Everything is in place. Doug Lancaster steps to the bank of microphones.

Yes, I was right, Luke thinks to himself. I'm being set up.

"I wish to make an announcement," Doug begins. His voice, amplified over dozens of microphones, booms out into the large grassy sunken amphitheater that is formed by the three sides of the courthouse.

Luke edges around the side of the massed throng, wanting to get a better look at the man. The sun is sitting way up in the sky, the sky so sharp, so brilliantly blue to look up at, it makes your eyes hurt. There are no clouds.

Luke feels the bile rising in his upper chest and throat. All these news crews were alerted for a reason, and it wasn't to hear Doug tell how he was the one who had really killed his daughter.

And then he sees her. Helena Buchinsky, the woman he interviewed in Malibu. Lancaster's mistress. Standing off to the side near the front, on the other side of Doug from the sheriff and the district attorney. Wearing a large floppy straw hat to shield her face from the sun. Dressed plainly, a simple shirtwaist dress, sensible heels. No jewelry. There is no erotic thrust coming from her.

Riva comes up next to him. She takes his hand. They grip each other firmly.

"An issue has been raised in this trial," Doug says. "About where I was on the night my daughter Emma was taken from her room, and subsequently murdered."

The crowd, most of which is press, is listening intently. This is going to be hot.

"In particular, the defense has raised this issue to try and cloud the true nature of this case. There has been a strong implication, because I wasn't home that night and gave a misleading statement to the police regarding where I was, that I was involved in my daughter's death." He pauses, clears his throat, looks over to Helena Buchinsky, who is standing rigid as a mannequin. She looks back at him briefly, then away.

"This is a horrible, scurrilous, disgraceful allegation," Doug says into the microphones. "But because I did lie to the police, on the day of her kidnapping, I have fallen under suspicion." A brief pause. "I did lie. I lied for a reason. It was to protect some innocent people.

"But I have decided, finally, to come clean about this, because I was not involved, in any way, in my daughter Emma's death, and I don't want the man who really killed her to be a beneficiary of my lie, even though, as I said, it was for a good reason."

It's warm out. He's dressed in a dark suit, starched white shirt, tie. He dabs at his forehead with a handkerchief.

"On the night in question I was, in fact, with my child. But it was not my daughter, Emma. I was with my son. His name is Mark. He is eleven years old."

The institution always knew where to find him. He made sure of that. The call came to the hotel late that night. His son had contracted some kind of virus very suddenly. He was extremely ill, there could be complications—his temperature was almost 105—he might die, given his weak condition. They were taking him to the emergency room at the hospital in Camarillo, the closest hospital to where the boy lived and was cared for.

He called the boy's mother and told her. Then he phoned down and ordered his car brought around. He threw on any old clothes and rushed downstairs. His car was waiting. He jumped in and peeled out of the hotel parking lot, heading for the freeways that would take him up the coast to Camarillo. It was late, slightly after one in the morning.

He got to Camarillo a little before two. She was already there; she lived closer, in Malibu.

The doctors were working on their son. His heart had stopped, but they had gotten it started again. His breathing was labored, they needed to help it with a respirator. It was going to be nip and tuck.

This had happened before. Someday the boy's heart would stop and there would be no way to start it again. It was a flawed heart, as so much of him was flawed. His brain was flawed—it was barely a brain, his IQ was unmeasurable, certainly below twenty. His tortured little body, when it had come from her womb, was all twisted and broken. He had so many abnormalities—spina bifida, hydrocephalus, bones so bereft of calcium that a firm poke could break them. Over his ten years, he had broken dozens of bones, sometimes from activity no more strenuous than rolling over in his sleep.

It took four hours of intensive work, but the hospital staff miraculously stabilized him. Got his heart working again, spiked the virus that had almost caused his brain to fry.

There was nothing more they could do for him. There had never been anything they could do for him, from the moment of his birth.

The boy's mother drove back to her Malibu beach house. He grabbed a cup of coffee at a Carrow's near the hospital, then drove back to Santa Monica. He was a wreck, physically and emotionally, but he had to keep up appearances. He had to play a round of golf with some business associates, a few hours after leaving his son, who had never spoken a word, who had never in his entire life given one sign that he recognized his father, that he recognized anyone.

And then, that afternoon, the call had come to say that his daughter had been kidnapped; his healthy, beautiful daughter, his legitimate daughter.

Doug Lancaster looks out over the microphones. "A dozen years ago, I had an affair. I was married, I had a baby daughter. Emma."

For a moment he chokes, then he continues. "The woman became pregnant. She was not married. She is married now, to a close friend of mine." He pauses. "That marriage is now in jeopardy, because of what I have just told you."

Luke is listening, and his knees are shaking.

"She couldn't keep Mark with her. Not because she wasn't married—she would have, under different circumstances, she wanted to, that's why she didn't abort her pregnancy. She's Catholic, she doesn't believe in abortion. But given his extreme condition, his multitude of acute, incurable physical problems, his total mental retardation, we had to find the best place we could for him, where he could be cared for as well as possible."

He swallows hard, goes on. "Mark has been institutionalized his entire life. He will be institutionalized for the rest of his life, which, God willing, won't be much longer, because he has suffered every day of his life. When he was born, the doctor asked if we wanted to let him go. It would have been easy. In hindsight, it would have been the humane thing to do. Certainly the expedient thing to do. We chose, his mother and I, not to let him go. And since then, we have done our best not to let him go."

He starts to break down, catches himself, presses on. "No one has ever known about our son. My former wife Glenna did not know. My daughter Emma didn't know she had a brother. No one in the world knew, except the few people at the institution who had to know—and Mrs. Buchinsky and me."

One last pause. Then his voice takes on a defiant cast.

"No one was ever going to know. There was no reason anyone had to—this was a private matter, between two people. And it should have been kept secret, forever." More angrily now: "But because the defense lawyer in this case decided to cast me as the villain in my own child's trial, I am now forced to come public with this terrible secret."

Brandishing a document in his hand, he says, "This is an affidavit from the director of the institution that cares for my son Mark. I will distribute it to the press after I'm done, so that you'll know what I'm telling you is true, painfully true. Thank you."

Ferdinand De La Guerra, who has been so unobtrusive as to be invisible in the actual trial proceedings, joins Luke in Judge Ewing's chambers—an unsubtle reminder that there are establishment heavies behind the scenes here, particularly the former head judge in the county's legal system.

As they were walking towards Ewing's cubicle, De La Guerra had commented on Doug Lancaster's devastating press conference. "Aren't you glad now that you didn't call him as a witness?"

"What's the difference," Luke moaned. "I got run over by a truck instead of being shot in the head. Either way, I'm still dead."

"The jury didn't hear him," the former judge reminded him. "Nothing he said is part of the trial record. Huge difference."

That is true; but it brings scant solace.

They're joined by Ray Logan and two of his top aides, his senior deputy assistant D.A., and the in-house consultant, who specializes in legal issues.

Ewing is hot under the collar—literally. His robe is off, draped carelessly on a chair. He's loosened his handsome new tie. His dress shirt, the top collar unbuttoned, is pocked with sweat blotches.

"In all the years I sat on the bench, including the dozen when I was the senior jurist," De La Guerra says to his former colleague, "I never saw such an egregious violation of professional ethics." Turning to Ray Logan: "What in the world were you thinking? Have you no scruples regarding your judicial conduct? Mr. Lancaster's utterances could be grounds for a mistrial."

"With all due respect, Judge De La Guerra," Logan shoots back,

"I don't think so." He's stung by the onslaught from a man who is considered above reproach. "This wasn't prearranged, I swear it. I didn't know a thing about this until Doug Lancaster corralled me on the way out after my summation and told me he was going to hold a press conference in five minutes and the sheriff and I needed to be there."

"It caught you as much by surprise as it caught me?" Luke spits back derisively. He turns to Ewing. "I'm going to have to ask for a mistrial and we're going to have to start this entire mess all over again, and this time you're going to have to get a new defense lawyer, 'cause those were my taillights you just saw vanishing in the distance!"

"What grounds do you have for a mistrial?" Logan asks, glancing at his legal expert, who nods in agreement: the office just did a blitz check on this, and they're okay, at least for the moment. "Lancaster's a private citizen. We can't control his actions. You show me anything in case law that makes the actions of a private citizen speaking up in his own defense grounds for a mistrial. I'd love to see it. We could be breaking new legal ground here." He shakes his head dismissively. "There's nothing there. You got outfoxed, and that's too bad. But there is nothing Doug Lancaster did, or my office did, that merits any stoppage of this trial."

He's feeling supremely self-satisfied. This is a defining moment in his career. That it should occur when opposing Luke Garrison only makes it juicier.

Judge Ewing looks to Luke. "Are you going to file a motion for a mistrial?"

Ewing himself had watched the doings from his office window. Like the prosecution, he too has done a quick check on what ramifications Lancaster's public address might have on any legal positions either the defense or, much less likely, the prosecution might take. He's found nothing.

"I'd like to file a motion, Your Honor, but I need to do some research on it first, to find out where I stand. If I have standing, which right now I don't know," Luke admits candidly, "I certainly don't want to have to give my closing today. Because frankly, I don't have one now."

"Your honor, I have to object—" Logan begins.

"Shut up, Ray!" Ewing barks impatiently. "Whether or not you knew it was coming, this incident reeks of unprofessional and tawdry behavior." He turns to Luke and De La Guerra. "I'm going to dismiss the jury until tomorrow morning. I want you to come back into my courtroom by a quarter to five this afternoon and tell me, if you can, what you're going to do. We're in trial—I'm not going to stop it. Unless you can convince me, with clear legal precedent, that Doug Lancaster's actions today are grounds to grant a motion for mistrial, we're forging ahead. You show me, or this trial goes to the jury for their deliberations by the end of the day tomorrow."

Sittin' on the dock of the bay . . . Luke and Riva, shoes off, his suit pants rolled up to the knees, walk along the water's edge at Butterfly Beach. The tide is way out, almost a hundred yards. Hand in hand, they walk past Channel Drive and the Biltmore Hotel, away from the afternoon western sun. The damp sand crunches under their steps. Her footprints, normally highly arched, are now, because of her pregnancy, completely flat, no definition except the toe marks.

"Luke . . ."

"It's okay. It isn't over."

She marvels at his stoicism. This man she loves so dearly has just had the rug pulled out from under him, his entire defense ripped to shreds. And before this latest, almost inevitable catastrophe, Luke has, during the course of their sojourn here in enemy territory, been shot at, discovered that his client is a liar and a child abuser, reencountered his ex-wife with all the psychology and emotion attendant on that, had to process the enmity of the members of his former staff and handle the overall hostility coming his way from the city at large, and, to top all that off, been sucked into the maelstrom of a situation that appeared pristine and pure on the outside but was actually dirty to the core.

"What are you going to do?" She can't help but ask him, even though she knows he's thinking, he doesn't want to talk. This walk on the beach was his idea—he wanted to make sure he was calm and that his mind was clear before taking his next step.

He stops, glances up at the sun. "I need to give Judge Ewing an answer in two hours," he says elliptically, avoiding her question. Picking up a piece of beach glass made smooth by countless caressings from the surf, he skims it across the shallow tendrils of the shore-lapping waves. "And while I'm figuring out what that's going to be, I want you to check on one more thing for me. We may have overlooked something, and if we did, there's still some hope." He holds his thumb and forefinger an inch apart. "This much, or less. But right now, it's all we've got."

He's in the middle of typing his brief when Riva opens the door to the motel room that's eight blocks from the courthouse. She rented the room under a false name days ago, for them to work in; he doesn't want the press bulldogging him at his office, checking to see what he's doing or who he could be seeing. So far, he's managed to elude them.

"Is she here?" he asks, fingers frozen over the keyboard.

Her smile is wide, open, and full of relief. "She's here." She turns, addresses the unseen woman standing behind her. "Come in, Mrs. Gonzalez."

Maria Gonzalez, eyes darting everywhere but on his face, edges into the small chamber. As soon as she's crossed the threshold, Riva pulls the door shut behind them. The curtains are drawn tight against the afternoon sun and any prying eyes.

Luke stands, comes from behind his makeshift desk. "Thanks for coming in," he tells her. "I can't tell you how good it is for you to do this."

The woman is trembling. "I'm scared to death," she admits.

"No reason to be," he says reassuringly. "You haven't done anything wrong, you have nothing to be ashamed about."

"I lied," she whimpers, sitting in the chair he slides under her. "In court."

"Naw." He shakes his head dismissively. "You didn't lie." He sits on the edge of the desk, looking at her friendly-like. With a slight motion of his head, he cues Riva, who crosses behind Maria to a small, low credenza on which there is a tape machine. Silently, she presses it on. "You answered all the questions anybody asked you. You just weren't asked all the right questions, that's all. That's not your fault, that's mine." He leans forward, touching her on the fabric of her sleeve. "Now I'm going to ask what I hope are the rest of the right questions, so we can get straight with this whole thing, once and for all."

Outside the courthouse, the press corps, print and television, hang around in small clusters, idly yakking with each other. Speculation runs rife. One rumor going around is that Joe Allison is going to change his plea to guilty in exchange for a promise of life without parole instead of the death penalty. Another is that there's going to be a mistrial. There's even some talk that Luke Garrison, having gotten his ass kicked from here to Ventura County, is trying to finagle his way off the case.

No one's leaving. Something is going to be decided by the close of the court day, and they all want to know what it is. They already have their lead story: Doug Lancaster's admission of where he was, and the fallout from it, both personally and how it will affect the outcome of this trial. But the press buzzards are hoping for a two-fer, another sensational revelation that will elevate this to the kind of cheap mythical status that a voracious tabloid-driven, gossip-hungry public has come to expect.

Checking of watches. Four-thirty. The court's day ends at five. Whatever's going to happen, it's going to happen pretty damn pronto. Where is Garrison? No one knows.

In the confines of his office, Ray Logan paces. Something's got to give. He hopes Luke doesn't come in with some whacked-out mistrial notion. There are none, none that his staff has come up with. And not only his people—the state attorney general has had his own appellate staff researching this madly, dozens of lawyers in Sacramento poring over every law book and statute known to be current, looking for any needle in a haystack. So far, with less than half an hour to go before Luke has to make his appeal, they haven't found one.

Time is running out on the defense. Logan wants it to run out faster.

* * *

Riva, checking the door to make sure no one is around, hustles Maria Gonzalez outside to her car, where she'll drive her home.

Luke is finished. He prints out his motion, only a few pages. He's already prepared the subpoenas. One was handed to Maria Gonzalez before she left. The other will be served as soon as Judge Ewing approves his motion.

If the judge approves it. That's the entire ball game, right there. A betting man wouldn't take that bet: Ewing has never gone for a motion like his, he looked it up. But he has nowhere else to go. He's out of options. Squaring his shoulders, shrugging into his suit coat, he leaves the sanctity of the motel room, briefcase and computer in hand.

Circling the far side of the courthouse, coming from the opposite direction from where his office at the law school is located (which he correctly figures is the direction all the reporters will be watching), he drives into the basement entrance of the courthouse garage, which is usually reserved for jail vehicles, but which he's been given special dispensation to use, to stay away from the press. Judge Ewing's orders.

Inside the judge's little private room, the air conditioner is going full blast. It's a west-facing room, it catches the afternoon sun. The judge doesn't use it much; he sometimes eats lunch there, or works at his desk when the court day is done. Now he sits and waits.

The telephone rings on his desk. Instinctively, he looks at the old Ingersoll clock on the wall, his father's old clock, the one that hung behind the counter in his parents' feed store in the Santa Ynez Valley. Ten to five. Listening, then: "Notify the district attorney and tell him we're ready."

Wordlessly, Luke hands a copy of his motion to Judge Ewing, another to Ray Logan. They open the envelopes simultaneously. Ewing, reading the cover heading, looks up in disbelief. "Motion to reopen? Luke, what is this? I can't . . ."

Ray Logan, incensed, throws his copy across the room. "This is amateur night in Dixie, Your Honor," he bellows. "There's got to be a limit to how far we can be pushed. This is absolute crap!"

Luke crosses the room and retrieves Logan's copy of his affidavit. He holds it out to his opponent. "I think you should read it," he says softly. "I put a lot of work into this. Humor me, okay? Just read it. Then you can toss it." He's smiling as he holds out the document.

Ewing has been reading it. He looks up at Luke. "The housekeeper will swear to this?" he asks, his voice quavering.

"Yes, Your Honor. She says she will."

Ewing reads further. Glancing up for a moment to Logan, he says, "You better read this, Ray."

Logan, alarmed by the tone of the judge's voice, snatches the document from Luke's hand and looks at it. He reads a few lines, then looks at Luke in alarm. "Where's this coming from?"

"Keep reading."

Ewing has finished. He lays the papers on his desk. "This is explosive material."

"I know, sir."

"It's awfully late in the day, Luke."

"A man's life is at stake, Your Honor. That supersedes anyone's schedule."

Logan, having finished, puts his copy down. His face is ashen. "This is horrible, if true," he laments.

Ewing looks at the district attorney. "Are you going to oppose this motion?" he asks gravely.

Logan's mouth flops open, like a fish caught on a hook. "I . . ." He sits down, buries his head in his hands. Then, looking up, he gives in. "No, Your Honor. In the interests of justice, I can't."

Ewing nods. He stands, buzzes his clerk and the bailiff to come in. They've been outside, waiting patiently.

The woman stands in the doorway, pencil and pad in hand. The bailiff is one step behind her.

"The defense has filed a motion to reopen, which I am granting," he tells them. "Type it up and distribute it. Make sure the jurors are contacted as soon as possible." He turns to Luke. "Are you going to issue subpoenas?"

"Absolutely, Your Honor. Our key witness is definitely going to be hostile. We've already served the housekeeper, Maria Gonzalez. I've got somebody standing by with my other one."

The deputy whistles. "First time I've ever seen this happen, Judge."

Another nod from the judge. "First for me, too." He scoops his coat from the rack. "I'll see you in court tomorrow morning, gentlemen." On his way out, he stops and turns back to Luke and Logan. "I'm issuing a gag order on this until tomorrow morning. No talking to the press about reopening the case. It's going to be tough enough once they find out. I, for one, would like one night of relative peace before they start to tear us all apart."

Sheriff Williams, seeing Luke leaving, pulls him aside. "What's going on?" he asks anxiously.

"I can't discuss anything," Luke tells him. "We're under a tight gag order."

"I know. Even Ray Logan won't tell me." He's bent out of shape from this, and isn't making a good job of not showing it.

"He's bound by the judge's ruling, same as anyone. Don't worry." He claps Williams on the back, hail fellow. "You'll find out soon enough."

The sheriff nods unhappily. He hates being out of the loop, like he isn't as important as some of the other players. "By the way. We're pulling your surveillance."

"Oh?"

"There's no threat anymore. Doug was our prime suspect."

"Sure, I understand. I appreciate all you've done."

Williams stares at him. "Stay low to the ground the next few days. No one's after you anymore." He offers his hand. "Good luck tomorrow. Whatever it is you're doing."

"Thanks. You too."

"He's pulling your protection?" Riva's nonplussed. "Now?"

"They don't feel there's a threat anymore. They're trying to save a buck."

"They're fools."

"He may be right." He pauses. With some foreboding: "Then again, he might be wrong."

"Don't go anywhere by yourself, especially at night," she cautions, as much for herself as for him.

They're in their house. She's started packing up—there are boxes scattered around the floors, she buys groceries day-to-day now.

"I'm staying put tonight. Right here. I'm not going anywhere."

She has the truck keys in her hand, her daypack slung over her shoulder, heading for the door. "Where're you going?" he asks, looking up from his work.

"Haagen-Dazs. I've got a craving for strawberry ice cream. I may stop at the market and get some pickles, too."

"I thought that was an old wives' tale."

"Even cliches were fresh once."

"Don't be long getting back. I worry about you." He touches her swelling stomach. "And Junior."

"I'll be fine. You worry about you."

"I'll be fine."

No protection. That's not good. She needs to know where Nicole Rogers is.

She goes into the bedroom to get a sweater. Making sure Luke isn't eavesdropping, she gets in touch with her technician friend. Nicole's Pathfinder is on the move, even as they speak. He gives her some streets to coordinate by, and wishes her luck.

Jumping into the truck, she barrels down the narrow, dark road. Please don't let this be happening, she's praying.

The woman pulls into the Von's shopping center parking lot on Coast Village Road. Her pharmacy is there. Since this trial started she's been on medication, Prozac, a heavy daily dose. Her prescription's run out, and she needs it refilled, right now.

The druggist hands her the container. She twists the top off, takes out a couple of pills, dry-swallows them. Feeling better, even before it actually takes effect, she walks back out to her car.

As she's unlocking the door, a man approaches her. He's holding a large legal-sized envelope in his hand. "Hello," he says cordially. But he isn't smiling.

She starts to shrink away from him, but he's got her pressed up against the door of her vehicle. "What do you—?" she starts to ask.

He hands her the papers, literally forces her to take them. "You have been officially served," he tells her. He turns on his heel and walks away.

She opens the envelope. She knows what it is before she reads the first line, but the dread and terror grab her by the throat anyway. *"You are hereby . . ."*

She crushes the subpoena in her hand, her heart pounding. No way is she going to testify, expose herself, be made an object of ridicule and hatred. Joe Allison had made it clear that their lives were going in separate directions. Now he's reaching out for her, from his jail cell. To help him, be there for him. What a bastard.

Trembling, she manages to drive home, pour herself a drink, turn on the television. Doug Lancaster's press conference is being replayed on all the channels, not only his own. She watches in fascination, horror, and revulsion as he reveals his secret life. What kind of man would do that to his family, keep something so important a secret? She feels for Doug, because he's lost his daughter, but otherwise she couldn't care less about him and his problems, including his retarded bastard son. He's a man with a massive ego, full of himself. And that woman with him, his "former" mistress. Had he stopped their affair after she gave birth to a retard, or when she had gotten married? Everyone who knew Doug knew of his promiscuity. He wouldn't stop seeing that woman unless *she* stopped *him*, and it was obvious, from her appearing with him, that she hadn't. A woman doesn't put her marriage, or any deep relationship, in jeopardy unless she's in love. Which she knows, all too well.

It has all gone too far. It has to end.

The sun is almost down as Riva drives to the location where the Lo-Jack had indicated Nicole Rogers's Pathfinder should be. And there it is, parked in the upper Village parking lot. She puts her hand on the hood—it's still warm. It hasn't been here long.

Nicole is easy to find. She's seated on the outside veranda of Pane e Vino, a popular and expensive Italian restaurant. Sitting opposite her is Stan Tallow, a senior partner in Nicole's law firm.

Riva edges closer. She doesn't want Nicole to see her.

Nicole and Tallow seem to be enjoying each other's company. Her hand on his, eyes on his face as she listens attentively to what he's saying. Riva catches snatches of the conversation: something about county zoning ordinances.

A waiter is at their table now, bringing them drinks, taking their dinner orders.

Nicole isn't going anywhere, Riva thinks with relief, except maybe to bed with her firm's rainmaker. For tonight, at least, she can rest easy.

Now the night has set in. The woman stands on the ridge across the canyon from Luke Garrison's rented house, sighting it through the high-powered telescopic lens attached to the rifle with which she terrorized the defense attorney at the ranch up north. She only comes here when it's night, when she can hide under cover of darkness. Through the infrared lens she sees him, sitting at the dining table in full view. He's alone in the house. The woman who lives with him isn't around.

His police guard is gone too. It was mentioned on the news, in passing: the sheriff had pulled his men from their surveillance. The county couldn't continue to keep their vigil up, it was costing the taxpayers too much money. And besides, the incident is well in the past now. Luke Garrison doesn't need the protection anymore.

Good. Let them think that. He's alone. She's alone, only her rifle keeping her company.

Now's the time.

She had been to the clinic to discuss a fund-raiser she was going to chair. The meeting went all right, but there was an undercurrent. She couldn't put her finger on it, but the doctors seemed uneasy around her—both of them, the man and the woman, but especially the woman, Dr.

Lopez, who was normally very friendly with her. Dr. Lopez almost shrank from her when they encountered each other in the hallway before the meeting. And they seemed cool to her, both Dr. Lopez and the other doctor.

The meeting ended and she rushed out to her car: she was on a busy schedule, she had a lot to do, she always had a lot to do. Reaching for her keys, she realized that in her haste to get going she'd left her purse inside, under her chair in the meeting room. She went back in, through the back entrance, she didn't like going through the front door, there were always so many poor, sick people in the waiting room, it depressed her to look at them.

The two doctors were still in the meeting room. She heard them talking as she approached. She didn't know why, to this moment she doesn't know why, but she didn't go in. She hung back and eavesdropped on their conversation.

They were talking about a girl who had been in earlier to get the results of her pregnancy test. The girl was young, fourteen. There were so many of them these days. This one was different, though. She wasn't poor, or working class, or Latina, or black. She was white, rich, privileged. She had only two things in common with the others like her. She was pregnant, and she didn't want her parents to know.

The girl was going to have an abortion. It was getting late, she was almost beginning her second trimester. If the clinic was to perform it, it had to be right away. She—Dr. Lopez—was going to do the procedure next Friday.

There was a gnawing in the woman's stomach, listening to this. She looked around furtively. No one was in the hallway.

"Thank God she wasn't here when her mother showed up," the male doctor said. "Can you imagine?"

"It's okay," Doctor Lopez said. "They didn't cross paths. The mother didn't find out."

She leaned against the wall, feeling like she was going to faint. Then she snuck back outside to her car, where she smoked a cigarette in the parking lot behind the building.

Five minutes later, she went back in again. This time through the front door, in plain sight. She spotted Dr. Lopez behind the counter, talking to a volunteer. "Forgot my purse," she said with a smile.

The doctor nodded, turned away from her. She fetched her purse from the meeting room where she'd left it and took off.

She went home and had a stiff drink, a bourbon on the rocks. Then she threw up.

Her daughter was pregnant. Who was the father?

Now it was the dead of night, hours after midnight. Lying alone in bed, unable to sleep. Her heart pounding, racing. Her husband a hundred miles away, fucking God knows who, her daughter pregnant, fucking God knows who, she's fourteen years old, still wearing a retainer. She was going to have an abortion.

Forget sleep. She needed a drink.

It was too late for bourbon. It was too late for anything, closer to morning than to night, but so what? Standing in the dark, empty study that overlooked the backyard, barefoot, wearing a flimsy nightgown, she poured herself a stiff cognac, knocked it back. It burned going down. It mellowed her out immediately. One more for the road, then she'd try to sleep.

The movement outside caught her eye. A man carrying something in a blanket in his arms, moving across the lawn.

They traversed the length of the lawn, down to the gazebo at the far end. She followed them. She didn't have anything on except her nightgown, she had nothing on her feet, but she didn't feel the cold. The blanket slipped a bit, and there was her daughter. Carrying her daughter, the man climbed the stairs to the gazebo. She followed, keeping to the shadows. She crouched at the foot of the structure, listening as they settled themselves above her.

As soon as they began talking, she knew that the man was Joe Allison, and she felt a knife going into her heart, into the center cut of her heart. She crouched there, shaking, listening to them above her.

They talked. She was pregnant, she was going to have an abortion next Friday, he was the father. She was matter-of-fact about it, she didn't want him accompanying her, she would take care of it herself, thank you very much. But she wanted him to know, which is why she'd forced him to come see her now.

Crouched at the bottom of the gazebo, underneath them, she could make out pieces of their bodies through the wooden slats of the floor. She was shivering, quietly hysterical. Quietly coming apart.

She heard her daughter say, "I'm going to have an abortion." And then she heard her say, "We might as well." And the sounds of lovemaking.

She cried silently, hating herself for crying, wanting to stop, unable to. She listened as they finished their lovemaking, listened as he pulled on his clothes.

He came down the stairs alone, looking back up at the girl, as if to say something, but saying nothing. She shrank back under the cross-structure of the struts that held the gazebo up. He didn't see her. He wasn't seeing anything.

Her daughter was smoking. She was humming a tune, some old show tune from the play her school had put on that fall. She had a sweet young voice. She loved to sing.

Go back, she told herself. Go back and pretend this never happened. Go back.

She didn't realize she had climbed the stairs until she was at the top. Her daughter's back had been to her. She was smoking the last drag on the cigarette butt she had found.

"What did you come back for?" her daughter had said, her back to her. "I don't want to do it again tonight. We're not going to anymore, that was the last time."

She stood there, trembling, and her daughter Emma knew it wasn't Joe Allison who had climbed up the stairs. She had turned, slowly, her face registering who was there—her mother, shivering with cold and fear and astonishment and anger.

"Oh, God!"

"How could you?" was all she could think of saying. "How could you?"

"How could I fuck your lover? Or how could I fuck anyone? Or how could I be smoking a cigarette at three in the morning?"

"You're pregnant." She felt like she was having an out-of-body experience.

Her daughter stared at her with hostility. No, not hostility. Hatred. "You were listening to us. You were spying on us? You were listening to us fucking, you sick bitch! How sick can you get?" She was on her feet. "Did you get off on it? Did it turn you on?"

She was whimpering, crying. "You're fourteen years old, for God's sake."

"I'm not the only one, Mom," her daughter had said, so matter-of-

factly. "There's plenty of girls my age. You're on the board of the clinic, you know that."

"Not like you." The words were coming out of her mouth, she didn't know what they were, or why.

"You mean, not 'nice girls'?" She had laughed. "Maybe I'm not so nice. Aren't you always telling me to be my own person?"

"I didn't mean this."

"Sorry, Mom. This is how I'm my own person."

She had failed her daughter. She hadn't been there, she hadn't seen it coming, and she should have, it wouldn't have been hard to see. If she had been there. Instead of being consumed in her own world, her own selfish life.

"It's Joe, isn't it?"

"What?" The words from her daughter snapped her out of her reverie.

"Joe. It's Joe being my lover that has you so bent out of shape, isn't it? Not that I'm having sex, but who I'm having it with." She walked up to her mother, stuck her face right in her mother's face. "You're jealous, aren't you? That I'm having an affair with your lover." She taunted her deeper. "Did you think you could keep him all to yourself?"

"Emma . . ."

"He doesn't even like you. He just takes pity on you."

The rage took over. All-encompassing, all-overwhelming. She reached back and threw a punch at her daughter, threw it as hard as she could, and it caught Emma flush on the face, and she fell from the force of the blow, fell off the edge of the platform where they were standing next to the stairs, and she fell straight down, fifteen feet, her head hitting the ground below with a dull thud, like a sack of potatoes. She twitched for a moment. Then she was motionless.

"Emma . . ."

There was nothing. She had caught her daughter with her lover and she had killed her.

She had killed her daughter, the fruit of her womb.

She couldn't leave her here. Not out here, in the cold and the dark. She tried to pick her up. Her daughter was too heavy, the ground was too slippery under her feet.

She couldn't leave her here.

She needed traction. She ran to get something for her feet. Her car was the closest thing. Her running shoes were in her car. She grabbed them out of the backseat and pulled them on, then ran back to the gazebo.

She could carry her daughter now. She slung her over her back in a fireman's carry and carried her towards the house.

She had murdered her daughter. She had killed her own seed.

But (her mind was racing out of control) her daughter was dead now. She wasn't going to come back to life, no matter what. So it was whether or not she, too, should die.

Emma wouldn't want her to die. Emma knew it was an accident. Emma knew she loved her. That her mother loved her, more than life itself.

She threw the body into the car and drove around aimlessly. Then she remembered a hike the two of them used to go on when the weather was nice, up Hot Springs Canyon. Emma loved it there. It would be a nice place for her to sleep.

She drove to the base of the canyon, lifted her out of the car, lugged/carried her up the trail. It was exhausting, but this is where Emma would want to be. She had to do this for Emma.

With any luck, no one would find her until summer, when the creek stopped running. By then all that would be left would be bones. Her soul, her beautiful spirit would have long gone on to a better place.

It wasn't until she got back to her car and looked down at her feet that she realized she was wearing Joe's shoes. He'd left them in her car the week before, after their run on the beach. In the dark she had grabbed them by mistake, instead of her own shoes, which still lay in the floor in the back. He had joked with her about how big her feet were, how they almost wore the same size shoe.

Someone had gotten her daughter pregnant. Someone didn't want anyone in the world to ever know that. Someone had killed her daughter. Someone wearing these shoes.

The next morning she took the key chain. She was going to plant it in his house, with the damning shoes, and make sure the detectives noticed them later on, when they came out to the house to begin their investigation. A few days until the tumult died down. Then she'd sneak over there, and plant the evidence. She had a key. She had been there many times.

He came to the house, to console her. He didn't know, but he had to be feeling guilty, overwhelming guilt. He was so loving with her, so gentle.

She couldn't frame Joe. Because she still loved him.

They were lovers now, more than ever. Especially after the divorce, they saw each other all the time. He was still "going" with Nicole Rogers, for appearance' sake, but she was in love with him, and she knew he was in love with her. He had to be. She still thought of Emma, her wonderful, loving daughter, but days would go by when she didn't.

He got the new job, in Los Angeles. They were going to move down there, start their life together. In the open, finally.

Except they weren't. He was going alone, making a clean break. What they'd had had been wonderful, he told her, but it was over. They both had to start fresh. She understood that, didn't she? It was better, for both of them. He was leaving Nicole behind, too, if that made her feel better.

He was having dinner with her husband and that woman, Nicole. She drank some bourbon to fortify herself. Maker's Mark, her brand of choice. Then she stole over to the restaurant. She had the bourbon with her, in case she needed more courage.

They were inside, having dinner. Having a great time, laughing. She could see them through the restaurant window. They were probably laughing at her.

The man who got her daughter pregnant had killed her. The man who wore those shoes had killed her. The man who had taken her daughter's special key ring had killed her.

She went out to the parking lot. There was his Porsche. It was open, the attendant hadn't locked it. She took one last swallow of bourbon for courage, screwed the cap on, and slid the half-drunk bottle into the car, sticking it behind the driver's seat, in plain enough sight. Then the key chain, in the glove compartment. Keeping a sharp eye out for the parking attendant, who was on the other side of the lot, listening to the ball game on the radio, not paying attention.

She had a key to his house. She let herself in, planted the shoes. Then out, to the road he would take to come home.

Sitting in her car at the side of the road, waiting. He drove by her, as she knew he would. He was alone. That was good. It would work if Nicole was with him, but this way was cleaner.

She watched his car head away from her, towards Coast Village Road. Then she picked up her cell phone and dialed 911. A drunk driver just passed me, she told the operator, telling her where this had happened. Maybe he's on drugs, too, you should check for that.

Then she went home, to the house where she lived alone, and passed out into a deep, exhausted sleep.

She stands on the ridge, looking at the house across the ravine. She has her rifle with her. She bought it last year. She's an excellent shot, she practices. Doug got the ranch property as part of the divorce settlement, but she kept a key to the gate, and came and went as she pleased.

You don't have to be a great shot at this distance, this rifle is so accurate, so easy to shoot. Doug had the same kind, he was always talking about how great it was to shoot, how easy. Even a beginner could be proficient at it in a short period of time, which she found out was true, she was proficient. And with the night scope it's like shooting ducks in a barrel. Like it had been out at the ranch, when she had shot him to warn him off.

He hadn't taken the hint.

He takes a break from what he's doing. Comes to the window, looks out. Then he slides the glass doors open and steps out onto the balcony, his arms outraised. Stretching? Maybe, she thinks, he's praying.

She raises the rifle to her shoulder, takes careful aim.

The shot rings out, the crack of the report echoing like a thunderclap across the canyon. The bullet hits home, a clean head shot, knocking the target backwards, dead before it hits the ground.

Across the ravine Luke, hearing the explosive repercussion, hits the deck.

Riva trudges across the hard ground, in her hand the .40 S&W howitzer that her old drug-dealing boyfriend had bequeathed her, which was hidden under the floorboards, just remembered. She looks down at Glenna Lancaster, lying still, a small hole in her temple, blood starting to ooze out onto her cheek and neck.

She had gotten the ice cream, dawdling over her choice, and was leisurely heading home when she saw it: a light, across the barranca, where she had seen the tire tracks.

She had turned around and driven in that direction as fast as the old truck would go, praying she wouldn't be too late. Stopping down the hill so as not to be heard, scrambling up the dirt road, slipping and sliding, feeling her belly, the life inside it. When she got to the top she saw Glenna standing there, raising the rifle to her shoulder. She took aim, and pulled the trigger.

She kneels down. "You got away with killing your own daughter," she says to the warm, suddenly inanimate body. "But no way was I going to let you get away with murdering the father of my child."

SEVEN

Riva is calm when she talks to the police back at the central sheriff's office. She had been driving home, she'd seen a suspicious light across the canyon from their house, she'd driven up to investigate. She had the gun just in case—she hadn't really expected to find any trouble.

Glenna had heard her coming, she says. She had called out a warning to Glenna to put the rifle down, but Glenna had turned it on her—she wasn't about to lay her weapon down. She had come here to kill Luke Garrison, she had called back to Riva, and if she had to kill someone else, too, then she would. One, two, or three, it didn't matter anymore.

Riva had fired out of instinct. Thank God for a lucky shot. If she'd missed, she would be the body lying there on the ground.

Ray Logan interviews her by the book, but keeps it as short as he can. Luke's by her side, protectively hovering over her.

"Justifiable homicide," Logan says curtly, when he's done questioning her. He looks over to Sheriff Williams, who nods confirmation. "We won't be pressing charges." He shakes her hand. "I'm sorry you had to go through this ordeal. You're free to go now."

Luke drives them home. They sit side by side, silent. Not until they're safely inside the house does she break down in his arms.

"She was going to kill you," she sobs. Her body's shivering, she can't stop it. He holds her tight to him, as tight as he can. "Five more seconds, and she would have killed you."

"But you got there, so she didn't," he says. "She didn't." Holding her head against his shoulder, he asks her, as gently as he can, "Did she really try to kill you?"

She looks up at him. "She was going to kill *you*. What difference does it make?"

He sighs. "None, I guess."

She looks at him. "I've seen the way the law works—and doesn't. I couldn't take the chance on that happening again. I wouldn't."

The police find Glenna's diary, tucked away in a desk drawer in her lonely house. It's all there, the whole story in detail, from the day she accidentally killed her daughter. The oldest story in the world, and still the saddest: two women fighting over sharing the same man. It didn't work for Sara and Hagar, and it's never worked since. Definitely not between a mother and a daughter.

Maria Gonzalez hadn't lied, as she explains to Judge Ewing, the following day, before a packed and hushed courtroom. She hadn't been guided all the way down the road, by either prosecution or defense. The prosecution didn't want to know, and because Luke Garrison had been caught flat-footed by her surprise testimony, he hadn't followed through as thoroughly as he normally would have.

She did see Joe Allison leave, like she had told the court earlier. But then she had heard quarreling, coming from the other side of the lawn, down by the gazebo. The voices of two women. She knew them instantly: Glenna, the mother, and Emma, the daughter. They were at it again, as they had been so many times in the past. The daughter giving back as good as she got. She was a wild child, Emma. Even by this age, fourteen, no one could tell her what to do.

She couldn't hear what was being said, but she could hear the rage coming from both of their voices.

Then the yelling had stopped.

She had a sick son waiting for her. She had to go home.

If either side had asked her if anything happened after she saw Joe Allison that night, way back when they were first interviewing her, everything might have turned out differently. But no one did. And although she was reasonably sure Mrs. Lancaster had killed Emma, or at least harmed her, she couldn't bring herself to voluntarily tell about it. She and her family owed their very existence to Mrs. Lancaster.

No one had asked. She wasn't going to volunteer anything, not in America. She had learned that from day one of being here—never volunteer anything.

The duty officer gives Joe Allison his effects, he signs for them. He had been the victim of a frameup, as he had claimed all along, from the day he was arrested until now.

There is no apology, no admission from the sheriff or anyone else that they'd made a mistake, that they had almost convicted an innocent man. They deal with him in silence. The only thing Sheriff Williams says to him is, "You were on your way out of town when we arrested you. If I were you, I'd make like this hadn't happened, and keep going."

Luke meets with Joe, one last time. They're in the small room in the jail, where they've always met. This time is different. Allison is dressed in civilian clothes, and he's a free man. He can walk out the door anytime he wants—the same door Luke's been walking out of these many months.

"I don't know how to thank you," Allison says awkwardly, to a man he may never see again for the rest of his life. "I really owe you."

"Yeah," Luke says dully. "You do owe me. But what you paid me—it wasn't nearly enough."

Allison looks surprised, and concerned. "It was everything I had. That's the truth, you know that. I don't have a job, and I don't know where or when I'm going to get one." He forces a smile. "That job you referred to before? When you were telling me how Doug Lancaster could ruin my career—reading weather reports in Nome, Alaska? That sounds pretty good to me right now."

"I'm not asking you for more money."

Allison's confused. "Then what?" He pauses. "You don't seem very happy, Luke. You just won a huge case, against tremendous odds. No one thought you had a prayer of winning. You ought to be ecstatic. You're the hottest lawyer around now. You ought to be celebrating." He smiles. "Let me take you and your lady out to dinner, okay? Anyplace you want, whatever you want. It's the least I can do for the man who saved my life."

Luke stares at him. His stomach feels as agitated as it did after his shooting. "I don't want to eat with you, Allison. I don't want to drink with you. I don't want to have anything to do with you, okay? If I never see you again, that'll be fine with me," he says sharply.

Allison is slow on the uptake. "Why are you angry with me? What did I do?"

The anger has been rising for months, ever since Luke discovered that his client was lying to him regularly in a case he'd agreed to take on even though it was supposed to be a stone-cold loser.

"Why am I angry with you? What did you do?"

He loses it. Without warning, even to himself, his hands are around Allison's neck, he's slamming the man up against the wall, gripping his neck like his hands are the talons of a bird of prey. "What did you do?" he screams. "You killed her!"

Allison is struggling, tearing at the hands that are choking him. "Leggo—" He tries to scream, to get someone to come in and save him, but Luke's all over him, way too strong, his voice is a hoarse rasp, barely a whisper.

"So you didn't commit the actual murder!" Luke cries out. He doesn't care if anyone comes in now. He doesn't care about anything at this very moment except to get it out, all of it. "But it's because of you that she died! It's because you committed statutory rape. It's because you were sleeping with her mother, a married woman, a sad, unbalanced, lonely woman who was in love with you! That wasn't Glenna Lancaster that knocked her daughter to the ground, that was you! It never would have happened if you hadn't slept with a fourteen-year-old girl! You and the other men who took advantage of her!"

"She wanted to," Allison manages to gurgle, from lips popping from the pressure on his neck. He's clawing at Luke's hands with his fingernails, but Luke's grasp is too strong.

"*She* wanted to? She was a *kid*—it's not her place to make those decisions. If she'd wanted to play Russian roulette, would you have let her? That poor girl had no chance, not the way you set it up!"

And then, as quickly as it came, his rage is spent, and he lets go. Joe Allison drops to the floor in a heap, gasping for breath.

Luke's done all the physical violence he's going to do. "There are two people dead and so many others whose lives are in ruins because of your childish selfishness, your preening narcissism." He looks down at Allison, quivering on the floor. "I saved your life, yes. And you know what? I'm angry about that. I'm enraged. I'm enraged at myself. For being a part of this."

He turns away. "We won. Technically, we won. But in the what's-real-and-right sense, everybody lost. And I'm going to be scarred with that, for the rest of my life."

Luke does have a celebratory dinner, of sorts, he and Riva with Ferdinand De La Guerra. A quiet dinner at Casa Donna, where the old money eats and he isn't likely to run into anyone he knows.

"What are your plans?" the old judge asks. He knows Luke is in pain. He's won big and lost big at the same time.

"I don't have any. Not professionally. Being a father, that'll suit me fine for a while."

He got the worst of his anger out of his system. This is the profession he chose, and this is how things work out sometimes. He did his job—he defended his client to the best of his ability. Anything else was out of his control. You have to let these things go.

"You could stay here," De La Guerra offers. "You could have a nice practice."

"Sure. The establishment lawyers love me."

"You did your job. Everyone respects that. Any one of them would've done the same thing."

"Except not as well," Riva says.

"Except not as well," De La Guerra agrees.

Luke shakes his head. "I don't want to do this. I don't know what I want to do now. But I know I don't want to do this, not right now. And I don't have to."

He'd sent Doug Lancaster's check back. The next day, a new one came in its place. The accompanying note read "I offered a reward for finding out who killed my daughter. You found out. I stand by my word. You earned the money. I expect you to cash this. Doug Lancaster." The check was for half a million dollars.

He doesn't know if he'll cash it; but he probably will. The man sincerely wants him to. And to be brutally honest, Doug Lancaster can afford it. Call it blood money, for the grief he caused Luke and everyone else.

They shake hands outside the restaurant. "I don't know if I did the right thing or the wrong thing," De La Guerra says. "But it was good to see you in harness again, Luke. You're still as good as they come."

"Thanks, old man."

The judge turns to Riva. "You take care of him. He needs someone good taking care of him."

"I'll try," she promises. "That's all I can do."

"I suspect you'll do very well," he smiles. "I think you'll do just fine."

The parking attendant pulls up in the Cadillac. One last awkward embrace between the old man and the younger one. *"Vaya con Dios,"* De La Guerra says. "And be careful."

"And you."

The old truck is packed. It's parked outside the rental house. Tomorrow morning the people from Bekins will come to get the rental furniture, and they'll drive away.

They stand on the balcony, looking at the lights of the city shining down below. "Are you glad you came back?" she asks. "After all is said and done, are you glad you did this?"

"Glad? I don't know if that's the right word." He's sipping champagne. Not because he won, that's too hollow. Because it's over. Because he and Riva are still alive. "But yes," he reflects, "I think coming back was a good thing. Maybe 'good' is the wrong word. A *necessary* thing."

"You conquered all your demons."

"Some of them. The ones that needed it."

"That's what I meant." She smiles. "I like it here. I could live here."

He regards her half suspiciously. "You think so?"

"Yes." She turns to him. "It's still your city, Luke. If you want it to be."

"I guess," he says, reluctantly half agreeing. He puts his arm around her, pulls her close. "I guess it could be."

She gives him a kiss on the cheek. "I'm tired. I'm going to bed."

"I won't be long."

She goes inside, turning the lights off behind her, leaving one burning in the kitchen to guide him. He leans against the railing, staring down at the city, the lights laid out like a constellation, a blanket of earthly stars.

He came home a loser in his own mind, and now he doesn't feel that way about himself anymore. And maybe, at the end of the day, that's enough.

This is his city again, if he wants it to be. He looks at the lights twinkling at his feet, and he feels some inner peace.

It's been a long time coming.

ACKNOWLEDGMENTS

David A. Freedman, J.D., assisted me with the legal aspects of the story, and was especially helpful in the areas of trial law. Terry Lammers, J.D., and Kristofer Kallman, J.D., advised me regarding California law. Chris Carter provided expertise about surfing and the central coastal areas north of Santa Barbara. Terry Cannon, J.D., from the office of the Santa Barbara County District Attorney, helped in areas regarding prosecutorial procedures.

Al Silverman, my editor, who has retired, was, as usual, terrific in working closely with me to make this a better book. I will miss him. Bob Lescher, my agent, was very supportive and helpful, both professionally and personally. I'm also grateful to Elaine Koster and Lori Lipsky at Dutton for their unflagging enthusiasm for this book, and for my overall body of work.